the SCENT *of* ORANGES

JOAN ZAWATZKY

Zawatzky, Joan.

The Scent of Oranges.
ISBN: 978-0-9707558-7-2.
Printed in the USA

Garev Publishing International, Inc. 2008

North American address:
1095 Jupiter Park Drive, Suite 7, Jupiter, FL 33458, USA
Tel: 561 697 1447

European address:
50 Highpoint, Heath Road, Weybridge,
Surrey, KT13 8TP, England
Tel: (44) (0) 1932 844526

Web: www.garevpublishing.com

Originally published in Australia by JoJo Publishing
ISBN 0-9757471-2-6

Cover and typesetting: SMK Design

Author's Note:

This book is a work of fiction. Names, characters, places and incidents are the product of the author's imagination. Any resemblance to actual events or locales or persons, living or dead, is entirely coincidental.

To the memory of
my mother, Ruth

I've come to take you home –
home, remember the veld?
the lush green grass beneath the big oak trees
the air is cool there and the sun does not burn.
I have made you a bed at the foot of the hill,
your blankets are covered in buchu and mint,
the proteas stand in yellow and white
and the water in the stream chuckle sing-songs
as it hobbles along over little stones.

From a poem for Sarah Baartman
by Diana Ferrus.

Summer 1958

The day we arrived at the orange farm I clung to Ma as the swaying truck loaded with our possessions turned into the dirt driveway. Pa pulled up in front of the red brick farmhouse. With bowed head he mumbled a prayer, 'May God bless us, keep us healthy and make this land prosperous as He did for my father and his father before him.'

Then Ma lifted me onto the ground. 'I'll find a place for you out of our way,' she whispered. At three I was a nuisance. She looked around quickly. 'It's soft and shady next to the bougainvillea. Sit quietly.'

I settled in the dappled sunlight watching the drama of the move unfold. Pa jumped out of the truck. My eldest brother, Connie, stood next to him. Vince, twelve, and Hannes, six, joined them. The four surveyed their land, from the orange groves to the crest of mountains in the distance. Then Pa put his fingers to his teeth, whistling shrill and loud.

From behind the bushes an army of black men rose to answer the call. They stood silently, eyes downcast. It was their job to unload the new *Baas'* truck and they accepted the order. Then, moving rhythmically in twos and threes, they lifted our furniture and placed it on the gravel driveway. Grunting in unison they moved the heavy table, beds, closets and boxes of smaller items and carried them into the house. Then each man took a chair and the job was all but done. Ma was so busy supervising the blacks' sweeping and cleaning that she forgot about me.

My brother Hannes was told to keep out of the way and he threw bougainvillea blooms at me until I wore a purple coat of them. When my podgy hands couldn't free the bits of petal stuck to my eyes and mouth, I wailed. Though Hannes had run away chuckling, he crept back when he heard my cries. He had a kind streak that lived on the opposite side of his nasty one. He eyed me with his head cocked to the side, shrugged and began to remove each bloom. Then he squeezed my hand and ran off again.

Later Pa carried me into the house. He opened all the windows and pulled off the sheets that had been gathering dust since Oupa died. I crept onto an armchair and slept while boxes were opened and furniture moved around me.

The red brick house, with white windows and trim, seemed strange and large compared to our last home. Flowering plants and tall trees were everywhere. Cows dotted the paddock and there was row upon row of orange trees. On the edge of the property near the orange groves stood the black workers' huts.

Once I found my way around the new house I explored. Past the bedrooms and up a short flight of steps was the attic, where the things from the past lived. Things that I had no name for. I wasn't afraid of them and sensed them in the same way one knows that someone is staring. They didn't speak but I felt them burning or icy, whizzing in my head. Occasionally I saw them. A sad black woman in a maid's uniform, I called her Daisy, cried every time we met. A girl with curly dark hair in a green striped dress with lots of ruffles, often rode a squeaky wooden horse that was broken when I tried to ride it. She'd nod to me and carry on riding.

The 'goners', as I called them, had their way of making their wishes known. Sometimes they visited me in my dreams and daydreams. A light on a door meant it should be opened.

The old captain, a regular, let me see him when he wanted his cap. The goners became a natural part of my life – a part that I kept secret from Ma, Pa, and even Hannes.

Part 1

Blossoms

Chapter 1

Spring 2005

I returned to South Africa when the farm was white with blossoms and wildflowers burst from the rain-soaked veld. It was a day when the sky was strangely luminous. Trees moaned and the wind swelled with fierce energy.

After nineteen years of good living in Australia I had needed a reason – possibly an excuse – to draw me back. It came one dark morning with a phone call. Pa was dead.

During the long plane trip my head was a muddle of longings I'd prevented myself from thinking or feeling since I'd moved away. Childhood memories competed with uncertainty about the reunion with my family but when the plane went into landing mode I tingled with excitement.

At first I'd called Pa and my brothers regularly but over time our connectedness withered and we spoke only on Pa's birthday and at Christmas. During our last conversation Pa's voice was as strong as ever and he did not complain of ill health. The news of his death had come as a shock.

We were all at the church service. The older farmers from the district didn't recognize me, and my nieces and nephews didn't know me. When I was introduced their faces were stony. How could I blame them? I had moved on and left them with the farm, our aging parents and the multitude of changes in the country. There would be time to talk and explain, if they were prepared to listen.

On the edge of the crowd, a group of Tswana men and women who had worked for Pa, stood with heads bent. Most still worked on the farm, now run by Connie. I recognized those who had been youngsters when I left. Once kind words and prayers were said, the group of workers moved forward. All eyes were riveted on them as they sang a Tswana hymn with such raw beauty that it could've carried Pa to heaven.

From the back of the group a black man in his late sixties stepped out and tenderly placed a box, the size of a matchbox on the coffin. He had put on weight and his hair was silver but I recognized Esiekiel, Pa's right hand man.

The small farm cemetery was so overcrowded that close family were shoved to the edge of the grave. I barely heard what the priest said as Pa was lowered into the cut in the ground. There was a scrape against the grave wall and then a jolting echo of wood on earth. Connie and Vince shoveled orange dirt into the grave until the coffin was covered. After some of Pa's old mates had a turn at filling the grave, Connie told three of his workers to complete the task.

After the ceremony the priest led the crowd to the farmhouse but I lingered among the blossom-speckled graves. When my sobbing was a whimper I moved to Ma's grave. Her simple oblong headstone stated only her name, date of birth and death. A bunch of roses I had meant to throw on Pa's coffin was still tight in my hands. I kissed the petals and placed half on Ma's headstone. Then I went back to put a handful of the remaining roses on the orange mound that signified Pa's grave.

My youngest brother Hannes' smaller white headstone stared up at me. I could picture Hannes with his slight build, fuzzy hair and oval face the color of unpolished copper and his eyes like almonds wet on the tree. He was murdered in 1965 when he was only fourteen. My memory of his murder and the period directly after it had disappeared. The harder I tried to grasp an occasional fragment, a shadow, the more remote it became. Finally I accepted my loss like a dangerous forest that I no longer attempted to venture inside.

After Hannes died, places on the farm where we had walked, talked and played together exposed the wound. It became easier when I married Wil, my childhood sweetheart, and moved to the city. Later, when we migrated to Australia, Hannes slipped into the background. I would choke up on his birthdays and occasionally when someone I saw resembled him and triggered thoughts and memories.

In the farm cemetery that day I longed to see him, hear him laugh or even whine and complain. Once more I kissed the roses left in my hand and gently placed them on the white marble.

As I turned to look at the graves, I felt a tender touch on my cheek, a strand of hair lifted from my teary eyes. A whiff of tobacco – the aromatic blend that Pa used to smoke. My legs were wobbly, my gut knotted. I told myself to get a hold of my emotions as I blotted the wet beneath my sunglasses and pulled my shoulders back. Quickly I closed the cemetery gate and followed the path to the farmhouse.

Almost there I stopped, leaned against a tree trunk and took a deep easing breath. Through the heathery scrub I glimpsed patches of the farm, the veld and the orange groves as they had been years ago.

'I'm back. I'm back,' I told myself as I dangled back and forth in time.

The sitting room or *voorkamer,* as Pa had called it, seemed enormous when I was a child but now it couldn't hold the funeral crowd. They spilled into the dining room and kitchen.

The guttural sound of Afrikaans came as shock, though it shouldn't have. It was the language of my youth but I hadn't spoken it or heard much of it for all those years I had been away. Occasionally in a shopping center, a cinema or on a bus I'd hear two people speaking Afrikaans about personal things, thinking that no-one else would understand them.

Here I was greeting people fluently. The language had a directness and simplicity with emotions expressed openly. I was no longer in the cooler Anglo-Saxon world or the regulated bureaucracy of the hospital in which I worked. It would be a brief but welcome change from subtleties of meaning and political correctness.

I looked back at my school days and thought how strange life was then. At our Afrikaans school we spoke nothing but *onse taal,* our language, except for our one period of English every day. The English pupils at their English schools attended daily Afrikaans classes. Separateness ruled all our lives – black/white, English/Afrikaans – and I didn't want to think of the others in their own boxes, such as Indians or mixed-race 'Coloreds'. A tupperware society. The government generated fear and hatred of our differences to drive apartheid but I didn't realize it then.

In my twenties I spoke only English except when I visited my family. It was my way of rebelling against the government and all it stood for.

I made my way past the food table to the drinks. A beer was what I needed. Burly men, skinny ones, wives and girlfriends I couldn't place stroked my arm, shook my hand or kissed my cheek in sympathy. On canes and walkers, Pa's old friends came to pay their respects. I smiled and nodded my thanks and answered questions about my life in Australia. From time to time I'd jab Vince or Connie in the side and whisper, 'Who's that?'

That afternoon Connie, Vince and I were bonded in our mourning and our memories of Pa. It hadn't always been like that and I doubted it would be in the future.

What a thrill it was to catch amusing incidents about Pa from his friends and to laugh with them. Every scrap of nostalgia brought Pa back to me for that moment longer. We sang his favorite song, *Sarie Maree*, with a gusto that filled the house. Again and again we drank to Pa, to his life and to what he meant to us. I downed more than I should have.

I scoured the crowd for two of Pa's oldest mates, Dieter Naude and Danie Van Jaarsveld. I asked Vince about them. His face crumpled.

'Dieter's son, Roy … his farmhouse was burned down recently. Roy and the kids were pulled out alive but … horrific burns. His wife Tracie died – asphyxiation. Dieter spends all his free time with Roy and the kids now. Keeps out of public places so … I guess that why he's not here.'

'How sad. And Danie? He was a bit younger than Pa.'

'He and his family were killed about two years ago.'

'Oh no. How?'

He bent down to whisper. 'A black gang massacred the lot of them. When the police turned up the bodies had no ears, tongues or … genitals. Word is that it was a voodoo killing.'

'Voodoo?'

'Ja. It's always been part of black culture ... animal sacrifice, witchcraft and that sort of thing. Now it's beginning to surface in human killings.'

Of course I knew about the increase in violence in South Africa, but learning about horrific murders of people I'd known shocked me.

'Someone round here that you know or care about is mugged or murdered every few weeks,' he added. 'It's impossible to police vast farming areas. Some farmers have taken the law into their own hands and clubbed together in commandos to patrol their farms.'

A solemn-looking man in a pin-striped suit interrupted. 'I'm Christian Myburgh, the family attorney.' He coughed before plucking a buff envelope from a thin leather briefcase. 'I promised your father that I'd deliver this letter to you personally if you attended his funeral or that I'd send it on to you in Australia if you didn't. When the doctor told your Pa that his cancer was spreading and he had only a month or two left … he organized things. Made a will and wrote this letter.'

The attorney coughed again before handing me the envelope. 'Your father's instructions were for you to read it immediately and then tear it up.' With the letter in my hand I edged towards the door. Connie put his arm out to stop me.

'What did Myburgh want?'

'Pa left me a letter.'

'It looks important.' He stood over me and fingered the corner of the envelope. Holding the envelope firmly, I ducked under his arm and joined a group next to us.

As soon as the crowd thinned I was up the stairs to the room where I had slept, dreamed and cried as a child. The smell of resins in the wood and floor hadn't altered. The wallpaper of pink roses and forget-me-nots and the ancient desk where I had done my homework were as I remembered them, but a more comfortable bed had been added. My old rocker stood before the window. When I had lived there I hadn't realized that the dark wooden door, edgings and furniture made the small room gloomy. Photographs of Ma and Pa, taken during their middle years, looked down on me from either side of the bed.

I had to remind myself that though I felt as if I was back in my childhood home, Connie and his wife, Raelene, had lived in the house for the last six or seven years.

Pa must've been in his seventies when he became too frail to run the farm and moved nearby. Though Connie took over the day-to-day operation of the farm, from the little contact I had with Pa, he made it clear that he had not relinquished control of his farm. Knowing Pa, I doubted whether he had left the big farming decisions to Connie.

I imagined how frustrating it must have been for Connie to have had to work under Pa's conservative and constant shadow, when Connie had learned a host of modern farming methods at agricultural college.

In Pa's plain handwriting the letter was addressed to: *My daughter Linda.* Underlined were the words*: To be read after my death.* Curious and excited, I tore it open and settled into the rocker to read. He'd written on grey paper and the letter was dated 23 July 2004.

My dearest daughter,

By the time you open this letter, I will have joined your Ma and Hannes in our little cemetery.

Though we have not seen each other in all the time that you have been away, I do hope you will be at my funeral. But if you cannot attend, my attorney has been instructed to send this letter to your home. This could mean that you will have to make a special trip to South Africa and to the farm in order to carry out my wishes. I am sorry if this inconveniences you but I must ask it. I have asked nothing else of you since you left.

As my death nears, you, of all my children, are the one I have chosen to fulfil my request. You, my daughter, are most like your Pa – straight, tough and you don't give up. The signs were there when you were a little girl.

Since I became ill, I've had time to weigh up my life, as I believe our good Lord will. As I prepare to go to my grave, I want to set right my wrongs. When my Will is read, you will become aware of the provisions I have made and I ask you to ensure that my wishes are carried out.

The next matter that concerns me is the three black men sent to jail for murdering Hannes. When Hannes was missing I immediately contacted people I knew in the police. Once his body was found, I drove them to hunt down Hannes' killer. I was so torn with grief that I was desperate for a result. Within twelve hours the police caught three young blacks and charged them with the murder. At the time I was relieved when the men faced court and were sent to jail. But after the trial, the word got out that the men had been forced to sign guilt statements.

I am clearly guilty of neglecting my duty. I ought to have voiced my concerns and acted on them but I didn't. If I still had strength, I would look into all this myself but these days all I can manage is to move from the chair to the bed. So many years later, I am still unsure if there was more to the murder than I first thought. I am leaving all of this for you to consider as you try to put wrongs right.

Thus I entreat you, my daughter, to ensure that my Will is honoured. I also ask you to look closely at the circumstances of Hannes' murder and to seek the truth. I tried to do good in my life, and I trust the Lord, but wrongs must be righted before I can rest.

Your everloving Pa

I felt a swell of love for Pa, an ache at his passing and a heaviness of guilt for not having been to see him before he died. There was another side to it. I admired Pa and for him to think I was most like him and to have chosen me for this task filled me with pride. I had to admit to myself that his grip on me was strong and that when he wrote the letter he must have been sure I would do anything he asked.

Over the years I had always accepted that the three men sentenced for Hannes' murder were guilty. Nothing had occurred since to make my views change. I wondered why Pa had doubts about their guilt and had waited until he was so ill before doing something about it. Could there be something deeper and more significant to this? Pa was usually so logical but this time there was a hole in his reasoning.

I read the letter a second time, and then, as he requested, tore it up. As I sat in the rocker admiring the late afternoon view of the purple Magaliesberg Mountains, I realized how enormous the task was that Pa had set me. My short stay of two months or so wasn't long enough to answer his question, but I had no intention of staying longer, drowning in a murky pool. I would do the best I could to make sense of his request.

The unplanned trip home had come after a period of emotional strain. Six weeks earlier I had signed the papers sealing my divorce from Wil. Part of me still loved him and I had held on for months, refusing to admit to myself that we would be yet another statistic in the divorce files. But I knew I had to let go. We had nothing left to share other than our son Davie, and he had married and gone to America to pursue a career in film. Unused to living alone, I worked harder and longer to fill lonely hours.

For now, I had old friends to contact and the countryside of my youth to explore with fresh eyes. I pictured long walks on the farm in the spring sunshine and possibly a visit to the Kruger National Park that was near the farm. I had a lot to look forward to.

Chapter 2

By the late afternoon the noise had abated. From halfway down the stairs I spotted Connie surrounded by a clutch of drinking buddies – all with bottles and glasses in hand. Turning back to my room I unbuttoned my blouse, unzipped my pants and hung them far back in the closet. I was in a hurry to walk before the light faded. Without disturbing the rest of the clothing in my suitcase, I took out a pair of jeans, runners and a tee-shirt and pulled them on. After unhooking my gold earrings and tying back my dark hair I was ready for the outdoors.

Soft rain tickled onto my face as I took the path under the blue ladies – my childhood name for the jacarandas. Around the swollen dam birds celebrated the rain and each thorn tree was alive with their twitter. Heading for the hollow of the orange groves, I cut across the veld, avoiding bristly leaves and cat's tails but was caught in overgrown lantana. I bent to pick wild freesias and shook the raindrops free. By the time I reached the orange trees my runners were caked with chocolate mud.

I had longed to be back and the farm had been the subject of my dreams for so many years. Pa was everywhere. I sat on the stone wall he and his workers had built to divide the orange groves from the rest of the property. Stripped to the waist, he had joined his men as they dug out the hard earth to create a dam. Then, using hoses, they filled it from the stream that ran through the property next door. His hard work and determination to succeed had created a flourishing farm.

The farm was small relative to others in the area and the huge orange estates. After the first harvest Pa asked his brother, Gerret, to help out on a casual basis. They had never been close but Gerret was out of a job and had worked on an orange farm before. The arrangement suited them both and the farm prospered. Pa even saved a little for leaner times when he battled to meet the mortgage. We were rich then, compared to the workers in their mud huts who had nothing.

Pa ran the farm according to his own rough program that followed the changing seasons, but Connie's methods of farm management were modern. He put his knowledge to good use, growing other crops as well as oranges on every bit of available land. As Pa had done he kept a few sheep, cows on the back paddock and a stable of horses. More precise, he established a task timetable that he adhered to strictly and since he had taken over, the production of oranges had doubled. Time ruled Connie and he drove his workers by the clock. 'We'll finish cutting back this lane of trees by lunch,' he'd say. 'This afternoon we must be finished the next one.' The workers had a different view of time. Things were done when they needed doing. The clash of cultures created an undercurrent of rebellion among the blacks.

Connie's priority was improving production and lifting profits but it wasn't as if he didn't attend to his workers' basic needs. He followed the example of every other farmer in the area, giving his workers no more or less. He provided them with sufficient food and beer, now and then helped out with a small loan to a father sending his child to school or took a sick worker to the hospital. Yet he was not popular with the workers. It might have been his detachment. They sensed he didn't care about them.

The farm flourished but Connie tried to influence Pa to purchase more than the few basics – a moveable sprinkler system and a new tractor. Pa preferred the security of a pile of money growing in the bank and Connie couldn't shift him.

There were few additions to the farmhouse and the workers looked as thin and poor as they had when I was growing up. I couldn't help comparing the running of the farm to Ma's old laundry – the elderly washerwomen using bars of yellow soap, concrete troughs and washboards. 'Why use machines when you have so many hands to do the work?' she said when I nagged her to buy a washing machine.

Sounds of chanting interrupted my thoughts. A line of about thirty men with spades sang as they broke up wads of earth and another group made holes for new trees. Singing in harmony made tough work easier and time pass more quickly. The scene was so African and I had missed it so much.

The rain eased and with no particular route in mind, I relished the walk. Through a row of fiery kaffirboom I saw the thatched workers' huts. The smell of beef and onion stew cooking for the evening meal hadn't changed either. To feed the communal fire women still carried firewood on their heads. Chatting during the preparation of the meal was as pleasurable as it had been years ago.

It was a relief that in the new and renovated huts electricity replaced candlelight and oil lamps. The new roofs were of colorful corrugated iron instead of the traditional fire-prone thatch but, retaining heat in summer and cold in winter, they couldn't have been as popular. Sanitation had been disgustingly primitive on the old farm, with no sewerage pipes or tanks from the huts and toilets were simply rigged up. I noticed that the luxurious flowering hedge which once served as a place 'to go' in a hurry smelled more fragrant now that a modern toilet block and running water had been added.

A black girl popped out from behind a hut and stopped in front of me. Her surprise turned into a wide gummy smile. '*Dumela* ma'am,' she said using the respectful greeting.

I returned the greeting and asked her name.

'Eva ma'am.'

'Who's your Ma, Eva?' I asked the child with long plaits tied up in loops.

'Miriam,' she said with a half curtsey. I didn't know Miriam but I would look out for her, I thought. Eva looked up at the sky and frowned.

'Rain no more but plenty *goggos* coming,' she said before running off.

Goggos – I hadn't heard the local word for insects for so long. I enjoyed repeating the word's sound. In minutes, a dense cloud of flying intruders buzzing frantically blocked the last rays of sunlight. Soon they lost their wings and decked the ground and the plants with their squirming bodies. We had always called them flying ants but they didn't look like ants to me.

Squishing them as I walked, I took the slim path behind the huts to a grassy patch where a white cross marked the grave of Zacharias, the Tswana headman in charge when I had lived at the farm. He died about five years after Hannes was murdered. He was seventy-five then and still in command. I smiled, running my hand over the painted wood, and remembered Zacharias for his kindness and his interesting beliefs. He belonged to a Pentecostal Church and at the same time he still worshipped ancestral spirits. He claimed to believe reverently in both.

Hannes and I loved Zacharias like a grandfather. We knew him when he was old with a bowed arthritic body but a mind as clear as a summer morning. We would clamber into his hut and sit on the floor in front of him while he told us about his past and the people he had known. Apart from his seven children and many grandchildren, at his age nearly all the people he spoke about were dead and had become spirits. He kept photos of his family on a low table and enjoyed showing us photos of them. We giggled at Esiekiel pulling faces at the camera and Nathaniel, his youngest, as a baby wrapped up in a blanket on his mother's back.

Our fascination with Zacharias encouraged us to visit him often. He taught us about the Tswana religion and their beliefs of good and evil. We were fascinated by the ancestral spirits, or *Bodimo,* and on each visit we nagged Zacharias to tell us more about them. When the Tswana died and entered the other world, they became *Bodimo,* he said. If the *Bodimo* were pleased with the behavior of those who were still living, they could intercede for them with the creator, *Modimo.* The idea of spirit entities communicating with their God to help those living and working among us seemed magical.

Hannes was three years ahead of me when I started junior school. Zacharias was so fond of us that he involved himself in our 'informal education'. After school he concentrated on teaching Hannes practical matters such as tracking and interpreting the calls of various animals, while he taught me how to use my intuition more accurately. I became aware of the hovering spirits of the departed and could describe them by their particular smell or sound. Zacharias was convinced that I had a psychic talent that might develop in later life. Hannes had none of my special perceptions and, jealous of Zacharias' attention, told me that I was imagining the spirits and that Zacharias' hut was filled only by ourselves, a flat mud wall and Zacharias' frequent farts.

Though I went to church, the idea of the spirits of the fathers didn't seem out of place to me. After all, I reasoned, Jesus was dead too and we worshipped him. Pa would've been horrified at my thinking and would've called me a pagan like the blacks.

I didn't realize then that Zacharias had given me the confidence to be more receptive towards the spirit world. I regularly saw spirits in the orange groves. They hung about the huts and several appeared in the attic but most of them were unrecognizable. When I was six and seven my beloved Oupa Eric, who had died in a mine accident, visited me when I was daydreaming in the garden. I knew him by the brush of his mustache against my cheek. Fortunately Ouma didn't visit. I didn't like her much.

After Hannes died I lost my spiritual connection. When puberty passed, and in the years that followed, I had only occasional encounters. After I left South Africa for Australia the demands of the physical world were too great and I became closed, my thinking less flexible.

I was thrilled to be back at the farm but the long journey and Pa's funeral had made feel unusually vulnerable – a prickling of tears behind my eyes.

I left Zacharias' grave, following along the path past the wild granadilla vines and up the ridge where a huge whitewashed boulder encircled with rows of flowers stopped me. I guessed that Pa must have erected and painted the boulder to mark the place where Hannes' body had lain all those years ago. Pa told me that it was there that, as a child, I had discovered his body. I stroked the rock and with eyes closed and jaw clenched I tried to force the shifting fog to render a memory of Hannes' murder or of the days immediately before or after it. But it was useless. The task Pa had set me would have been extremely difficult even with a clear picture of the murder.

Unexpectedly the air turned icy and dense with the energy of an impending electric storm. I shivered, my head buzzed and I detected a high-pitched wail. Was it my imagination? My feet locked, my arms stuck at my sides and my breath came faster than usual. Then it was gone. In just a moment I was free again, the air cleared and I was able to move. I kicked an empty soup can lying among the flowers. I tore at tiny yellow and white daisies peeping between the weeds and added handfuls to the flowers beside the boulder. Zacharias' teachings about spirits of the ancestors jangled in my head.

'Sometime spirit visit. They want some thing. He no rest then he no let you rest. He not finish work then he want you must finish work for him.'

A crunching sound startled me. 'Who is it? Who's there?' I called out.

A muscular man with a smiling face held up his hand, his palm facing me in greeting. 'Missie Lindie. Missie Lindie. Hello.'

'Wow Nathaniel, you gave me one hell of a fright!'

He laughed until he held his chest. 'Oooh oooh, you think I'm spirit talking to you! No Missie Lindie, just me.'

I laughed too. 'So good to see you,' I said. I wanted to hug him. I sensed he wanted to do the same but we stood facing each other, soldier-like.

'I too am very pleased see you.'

'Are you head of the *kraal* now?'

'Ja. For long time. Esiekiel say it my turn.'

'Zacharias would be proud of both of his children.'

'We trying hard for him.'

'I used to enjoy listening to your father's stories.'

'Father tell too many long stories,' he laughed as he sat cross-legged on the grass. I cleared a spot of leaves and twigs and joined him.

He tugged at the spikes of kikuyu grass. 'You been away too long.'

'I know.'

'But now you come back. You come to bury Pa.'

I nodded. 'I saw Esiekiel at the funeral.'

'My brother and me, we come to ask *Bodimo* to look after *Baas* Piet.' He pointed to the heavens. 'The *Baas* was good to us. Tonight we kill two goats and put them on the fire for him. It will make *Bodimo* very happy.'

The sacrifice of two precious goats to please the tribal ancestors and ensure Pa's safety in the afterlife was touching. The workers had thought well of Pa.

After Nathaniel had updated me on his family news, I remembered Pa's letter. It was an intuitive tug, a reminder.

'I'm trying to find out more about Hannes' murder. Before Pa died he worried if the men the police caught were really the murderers. He left me a letter asking me to find out. Maybe you've heard something that could help me?'

'After murder, people say boys in jail didn't do it. Chief go lots of times to jail to talk to man in charge. But nothing happen.'

'Can I meet the chief and talk to him about it? It's important for the men in jail … and for our family too,' I said.

'That chief is dead now.'

'Can you help me?'

He looked away. 'My brother know more than me. He work on the farm the time Hannes is missing.'

'Could you try to think of anything unusual that happened that night? Have a think, and in the meanwhile I'll talk to Esiekiel.'

'Better I go now. I be late back to job,' he said, brushing some stray grass from his legs as he rose.

An acrid smell occupied the space where Nathaniel had been sitting. I recognized the pong of marijuana. He had been a pothead since he learned how to roll his own cigarettes.

By six o'clock tiredness had caught up to me and my legs ached from walking. I crept past the sprinkle of drinkers to my room.

Stripped of my damp clothing, I lay under the same floral cover I had lain under as a child. The familiar rustle of bougainvillea and the echo of the wind against the thorn trees toying with the veld grass carried me into a brief but deep sleep.

The room was almost dark when I woke but I could sense Hannes was there – a gentle swirl of energy, the sweet Hannes.

'Hansie, I know you're there,' I called out. 'Who did this terrible thing to you? … and why?' I felt a warm buzz but received no answers.

At seven or eight a sweetness shone through his mischievousness and our bond was strong. Occasionally we were able to tune in to what the other was thinking – laughing simultaneously or finishing each other's sentences, but this didn't last. Within a year or two a scab grew over his gentleness, making him sharp, petulant and constantly seeking attention any way he could get it. Like a Stradivarius violin, he had to be cared for and stroked right. The trouble was that Hannes was not treated with love and care. As he developed he hit a wall of indifference from Pa and his brothers and he was jealous of the attention I received as the only girl.

Learning to defend himself with a smart mouth sharpened Hannes' wit. At Christmas time or some Sundays when we were all together he'd grab the stage and have us laughing until we hurt. He'd mimic people we knew like the priest or shopkeeper and change his appearance by using Pa's pipe or one of Vince's caps.

It wasn't as if he was the only child at the school who had mixed blood. I could think of at least six children and possibly there were more with coffee or caramel skin tones, woolly hair or unusually broad features. They too were jeered at and bullied but eventually they were accepted. What was it about Hannes that initiated the swell of antagonism against him?

While the other children of mixed blood waited passively for the storm of abuse to abate, Hannes' anger festered.

He protected himself against taunts by yelling remarks so vitriolic that dislike of him may have caused more antagonism than any of his physical characteristics. Later he developed his natural athleticism with muscle strength. He was so determined to defend himself physically that he exercised daily. I noticed the difference when his tap on my arm threw me off balance and made a pancake of me.

Of all my brothers Hannes was the smartest and the most creative, with a brimming imagination. He drew the ships and planes of his imaginary air force and navy and stationed them on the farm. Copies of some of his drawings he sold to children at school for a few shillings. Like many other bright children, school bored him and he didn't bother with it. His battles in the playground and after school worsened the situation. He learned to be secretive and devious and by the age of twelve could outsmart his antagonizts with a nasty scheme to upend them. 'I'll have my day,' he'd say, '*agter os kom ook in die kraal*.'

At home he'd confuse us all by locking his bedroom door and then climbing out of the window and down the drain pipe with the gnarled bougainvillea to cling to. Where he went and with whom none of us knew. Eventually Pa hid Hannes' bedroom door key. He retaliated by seeking out an old door with a latch and nailing the fitting onto his door. Pa threw up his hands and gave up.

By the time Hannes was thirteen he was disliked by many outside the family. Only Zacharias fully accepted him. I loved him but I didn't trust him.

Chapter 3

Connie looked up as I entered the sitting room. He was reclining in one of those double padded leather rockers that made his tight roll of gut fat roll each time he pushed the lever. It was the only padded chair and no-one else in the room was likely to be as comfortable. Well positioned, he had an uninterrupted view of the door leading into the dining room, the kitchen and the sliding glass doors that opened onto the garden. He was also close to the low wooden table that Raelene stocked with nibbles.

Groaning, Connie dragged himself up. 'The prodigal sister,' he said placing an arm around my shoulder. 'Come. Sit.'

Once he had been classed as a catch, a looker – tall and strong, with curly black hair, full lips, a well-defined jaw and the short neck of a soccer player. Though his features had coarsened, his trimmed goatee beard, a new addition, suited him.

Connie had been the only one for three years until Vince was born. I'd heard Ma and Pa complain about the regular battles between my older brothers but as Vince grew stronger he kept Connie in check. When Hannes came along six years later, followed by me, I was harassed by Connie in the same way as Hannes had been.

I despised him. In front of Ma and Pa he'd make a show of spoiling his little sister, but in the shadows his nasty side emerged. Once I caught him out telling fibs and I threatened to tell Pa. Connie punished me by locking me in a cupboard all morning. And I won't forget my terror when he pushed me into the dam for standing up to him. Geese were mating that day and I was lucky to escape with my calf nipped. A bully at home and at school, he made younger and weaker children's lives a hell.

That was then but I had to admit to myself that I still had no love or even liking for Connie. He didn't try to hide his aggressiveness but let it rip, almost as if he felt he was the one in the right. As my oldest brother, when he invited me to stay on the farm I felt obliged to accept. I could only hope that, at sixty-five, a mellowing of his temperament had coincided with his greying strands of hair.

'Did you have a good rest? It's a long flight and it can take it out of you,' my sister-in-law Raelene said, crinkling her brow in concern.

'My head's like cotton wool but a few nights of sleep will fix it.'

Connie had moved to the modern wooden bar he'd built in the corner of the room. 'A beer, Lindie? That is, if you still drink beer?'

'Just what I need.'

He poured my beer into a glass. Raelene offered a platter of sandwiches. My sudden hunger pangs reminded me that I hadn't eaten since morning. The brown bread tasted nothing like the bread I ate at home. Its nutty graininess and the flavor of the sweet cheese couldn't be duplicated. The beer was different too, fuller and smoother. I ate and drank far too much.

'Thank heavens they've all left. Pa had a good send-off don't you think?' Vince said. He yawned, tapped his mouth and then yawned again. His bony frame sank into the couch as he sipped his beer with half-closed eyes. Then, stretching his arms, he shuffled forward on the seat. In the way he moved and in his expression he could've been Pa.

Vince had been my favorite brother. He was the taller, wiry brother with the sweeter nature. At sixty-two his face was thinner and more angular and the ginger in his hair splotched with silver but his grey-blue eyes were as alert as ever.

'Ja. I think Pa would've been pleased with the turnout,' Connie said.

'All his old cronies I haven't seen for years turned up,' Vince said.

'For me,' I said, 'it was great to catch up with people and my past.'

Jeanette, Vince's wife, complained that she was tired and went to bed, with Raelene following soon after. My brothers and I were alone. I glanced round the room. Knickknacks from my childhood had remained on the walls and on the shelf over the fireplace were copper bellows, two masks from Kenya, a small statue of a pelican, a clay pot and a brass elephant in the positions Ma had originally placed them. Raelene had added two fluted blue Venetian vases, a porcelain sculpture of a boy on a bicycle and several standing photographs of her grandchildren.

'Relax, Lindie,' Vince squeezed my hand. 'You've been away for ages and you'll need to get used to the place again. And us, of course.'

As he said 'relax', I was instantly aware of the tension in my shoulders and back. Connie joined us on the couch.

'Have you read Pa's letter yet?'

He took the two sandwiches left on the plate, put them on top of each other and stuffed them into his mouth.

'Ja.'

'So can we see it?' he probed.

'I've torn it up as I was asked. Anyway it was personal,' I said, moving back into the cushions.

'It has to be about Hannes' murder. Pa was always going on about it. He went weird towards the end … all religious … quoting biblical verses and psalms. I wouldn't take too much notice of the letter and spoil your holiday,' Connie said.

'I'll try to do what he's asked, as best I can.'

'Was there a date on the letter?' Connie scowled.

'July 23rd.'

'About six weeks before he died. He was on and off morphine then but he had lucid times. And yes, he was obsessed about Hannes' murder,' Vince said.

Connie stood, swaying on his toes, glowering down at the two of us seated in the low couch.

'Do what you bloody well like Linda but you're wasting your time. A judge and jury gave that verdict. They weren't idiots.'

I didn't answer. Connie was downplaying the letter, implying that towards the end Pa had lost his reasoning and that I should ignore its contents. Why was he so insistent? Morphine was a wonder drug but in the hospitals I'd seen the other edge to its sword – the hallucinations and delusions it wrought. Vince said Pa hadn't been drugged all the time and that he had periods of clear thinking. How was I to know what really happened to Pa? I had always trusted Vince as the more genuine and balanced of my brothers. As the letter appeared to be perfectly rational and Pa's concern for me to investigate Hannes' murder was clearly stated, I would accept it at face value and do as Pa asked of me.

'Shush,' Vince said leaning towards the window. 'Can you two hear that wailing sound? '

'Baboons,' said Connie. 'They're close by … on the Mopane trees, too close to the house. Haven't done that for ages. 'If they don't *voetsak* I'll fire up into the air to shift 'em. We don't want a whole troupe of 'em hanging round here.'

I hadn't heard Afrikaans slang for years. One couldn't translate it. The closest acceptable phrase I could think of was 'get lost'.

'Oh Connie ... don't. They're terrified of loud noises. They'll leave when they find nothing to eat.'

Connie dipped his hand into a bowl of peanuts, chewed, swallowed and then, snake-like, spat out a question. 'So Linda, tell us, why did you leave?'

The room seemed to contract. In the heavy silence Vince looked uncomfortable. Connie's head was turned away from me but I could just see his flushed neck. Tears wet my cheeks.

'You know damn well why Connie.'

Connie's eyes turned from me and focused on his highly polished boots, Vince continued sipping his beer. None of us spoke for two or three minutes but it seemed longer.

They had seen the advertisements for nurses in Australia and knew why I had applied for a position. When I secured a job in Melbourne Connie had even made foul jokes about me nursing kangaroos and pointed out to Wil that his South African law degree wouldn't bring him a job in the new country.

It wasn't as if my brothers weren't aware of Wil's background – both his mother's and father's involvement in the Communist Party in the 60s, the dawn raids at their home by the 'special branch' and the time Wil's dad was taken into custody for questioning, only to be freed later that day as he wasn't regarded as a danger to the state. Wil and I found the government's apartheid policy repugnant. We sympathized with the blacks and admired them. Imbued with his family's ethos Wil studied law. He was determined to fight race discrimination and segregation, but the system ruled and he rarely won his cases.

He did save some from the gallows, improved conditions for those in jail and occasionally shortened their sentences.

I wondered if my brothers looked back, as I did, to those political wars over the Sunday dinner table with Wil and I on one side, Pa, Connie and Vince on the other and Ma on the fence. We all ended up angry, with no-one winning. I smiled, thinking that Pa would have been livid if he'd known about the anti-apartheid marches I joined at university, the sit-ins and the placards I'd held.

After the Soweto Riots in 1976 and the continual cycle of violence and repression in the 1980s we knew that nothing we could do would alter the situation and we made no secret of our thoughts of joining friends in Australia. My brothers told us we were crazy to leave our 'God-given country' and Pa tried to dissuade us. With the declaration of the first state of emergency in 1985 we made our decision to leave, and by 1986 when the government expanded its powers we had our papers.

Connie's clasped fists were white when he spoke.

'Admit it. Once the government changed you could've returned. There was nothing to stop you but the truth is that you didn't want to come back.' His eyes burned accusingly.

'For God's sake Con, let it go,' Vince said.

I wiped my face with the back of my hand. 'When I was able to return, I was still upset by Hannes' death and I couldn't face coming home to a family that hadn't got over it. Anyway, I like living in Melbourne – I enjoy my work, have a comfortable home and I've made friends. I have no intention of uprooting myself.'

Connie sighed and then looked at his watch. 'I'm bushed. I'm going to bed.'

At that moment I felt like throwing the dregs of my beer at him. My brothers' faces spun before me as I yanked myself from the chair. I walked quickly towards the staircase. Halfway up I stopped to glance back at them. With misgivings about the time I was to spend with my brothers I made for my room.

It was 2.30am but I wasn't ready for sleep. My body was still on the plane and it ached for rest but my mind was electric. I hadn't left Melbourne yet. Not really. I was hovering in limbo.

The intense smell of blossoms, the familiar insect hum, and sounds of animals seeking mates floated in the night. I'd forgotten how seductive spring nights on the farm could be. I shooed away moths hovering around the light bulb. On the window ledge shoots urged themselves into the room.

When at last I went to bed, I tried to concentrate on the sounds of the abundant outdoors, but the image of the rough mound in the cemetery kept asserting itself. The orange dust had clung to my hair and nostrils even though I had showered. I heard the priest's solemn voice and the thud of the coffin again and again. My tears for Pa exploded in sobs, shudders and then whimpers.

As my eyes fluttered closed, Pa visited. His calling card was his blended tobacco and a gust of energy, as powerful and demanding of me now as it had been in life. Hannes was more quirky – either tearful or giggly. Alone or together I could tell them apart.

It was Pa who had comforted me when I was sad and sang me to sleep when I was ill. My older brothers made pointed remarks about me being Pa's favorite but then laughed it off. Hannes was rightly jealous. He was needy of his father's love but Pa lavished attention on me and ignored him. When he saw Pa smile in the tender way he reserved for me, Hannes ran away.

'Silly boy,' Pa would say, but he would not make an effort to reassure his son of his love.

Pa's visit was too brief. If only he would've stayed long enough for me to see his stern face soften or to kiss my forehead and tell me he loved me.

I had slept lightly and looked at the clock. It was 4.35 – about the time Pa used to rise. My mind was too active for sleep. At the open window, I watched the dawn devour what was left of the night sky. In the distance the violet Magaliesberg Mountains created one boundary, the road to the nearby town of Rustenburg formed another and the orange groves defined the other edges of the property.

Dewy fronds of bougainvillea and the fragrance of jasmine brought back nagging questions about our family's past. Whispers of Hannes being a *kick back* or that he had Bushman blood had upset me as a child. But I was too young then to know about genetics. I did know that he looked distinctly different from the rest of us and that he put up with constant name calling and prejudice. At school he was bullied relentlessly.

I thought of the awful apartheid years when the yellow-skinned Bushmen in the Northern Cape and Kalahari were regarded as vermin, lower down the human scale than any of the blacks in the country or those of mixed race. How dreadful it was that the first inhabitants of the driest areas of Southern Africa were dispossessed of their land and hunted down like wild animals until they were almost wiped out. In those days anyone having Bushman features and coloring was treated with disdain.

I wondered where and when one of our ancestors coupled with a Bushman and who he or she was. Our relatives called Hannes our little black sheep, friends said he was our dark beauty and some unkind folk said he had a touch of the old tarbrush. Neither Ma nor Pa discussed Hannes' color and so its origin was guarded. Pa had always been so secretive about our family background.

The idea that Ma and Pa met when she was on holiday was romantic. It was hard to imagine the uproar their marriage had caused all those years ago. The Van Wyks were horrified. Though the Boer War was long past, it was not forgotten by many Afrikaners and anything English or anyone with ties to England was taboo. Pa's family saw the union with an English family as an affront. Neither his parents nor his close family members attended the wedding celebrations, but after two years, my grandparents relented and welcomed Ma into their home.

The question of family had plagued me in recent years. I had spent hours attempting to trace my relatives through genealogical sites on the internet. So far I had traced my mother's family tree back as far as the 1500s. All of her ancestors came from or around Winsford, a village in Cheshire, England. Some aunts and uncles who had settled in Cape Town were still alive and I'd found cousins I hadn't known about.

On Pa's side my search for relatives reached a wall after his great grandfather Cornelius, a General during the Great Trek. A few years ago, I wrote to Pa asking for information about our family history but he avoided my questions. I hoped that Connie and Vince knew more than I did about our family background.

I looked out again. A pale sun had risen but it was far too early to shower and dress. I slipped back to bed, pulled the sheet up to my chin and within minutes was asleep.

Chapter 4

A cruel flash of light woke me as the curtains were flung open. Squinting, I struggled to focus. A smiling maid in a pastel blue uniform and frilly white cap set a breakfast tray of eggs, bacon, toast and tea on my lap.

'Morning ma'am. I'm Nettie.'

I luxuriated in being spoiled. At home there wasn't time for these niceties. When Nettie came in to collect the tray, I yawned and stretched.

'You still tired ma'am?'

'I think I could sleep all day.'

Her rounded body and generous smile reminded me of my nanny, Tansie. Years ago I'd written to her in the township and tried to find her through her family but without luck.

'Lot of people remember Missie Lindie.'

'I remember many of the people who worked here too. There's one person I've been trying to find for years. Maybe you can help. Her name is Tale but some people called her Tansie. She was my nanny.'

'Is she Tswana?'

'Ja, Ja. She's a Hurutshe and her family came from around here. In the old days she and her children had a hut on this property. She must be at least seventy now.'

'I'll ask for you.'

As I dressed, my thoughts were on Pa's letter and the task he'd set me of finding Hannes' murderer. I would follow

Nathaniel's suggestion and visit Esiekiel, who had supervised the harvest workers at the time Hannes was murdered. I'd ask him if he remembered anything unusual happening on the farm back then.

Out in the morning air I strode out to the workers' huts. I glanced at the sky. The rays of the morning sun radiated in the cloudless blue with a clarity and energy I had only seen in children's picture books. Pa had told me how primitive farm life had been when he was a child. Oupa Eric's farm didn't have electric light or running water in those early days. Water was carried up to the farm from the stream. He smiled when he described learning to carry water on his head like the women did. They told him that it wasn't right for men to carry things but he could since he was still little. Ouma had to heat water on the stove for cooking and bathing but the workers had to heat their water on a fire. The toilet was outside the farmhouse and the sewerage had to be disposed of manually.

Warm from the brisk walk, I stopped when I reached the new modern huts, built to the side of the original mud and stone ones. On the small porch of one of the newer huts an attractive black woman, tall and cat-like, was enjoying the morning sunshine, her firm body arranged not to miss a ray of light. She was pale skinned for a Tswana and wide expressive eyes dominated her face. She took her time to stand, stretching slowly until even her fingertips were greeting the sun.

We were strangers and though I was aware of my feet firmly placed in the direction of the farmhouse, inexplicably I knew I had to stop to speak to her. I introduced myself.

'I'm Miriam,' she replied. 'So you're back from overseas?'

'That's right.'

'I've been living here on and off.'

Through the door I could tell that her hut was well-appointed with a kitchenette and divided living and sleeping areas.

'You want to see inside the hut?' she said watching my inquisitive eyes. 'Come.'

The hut looked comfortable and had been decorated with a mixture of wood, leather and African knickknacks.

'I like the way you've decorated it.'

Miriam smiled. She offered me tea and we talked about her children. Thomas had an engineering degree and was working in Rustenburg. Tania was a teacher. I told her that I'd met Eva.

'She's my sister's girl. She's with me now. My sister died two years ago … the bastard AIDS got her … but little Eva's well.' She put her hands together in a prayer gesture and looked up at the sky. 'She's settled down with us.'

We talked about Eva for a while and then I left. As I looked for Esiekiel's hut my thoughts were about Miriam. She was an attractive and pleasant woman who spoke well and yet she was perturbing. She had deftly steered me away from discussing herself. And I wondered why she lived on the farm when her looks and abilities could have offered her more. The opportunities were out there for her now.

Esiekiel didn't hear me approach. He was in front of his hut, busily working on a low wooden bench. When he did notice me he beamed and lifted his hand in greeting. 'Missie Lindie! Happy you come.'

'I'm glad to see you too.'

'You stay away long, long time.'

'I know.'

I wondered if Esiekiel knew that Pa, like most of the Afrikaans farmers in Rustenburg, had been a member of the secret pro-white and anti-British *Broederbond*. He did resign though after Hannes died. Children at school talked about the Bond in awed tones. '*Van heinde en verre*, from far and wide, they'll know about us Afrikaners.'

I was about eight years old when Vince tried to explain why it was important for Afrikaners to be members of the society. 'We're caught between the bloody English on the one hand and the bloody *kaffirs* (blacks) on the other. Both would squeeze us out if they could. I look at it like this; we trekked through this land, found it empty and developed the countryside while the English were making money in the cities.'

The fanatically pro-Afrikaans secret organization didn't fit with my image of Pa. I argued that the blacks had been on the land long before the trekkers arrived. It had been their land. But Vince ignored that statement and went on to tell me that the Afrikaans language and culture had to be preserved. It was time for Afrikaners to run businesses as well as farms, and to protect themselves against the growing *swart gevaar* – the black menace. They outnumbered us in the millions.

Later Hannes told me that Esiekiel and most of the other blacks on the farm belonged to a secret anti-government organization of resistance, *Umkhonto Sizwe* – Spear of the Nation. Surely Pa knew about their membership. Perhaps he chose to ignore it.

Pa, like many of his farming mates, had grown up in the 1930s and '40s on his parents' farm with the children of blacks who later became workers on their farms. In the background, the traditional paternalistic approach towards blacks was passed down from father to son. Oupa Eric used to shake his head sometimes when he sat down to eat at night after a day on the farm.

'God help me, I try not to shout at the boys … they're slow and lazy sometimes ... but they can't think like us … understand our ways.'

This fatherly approach to workers had virtually disappeared by the time I was in senior school. The *swart gevaar* had grown and to stem its roots apartheid took hold and increasingly repressive laws clamped down on the blacks.

All that had occurred in this land seemed unbelievable. Right then I could find no reasons, other than obvious economic ones, to explain how in spite of enormous past differences and bubbling resentments, farmers and their black laborers continued to work together. Nor was there an explanation for the many long and lasting ties that developed between whites and blacks on the land, that went beyond mutual need.

As Esiekiel moved one of the tools on the bench my attention returned to the present.

'I see Missie is sad. I also sad Pa die. But Missie not worry ... Tswana fathers look after him.'

Esiekiel was more practical than his father and brother. He was gifted at cultivating, building and fixing most things. The workers respected Esiekiel and even though he worked part-time now his presence created stability on the farm. Where would Pa have been without Esiekiel rallying the workers when morale was on the slide during the apartheid days? There had been a bond between Pa and Esiekiel. They had worked together on delicate tasks like grafting or transplanting trees but it was more than that. I remembered Esiekiel tearing his shirt into a bandage to staunch my bleeding when I stepped on sharp twigs and cut myself. He carried me on his shoulders to the house. This kindness was repaid more than once and Pa lent Esiekiel money to pay sharks chasing him for gambling debts.

The workbench held boxes of matches, tubes of glue and a number of intricate matchstick sculptures. He was about to complete one of a horse in motion.

'Two matches and finish,' he said, sticking the bits into place. 'Work half-time, play half-time. Now wife Esa is dead, got plenty time,' he laughed shyly.

Esa had been small and skinny and whenever I passed their hut she was beating carpets or puffing up pillows. She was a lot like my Grandma Lillie in age and nature and I didn't like her much.

'I make presents for grandchildren,' he said proudly. 'Come see inside.'

The hut was packed with tiny matchstick animals, miniature huts and double-storied houses. His talent amazed me.

'You're very good at this. You could easily sell them to the tourists.'

'One day. Maybe.'

On the wall opposite the door was a large map unlike any of the maps I'd seen.

'What's that?' I said pointing to the map.

'It Hurutshe land long ago before Voortrekkers take it. See it go all here over river and up mountain.'

It took me a while to understand the map. Its symbols for paths, rivers, streams and mountains differed from ours and there were no roads when it was drawn. Once I had located the mountains and rivers it was easy to find which square of land represented our farm. I had my finger on the map.

'This farm's on Hurutshe land.' I looked down, feeling uncomfortable.

'We go outside now,' he said with a catch in his voice.

I followed him into the sunshine.

Esiekiel had resumed his seat at the bench and was spreading matches into shapes when I couldn't contain my curiosity any longer. 'What was in the box you put on Pa's coffin?'

He put a finger to his lips. 'The spirit of the *Baas'* land.'

I nodded.

I had left the most important question until last. When I asked him what he remembered about the period prior to Hannes' murder, he knocked his pipe several times against his shoe to empty its tobacco, then refilled it before answering.

'Little Master Hannes and two other boys have competition who can pick most oranges. Little Master and boys work hard, pick lots and lots oranges – fill up bins. End of day, Little Master win with most oranges. *Baas* very happy with big drums full. When light is gone, we pack up. I see Little Master pick up bag and go behind trees near dam. Is last time I see him.'

'Did you see anything else that could be important?'

He lit his pipe and puffed on it. 'I tell police I see white man carry something very heavy over veld. It maybe body of Little Master.'

'What happened?'

He sighed. 'Police very fresh, ask lot of questions. What time you see him? How you know he white man? What he look like? I tell police it was end of harvest and early star come out. I tell them there plenty light and I see white hands, white face but he wear cap.' Esiekiel showed me with his hands how the cap covered part of the man's face. 'I tell them he big man.'

With his hand Esiekiel indicated a height about a foot taller than himself, approximately six feet.

'He not so young. Big nose.'

'And so?'

'Police they laugh. Not enough details, not good enough ... When they find three men with blood on knife at Magaliesberg Road they happy to say found killer. Police not like believe what black man say. Black man always first suspect,' he said bitterly.

'What do you think about it now?'

'I still sure he was white man but not sure which one.'

'Thanks. You've helped to narrow my search down.'

He nodded.

'Missie find body?' He put his hand close to the ground to indicate that I was young at the time. His eyes questioned mine.

'Ja. But my memory … is full of clouds.'

'It a very bad time. Very sad. I also not want remember. I cry for Hannes, for *Baas* Piet and Madam.'

I felt my throat tighten.

'I also put little box on coffin for Little Master.'

'One like the box you gave Pa at the funeral?'

He shook his head. 'Different box,' he whispered. 'I make eland for Little Master … from matches. Put eland inside box.'

'Why the big buck for Hannes?'

I waited.

'Special animal Bushmen people hunt. For Bushman eland is very high spirit.'

I touched Esiekiel's shoulder and he smiled. He picked up the matchstick sculpture of the horse he had made and handed it to me.

'Present for Missie.'

Then he continued arranging his matchsticks. Thanking him, I left carefully holding the miniature. As I walked I mulled over what Esiekiel had said about the large white man he'd seen on the night of the murder. Perhaps Pa had been right in doubting that the three blacks the police caught had murdered Hannes. I could see myself spending all my time here searching for answers. Increasing my pace, I headed for the house. I passed a rocky outcrop surrounded by dense self-seeded trees and prickly blackberries. Pa hadn't attempted to clear this area and neither had Connie. It had always been a part of the farm to be avoided. Tansie had told us that it was a place the spirits went to when they couldn't find heaven and were lost.

'Bad spirits live there. Missie must keep away,' she waggled a finger at me. 'Dogs, cats they go inside … never come out. One day the girl of Doris – the one who do ironing for madam – run into trees to find ball. Next day Doris find her girl lie dead outside bushes.'

My expression had shown my disbelief.

The house was noisy. Nettie hummed as she dusted and cleaned. The *voorkamer* had been aired and sprayed with real lavender water. The smell was pleasing and it looked different without the smoke haze of the night before. I noticed that Connie had moved Pa's traditional Afrikaans couches made of crossed strips of leather or *riempies* into the hall and replaced them with leather sofas. All Ma's flower paintings were still on the walls. The fireplace that once dominated the *voorkamer* had been rebuilt and surrounded with stone. Two gold-framed photographs stood on the ledge above it. The large colored one was of our family, Ma, Pa and us four children, taken when I was about three years old. Ma had been a beauty then. The other, in black and white, was a family photo with our maternal grandparents. Pa was noticeably absent.

I sat on one of the padded tapestry chairs. Each carried motifs of birds and was made by a deceased maiden aunt of Ma's. They were the show chairs that no-one sat in unless we had visitors. I sniffed, recognizing the antiseptic smell of the shining parquetry. Ma had insisted the floors be polished once a week and be swept and buffed daily by the servants.

The low cabinet where Ma had kept chocolates and imported sweets had been locked. 'To keep the servants – and you children – from pinching.' I remembered the bunch of keys protruding from Ma's pocket. Then, all food stores, including the fridge, had padlocks. I tried the door of the antique cabinet. It was still locked.

Indoors the changes Connie had made were superficial. It looked much like the house in which I had slid down banisters, hidden in corners and run down passages. Memories connected to the house and the people in it were still drifting back to me.

A brush against my leg startled me. It was a fat marmalade tabby.

'What's his name?' I called out to Nettie.

'Madam call him Marmaduke or just Duke,' she shrugged.

I bent to pat Duke, who was circling my ankles and giving me occasional rubs. In the end I sat on the couch and he padded round me waiting for the suitable moment to jump on my lap. I devoted myself to petting him. A dog can't fit itself into the hollows and angles of the human body like a cat does. Duke responded with purrs that rose in decibels. Then with ears cocked and whiskers quivering, he jumped down, abandoning me. His body low, he stole out the door.

'He chase fancy black cat, Queenie, next door. She drive Duke crazy. But she expensive cat … only eat chicken,' Nettie said with disdain.

'A spoiled pedigree?'

'She know woman's tricks,' Nettie said.

A woman's tricks? For some reason I thought of Miriam.

'I met Miriam this morning. Are you friendly with her?'

'No way. She think she too good for us.'

'Too good? Why?'

Nettie pulled herself up to her full height.

'She same as Queenie – like white meat.'

'You mean she's got a white boyfriend?'

'Oh Ja. Very special boyfriend.'

'Who? Tell me Nettie. Please … please tell me,' I pestered.

'Nuh. Sorry not tell.'

Miriam was definitely an interesting person. I wanted to find out more about her.

I followed the aroma of fresh baking to the kitchen, where Raelene's biscuits and cakes stood on cooling racks. Her mahogany tinted hair, usually piled on her head in neat curls, fell lank on her shoulders and her shirt was slightly askew.

'Have a *koeksister*.' She pointed to one of the racks.

Hungrily I snatched a traditional doughnut-like sweet pastry. I hadn't eaten one since I'd been away. I stuffed another into my mouth. They were delicious.

Raelene boiled water for coffee and continued whipping egg whites for a cake.

'Are you still working part-time?'

She sighed, pushing stray hairs from her forehead. 'Nup. My job went to a black woman less experienced than me.'

'Why?'

'Blacks are replacing whites in the workforce and given preference at universities and colleges. It's their country now and I suppose one can't blame them. I'll find something useful to do with myself.'

Her voice had lost the optimistic tinkle I remembered.

'And you … still nursing?' she asked, wiping her hands on her apron.

'I've been working part-time and I'm painting a bit. It's a good arrangement.'

'You're the lucky one to inherit artistic talent from your Ma.' She steered me towards the deep pantry. 'I had this pantry specially built when I re-did the kitchen. I wanted to store things when I'm in the cooking and baking mood.' She pointed to a tall freezer. 'Lots of it goes in there as well.'

I looked at the new kitchen bench-tops, the shiny tiles and wooden cupboards and muttered appreciatively. The kitchen was choked with food.

I left Raelene and hunted for the heavy-duty flashlight. It was on the hall dresser as it had always been. Then I headed for the slim door at the top of the staircase to the attic. Inside the door a sticky spider web greeted me. Breaking it, I moved into dark mustiness. The light switch had been on the left wall next to the door and I slid my hand up and down the wall until at last I found it. My eyes took time to accommodate to the single small globe. When I clicked on the wide flashlight beam it added the light I needed. A stinkwood lamp, a broken table and stringless guitar cluttered the entrance. I moved them aside and eased myself past.

I bumped into something that jabbed me. It was my tricycle, a present for my fourth birthday.

'Happy Birthday my big girl,' Pa had said with a kiss. Ma wheeled the tricycle towards me. 'Extra legs for our darling.'

'A silly present that you'll grow out of in a year,' Hannes had said, trying out the tricycle. He had been given a boring gift of clothing for his birthday and was clearly jealous.

I recognized a dusty suitcase tied with rope. It was Ma's. Forgotten or dumped in the attic, it waited to be given away. The rope snapped in my fingers. With my touch the layer of tissue paper covering Ma's clothing crumpled to powder. I caressed an unwashed silky blouse retaining the faint perfume of Ma's soap. I longed for her.

Ma was always busy, doing more than one thing at a time, but somehow she found time to paint. She must have been quick and efficient to manage so much. I doubted that any of us appreciated the skill of the tall skinny woman we knew as our Ma. I couldn't understand the force that drove her. She had turned a congested box room downstairs into her art studio. None of us, not even Pa, could steal her attention once her mind was on a canvas. Her work was appreciated by the small community of artists in the area but not by Pa, who made jokes about her time-wasting hobby.

Deeper in the attic, an easel and paintings stacked against an old dresser caught my attention. I held the flashlight to them. There was a sudden hum, the beam swiveled and the light flickered. They were Ma's paintings, together with her paints, crayons, pencils, brushes, turps and sketchbooks. Fury surged from my gut. Ma lay in her grave while her work was entombed in the attic. Why had it been tossed away? All her paintings would have to come out of the attic and be seen in natural light. I would ask Vince for help.

The flashlight burned my hand. A painting propped up on the dresser portraying Hannes with tears rolling from his eyes glowed eerily. My gaze slipped as I changed my grip. By the time I shone the flashlight on the painting again, my heart was beating uncomfortably fast and I was breathing hard. I rushed out of the attic careful not to trip over or bang into anything. Down the stairs I raced, clanging the front door behind me and into the light. I gasped the fresh morning air until I felt calmer. That had to be message from the spirit world – a kick in the butt reminding me to find out more about Hannes' murder.

Chapter 5

My mind was a pot on the boil as I paced Connie's manicured garden with its sharp edges and beds of daffodils and irises planted with geometric precision. 'How could I satisfy Pa's wishes?' I asked myself. All I had to work with so far was Esiekiel's memories of the night. Could I trust his memory? And how was I to find out if what he had told me was true? I had been set a weighty task but asking questions and following up every scrap of information was all I could do.

'Why would Connie want an English park with daffodils and iris?' I muttered to myself. They were pretty enough but looked out of place on the farm. Gratefully I sat in the shade of a well-placed wrought-iron garden bench, enjoying the view beyond the garden to the orange groves and the mountains. My mind, which had been so full, slipped into an empty space, and if the breeze hadn't stirred the dew-laden leaves enough to spatter my face I might have been there for longer. I was watching snails leave crisscross trails on the grass and a thick line of ants leading to their earthy home when a hand touched my shoulder. I hadn't seen Vince behind me.

'I took a few days off work so that we could be together,' he said, pulling me up from the bench.

'That's good,' I said, giving him a hug.

We took the shortcut through the veld to the dam. Reeds and marsh grasses grew in clumps along the dam wall and dandelions danced in the breeze. We lay on the bank under wide-leafed loquat trees that Pa had planted for their shade and tart fruit. We watched ducks and geese frolic as they courted, fluffing feathers and spraying water with their flapping wings.

'They're gorgeous, aren't they?' Vince said.

'We've got to talk.' I could feel the strain in my voice.

'Cool it Lindie, you're supposed to be on holiday.' He squeezed my hand.

'But Vince … it's important.'

'Shush … shush. I heard a rumor,' he said with a mischievous smile. 'The blacks are saying that they saw a leopard run through the veld about a week or so ago. They apparently found tracks in the mud here near the water's edge.'

'Those stories did the rounds when we were kids,' I said sharply.

'Ah come on,' he laughed.

'I think the leopard must've had its drink and moved on.'

Vince lolled back on the grass. He wasn't taking me seriously and I doubted he had even thought about the task that Pa had set me. His casualness made me feel ridiculously serious. I didn't want to come across that way but I was carrying a load that the other two didn't have to bear.

'Now *listen*!' I thumped the grass.

'What's so important?'

'I was in the attic.'

'Oh … so you saw Ma's paintings stashed away?' he said with the defensiveness of a naughty child being caught out.

'Why, Vin? Why are they locked in there?'

He looked at the palms of his hands. 'Those paintings of Hannes were more than we could handle … but we shouldn't have dumped them there … not like that.'

I dug my heels into the soft red sand. He was silent for some time.

'She painted them shortly after he died.'

'Ma's paintings have got to come out of the attic.'

'Okay … okay. I'll ask Nathaniel to help and we'll make a start on it later.'

I shook the dust from my pants. 'Come on, let's go down to the orange groves.'

Connie and his manager were supervising a group of men spiking the ground around the orange trees so that they could hold water and nutrients through the summer. There wasn't any dirt on Connie. When Pa worked the land his clothes were stained with earth and sweat. Connie lifted his arm in greeting. 'Linda, let me introduce you to Frikkie Lourens.'

Frikkie shielded his eyes from the sun, then wiped his hands on his jeans. We shook hands. '*Aangename kenis* – pleased to meet you.' The introduction had been so formal – I'd forgotten how stiff older South Africans could be in comparison to laid-back Australians.

Connie, Frikkie and Vince gravitated towards each other. Their conversation shifted from the weather and the farm to the final soccer match that weekend.

After examining the lush leaves of the healthy plants, I sat in the shade of an old tree. Suddenly I was five years old again, sprawled in front of the fire listening to Ma and Pa's conversation. They were lying next to each other, touching.

'What do I know about growing oranges? I'm a sheep farmer and all I've ever grown is *meilies,*' Pa said, tensing his hands into fists.

'*Ag,* come on Piet. We haven't been here a year yet and you expect miracles. You'll get the hang of it. You always do.' Mum put her hand on his.

'I've been thinking of asking my brother to help. He worked on an orange farm once … bigger than this one. He's out of a job and it might suit him.'

A week or so later my uncle had started work at the farm. Uncle Gerret was a big brawny man in his mid-forties with heavy features but glorious blue eyes. He shared his knowledge, helping Pa to prepare the trees with fertilisers, foods and sprays to produce a bumper crop. He set the workers firm limits but earned their respect. After a year Pa gave his brother the title of manager and a slice of the profits.

'Come, sleepy head. I'll show you around,' Connie said, breaking into my reverie.

Connie proudly showed off his thriving orange groves. Some of the workers looked familiar. Possibly they were children or relatives of the workers I'd known. One or two smiled or nodded.

I admired the rows of healthy plants.

'Things are going well … except we're three days behind with cutting back this lot. A bit of catching up to do.' A scowl clouded his face.

Brushing against low-hanging branches, I twirled round and round, touching the orange blossoms and sniffing the perfumes as I had when I was a child. Vince watched me and smiled.

'Orange blossom fairy,' he laughed. 'Remember the year we had an Orange Blossom Queen? It's crazy to think of the secret ballot … a few names placed in an empty beer can.' He laughed again. 'And we made Hannes Blossom King. How cute he looked with that white suit with a crown. He loved it. Good memories, eh?'

Vince snapped off a branch of blossoms for me as we left the orange groves and walked towards the house.

'I saw that boulder Pa erected as memorial to Hannes. You know I can't remember a thing about the murder. It's a blank … always has been.'

He picked up his pace. 'I was away at school camp when it happened. By the time Pa called me back Hannes' body was already at the funeral parlor. Connie organized everything.'

'But tell me what you remember?' I insisted.

Vince sighed. 'The funeral was heart-wrenching. Hannes' death hit our family like a landslide. We needed each other so much yet we remained alone in grief, afraid to cry or say something upsetting. It was dreadful.'

I took his hand.

'You didn't speak for weeks and Ma had to virtually force food down you. Ma and Pa were so concerned about you that they took you to see a specialist in Jo'burg.'

'A specialist?'

'Ja. A psychiatrist. You were almost half your size and spent the day in the cubby we boys made.'

'I can't remember that either.'

'I think the shrink may have given you pills. Anyway you started speaking and eating again.'

'And how did you handle it?'

I had been self-absorbed, not thinking of my brothers' reactions. Vince swallowed. 'Ah well, I tried to get on with normal life as best as I could. What else could I do?'

'What about Connie?'

'He carried the farm. At night he drank a lot, then locked himself in his room. He didn't talk about it or show his feelings. But that's Connie.'

'And Pa?'

'He aged after the murder. He couldn't look after the farm any longer so handed most of the work over to Gerret and Connie. Esiekiel was there to help. Pa spent a lot of his time down at the huts with old Zacharias, smoking their pipes and talking. Ma tried to get a grip on things by teaching at the farm school. She was a natural teacher. Slowly she started up her painting again.'

'Poor Ma must've died from grief,' I said wiping my moist eyes.

'Ja. She was dead at forty-five.'

'I was tied up with myself and Wil. It was just after we left that she passed. I should've been here for her.'

Neither of us spoke until we neared the house. Then I asked. 'What did Pa say about the murder before he died?'

'I didn't take enough notice then. Maybe I should've. He said something about the police locking up the wrong men. You're not going to relax much with all of this on your plate.'

'Ja. I know.' Pa had given me an overwhelming task, knowing that my brothers wouldn't be much help. But anything to do with Hannes had been complicated, even when he was alive.

Raelene had turned Ma's old studio into a craft room. She had been through phases from Chinese plate painting to making dried flower decorations. Cloth dolls were a more recent hobby. Her work wasn't original and it wasn't art but she was talented and the dolls sold well. Intricately made dolls of all types and vintages decorated the cupboards. I couldn't help picking up a wide-eyed blonde one with long plaits and cuddling it.

The airy room with picture windows was nothing like Ma's raw-brick studio. It was as if Raelene had scrubbed out every vestige of her mother-in-law. The concrete floor spattered in a rainbow of paint where I'd sat and crawled had been replaced with beige linoleum and the once dirty walls, which had been stuck with sketches and pages from magazines, were now pristine. It was a boring room that served its purpose. The long row of cupboards would be ideal for displaying Ma's paintings.

Dragging sounds announced Vince and Nathaniel carrying the paintings down from the attic. Nathaniel put the first lot down in the corner of the room and returned to the attic for another load.

'I've brought all Ma's sketchbooks down. There's tons of them,' Vince said placing them in the opposite corner.

When the paintings were spread against the cupboard, I immediately recognized Hannes – slim and golden skinned, with fuzzy black hair and a halo round his delicately boned face. Rather than hide his Bushman-like appearance, Ma had embraced it. I scanned the twenty or so paintings. In each of them her subject was Hannes. In one Hannes was a baby, a toddler in another and in some he appeared ghostlike. Most disturbing were the paintings of Hannes dying with blood seeping from a wound and a pool of blood collecting around him. I shuddered.

Blood. Such a lot of blood. I could almost smell it. A flash of memory snapped at me – the stench of a sodden heap of debris. I tried to grab hold of details but my memory door closed on me. Perhaps I was meant to find Ma's paintings of Hannes. At least a small chink had opened.

Vince put an arm around me. Not only was he the most affectionate of my brothers but he was the most open. There had been few secrets between us when we lived together in the farmhouse.

'They're such powerful paintings, maybe Ma's best. Others must see them,' I said.

'We'll have to do something about showing them … maybe organize an exhibition.'

'Will you do it?' I said putting my hand on his.

'Let it go for now and get ready for the *braai* tonight. We'll think of a way.'

How could I let it go? Alone, I studied the paintings more intensely, trying to grasp Ma's pain through her choice of color and brushstroke. Paint was slashed on the canvases with short sharp jabs. In her previous work her strokes had been soft and flowing. I was aware of her anger and pain. They were disturbing paintings, yet they demanded my attention and brought Hannes back to me. As memories of him came and went a cloud of vinolia soap enveloped me. I sensed her close.

'Ma, Ma?' I called out gasping at the scented air. As it had come, the sweetness edged away. The scent mingled for only a second or two with the peanutty smell of her chestnut hair. My memory flashed pictures of her from when I was young. She was beautiful to me and I'd noticed men glancing at her and turning to look again. Mostly their eyes fixed on her long legs and high breasts. No wonder Pa didn't like her going places without him.

They were opposites. Ma laughed and said, 'Chalk and cheese but together we make a whole person.' Ma kept her emotions in check and reasoned things out but Pa blew up like a land mine. At night, through the thin plaster wall near my bed, I heard their muffled voices, but if I put my ear to the wall I could make out most of what was said. Pa would never have admitted it but in the early years of running the farm, he discussed his farming problems with Ma. She supported him and made it seem as if he had found the solutions without her help. Pa appeared so strong and decisive that others would never have guessed Ma's quiet role. I knew from the softness in her voice and the way she looked at him over breakfast that she must have loved Pa a lot then.

Most obvious was their different views towards our upbringing. Pa believed that children learned the hard way, like he had. He hit first and talked afterwards. If Ma considered we'd crossed the line of her expectations, she would march us upstairs to her bedroom. There we would have to sit on the carpet while she talked. Sometimes the lectures lasted so long that my mind traveled down to the orange groves or for a swim in the dam.

Hannes must've spent hours being lectured to in the bedroom. I'd listen at the door and after a while become bored and run off.

'When you grow up I want you to be a decent God-fearing man, who cares about others. You'll have to learn to tell the truth and take the consequences of what you do. One gets tangled up in lies and they bite.' After a long session with Ma, Hannes would emerge from the room looking exhausted. 'At least Pa's hand is quick,' he'd say.

The smell of burning coals drew me downstairs. The *braaivleis,* or barbeque, had been arranged for relatives and friends who had remained in Rustenburg after the funeral, and for others who wanted to catch up with me. Peeking from behind the velvet curtain, as I had when I was little, I watched the first guests arrive. There wasn't a dark face among them.

The *braai* had been set up across the full length of the *stoep,* or porch. Coals glowed orange, ready to receive from the heaped pile of meaty offerings. A red-sashed attendant had the job of feeding the fire for the evening. The smell of *boerewors* – the homemade sausages that we used to help Pa to make – was intoxicating. Onions, garlic, coriander and whatever else went into the fatty pork sausages made them delicious to eat but nauseating to make. While most things associated with cooking in the kitchen were regarded as a woman's job, anything to do with cutting meat, making *boerewors* or drying meat to make the delicacy *biltong* was a male preserve. I wanted to enjoy my meal and battled to divert memories of Pa forcing me to take a handful the gooey pink mince dotted with fat that I had to stuff into intestines, he called skins.

The servants had laid out a long table of salad, fruit and a variety of breads. Nettie had gone to a great deal of effort decorating food platters exotically with leaves and edible flowers. I had brought my camera down with me and couldn't resist a snap of the table with Nettie smiling next to it. Her smile was wide and proud.

In the breeze fireflies dazzled on the veld below. Connie, dressed for the part in an apron and chef's hat, turned the *boerewors* and Vince added marinated steaks and chops to the fire. Sounds of sizzling meat, talking and laughing hovered in the night air. Running, jumping, noisy children were everywhere. I recognized Connie's and Vince's grandchildren. None were denied hugs and kisses from their 'new auntie' as they called me.

I was pleased to see old school and university friends but we had less to talk about than I expected. After a catch-up about marital status, children, health and careers we lost our connection and there was nothing left to say. I overheard snippets of frightening conversation about hijackings, muggings and people murdered on farms by blacks. A small group was discussing a favorite topic – the pros and cons of immigration. The longer I stayed on the farm the more aware I became of the dangers of life there.

I was eating a chop with my fingers when Raelene approached me on the arm of an elderly man.

'Let me introduce you to Pa's friend, Cobie, or ex-Detective Inspector Mulder if you prefer. He was in charge of Hannes' case … his murder. I thought you'd like to meet him.'

I remembered the name but wouldn't have recognized the elderly balding man with a well-trimmed mustache.

'You're just the person I need to see,' I said.

'I'll leave you two. But don't hassle Cobie with too many questions.'

'So how can I help you?' his tone was honeyed as he pulled his chair up next to mine.

'Pa left me a letter. He wanted me to look into Hannes' murder. Did he mention it to you?'

'No, sorry. Your Pa had a thing about Hannes' murder but wouldn't talk about it. Not to me.'

'Pa could be secretive.'

Cobie nodded. 'Generous … but a closed book about himself and his family.'

'It happened all those years ago and the trouble is I don't remember a thing about it.'

'It's shock my dear – it zaps your memory. Seen it lots of times. You could be lucky … sometimes it comes back.'

'Do you think I'll ever get it back?'

'I'm no expert … but … sometimes something seems to trigger off the memories and then they roll in. Sometimes they come back with a bit of an explosion,' he patted my hand.

'I'll be waiting for that trigger.'

He clicked his tongue. 'Patience, my girl.'

His tone irritated me and I looked away. He patted my arm again. I wanted to yank my arm away but I didn't – I needed all information I could get from Cobie.

'I hope you won't mind some questions.'

'I'll do what I can to help a lovely lady. Fire away,' he said, running his hand over his bald patch.

Cobie must've been about eighty but he was dressed impeccably in beige moleskins, a brown corduroy coat and shiny tan boots.

'Is there anything about the inquiry that stands out in your memory?'

'I can still see him, lying in his blood on the grass strip along the farm road. He'd been stabbed with a sharp object. We combed the area and about two or three miles from here along the Magaliesberg Road. We found three blacks, still drunk from the night before. One was carrying a knife with bloodstains. Tests confirmed that the blood was your brother's. We arrested the three and they confessed to the murder.'

'No doubt it was them?'

'Looking back … it's hard to be certain. No DNA in those days. I suppose the blacks could've picked the knife up on the farm as they first said. My boys knew how to coerce prisoners into confessions.'

'Picked it up on the farm?'

'Ja, but we thought they were fibbing. We didn't follow it up.'

'Did the three blacks say why they did it?'

'Never.'

'It's odd, don't you think, that they had no motive?'

'Ja, but they were drunk.'

'Even if they were drunk … why would they kill Hannes?'

'Ja, this is a tough one,' he stroked the pocket of his corduroy jacket. 'It's going to be too hard for you to sort out alone. I imagine you'll be going round in circles with it. The least I can do for my old pal's daughter is to get you some help. I'll speak to Detective Inspector Swart. He's at the Rustenburg shop now but at the time of Hannes' murder he was a new recruit. I'm sure he'll remember the case.'

'But he's a busy …'

'Not to worry. He lives near here and could pop round.'

'That would be wonderful.'

'My pleasure,' he bowed. 'Now that I'm retired I enjoy talking about my old cases now and again,' he said. I watched him make his way towards the drinks table.

After speaking to Cobie my uncertainty melted slightly. I saw a break in what I thought was a steel band around my task. The desserts were scrumptious and I was filling my plate with a second helping when a silver-haired man in a tweed suit and tie approached me.

'I'm Dr Parker,' he said. 'I don't know if you remember me.'

'Oh yes, lovely to see you again.'

He had been our family doctor. Outwardly he hadn't aged that much – still slim, bald and florid in complexion. Though he spoke English and Pa would have preferred an Afrikaans doctor, we put up with Dr Parker due to his gentle manner and ability. He expressed his condolences about Pa's passing and went on to talk about our families.

'I've always wondered what really happened to Hannes,' he said. 'The police reports weren't satisfactory.'

I agreed and explained that I was investigating Hannes' death.

'There were times I was worried about Hannes – he was very anxious, you know.'

'Ja. He was.'

'The last time I saw Hannes was when your mother brought him in with a sprained ligament in his arm. He seemed very upset that day … and I felt sure there was something more to it than his sore arm … but he wouldn't open up to me. I told your Ma I was concerned and she said she'd have a chat with him.'

The doctor altered his stance and placed his hands behind his back. I could picture Hannes with his uptight face with strain around his eyes. I'd go upstairs to his room to look for him. In those moods his door would be locked and he'd grunt, 'Leave me alone'.

I watched the black waiters with the eye of a visitor. They were all Hurutshe Tswanas, employed in the house or farm, dressed in white coats with diagonal red sashes. Since the 17th century the Hurutshe tribe had lived under different chiefdoms around the area we call Rustenburg. In those days they were rich traders with other black tribes and owned large herds of cattle. They were Iron Age people who mined and sheltered copper and iron. Archeologists discovered smelting furnaces as well as some of the implements they made. Some groups wove cloth and made pots and urns. The circular huts, like the ones on the farm, were made from clay and cow dung with thatched roofs.

Disputes with other tribes hungry for land weakened the Hurutshe and by the time the Zulus attacked, under Shaka, they were decimated. Survivors fled, leaving their villages and huts in ruins. When the *Voortrekkers* came down from the Cape in the 1840s, they searched for farmland, a place where they would be free of British domination and be able to practise their religion. A group of trekkers, including my Great Grandfather Cornelius, rode with their leader Paul Kruger. The Rustenburg area was virtually depopulated and rich, with suitable land for farming. They seized it and soon formed a republic headed by Paul Kruger.

Kruger's original cottage, on the farm Boekenhoutfontien, was a short distance away. When we were children Pa took us there on several occasions. He treated the farm and its buildings with the reverence reserved for a shrine.

'It's our history and you children should be proud to be blood relatives of one of the men who was at Paul Kruger's side and saw the value of this land.'

Guests drifted home and Jeanette and Raelene lingered in the kitchen while Connie, Vince and I moved to the sitting room. We had a few beers and we chatted politely but the tension between us was unmistakable. At about 10.30 Connie looked at his watch and put his hand to his mouth like a little boy who'd forgotten something. He gulped down the remains of his beer and dashed from the room.

'Where's he off to in a hurry?' I asked Vince.

'Probably looking after security stuff – setting the alarm system and checking if the barn door's been bolted. There was an attack on the farm five years ago. Livestock and a plough were stolen and two of the workers beaten up. That's when he put in an expensive new security system,' said Vince. 'He's been sleeping with a gun under his pillow for years. His dairy cows and sheep are kept indoors now and the horses are guarded. One of the workers sleeps near the livestock with a rifle in case thieves break in. It's Nathaniel's job to keep an eye on the orange groves in case of damage.'

'Was Connie attacked?'

'No, thank goodness. But if Nathaniel hadn't been near he might not've been so lucky.'

Connie had been gone for almost an hour when I dragged myself out of the chair and stretched. 'Sorry Vince, I can't wait any longer. I'm off to bed.'

'I'll have another beer or two and wait up for him.'

The moon was at its roundest that night and the light-sprinkled sky dazzling. The sweetness of jasmine was in the air. I couldn't relax enough to fall sleep. Raelene, as a thoughtful gesture, had left a bottle of red wine and a glass on the dresser. Duplicate keys for her car and the wine cellar lay next to the bottle. I'd forgotten the habit of locking things away from the servants. After at least half the bottle I must've fallen asleep.

Shrieks and booming sounds in the trees outside my window woke me. Baboons were calling. Soon the dogs caught their scent and settled at the bottom of the clump of trees barking.

Each Tswana group chose an animal as their identifying totem and baboons were the sacred protectors of the Hurutshes. They welcomed visits from baboons and wouldn't consider harming their totem animal. Fortunately the dogs lost interest in the clever creatures too high for them to reach. After about a half an hour I must've fallen asleep again with baboon chatter in the background.

Chapter 6

Nettie placed a breakfast tray on my bed. 'Morning ma'am, I got good news for you. I find your nanny. She living with her sister, Nandi, nearby here … but she very sick.'

'What's wrong with her?'

'Nobody say but she sick long time.'

Her tone was heavy. She handed me a piece of paper with the address. Nandi's house was in an area that had been called a township, a poor area where blacks lived. Those were the apartheid times when the Group Area's Act prescribed areas for different races.

My mind raced through all the illnesses Tansie could be suffering from. I'd have to wait to find out. As I lay back against the pillows an image of her came floating to me – young and energetic, her eyes shining with vitality. She was neither fat nor slim, but firmly rounded with the bearing of a woman who had balanced heavy items on her head. Ma complained about my ability to run or play from dawn until bedtime but Tansie laughed as she kept up with me. Each day we had a battle over milk. I disliked it no matter how it was flavored. 'Drink milk, Missie Linda … one day you be strong like Tansie,' she'd say, smiling broadly with her perfect set of teeth that had never seen a dentist.

I had grown to love Tansie and in the time spent in her care she became as important to me as my parents. The first time Tansie smiled at me I felt safe. Her capacity for giving was an endless spring. She listened and said little, and seemed the same each day irrespective of her mood or her troubles. She expected nothing from me other than my respect and I found myself wanting to please her. If she was displeased with me I wasn't afraid of her. She had the widest lap and tightest hugs. Her voice was sweet and she often sang to me when I was young. *Tou-la tou-la baba, tou-la tou-la baba.* I understood her songs and later began to understand and speak her Tswana dialect. It was from her, not my mother, that I learned to love unashamedly. My love for her was deep-rooted, different from my feelings for my parents. I hoped she cared for me a little too. After my bath when I was pink and soft she'd hold my feet in her huge hands and kiss them. There were moments when, half-asleep, I felt the kiss of a butterfly on my forehead.

I had dozed off again when Nettie shook me. 'Wake up quick,' she urged. 'Police here for you.'

A police car was parked in the driveway and a lanky, dark-haired man in his forties leaned against it smoking.

'You must be Linda, late Hannes' sister. Detective Inspector Arnie Swart.' He extended a tanned hand. 'I had a call from your Pa's buddy Cobie Mulder. As a special favor he asked me to help you out with your … investigation.'

'Thank you ... but you must be an extremely busy man. I don't like taking up your time.'

Cobie obviously still held a lot of clout to organize for a Detective Inspector to come see me about an amateur investigation – and one about a crime that took place so long ago. Surely Cobie wouldn't have wasted his time unless he thought having another look at the murder might be worthwhile.

'Don't look the proverbial gift horse in the mouth, lady. There's chaos at the station … murders and rapes, hijacking and every other kind of violence. I'm happy to get out of there for any reason.'

'Mmm.'

'It's a break,' he said, giving me a swift look over – breasts, legs, face. He smiled.

'We all need time out.'

'I did something for you I don't usually bother myself with. Let's say I did it for your Pa. Got one of our newies to dig into the archives. And guess what? We're in luck. She found my old case notes from Hannes' murder. Nowadays everything's on computer.'

He opened his briefcase and pulled out a bunch of yellowed pages.'

'Thank you so much.'

He lowered his eyelids and gave me a slow long look. If I was reading him correctly, he knew how I could thank him.

'Reading this stuff brought the scene back to me. It was one of my first cases.'

'I heard so.'

'The three blacks carrying a hunting knife with your brother's blood on it were apprehended near the property along the Magaliesberg Road and charged with murder. They had no alibis. Once they had been questioned at the station they signed statements admitting they'd killed your brother. At the time we were convinced they did it. Maybe we missed a few things. Didn't spend enough time looking elsewhere.'

'A-huh.'

'Have you any new clues?' he asked with half a smile.

'The word on the farm is that those men didn't kill Hannes.'

'Sure, but it's gossip not fact ... and anyhow it's too late now to reopen the case. With the number of new unsolved crimes, we just don't have the manpower.'

'I understand but it's a pity.'

'I'll do what I can.' He crushed his cigarette end in the dirt. 'I can read our case notes to you ... if you want to hear them.'

'Of course I do. Let's move to the *stoep.* It's more comfortable there.'

The heat was overwhelming and I was feeling dizzy. The detective made a point of locking his car door and brought his notes with him. We arranged ourselves on the cane chairs and I offered him coffee. He glanced at his watch, thanked mc and shook his head.

'The coroner's report ...' He scanned the page. 'Stop me if you want more details. Let's see, there was a bruise to the left side of the face, close to the temple.'

'Stop there. What about that bruise?'

'I suppose there must've been a scuffle of some sort and the attacker punched Hannes. The report says it occurred while he was still alive.'

'Was Hannes trying to defend himself?'

'There's no way of knowing. It's possible. I'll continue. There were two cuts to the abdomen – described as slices – that were fairly superficial. But the knife was plunged into the chest cavity eight times. To me that's a particularly brutal stabbing.'

'Whoa! You're saying that the person who stabbed him did so viciously ... with violent emotion?'

I tried to imagine I was talking to the detective about someone I hadn't known but it didn't work. The knot in my stomach had already wound itself up and I could taste the acid in my mouth.

'On the button. It wasn't simply a stab and run thing,' he pursed his lips and frowned.

I hunted for the right words. 'Why would someone kill a fourteen-year-old in such … a frenzy? Surely there had to be a reason?'

'You're talking about a motive?'

'I guess so.'

'There's nothing about motive in the notes.' He lit another cigarette.

'Can I have one of yours?' I pointed to the cigarette.

'Sure.' He opened the pack and held it towards me.

'So those three were charged with the vicious murder and they didn't even have a motive? You let it go at that?'

He shrugged.

The Detective Inspector had given me an awful picture of Hannes – slight and small for his age, stabbed so violently yet he didn't want to discuss who had committed this vile thing or why. To me, the motive was the key to the murder.

'Let's move on with the report. About the knife – probably a hunting knife. Longish, with a broad blade, and it was sharp at the tip. Hence the deep gashes.'

He scanned for more information and turned the page.

'This is strange. They didn't find as much blood as there should've been from such deep cuts. There are notes about drag marks. The body was dragged a little distance away from where the killing took place.'

'Where was he killed?'

'We couldn't put a fix on the place. After searching the property we found no blood droplets in the veld or along the grass. Maybe he was carried in something that soaked up the blood like a blanket but we couldn't find that either.'

'Back then there was a lot you people couldn't find.'

I could feel my scowl as I wiped the sweat from my forehead with a crumpled tissue.

'Well ... time and manpower, you know.' He scratched the side of his face. 'Later, forensics confirmed the blood on the knife the three black boys were carrying was Hannes' blood.'

'I see.'

He checked back through his notes.

'What about footprints?' Footprints were always important in murder mysteries.

'There's a note here that it was difficult to distinguish footprints. There were human prints – rippled prints from boots – and several animal ones ... and ...'

'It was just too hard,' I interrupted cynically. I was sure the police didn't bother to investigate further once they had black suspects. You need this cop, I told myself. You'll put him offside and then what? I took a deep breath, pushed my sticky fringe from my forehead and tried to arrange my face with a more receptive expression.

'As I said ... it all takes so much time.' He went on looking through the case report.

'Anything about tyres or skid marks ... bicycle or car treads on the dirt road?' My questions came from the many detective stories I had read.

He shrugged. 'Sorry ... no. We don't know if the killer walked, drove or rode into the farm. You're right there – it would have helped knowing if he was on the farm at the time or came in from outside.'

'I suppose your lot didn't look for things like fibres on and near the body or even prints on the knife?'

He tapped the glass table and didn't answer. 'There were some weird things we never figured out … red wine thrown on the body after death was one of them.'

'Red wine?' I interrupted.

'A cheap quality red wine and a lot of it too … nearly a bottle poured over the body.'

'You're saying he was dead when the wine was poured over him?'

'That's right.'

'Strange.'

'Another thing,' he looked up at me. 'Your brother was wearing lipstick … red stains on his lips were still there.'

'Couldn't it have been a red stain on his lips from a sweet or food?' I asked hopefully.

'No, it was tested. Lipstick … definitely lipstick.'

Ma's old lipstick and powder. Memory fragments of Hannes playing, dressing up in old clothing and putting on make-up slid back and forth but it made no sense at all.

'If you won't have coffee, what about a glass of iced water?'

Nettie, anticipating our thirst, had left a jug of iced water and glasses on the cane table. No tea or fresh lemonade and cakes for a white policeman.

'About that lipstick. Your late brother … was he … um … gay … homosexual?'

'I doubt it. After all, he was only fourteen when he was killed. And he didn't show any interest in boys. Well … not in front of me.'

I felt the stub of the unfiltered cigarette burn my fingers and ground it into the metal ashtray on the table.

'Uh-huh.'

'Did they find any … sexual … interference on his body?' I asked tentatively.

'Rest easy. According to the coroner … none.'

While we sipped the water he insisted on going through the basic steps of solving a crime. After living in Australia for so long, I'd forgotten how charmingly patronizing South African men could be. Connie wasn't all that different. I had to acknowledge that talking to Arnie Swart did help to focus my mind on the lack of motive in the murder. He posed questions. Did Hannes antagonize someone sufficiently for them to kill him? Or was it a random attack? As before, there were no satisfactory answers. He pulled his chair closer to mine as we discussed possible suspects other than the three men in prison. It led us nowhere. Then he stood, placing his hand on my shoulder and gave me another long look. I turned away.

Pacing the *stoep,* he made suggestions I'd already thought of. One, about picking through lists of children in Hannes' class to find a possible killer, seemed worthwhile. I walked him to his car.

'All this happened so long ago and it needs more time than you've got. You've taken on a hell of a difficult job … We could always discuss things over dinner.'

He smiled again but his eyes bothered me – tired flat eyes. He was arrogant, but attractive in a way. Tall skinny guys appealed to me. But a night in bed with him? Oh no.

'I appreciate your help,' I said.

'Pleasant chatting but it's back to chaos for me now.' He gave me a wink and a wave.

Red wine and lipstick? Hannes' murder wouldn't be solved in a linear way. I knew it. Figuring it out would be like unraveling knotted wool.

Immediately after dinner and a quick coffee, I excused myself. I craved time alone for my thoughts to crystallise. By midnight my usual remedies – a shower and a glass of wine – had failed to settle me. I slipped on the gown I'd borrowed from Raelene and went downstairs. All the lights were out except those in the lounge. Connie was in his favorite chair, sipping beer from a can. Empty beer cans were littered on the carpet.

'Joining the sleepless?'

'Too much on my mind.'

'Want to talk about it?'

I sat on the sofa opposite Connie and lent against a velvet cushion.

'What's been happening in the rainbow nation?' I asked, keeping my concerns about Hannes' murder to myself.

'Let's start with Mandela. You know how much he is loved. The day he came out of jail to lead the nation was the turning point. The kids round here went crazy that day. They adore him.'

'Well, he is an exceptional human being,' I said.

'Lately the country has changed so much that you won't recognize it. The myth now is that the blacks are running the country and we're all living happily together and everything is working out fine, but the truth is that there's one hell of a mess ... poverty in the streets and corruption in high places,' Connie stroked his goatee.

'It's hard to believe it's as bad as that.'

'The infrastructure's breaking down. Nothing works as it should – the post is unreliable, roads aren't maintained, streets are littered with rubbish, there are frequent power failures ... to list a few things. There aren't enough cops and they're underpaid,' Connie said.

'Do the blacks with jobs earn a decent salary these days?'

I asked.

'I pay my workers the going rate but there's mass unemployment and you just have to drive around to see the beggars and their shacks along the roadside.'

'I've seen it and it's awful.'

'It will take time. Things have to settle down you know. Mbeki's taken over and trying to control the black thugs but without much luck so far. He's no Mandela.' Connie said, leaning forward and placing his hands on the coffee table.

'So things aren't that easy?'

'In the cities some are making money behind their alarmed fences but out on the farms ... it's another story. Farmers all over the country have been attacked or killed, their livestock and equipment stolen. It's too dangerous out here for farmers to leave their families unprotected.'

Connie painted a scary picture of South Africa that was nothing like the country I had grown up in and known for so many years. The repressive government and its laws had disappeared but with change came all these problems. If not for the black people, the smell of the earth, the mountains, rivers and the farm itself, I could've believed I was elsewhere in Africa.

'Vince told me you've had your problems.'

He took a few slugs of beer and shrugged.

'You've done wonders with the farm.'

'The farm is my life. I won't leave and no *kaffir* can make me.' Connie tilted his head back to swallow the last of his beer. 'So what's really bothering you?'

I didn't answer.

'This hunt for Hannes' murderer is going to cause trouble. Mark my words.'

'Why should it?'

'Leave it alone, I say. Why dredge up all this old stuff?'

'Pa asked …'

'By the time Pa wrote that letter he was gaga.'

'That's not what Vince said.'

'Look, I'm telling you, leave it bloody well alone.' His eyes were stony.

'I can't Con.'

'A fucking bulldog – just like Pa.'

'Maybe.'

He stood and glared down at me. 'Let it go.'

I ducked past him quickly, hovering inside the door to the kitchen. I felt more secure with some distance between us. His belligerence must be the drink talking, I told myself.

'I'll get some milk and something to nibble and go back to bed.'

Part 2

Buds

Chapter 7

Even if I had the key to Pa's request, I had no idea how to tackle a murder investigation. All I could do was to remain vigilant – an early morning sparrow, picking up titbits of information, hungrily following any leads that presented themselves.

Dairy cows grazed as they had always done and I was curious whether Connie still operated the farm dairy. I found the small dairy attached to the back of the house was still a dank place that smelled of curds and mildew. The milking stools could've been the ones I'd sat on and the bloated cows may as well have been called Lucy, Daisy, Bettie and Sue. I drank from the froth offered me in the can. Its deliciousness was as I remembered. Licking my creamy mustache, I went out into a stream of light.

I took the path to the orange groves to look for Nathaniel. I hoped he'd asked the workers if they remembered the murder and found out something of interest. When I couldn't find him down at the orange groves I asked two workers on their way back to the huts if they'd seen him. They shrugged and threw their hands in the air.

When I returned to the house, food was what I wanted, not needed. The pantry was well-stocked and after some deliberating, I made my choice – an oversized chocolate muffin. Nettie's singing carried into the pantry as she tidied, cleaned and buffed the marble kitchen tops. As a gossip she made it her business to know as much as possible about the farm and the movements and intentions of the people on it.

She had moved on to her next chore, preparing a chicken for the evening meal, and made polite conversation. When the spicy chicken was in the oven I asked her about Nathaniel.

'He been in hut for nearly two days. No good for headman to lie in the bed.' She clicked her tongue. 'They say he come back to work tomorrow.'

'Is he sick?'

'Nooooo. He got too much *dagga.*' With her fingers she imitated the rolling of a paper to smoke marijuana.

'Does this happen often?'

'Mina already so cross she take the children go back to her Ma.'

'Where's Mina from?'

'She high-born Tswana like Nathaniel, from other side.'

'I would've liked to meet her and see the children.'

'Maybe she come back next week after she teach him lesson.'

'I bet Connie isn't pleased with him.'

'He can do nothing. Nathaniel is headman.'

'I suppose so.'

The blacks grew as much marijuana on the farm as they could. If Pa discovered the plants under trees or tucked behind fences he made the workers uproot and burn them. But as soon as one crop was destroyed another would appear and was taken to be dried in a secret area. In this way a constant supply was available.

Nathaniel learned to roll his mix of marijuana and tobacco from the other teenage boys and smoked with them from time to time. Later he grew his own or bought a supply from a neighbor with a less vigilant boss. I knew he was a regular smoker for relaxation after work but he had not smoked excessively and had never been unreliable. Was something wrong? Could it be the job? Nathaniel had been the most intelligent boy at his farm school. Could he have felt trapped in an unsatisfying job with no stimulation or future?

'Pity they smoke *dagga* … leaves poison … make them sick or mad if smoke too much.' She gave the workbench an extra rub.

The flower-laden breeze through the open window was urging me out but after scrolling through the activities I could follow, I realized there was nowhere to go that would advance my investigation of the murder. Though I had expected to spend time relaxing, I couldn't concentrate on a book or sleep. Hannes' murder was nibbling away at me.

I spotted the scrap of paper Nettie had given me with Tansie's address lying on the table next to my bed. It was midday when I set off. Fortunately it was only a ten-minute walk from the farm along the Rustenburg road. Striking red kaffirbooms and mounds of daisies edged the pavement and honeysuckle covered the wire fence. I was amazed. It was as it had been before.

The house was in a poor part of the town but the people living there were not the worst off. Compared to the shanties I'd seen a little further along the main road, it was a stable community of mainly black residents. The houses had originally been built forty or fifty years earlier for workers on the farms and platinum mines and it wouldn't have surprised me if some of those residents or their families continued to live there.

I had been told that the shanty town housed itinerants who had no other accommodation and had to be near their work. Many without jobs camped out there too and hawked goods on the street. The humpies were virtually thrown together from whatever materials were available – corrugated iron, plywood and so on. Life there was without almost every basic amenity and disease spread easily. There was no electricity, sewerage or enough water. It was an insecure life where crime was rife.

The small boxy houses in Tansie's suburb were built identically – they had two bedrooms, a lounge or dining area that led into the kitchen and a laundry and toilet outdoors. In South Africa then, houses were built solidly from brick, and not the brick veneer popular for building homes in Melbourne. Some of the houses wore bright fashionable colors and were adorned with a trellis or shutters. Others had enclosed narrow *stoeps* to create an extra living area or had used the small backyard for an added room and inside toilet. Many were individualized with a decorative plaque on the front door or wall, a weather cock or neat fence around the strip of front garden. In the narrow lanes music still blasted and young people lolled on street corners.

As Nandi had a corner house, her garden was larger than the rest and I could see that pot plants overflowing their containers were on either side of the front steps. In the backyard, jammed between the chickens and the clothesline, a bed of earth was exactly divided. In the one half vegetables grew and in the other flowers bloomed. Tansie's liking of flowers made me think she must've planted the garden.

I stood in front of the house wondering how ill Tansie was. Would she recognize me? I knocked on the door and Nandi opened it. She was wrinkled and thinner.

After looking at me a few times she shook her head. '*Hauw*! Is Missie Lindie here from orange farm,' she shouted excitedly.

I heard a thin but unmistakable voice from the backroom. 'You bring her here quick quick.'

Nandi whispered to me as she led me into the house, 'She very sick Missie.'

The house was newly painted in a pale pink and there were matching floral curtains and a thick rug on the floor. In the corner was a deep rose rocker. Tansie was older of course and lined, but her smile hadn't changed. We hugged, holding each other for some time.

'Why you wait till Pa die to come back?'

'I wanted to come before but …'

'I very happy to see you.' Her eyes shone with pleasure. 'You good present for me.'

'I wrote to you but the letters came back.'

'After you go I leave Rustenburg for Jo'burg with a new man. I think maybe I marry him but he turn out no good. He drink, hit my children just like first one … so I come home.'

'Your children … how are they?'

'Ah, they very good. You remember them?'

'Of course. We used to play together.'

Her voice was hoarse and she gasped for breath as she spoke.

'Rosie pay for everything,' she said, waving her arms round the room, 'house painted, new curtains, special chair that push up and down and new mattress ... and …'

'I'm happy for you,' I interrupted and placed my arm on hers.

'Rosie very clever. She doctor now in Jo'burg General Hospital!'

Rosie had always been a bright spark. When we were kids she made up games and set the rules. I knew she was the smartest of us all – her vivid imagination was a match for Hannes'. After five years in a combined farm school run by nuns she was the only black girl in the area to win a scholarship to a black high school in Pretoria. While she studied, Rosie stayed with her aunt and uncle, who lived and worked on a dairy farm outside the city. Each month Tansie struggled to pay towards her keep. Once Tansie showed me the red-rimmed tin for her savings that she hid in a deep vat of *meilie* meal.

When I told Ma about the tin with only a few coins in it, she was determined to help. 'There are so many black children out there with talent and ability with families too poor to even consider further studies,' she'd said. 'The least I can do is to give one I know the opportunity of an education.' Every month she gave Tansie sufficient money and books for Rosie's studies. Ma told me that the money came from the paintings she'd sold. 'It's our secret. Better not to tell Pa.'

Every week Tansie picked a huge bunch of veld flowers and leaves for Ma's studio. Arranged against a colorful backdrop with fruit and trinkets they formed the core of Ma's still-life studies.

Rosie's scores in her matric exam were so high that the University of the Witwatersrand, or 'Wits' as it was called, accepted her for medicine. At that time Wits was the only university that had a few black students on campus. Wil was studying law there and when I met him over lunch the black heads stuck out like crows in the snow.

'But I wish she married.' Tansie clicked her tongue and looked down. 'Zebedelia was young when you leave. Now she work in big government office. She got three boys!'

Tansie stretched across to the table next to her and handed me a photo album.

'Look, I got lot of pictures.'

Rosie, my childhood friend, smiled into the camera. We had played with pebbles, made people shapes from wire hangers and tied up coke tins to make a din. Would she be interested in seeing me again? She may have had her fill of whites by now. Would we have anything to say to each other?

'I'm surprised you're still living here.'

'Rosie find house on other side – close to shops, close to bus, big house for me and Nandi with beautiful garden ... Young Zulus one side, whites other side. I not know them. They not my people. This street – all Tswanas. We together from young … helping when we have babies, for sickness and we cry when old ones die. I church elder here. I tell Rosie … better to make this house nice and we stay here.'

I hesitated. 'So how are you?'

'Very sick Missie Lindie. Rosie say I got TB. Must be the devil bring it.'

I had read that a tuberculosis epidemic was raging throughout the continent and that it was the largest infectious killer in South Africa. Two-thirds of the population were thought to carry it without symptoms but more and more were developing the active symptoms in a new and deadlier form.

'Oh Tansie I am sorry.' I felt a stab in my guts.

She pulled her shoulders back and lifted her head proudly. This was how I knew her when she spoke of her heritage, of being Tswana. I squeezed her hand.

'How long have you been sick?'

'Rosie say she don't know. Maybe it lie inside for long time. Last year I go in hospital. But my Rosie, she look after me good. She here to see me yesterday with tablets but they make me more sick.' She pulled a face. 'She promise that one day they make me better … but I sure I die soon.'

She stopped talking, placed her hands on her lap and looked at me. 'I see your eyes ask question. You want ask me something?'

As ill as Tansie was, she still concerned herself with others.

Miriam's face formed a picture in my mind. 'Miriam,' I said tentatively. 'Do you know her?'

'Ooooo that Miriam … she big trouble.'

She coughed once and then again. She was tiring, lying back with her eyes closing every few seconds. I wanted to ask more but felt I couldn't.

I stroked her arm. 'You must rest.'

'Please, you come back very soon Missie Lindie.'

Nandi was waiting for me outside Tansie's room. Her lips were tight and her head to one side as she looked at me. She motioned for me to move away from the window.

I'd always thought of Nandi as my nanny's sister but Tansie had once told me that Nandi was a midwife and also a healer who had powers through her links with ancestral spirits. Nandi hid her spiritual strength, as women healers in the black community were often regarded as evildoers and witches. Any healing acts she performed were secret, so she wore ordinary clothes, not the beads and feathers of witchcraft that might draw attention to her. The ancestors and their spirits were so much part of African life that as a child I learned not to be afraid of them.

Nandi's eyes burned into my forehead. She must've known something about me that I didn't. Before I could resist she shoved me towards the corner of the room, so as not to be seen by onlookers. Next to me a portion of wall had been roughly covered with a worn piece of cardboard. She jerked at the cardboard to reveal a wallpapered niche cut into the wall. Inside was an oil lamp. This was Nandi's shrine, the place where she knelt and called on her ancestors.

She moved quickly to light the lamp and then delved into the pocket of her wide print skirt to extract a small glass bottle.

Though I pulled my nose up at the sight of the reddish stuff in it, I was intrigued. She shook the bottle vigorously, explaining that it was part of the afterbirth that she had removed in a recent birth. She told me that it was strong medicine that had its use in spiritual matters.

With eyes closed, she mumbled a refrain. At that moment I felt an icy shiver. It was like being under a cloud that passed the sun on a hot day.

'The spirits they come,' she said in a voice that sounded nothing like her usual one. A ribbon of wind swirled past me. I shuffled towards the door but Nandi put both hands out to stop me. 'You walk very careful Missie. Someone scared you see the past.'

Then she stood back, allowing me to pass. Whoever had been visiting had left.

'Can't you tell me more?'

'She shook her head.

'Nandi,' Tansie called from her room, 'You leave the spirits alone!'

Nandi muttered to herself in Setswana and slipped the bottle back into her pocket.

Nandi's psychic predictions and prognostications had been a source of amusement to both Hannes and me. She was rarely accurate and we ignored her warnings. However, she was correct when we least expected her to be. Once she warned of an evil wind on its way that would tear off roofs and kill livestock. The wind came the next day causing havoc.

'I'm going back now,' I could hear the edge in my voice.

'You come by yourself?' Nandi asked.

'Ja.'

Nandi warned me of the dangers lurking in the narrow streets and wouldn't allow me to walk back alone. I waited inside while she called her neighbor, Phinias. He must have been Nandi's age and would've been little use if a mugger had attacked us.

Arnie Swart's description of the awful stabbing remained in my thoughts. A fourteen-year-old boy was stabbed brutally and yet the police had made few investigations. It didn't add up. Surely questions were asked. Had Arnie told me the full story? Perhaps he would fill in some gaps if I prodded. When I phoned him he seemed pleased to receive my call and said he would try to drop in that afternoon.

It was almost dinner time and I was sipping a beer on the *stoep* when Nettie gave me a message that someone from the police station had phoned to say that the Detective Inspector was too busy and would come another time.

Connie rushed past me into the house, leaving his caked footprints on the slate and his sweaty smell behind him. I thought of Pa drinking cold beer as he listened to the radio after work. The news broadcast would be blaring and none of us were allowed to disturb him. When he had heard all he wanted he'd twiddle the dials to find music, preferably a military brass band. He enjoyed describing the different instruments and their sounds to us but we slipped away as soon as we could. Pa had played the trumpet in the school band and at concerts had solo spots. As an adult working the land he had no time to practice. His trumpet lay unused, its red case gathering dust in the attic.

At the dinner table crammed thoughts killed my appetite. Raelene had made curried chops for the main course. Fascinated, I watched Connie eat with his fingers, gnawing and pulling at the meat. He scooped his rice and vegetables into his mouth with a spoon and then sighed. I tried to eat to please Raelene but left most of my food on my plate. Peeved, she eyed me from under her lashes. I'd noticed that she and Connie seldom spoke to each other and were rarely in the same room together except during meal times.

Raelene had disappeared into the kitchen and Connie and I had retired to the lounge. He'd put down at least three beers before he spoke to me.

'Have you been having a good time?' he asked with a warmth that had been missing since my arrival.

'I've enjoyed being back here but I haven't had time to relax yet.'

'Well … you've been playing detective.'

'It's tough going and I haven't found out much. That's where I need your help. I want to know details … about the day Hannes was murdered. It bothers me that I can't remember.'

As the eldest sibling I expected him to have a different and helpful perspective on the murder and the events prior to it, although I knew his attitude to my investigation was bound to make him defensive. His face tightened and the pleasant expression vanished.

'You never could leave well alone, could you?' He snapped the cap off another bottle of beer and gulped some down. 'All I can give you is a vague outline.' He paused, thinking. 'After school Hannes helped with orange picking. We had the usual group of casual pickers – school kids and a few backpackers. At sunset they all left but Pa, Vince, Gerret, Hannes and me. I think Esiekiel, Nathaniel and one or two of the other blacks stayed too. We worked on until the light faded and when we packed up for the night we noticed Hannes wasn't around. We called out for him but when he didn't answer we thought he'd gone off with some of the school kids so we left for the house. That's it.'

'Even when you tell me about it I can't remember a thing.'

'Ah, well. That may be how God meant it to be.'

'Maybe.'

Connie tapped at the glass top on the cane table. 'Can you leave me in peace now?'

His voice was edgy as he picked up his bottle of beer. He drank most of it and sank into the chair. Communication was closed. There was no point in explaining the urgency I felt to find out more about the murder.

With a soft thud Duke was on his lap. Connie's frown lifted as he stroked the cat's head and spoke to it soothingly. Shifting position, Duke snuggled into his body. With eyes closed Connie rolled the cat over and expertly pleasured the exposed tummy.

I saw Vince standing in the doorway. He smiled at me and pointed at Duke on Connie's lap.

'A tender moment.'

'Where did you blow in from?'

'Rae let me in through the kitchen. Thought I'd pop in for a coffee and see how you're enjoying your break. Been standing here listening for a while.'

He sat on the sofa next to me. Minutes later Nettie carried in a tray with fresh coffee and a platter of biscuits.

'So how's the sleuthing going?' asked Vince as he stirred his coffee.

'Slowly. Much too slowly.' I laughed.

'So how far have you got?'

'I don't want to bore you two.'

I directed the comment mainly at Connie.

'If you've found out anything new we want to hear it,' Connie said, prizing the cap off another bottle of beer.

'You would've heard all the local gossip at the time … that the wrong men were arrested,' Vince said.

Connie muttered inaudibly.

'I have to get to the truth.'

'It's what Pa wanted … but it's all ancient history. Can't you let it be?'

'You know that I can't.' I battled to control my temper. 'I want to talk to the convicted men. Do either of you know where they are being held?'

'Pretoria Central,' Vince replied.

'I want to talk to them.'

'I'm hearing right? You want to visit the jail?' Connie said.

'I suppose I can take you,' Vince said. 'I'll rearrange a few things and make the time.'

'Thanks Vince.'

'You haven't changed. Not one bit,' Connie said sulkily.

'None of us has changed.' I glared at him.

'Cool it, the two of you,' Vince was playing mediator, the role he had played years ago.

Chapter 8

I woke feeling compelled to return to the heart of the past – the attic. Though drawn to memories of my discoveries there, I was repulsed by its creepy atmosphere. Attempts to slip back into escapism had failed. I threw the doona back, almost stepping on my uneaten breakfast. I bent down to a buttered slice of soggy toast and gulped back cold coffee. At least I had filled the tank sufficiently to sustain me. After a shower I avoided the kitchen and Raelene. A long chat with her and her tempting baking could have easily distracted me.

I took the wide-beamed flashlight from its spot at the foot of the stairs and climbed the short flight to the attic. The door was ajar. Was this a welcoming sign or had Nathaniel been forgetful? Whenever Hannes and I left the attic we closed the door as tightly as we could and even went as far as giving the doorknob an extra turn each to keep the 'nasties inside where they belonged'.

Navigating around broken furniture and useless household bits and pieces was easier than it had been times before. Though I moved without scratching or bruising myself against hard angles, new shimmering cobwebs cut across my path. I cursed as I broke through them.

As it was directly under the roof, the attic was a spacious area that followed the shape of the house. Though Hannes and I had worked our way through most of the junk, on each visit we found something we hadn't seen before. The oldest and most prized things were at the furthest point from the door but the thought of going down to the 'far end' to search them out had always been scary.

With no idea why I had been drawn there or what I was expecting to find, I reached the dusty space where Ma's paintings had stood. Logic didn't drive me beyond that point, it was a whiff of Ma's Vinolia soap. Entranced, I followed it. Moving deeper into the attic was like making my way through an inhospitable jungle. Taking careful steps and holding my arms close to my body I crept forward. Then I stopped. Sticky sweat had collected on my skin and I was breathing too fast. I swung the flashlight round but saw nothing out of the ordinary. Then, as I was about to turn back, I spotted six unframed paintings and shone the flashlight on them. Ma had painted life size portraits of each member of our family. I gasped. No superlatives could have described them. Not only had she captured resemblances but it was as if she had been inside our secret selves.

The first portrait was of Connie, the captain of the soccer team with his short neck and dark curls. She had caught the aggressive tilt of his chin, tight mouth and the ambitious glint in his eye. Vince's portrait stood next to Connie's. He had Ma's dreamy eyes and with a ray of light she had focused on Vince's hands with their long fingers. Ma had known about Vince's healing hands long before he studied physiotherapy.

Hannes was an imp. His eyes glinted with excitement and his mouth grinned naughtily. It was the way I liked to remember Hannes. Once again Ma had emphasized his golden skin and Bushman-like features.

My hair was in ringlets and I wore a frilly dress but the way Ma had portrayed my face surprised me. I had Connie's glinting eyes, the high cheekbones and my mouth was pursed in decision making. I laughed at her portrayal – she'd given me something to think about.

Ma's self-portrait accentuated her fine bone structure and her pale English complexion, her deep-set grayish-green eyes had her forthright stare. She looked dissatisfied, her mouth drooping slightly at the corners, and her jaw muscles were tense. Pa's portrait was last. Dressed in his khaki work clothes, he was wet under the armpits and had beads of sweat on his sunburned forehead. Pa had the familiar dark curly hair but his face was longer than any of ours and his eyes deep set, with his gaze distant. In Ma's portrayal Pa resembled his father, our Oupa Eric. The most striking part was the armband with an emblem that reminded me of a swastika.

On the first Thursday of every month Pa attended a meeting of the Broederbond. When we asked Pa about it he'd put a finger to his lips and say nothing. I can't imagine how Ma must've felt when she discovered that Pa had joined the anti-English Bond. Though she had lived in South Africa since she was about ten years old, her parents were British and her language was English. She must've been horrified when, during World War II, some Bond members expressed Nazi sympathies.

No wonder members had to meet in secret.

When she married into the Van Wyk family she improved on the Afrikaans she'd learned at school and embraced the family's ways but she made a point of speaking English and telling us about our English ancestors – the town where they lived and their history. She said she wanted us to have good manners and that she didn't want us to grow up like rough *boertjies*. 'There's more to life than soccer, *braaivleis* and the farm.'

Viewing the portraits had been so absorbing that I forgot I was in the dusty attic. When I left I closed the door behind me with the ritual double twist. On my way to my room I tried to work out when Ma had painted the portraits. They showed us at different times in our lives, as though painted in retrospect. I'd ask Nathaniel to free them from the attic and place them with the rest of Ma's work in the craft room. I expected the reaction from my brothers to be interesting.

That night Raelene made the viewing of the portraits an event by inviting Vince and Jeanette for coffee and cake in the craft room. Intrigued, I watched their reactions. Connie walked away from his portrait with a sour face but Raelene burst out laughing.

'A mother knows,' she said.

Vince looked at the light on his hands and shook his head.

'Amazing. I don't know when she painted this but from the softness of the face I must have been about sixteen. I hadn't decided on a career yet and physio wasn't on my list.'

Everyone agreed that Ma had me to a tee. The portraits of Ma and Pa triggered memories and conversation until late that night. Ma was giving each of us one of her lessons about ourselves again. The portraits cut deep, but they were excellent. I would take mine home with me. The rest would have to be framed and placed in my brothers' homes. That is, if they wanted them.

Chapter 9

Hannes had been in my dreams and when I woke he was still with me. 'Had I really known him?' I asked myself. I sifted through memories for answers.

There were three years between us but when I was little Hannes had seemed far older. He was bewildering. Whenever I thought I understood him, it was clear I didn't. Often the butt of jokes or nasty comments, he defended himself by snapping back or telling tales. He was secretive too, hiding sweets in his socks and his choice indulgence – chocolate – was often sandwiched between his books or toys so that he wouldn't have to share it. But I knew he was sweet underneath.

We were closest when he forgot he disliked me.

Some days I'd find Hannes sitting alone. When his dark eyes lost their gloss I could tell he was unhappy.

'Poor Hansie's sad?' I would say, putting my arm on his shoulder.

He'd shake his head.

'I'll make it better.' I'd give his cheek a kiss but he would push me away and give me a smile, pretending to be happy.

He'd play with me if it suited him. We'd race giggling through the house, but he had to be best at everything and was rarely satisfied with having fun. If he made hurtful remarks, I retaliated and we'd punch, scratch and slap, often ending up rolling down the stairs shrieking. Ma would yell at us both.

Nettie put the tray of breakfast down on the doona with a thump. She had a message for me from Vince to hurry up so that we could leave early for Pretoria. I washed and dressed as fast as I could and found Vince waiting in the car listening to cricket scores. He turned the radio down when he saw me. Smiling he clapped a slow clap and then looked at his watch. 'Here at last.'

Breathing faster than usual from hurrying, I dropped into the car seat.

'Visiting the jail is likely to be a waste of time but if you must, we'll go.'

'You never know.'

'Just like Pa. Once you get hold of an idea you won't let go,' Vince said.

'Is that a backhanded compliment?'

He cleared his throat and went on talking. 'I thought we'd go past Oupa Eric's place if you want to. It's on our way.'

'Good idea. I'd like to visit the old farm.'

He turned on the ignition.

'Please … wait a moment. In my rush I forgot my camera … and I want to pick some flowers.' I wanted a generous bouquet for the family graves.

The farm was ten minutes away along a little-used dirt road. I'd been to the cemetery there often with Pa to pay respects to family who had passed on. As we turned into the bumpy driveway I closed my eyes and held the edge of the seat. I opened them onto paddocks high with a grass wilderness and masses of pink and white flowers that bobbed like floating marshmallows. The once whitewashed house seemed to have shrunk and the green iron roof with its twisted gable was orange with rust.

Through a crack in a partly boarded-up window I peeked at a tiled fireplace, rose ceilings and greyed sheets covering the furniture. I thought of Oupa in his cane rocker under the striped awning that was no longer there and the fat golden Labrador that had lain at his feet. Vince's footsteps jiggled the broken mosaic tiles.

'Oupa's farm belongs to the three of us, so you'll have to tell us if you think we should keep it in the family or sell the land. We've had lots of offers.'

'Come, let's go to the graveyard,' I answered slowly. I needed to think about his question.

Oupa's family cemetery was far older than the one on Connie's farm. Our oldest known ancestors were buried there. Holding back the overgrowth, Vince helped me along what remained of the path.

Our grandparents were buried side by side. Mud, stones and weeds had wound themselves around the base of their tombstones. I felt a tug for Oupa Eric. Tall and burly, he used humor to take the edge off a tough farming life and spells of near-poverty. He fussed over Hannes almost as much as the three pedigreed Persians he spoiled relentlessly. At nine or ten Hannes would still sit on Oupa's lap to be petted like one of the cats. It was the love and attention missing from home that Hannes reveled in.

Oupa spoke of retiring, but chose to continue working part-time at the platinum mine close by. It was a mine accident that killed him and robbed me of the opportunity to spend time with him when I was older. I walked quickly past Ouma's grave. She was a finicky woman whom I didn't understand. I felt guilty about not spending more time with her.

We stopped at our great grandfather Louis' grave. The only times I saw him were after church or on birthdays and he always wore a black suit, tie and hat. He was a stern man but Georgina, our great grandmother, was gentler. I could picture her in her long dress nipped in at the waist and her hair piled on her head.

A tall crumbling headstone was inscribed with the dates 1832–1904. It was the grave of Cornelius – our great great grandfather.

'Our hero from the Boer War,' Vince said.

An icy blast swirled around me and I recognized Pa's signature scent – aromatic tobacco.

'Do you notice anything?' I asked Vince.

'Nothing. Just family graves,' he said looking puzzled.

'Never mind.'

I tried not to get rattled by visits from Pa. I took photographs of all the graves and of the cemetery so that I could place the photos together with the information I had gleaned about my Van Wyk ancestors. I explained to Vince that I had been researching our family tree and that I'd been successful in discovering Ma's relatives but not Pa's.

'Did Pa tell you anything about our family before Cornelius?' I asked.

'He said that they came out with the Dutch East India Company but he didn't mention names.'

'I wonder why.'

'Probably no reason other than he didn't know their names,' said Vince.

'Do you know anything about our great great grandmother Francina?' I asked.

He shrugged. 'During the Boer War women had very hard lives. I remember Pa saying that one of the women in the family was in a concentration camp in the early 1900s. Pity Pa didn't fill me in with details. I'm sorry now that I didn't ask.'

No wonder the British were hated, I thought. During the Boer War they scorched the earth, Afrikaans farms were destroyed and they put women and children into camps. As a result of overcrowding, poor nutrition and unsanitary conditions disease spread and thousands died.

We pushed on through the weeds. I spotted a row of unmarked mounds headed with rough crosses.

I pointed. 'And who lies there?'

'They're black servants' and loyal workers' graves.'

'No names?'

'Their families can identify them. I've seen them here. They're all Tswanas who worked on this farm and most are related to the workers on Connie's farm.'

As I placed flowers on the family graves, I said prayers for the dead, a ritual from childhood. Then impulsively I stood on my toes to hug Vince.

'Blood is thicker than water *sis*.'

We closed the rickety gate. The car was a refuge from the wilderness the farm had become.

'I'd prefer not to sell the land. Keep it in the family. ' I said.

'We could shift the graves.'

'Never. I'm not happy about that.'

'So what'll we do? The land is worth a few million.'

'If we sell, the buyer must agree to maintain the cemetery as it is.'

'That's a possibility.'

'It's about family. If we don't sell we could start up another farm for one of the children if you like. I don't care about the money.'

'That's an idea. Or either of us could pay you out.'

'Whatever you decide. It doesn't bother me as long as the dead are left in peace.'

We turned onto the highway, driving in silence.

'Look, that's where Ouma Lily spent her last days,' he said, pointing to a retirement home.

'Slow down, I want a look at it.'

The main building had been modernized and the two wings that fanned out from it were rebuilt. The landscaped garden was a delight.

'She never got over Oupa Eric's death but at least she spent her last years in comfort.'

'You must've been nine or ten when she died,' Vince said.

'Mmm.'

'Did you go to see her with Pa?'

'He made me go there with him. I didn't want to go but it was just as well I went that day. She died a few weeks later.'

'Pa could get anything he wanted out of us. You know that look of his?'

I pictured Pa looking down at me. Being tall, whatever age I was he looked down on me. He'd say nothing but lower his eyelashes and stare through them at me. How he maintained that fixed look I don't know but he did until I agreed to do whatever he had asked of me.

'Ja. Pa was a master manipulator. The day I went with Pa we found Ouma Lily crocheting in an easy chair. She was in a mess – hair uncombed, blouse partly unbuttoned and skirt caught up. Her clothes were strewn on the floor. When Pa went to speak to the nurse in charge, I was alone with Ouma. She was making an exquisite mauve shawl for Ma, following the intricate pattern she had used over a lifetime. She promised to make me a shawl but she died before she could start it. It was nice to have her promise.'

'Connie's a bit like her,' Vince said.

'Finicky. Back in the old days when she and Uncle Eric had their farm she was obsessed with cleaning.'

'I know. She was never without a cloth in her hand. She gave me hell for leaving finger marks all over the smooth surfaces. I shouldn't have done it but when she wasn't watching me I'd put a thumbprint or two on the glass coffee table to have the pleasure of watching her rush to clean it. Hannes was banned from her house for breaking those porcelain dancers in the showcase. If I'm right, Connie was good at borrowing money from her.'

We laughed so much that Vince had to slow down.

Chapter 10

The road to Pretoria was unrecognizable. Factories, modern shopping centers, housing complexes and hotels had sprung up to replace the trees and farmland I once knew. We passed a sprawl of large houses with landscaped gardens.

'Mainly white suburbs … but blacks can live wherever they choose now if they can afford it,' Vince said.

Some streets were closed to outside traffic and the large houses and gardens of the more affluent were surrounded by the high walls and razor wire that I'd been told about.

'This is ghetto living and I hate it,' I said.

He shrugged. 'That's life here. In spite of the dangers, lots of people have moved away from the city and have established themselves out here.'

Shops with expensive-looking goods, gyms, hairdressers and other facilities displayed their signs. Minicab taxis stood in line for customers.

'I'm impressed with all the development but what about all the violence and the mass of starving blacks?' I said, pointing to the rows of hawkers behind tables selling clothes, fruit and food. There were buskers and women displaying meat and corn they cooked over open braziers. Beggars were everywhere. Vince caught my horrified expression.

'Poverty is such a huge problem that the government doesn't know how to start dealing with it.'

I noticed Vince looking at his rear and side view mirrors every few seconds. He drove fast, avoiding clumps of cars and screeching away from traffic lights.

'Don't ask me to stop or slow down near here. We have to be on the look out all the time. Black gangs hijack cars … and if they catch you …'

He felt his leg. I noticed the bulge.

'You're carrying a gun?'

'Of course. I have to protect my family and myself.'

'But you're a physiotherapist.'

'That doesn't stop someone breaking into my rooms or my car and attacking me.'

'And Connie?'

'He carries one too.'

He saw the puzzled look on my face.

'I don't think you have any idea how much violence there is in the country and how dangerous it is. Black thugs carry guns and knives and there have been murders and rapes round here.'

'It's a lot to live with.'

'Oh well. You have to push it out of your mind and get on with things. What else can you do?'

As we entered Pretoria the loveliness of massed blue jacarandas lining wide avenues wiped away our talk of violence. When the jacarandas were in bloom only the tops of buildings peeked through. The old city with its European facade planned by Afrikaner forefathers had been the heart of apartheid fanaticism. I had often accompanied Pa when he visited Pretoria for supplies unavailable closer by. The once familiar mind map of the locations of streets and buildings in the city center had left me.

'Please drive through slowly so that I can see it all,' I said.

'Yes ma'am.'

Church Square. It had been drummed into my head at school. The Square was the place the Voortrekkers camped, to rest their animals while waiting to attend the Dutch Reformed Church's quarterly Holy Communion or *Nagmaal.*

The commemorative bronze statue of Paul Kruger, the first president of the Republic, dominated the square. The old civic stone buildings created in the early 1900s – Government House, the Supreme Court and the Reserve Bank – no longer shone in the sunlight. I hadn't appreciated their Baroque elegance in the past and even though they looked grubby, I now wished I had time to explore.

We passed the Court House, where in 1955 people believed to be undermining the apartheid government were charged with treason and tried. Nelson Mandela was among them.

'We're here. Pretoria Central,' Vince said raising his voice.

'It's creepy to think that prisoners convicted of sabotage were hanged in this jail,' I said.

'The bad old days,' he sighed.

'Only twenty or so years ago.'

'I phoned the jail early this morning to set up an interview with the prisoner you want to speak to. Though he's due for release, he's in the hospital wing. I had to do quite a bit of explaining to get us in there but when I told the officer you were the sister of the murdered boy, he agreed.'

We moved slowly towards the prison – a maximum security section, the general prison for sentenced prisoners, the female prison and the block for those yet to face trial were all lumped together. A steel grill clanged behind us once we passed the checkpoint.

Inside the general prison, the noise of men singing and calling each other echoed eerily against the walls. An officer led us up to the hospital section. Groans and tubercular coughs pierced the background noise. The number of rows of gaunt men lying in bed covered with blankets shocked me. Some hobbled about but the expectation of death hung around the dormitory.

'What I do for you,' Vince muttered unhappily.

The officer called an orderly aside. They spoke too softly for us to hear but I noticed the orderly's shrug.

'So you want to see Nico Diswi?'

'Ja, please.'

'He's due for release but I doubt he'll be going anywhere. Too sick.'

'Are you saying he'll die in here?'

'Like the rest.'

The man had been in prison for about forty years. What with harsh treatment, poor food and overcrowded conditions it was amazing he was still alive.

'Don't expect to get much out of him. He can go days without talking.'

'Not much to say in here.' I looked through glass at the drab surroundings and rows of sickbeds.

'Here – two masks,' the officer said, passing them to us. On our side of the glass masks hung from all the staff members' necks, while those moving among the beds wore them.

'We've got a TB epidemic in the country. It's all over Africa but figures say it's worst here. With all of them cooped up, sick or frail, it's spreading like bloody wildfire. It's everywhere, so wear your masks. Follow me.'

I put on the mask, flung my head back and squared my shoulders. The orderly led us into an interview area where an emaciated man with his head slumped on the table was waiting for us. His face was scarred and he smelled the vile smell of the sick.

'He's all yours.'

Nico Diswi half opened his eyes and shut them again, showing no interest in us. Then he moistened his cracked lips with his tongue. I noticed he had no front teeth – possibly no teeth at all. Of all things to bring him, *biltong* – the dried meat delicacy – was a poor choice but it would be snapped up by another. A chocoholic for years I always carried chocolate in some form. I had a large block, missing the top row, in my bag. I sealed the foil.

'We brought you some chocolate and sliced *biltong*, Nico,' I said placing them in front of him.

He nodded, slowly lifting his head and took both. Shakily he stuffed them into his pocket.

'You talk to him,' Vince said moving a few steps back.

'I'm Linda and this is Vince. I don't know if they told you why we're here.'

He stare was glazed.

'We are the brother and sister of the boy you were jailed for killing. We're here to ask you about the murder.'

'Ja?' His voice was a whisper.

'Do you remember what happened the night of the murder?'

'Ja.'

'Can you tell me anything about it?'

He half closed his eyes. 'Ja,' he sighed.

'Please.'

He peered at me. 'It long time ago.' He was seized by a spasm of coughing.

We waited.

'We drinking.' He swallowed. 'Take a shortcut.'

'Across the Van Wyk's land?'

He shrugged. 'We no kill boy.' He stared ahead.

'Maybe you've forgotten.'

'Inn-o-cent.' Tears and coughs mingled. He wiped his eyes on his sleeve and after several sips from the glass of water next to him his breathing was still wheezy. After a few minutes he propped his head up with one hand and looked at me again. He cried, first softly, then louder. 'No, no, no, we not kill anybody. We innocent … inn-o-cent.'

'All criminals say they're innocent,' Vince said.

There was no point in answering.

'We eating at my father's house,' he said in a weak voice. 'We there six o'clock to eleven o'clock in night. Police doctor, he say murder was eight o'clock. We not there. You tell me how we can kill boy.'

'And the knife?'

'We find the knife lying in grass on the farm. Is a good knife, we say. We take it. The police say we kill the boy with the knife. We say no … they say we lying. They hit us … till we sign paper.'

He lay back in his chair gasping for air.

'Did you have a attorney for the trial?' I asked.

His voice was just above a whisper. 'Ja but he not help. The court say my father, he lie to help us and we use knife to kill boy. Not true.'

There was nothing I could say.

'I in jail very long time. I get old and the TB find me. I die here soon, for sure. Two others charged now dead. One die year before last and other die two months back.'

'If you three didn't kill Hannes, do you know who did?'

Exhausted, his head slipped back onto the table.

'I too tired now. You go. If you find out killer ... is too late for me.'

Hurriedly we left the building. I took several deep breaths.

'I hope you spend the rest of your time here relaxing. Visiting jails filled with the dying is heavy,' Vince complained.

I gave his arm an affectionate pat. 'At the *braai*, Cobie as much as admitted that the confessions of those men were made under duress.'

'Was it worth the hassle … something you won't be able to do anything about?'

'Ah, Vince. Really!'

'You know I wish we could find the real murderer and make him pay but … it's an ancient story.'

I cut in. 'While I'm here I'll do everything I can to sort it out. It's the least I can do for Pa and Hannes.'

'Good luck. And in case you don't know it, things are different here now. Justice moves even more slowly than it did before.'

During our return journey, Vince turned on the car radio. A cricket match was being broadcast.

I recognized the tall ugly monument rising above garlands of jacarandas. The Voortrekker Monument had been erected to remember and honour the Voortrekkers who opened up the country. They had traveled from the Cape to the Transvaal in their covered wagons in search of a place to set up farms and practise their beliefs free of British interference.

I pointed at the monument. 'Is there time to ride past for old time's sake, and have a look at the nature reserve? I've heard great things about it.'

'Another time. I've had my fill of Pretoria today … and I do have to get back to work.' He increased the radio's volume and put a finger to his lips.

I asked myself what Hannes would've thought of the city now? Would the throngs of people and the exotic smells and variety of sounds have excited him?

My inner voice warned me to stop torturing myself. I had learned to heed that inner voice and slumped against the padded leather. With snippets of the cricket in the background, my eyes closed and eyelids fluttered.

The visit to the jail had left me flat. I was satisfied that the three men were innocent but I had no idea of my next step. Arnie Swart's information and the snippets I had gleaned on the farm had provided me with nothing substantial to work with. I wrestled with myself, trying to justify dumping the investigation. After all, I had gone as far as I could with it – what more could Pa have expected of me?

Over the next two days I made relaxation my aim. At least I began the day with that intention. I'd sleep late, pass up breakfast, then pad downstairs to the kitchen to chat with Raelene over coffee and try her latest sweet delicacies. The extra sleep made me aware of my tiredness. On the *stoep* in a stripped swing I unwound. I swung to my inner tune, to the wind or a bird's song, sleeping and daydreaming. A pile of Raelene's detective novels by Patricia Cornwell, Agatha Christie, Ian Rankin, Nicci French and some others lay unopened next to me.

I was restless and went down to the orange trees. From a safe distance I watched the bees swarm over the fragrant blossoms. When I was little and Pa was struggling to get the farm going he kept bees. Orange blossom honey fetched a top price at the market and he and Esiekiel collected it in spite of being stung through their protective clothing. Ma adored the delicate flavor of the honey and called it angel juice. She spread it on her toast and mine each morning and I developed a taste for it too. When the trees yielded a full orange crop Pa was delighted to stop collecting honey from 'the stinging little devils'.

As hard as I tried I couldn't block out Nico's face – ulcerated, scarred, his yellowed eyes large with fear. The jail and his illness had stripped his humanity away and he'd grabbed at the *biltong* and chocolate like an animal. The antiseptic smell that couldn't disguise the stench of rows of ashen-faced men huddling under grey prison blankets waiting to die had remained in my nostrils.

On the afternoon of my second rest day, a walk past an ancient wisteria creeper, lusher when Hannes and I were children, was a reminder of the hide and seek games we'd play behind the trellis. We had telltale lilac all over us after the game. I was surprised that the gardenia Hannes disliked for its sweetness was still flowering. It swept back thoughts of him. If Hannes had lived would he have developed into the devilish man his teacher, Tillie Meintjies, predicted? I doubted it. He certainly wasn't meant to be an artist or musician, with his mechanical style of playing. Would he have studied further – gone to university? I was certain he would have. Perhaps he'd have studied law. That sharp tongue, his agile mind and taste for drama would've made him an excellent lawyer. If only he'd lived.

The warm breeze stirred, turning into a sharp gust that blew sand on my face. Hannes was with me again. Throwing sand at me when I was in one of my dreamy states – one of Hannes' ways of getting my attention.

'Rest, Hannes, rest,' I said gently.

But more sand came at me. This time it was thrown on my back.

'Alright. I'll do my best to find your murderer. Don't ask me how I'll manage it, but I'll try.'

The air was warm and breezy again as I made my way back to the house.

Chapter 11

From the day I arrived the sky had been speaking to me and the wind was wild. At first I thought it was my fresh eyes seeing the farm with such intensity. Later I was certain that there was something odd about the farm's atmosphere.

I was relishing an early walk, with no desire to visit the cemetery again, yet my feet were drawn to it. The push was too strong to ignore. I crossed the veld and went through the cemetery gate. On the grass near Pa's grave I sat staring at the rough sand. My eyes were open and as much as I was present I felt as if I wasn't there at all. The aroma of Pa's tobacco was around me.

'Find the devil that killed our Hannes,' Pa's voice said in my head, as a bubble of light swelled over Hannes' marble tombstone. A breeze swept a white flower over the tombstones and landed it at my feet. As I bent to pick it up a ripple tickled my back. It had to be Hannes. He would tickle until I cried.

Gasping, I ran from the cemetery and from the tall cypresses surrounding it. In the house I argued with myself. Did I hear Pa's voice or was it a memory of his voice? Could it be Pa's spirit or was it all my imagination, a daydream? And what about the flower and the back tickle? Perhaps I was losing my grip, feeling vulnerable. But I was well, I told myself. I'd seen enough psychotic people during my time as a nurse to know irrational thinking – delusions and hallucinations. Of course, if I was psychotic I wouldn't know it, I chided myself.

My argument with myself shifted into another circle. I had been intuitive all my life and as a child I was adamant that I had seen ghosts on the farm. Throughout Africa people believed in their ancestral spirits. Death and spirits were part of their lives. I couldn't find a logical answer and for the time being I decided to let it unravel itself.

Raelene was in the kitchen. Usually she dressed early but this morning she was still in her dressing gown.

'Everything okay Rae?'

She wiped her eyes and carried on whisking egg whites.

'I feel lousy. Flat, you know. I used to be a happy person,' she said as the whites stiffened.

'I think of you as bright and happy.'

'I suppose it's something to do with losing my job at the library. At least I felt useful working.'

'Mmm,' I tried to find the right words but didn't know what to say.

'Connie's no easy baby. Has to get things his own way or he gets into a hellish mood.' I sensed she didn't want to say he could be aggressive. I hoped he hadn't hit her. She gently added the egg whites to a mixture in a large bowl. 'I'm rattling on but I really wanted to ask you about your old nanny. How is she?'

I told Raelene about Tansie's illness. She'd met Tansie once or twice with Nettie. Tansie was one of the few blacks Raelene liked. Mostly Raelene found the changes in the country difficult to take and was still living in the old days where blacks knew their place. Fortunately for Tansie, Rae agreed to give her some of her bottled preserves. I packed a full basket, keen to take them to her.

'You're not going out of the house on your own again. We want to send you back to Oz in one piece.'

'Don't fuss about me. I'll be fine.'

'Nonsense. Ralph will go with you.'

I'd spoken to Ralph a day ago. He was older of course, around sixty, but his slim muscular body had hardly changed from the way I remembered it as a child and not a single grey hair was visible. He was one of Nathaniel's friends and had played with us occasionally.

I tapped my fingers on the kitchen table while I waited. Raelene put an arm round my shoulder.

'Connie told me you're looking into Hannes' murder. It won't be easy.'

'No it won't.'

It struck me that Raelene and Connie had married a few months before the murder. In the eighteen or so months of their engagement Hannes had chatted with Raelene often while Connie was watching soccer on TV. He spoke fondly of her and said he looked forward to her living on the property.

'Did you see Hannes on the day of the murder?' I asked.

'It's stuck in my mind because it was the last time I saw him. He popped in for something to eat and a chat after school. He was agitated and angry about something. All I remember him saying was something like, "That bastard will pay, I'll see to it." He wouldn't say more.'

Raelene watched the oven timer while I wondered what Hannes could have been agitated about.

'It's ready,' she said opening the oven carefully and placing a golden cake on the rack. At last Ralph arrived.

'We go,' he said.

At Nandi's house, Ralph handed me the basket filled with Raelene's preserves.

'I sleep outside for little bit.'

Nandi smiled a warm greeting and without a word ushered me in. Tansie was dressed and seated in a chair. I gave her a hug and fussed round her.

'So how are you today?'

'I see you, I feel better.'

'Good.'

'I wear green scarf special for you today. Your Ma give it to me long, long time ago. At same time she give me big pan for frying and big pot for boiling.'

'Oh.'

'She very good to me.'

I hadn't known that she loved Tansie too. I unpacked the basket.

'Healthy food for you to get well,' I said explaining that the food came from Raelene. She clapped her hands in front of her chest in the old fashioned manner and took the basket from me with both hands. Then Tansie stared at me, her eyes traveling over me.

'I see you have visitors. Pa and Hannes come to you today.'

She said this as if the auras she saw were an everyday occurrence. I slipped in a question about Miriam. Tansie hadn't given me a direct answer last time I asked about her.

'You leave her alone. She big big trouble,' she answered sharply.

'Why?'

Tansie ignored my question and twisted her body towards the window. 'I listen for car,' she said pulling back the curtain. 'Rosie, she got afternoon off and come today. She say she want see you.'

It wasn't long before a car drove up and a slim woman in a white doctor's coat with her hair pulled back and high cheekbones rushed into the room. At that moment she hadn't changed. She was still the skinny black girl in the torn dress, my best friend. We hugged, kissed and cried. Holding hands, we sat on the couch. Talking fast and over each other, needing questions answered, our words mingled. We giggled and hugged again. Then more slowly we asked each other about our jobs, our lovers and friends. We discovered we both worked in hospitals and thought it a weird coincidence. After years of study Rosie had become a doctor, one of the first blacks to specialize and certainly one of the few who were women.

'I must take this off,' she said pulling at her white coat. I was in a hurry to leave.' She straightened her clothing and ran a comb through her hair. 'So tell me, how's Willie? Still such a love affair?'

'We've split.'

'Aah,' she touched my shoulder. 'I can't imagine being with one person all the time for years and years. Boyfriends are enough for me. And there have been no shortage of them,' she said, putting a stray hair in place.

'Career first?'

'It has been that way but I've missed having children. I envy you Davie.'

'He's filled our lives. He and I became close, too close. Now he's gone to the US with his young wife.'

'Oh well, you must have some sorting and growing to do.' Her smile faded as she turned towards Tansie. 'You okay Ma? We're being very rude, ignoring you.'

'Much to talk after such long time,' Tansie smiled.

Rosie switched into her health care mode for a few minutes as she fussed over her mother. Then she went to the car for her doctor's bag.

'I didn't notice him a moment ago when I first rushed in but there's a man asleep outside,' she announced.

'That's Ralph waiting for me. Raelene won't let me out of the house alone.'

'That's wise. It's not even safe out for black women with so many rapes occurring every day.'

Rosie examined Tansie quickly. Then she kissed her. 'You're doing really well Ma.'

Tansie heaved herself up from the armchair and walked away, sighing.

'Ma's been doing quite well compared to others I've seen and is responding to medication, but unfortunately I doubt she'll recover ... She may've been carrying the TB bacteria around for years, so many of us do. But she's been sick a lot lately and her age is against her. It's not surprising it took hold. But I'm hoping she'll be with us for some time.'

Rosie told me that she had been tested for TB and found she was carrying it. She thought it was her work that had exposed her to the bacteria and that she was taking medication and monitoring it.

Nandi brought in two mugs of coffee. My mug was chipped so I drank from the other side. I felt close enough to Rosie to tell her about Pa's letter.

'Hannes never fitted in, poor kid. Do you remember the day we were playing that game of ours with the stones when we heard crying? He was huddled on a mat behind old Zacharias' hut. One eye was purple and he had a bleeding gash on his leg.'

'Ja, ja.'

'You must've started your nursing days then,' she laughed. 'You tore your dress and made a bandage from the material.

'When Ma asked him what had happened he told her he'd had a fight with Pierrie du Toit over marbles. I knew he'd given his marble collection away months earlier. Poor Hansie, he made Ma and me promise we wouldn't say a word about it to Pa, the principal or his teacher.'

'That wasn't the first time he was attacked, was it?'

'It goes back as far back as my memory takes me,' I said.

'If I can help with your investigation, just ask.'

I put my arm around Rosie as we sat basking in friendship. Rosie had been Hannes' friend too. He called her his girlfriend. I knew they had told each other things they didn't share with me and at the time I had been jealous. But when Hannes had such an awful time at school, how could I begrudge him the extra care and love that Rosie gave him? I had seen them hold hands and even kiss. They were both in their early teens then and I had no idea if they had moved on to a sexual relationship.

'By the way, how's Connie these days?'

'Maybe a bit more aggro than before.'

'That's for sure. I heard he'd beaten up one of his workers a few months ago. Insolence apparently. Anyway the worker was in a bad enough state to have his wounds dressed in hospital.'

'How did you hear about it?'

'Hospital drums work like the old grapevine.'

'Is Connie crazy? Why do you think he did it?'

'Too many beers, I think … and Franz can be rebellious. I know him … he's got a big jaw that gets him into trouble. Something else. I hate to tell you this but I saw Raelene in the town a few months ago in dark glasses that couldn't cover the bruise on her face.'

'Oh, no,' I murmured, horrified.

Rosie topped up our coffee and told me about her work. How swamped their casualty departments and hospitals were with long queues outside. Apart from those with AIDS, hepatitis and TB, the increase in poverty caused illness to spread more easily. Alcoholism and drug-taking were on the increase, with more and more children coming into hospital abused by their families. As she talked, I wasn't attending as well as I should've been. My thoughts were on Connie's aggression.

'I'm late,' Rosie said looking at her watch. 'I must go back to work.'

We woke Ralph and Rosie drove us back to the farm. As I walked into the house my anger about what Rosie had told me about my brother intensified. Connie had always been arrogant and authoritative but I couldn't imagine him attacking Raelene. Beating up an impertinent worker was easier to picture. Ma and Pa had argued a lot but Pa had never called Ma ugly names or abused her. If Connie had hit Raelene, whatever the reason, there was no excuse.

I had expected Connie too look older but not so bloated and pale. From the brief time I'd been at the farm I'd seen him drink a lot. I had no idea if he drank as much every night or if he was drinking more due to Pa's death. I had lost touch with him during all these years. In the past Wil had been closer to Connie than I'd ever been. He could've spoken to Connie about it. I couldn't.

I turned my thoughts to Raelene. I wondered if her virtual obsession with cooking was the result of problems in their relationship and not the loss of a job. Raelene enjoyed craft work yet she had not turned to it for solace. Food was her comfort – cooking and eating it. Her unhappiness concerned me. She had hinted at difficulties with Connie and the air between them was tense. They acted with forced politeness, barely talking over meals. I could only wait and watch.

Chapter 12

Too much wine the night before left me feeling seedy the next morning. I put the bacon and eggs aside and faced the toast and marmalade with little enthusiasm. A cool shower and a drink of water revived me.

My morning was consumed by chores. I dutifully accompanied Raelene on her rounds of food collection, from butcher to fishmonger and to the supermarket. She bought with an eye for quality rather than price, squeezing and smelling produce and checking use-by dates so that by the time we returned to the farm we had a car full of what must have been the best produce available.

Though I told myself that trying to find Hannes' murderer was a waste of time, it didn't work. Even though I had no leads, I felt guilty about not doing enough. By midday my frustration peaked. Back home I was organized and efficient – I worked through a prioritized list and then carried on to the next thing. The way to go is to start at the beginning with what you know and think that through again logically, I told myself. That was the way I had achieved results in the past. Mentally I ticked off my snippets of information. I thought about Arnie Swart's visit and his glib reading of the crime reports. The coroner during the period of Hannes' murder was still alive. I'd seen him at the *braai.* Perhaps I would learn something from a talk with him.

Luckily, Vince wasn't busy with a patient when I phoned. When I asked if he knew the coroner's phone number and address, he laughed. 'Cecil Redlinghuis is a cynical old bastard but he loves to talk. You never know, you might get something out of him. And if you don't, you'll enjoy the visit.'

'He sounds interesting. You know, a chink of lost memory's just come back to me. When Hannes was buried I had this feeling that Cecil and Pa were up to something. I remember them whispering in a corner.'

'Be prepared to spend a few hours.'

Dr Cecil, as he liked to be called, agreed to see me that afternoon. He had a cottage in a retirement village that faced the Magaliesberg Mountains.

He opened the door a second after I had rung the bell and, grinning broadly, he asked me into his lounge. He must have been in his early eighties but still had most of his hair and walked without a stick. The small room was furnished tastefully with antiques. A tall cabinet was filled with collector's items from all over the world – cups and saucers, plates, thimbles, cats and miniature shoes.

'What a delightful room,' I said.

'It's the showpiece of this retirement village. Quite frankly I'm tired of people coming to look at it.'

'I'm sure,' I mumbled.

'Sit and relax. Doris will bring us tea and cake soon.'

I tried to sink into the brocade cushions but they were too stiff to be comfortable.

'So tell me my dear, what brings you here? This can't be a social visit, though I am pleased to have your company – I get visitors so seldom.'

'I'm having another look at a murder that took place in 1965 – the murder of my brother Hannes. I was hoping you might remember the case.'

'Oh yes … as if it were yesterday. A vicious stabbing and that lipstick wiped off. Your poor Pa. I can't remember most of my cases from all those years back but this one was different because Hannes was your Pa's boy and your Pa and I were old friends. We were at the same school. He was ahead of me but you know what those farm schools are like with all the grades combined. We became friends then went our separate ways but we still had a drink together at the Burg Hotel now and again. I came immediately when I heard that Hannes' body had been found – I wasn't going to leave it to the other bloke. It was a brutal murder and I had to do my best for your Pa. That's the least I could do.'

'Detective Inspector Swart went through some details about the murder in the police reports . . . but I thought that perhaps there was more to it . . . and the whole story wasn't written down.'

'You should know, in these situations the truth lies somewhere between the lines.'

'What do you mean?'

'Every family has secrets. Your family is no different.'

'The days leading up to the murder, and those immediately after it, are virtual blanks for me so I don't know what you're talking about. All I can remember are a few shadows. I've been told it's shock or trauma ... whatever you want to call it. I'm hoping my memory'll come back as I hear more about it.'

'It's a fairly common reaction to an extremely painful situation. If you haven't retrieved the details by now ... well, I don't know. It's a long time but experience has taught me how strange memory can be.'

'About the secrets?'

'Your late Pa was worried and I helped him out by keeping my mouth shut. I can't tell you about it. Patient–doctor confidentiality.'

'So you're saying you can't tell me. Not even after Pa is dead and all those years have passed.'

'Sorry, but no, I can't.'

Doris served tea in fancy gold-rimmed cups and her fairy cake was high and light. For the next hour we talked about people we knew and memories of the past. He certainly enjoyed talking. I had one more bite at trying to urge him to tell me more about the murder but I was wasting my time. The doctor's reluctance to talk about a murder that took place so many years ago only confirmed my suspicions. Facts must've been diluted or covered up.

It was sunset when I returned to the farm. Connie and Raelene were about to start dinner when I walked in through the back door. I joined them at the table. Raelene talked a lot and fast but Connie was silent.

I sat talking to Raelene in the *voorkamer* over coffee. The conversation slid back and forth. I realized how difficult it would be to find a way of asking her if anything was bothering her. Then, yawning and complaining of tiredness, I went upstairs. The room of my childhood had become my refuge. With the help of a few glasses of wine, sleep came quickly.

It was past midnight when I woke. Too alert to go back to sleep I turned on the bedside light and pulled back the covers. As I sat on the bed shuffling for my slippers, I met Pa eye to eye in his photograph. I touched the gold frame and stretched to kiss him through the glass.

'Pa,' I whispered. 'You were so sweet-tempered as long as we all played your game. Each one of us loved you in our own way and I'm sure you knew it. You've asked a lot of me, Pa. You knew I'd do anything you'd ask of me and try my best but … this may be too much.'

Pa and I were so alike that he must've gauged my reactions and known that if I began the investigation I would be hooked.

I looked at Pa's photo again. He had been a strong, dominant man and it showed in his mouth and eyes.

During the night I dreamed of the way Pa urged me to study when I didn't want to. He was persuasive, his voice loud and definite, and I didn't dare argue.

The shrill of an alarm jolted me from sleep. Lights blazed outdoors and people shrieked. Too afraid to put on the bedside light or move, I hid under the covers. Beneath my window I heard thumping, banging and running feet. Connie's voice was shouting orders. By the time Raelene came into the room I had imagined a variety of unpleasant scenes.

'It's nothing serious. We've had an attempted break-in that triggered the alarm. It happens … but we've got a top-of-the-range security system. Connie should've warned you.'

'Where did they try to get in?'

'The garage. They must have been after the Land Rover and some of the equipment but they ran off when the alarm blasted.'

'Have you called the cops?'

'No. Waste of time. Connie, Nathaniel and Ralph have gone after a blue Escort they saw driving away. If they catch 'em they'll call the cops. There are too many break-ins now for the cops to handle.'

'Does this sort of thing happen a lot?' I asked.

'Every few weeks or so. We've had a few close calls, but as long as no-one's hurt, we can handle it.'

'I hope Connie and the others will be careful.' I wasn't used to this vigilante approach.

'We all have to be careful, especially driving. Don't forget, if you're on your own, try not to stop at red lights – you may be held up by muggers. Go through the intersection cautiously.'

'If another car doesn't hit me, the muggers will?'

'Something like that. My car has a top-of-the-range burglar alarm. It's almost impossible to deactivate it. I'll show you how to set it.'

'Phew!'

'We haven't installed some of the popular anti-theft devices like flame throwers. They're too dangerous. The driver could end up burned as well as the thief. Connie has put in the best possible alarm system but not even that's foolproof.'

'So how do you live with knowing you could be mugged or burgled or worse?'

'Prayer. Once we've taken all the precautions we can, the only thing that helps is prayer and a sense of humor,' she smiled wryly. 'I'm making some cocoa ... want some?'

'I'll come down to the kitchen.'

An hour or so later I heard Connie drive in and the voices of men talking.

'It doesn't sound like they got them,' Raelene said.

Part 3

Fruit

Chapter 13

I woke to birds calling and the shush of breezes tickling the veld. Part of me could've stayed on the farm forever and yet there was a pang of longing for home, with its rosy dawn stirring the spring bush, the breeze rattling through the silver wattles and the crazy magpies.

Vince had invited me for lunch. We agreed to meet at his consulting room and to grab a bite at a café close by. He warned me that he didn't have the time for more than a quick sandwich. All I wanted was to see where he worked so that I could carry that picture home with me.

Vince was the quietest, most studious and best-looking of us four. He starred academically and was good at the sports he enjoyed – athletics, swimming and tennis. Unlike Connie, he wasn't interested in soccer or cricket. Ma said he was too gentle and clever to be a member of the Van Wyk clan. She adored him and called him her 'perfect' boy. Vince had a kind way of talking to me when I was little. Speaking softly, he'd put his head to the side as he did when he explained things, rather than yelling at me like Connie did. But for all his qualities, he didn't have Hannes' sense of humor and imagination, Connie's toughness, or any of the artistic abilities that I had inherited from Ma. He wasn't cut out for farming either. Pa said that Vince was too soft for a farming life – and he was probably right. After Hannes died, Pa accepted that only one of his sons would help him on the land; the other would help members of the community.

Vince's practice was on the second floor of a modern cement and glass building. The clinical-looking building housed only doctors, psychologists and physiotherapists. I walked up the stone steps and along the corridor to number eight. When I opened the glass door with Vince's name on it in black letters, I felt proud. The waiting room was light and bright with blue couches and tubs of decorative plants. A patient was reading a magazine while he waited. Another, head in hands, stared at the carpet. The inner door opened as Vince supported the arm of a middle-aged woman walking in obvious pain. I saw the healer in Vince, a side I had rarely seen.

Lunch was hurried, with hardly any time to talk. We took the long route back along brick-paved paths where trees were generous with their shade. I felt comfortable with Vince and I tried not to think that I would be leaving soon.

A lanky dark-haired boy of fourteen or fifteen, tugging at his rucksack as he passed us, reminded me of Vince at that age. He had been a prefect, smart at his schoolwork, top scorer in the athletics team and girls chased him even though he wasn't interested in them. Not then. Many of the boys were jealous of Vince. From behind their hands they whispered that he was too full of himself. To his face they called him a swot and accused him of brown-nosing the teachers.

After weeks of ignoring the name-calling Vince thought up a plan of retribution. It was the scraping and running sounds under the floorboards of the farmhouse that gave Vince the idea. Since the last time Pa had set mice traps the mice had been breeding again. I liked mice and stroked their sleek bodies and held the babies up by their tails. Vince watched me and shuddered. His plan was to collect as many mice as possible in shoe boxes. First he made breathing holes in the lids, then he lifted Boris, the big grey-and-white cat, out of his basket and put him under the manhole. Boris purred loudly as he rounded up the mice. Lannie the sheep dog would've been proud of him. Wearing Ma's kitchen gloves, Vince scooped the mice up and pushed them into the boxes. With four boxes tied together with string he easily carried them to school at the back of his bike.

I'm not sure how Vince lured the boys who had bothered him into the school store room but once in there he turned off the lights, freed the mice and locked the door. The boys' screams carried through the school.

Over coffee we laughed about the episode. Vince returned to work and I shopped in the malls and alleys before driving home.

I was curled up in the leather couch reading a book when I felt an overwhelming urge to leave the house. Out I went, across the slate *stoep* and down the steps. I couldn't tell where I was directed or why. Like a dog on a lead I went through the garden and along the blue-blossomed path to the dam. At the dam edge where the green carpet was lushest, I stopped. There was nothing, apart from water surrounded by willowy trees and bushes bursting with blooms. Down the slope was a rusty wheelbarrow, the farm manager's cottage and the orange groves silhouetted against the mountains.

'Why did you bring me here? Stop playing fucking games with me! Tell me Hannes … tell me why you brought me!?' I yelled.

Perhaps the birds and grubs heard me. My thoughts were tangled and my body feverish. The water, dotted with fallen flowers, was inviting. I didn't mind that it was a bit murky, I thought. A trickle of overnight rainwater from the hills had filled it. I screened out all thoughts of nasties inhabiting the water. I'd have a dip and keep my head up.

Glancing about, I checked. I was alone. In one movement I pulled off my sundress but kept my bra and knickers on. I threw my dress, sunglasses and watch onto the grass and waded in over flat green spikes, past pollen-filled rushes and into the squish. Discomfort didn't register. I gave myself to the cool wet and the perfume of the flowers.

I floated on my back, forgetting to hold my head out of the water. The chatter in my head stilled as I basked in the filtered sunlight. Lazily I turned, dipping into the water and floating again, my body tingling as my mind drifted.

I imagined I was hiding behind the bushes with Hannes, watching black couples splashing and teasing until they collapsed in a shrieking tangle. We moved closer as their excitement grew and watched as they pleasured each other in ways that we thought disgusting. For us, sex had been relegated to animals in the paddock. In humans it was both hideous and yet amusing – arms, legs and bodies clumsily flaying and thrusting. We laughed until we couldn't pick ourselves up.

The grasses on my bare skin tickled me into the present. Thoughts of the murder were back. Perhaps I had overlooked essential points? I had been painting Hannes as a misunderstood youngster, racially abused and bullied. Was it the whole picture?

Hannes had learned to stand up for himself and not only in childish ways. He could be vindictive. If attacked, he was far from weak or helpless and fought back with stinging wisecracks that cut deep. His small but wiry body was stronger than it looked and he was capable of inflicting harm. I'd seen him beat up a boy at school. Perhaps there wasn't a motive to his murder – someone may have been forced to defend themselves from his attack and in doing so killed him. It was a possibility and I couldn't rule it out.

A branch cracking and the rustle of leaves nearby alerted me. I couldn't see anyone but there were so many places to hide. Crouching, I attempted to cover my revealing wet underwear. I hurriedly retrieved my crumpled sundress and pulled it on. With my sandals unbuckled, I left, choosing the fastest route to the house through the veld.

I was moments away from the *stoep* when I heard a piercing scream, followed by another and then a lot of yelling. Running the last few paces, I was on the steps of the *stoep* in seconds. Raelene and Nettie's voices were shrill with fear. I didn't have to ask what had happened. I saw the vile thing. A hideous doll more than a meter tall was propped up in one of the cane chairs. Its head and shoulders were covered in rough white cotton and the lower half was made from a woolly floral material. It had arms and legs but no hands or feet and its hair was of straw. It had a slit for a mouth and two round grey buttons the size of cherries were the eyes. They weren't eyes though; those grey buttons didn't glint in the light. From a few paces away, I could see that it had been stuffed with kapok or something similar and that it was badly sewn by hand. Adults collected special sorts of dolls and children played and loved them like little friends. This crude thing wasn't a doll, I thought.

Horrified, I kept my distance but Raelene motioned me to come closer. It stank. Tearfully she pointed to three long pins piercing the doll's body, one in the forehead, another in the heart and the last in the womb. Whoever had inserted them had also rammed a stick into its head carrying a note that said '*For Linda*'.

My head whirled and my legs buckled. I felt myself melt. The last thing I heard was, 'Watch it – she's going to faint!'

I was in my bed when my eyes opened. Though Raelene had placed several blankets and a doona over me, I shivered. I could hear her asking me how I was feeling but my mouth couldn't move to answer. She tried to tempt me to sip some of the steaming liquid she held in a cup and when I didn't make a move to drink it, she lifted my head and put the cup to my mouth. After I swallowed some of the very sweet tea, she allowed me to slip back on to my pillow and sleep.

I was gently shaken and when I opened my eyes the bright lights made me shut them. When I opened them again a strange man wearing a tie and tweed coat stood over me. He felt me, took my blood pressure, listened to my heart with his cold stethoscope and then turned me onto my stomach. I felt the sting of a needle and nothing more.

Chapter 14

Nettie shook my shoulder gently. 'Is ten o'clock Missie. How you now?' Her face was creased with concern.

'I'm still a bit shaky.' My head ached and my throat was tight. 'I think I'll stay in bed a bit longer.'

'It okay now Missie. Police come yesterday and take it away. All gone now.'

'Police?'

'Madam call police. The big one here before.'

'Inspector Swart?'

'Ja, him. Say he come back today, talk to you.'

'I'll have to get up then.' I would've preferred to stay in bed.

'Madam is gone to shops but she leave special breakfast for you.'

'Sorry but I can't eat. Not yet.'

When I stood I was wobbly. In the shower I attempted to wash away the feeling that someone wanted to hurt me but the image of the vile doll wouldn't shift.

I dressed slowly and by the time I'd laced my runners I felt stronger. I was in the kitchen picking at one of the croissants Raelene had left for me when Arnie Swart arrived. I offered him a croissant and Nettie made fresh coffee.

'You're looking pale but it's good to see you up and about today.'

'Do you know who sent me that … abomination?'

'I looked at the doll. It's made of the sort of material that doesn't hold fingerprints and with no smooth surfaces we're out of luck. The message was printed on a computer so it's untraceable. The pins are the kind found anywhere and the stick is from a tree in the area, so unfortunately we can't be specific.'

'It's witchcraft, isn't it … telling me I'll be hurt if I keep meddling?'

'Ja. I reckon that's the message.'

He explained that the use of dolls by witches to injure or harm began in Africa. When the African slave trade spread to other parts of the world the practice was called voodoo.

'It's intimidation. I'm expected to feel scared, aren't I?'

'Those dolls do scare people.'

I sensed he was choosing his words. I tried to put on a good show of bravado but beneath it I felt panicky.

'Maybe the murderer is still alive and is warning me.'

'It's possible – perhaps you should let your investigation go.'

I could feel my nails digging into the flesh of my palm. 'I'm no quitter. I'm obviously on the right track or the murderer wouldn't have bothered.'

Arnie dusted crumbs of flaky pastry from his pants and stood. 'I'll let you know if we find out anything useful. In the meantime, take it easy.'

He waved and the screen door banged behind him.

After a long walk and a substantial lunch I felt less afraid and my usual energy returned. I was determined to find out more about the doll. It was Nandi I wanted to see, as she was the only person I knew who practised her secret form of sorcery. Tired of being chaperoned I drove the car to her house. Three children playing in the streets were eager to take my money to watch the car.

At my knock Nandi opened the door halfway. She whispered that Tansie was asleep after a bad night and she didn't want me to disturb her.

'It's you I've come to see today.'

'You come talk about doll?'

She explained that Nettie, whose sister lived two doors away, had already told her about it. We tiptoed into the front room and spoke softly.

'When I was a child there was plenty of good dolls for healing. Good *ngaka* use dolls plenty times with sweet grass and medicine. Now not see them. People want make evil … *juju*,' she said wringing her hands.

I guessed she was talking about voodoo. Friends who had visited the country recently brought back stories of awful attacks and gruesome voodoo killings.

'I'm scared.'

Nandi came over to me and put her arms around me stroking my head. I had never seen her so demonstrative. A touch on the shoulder was the only sign of affection I'd ever had from her.

'Please, Missie not worry too much. I see spirits of brother and father sit tight round you. They look after you real good.'

'Are you sure?'

'Hundred percent.'

The stuffing in my head was still fear but I left grateful for Nandi's reassurance.

Back on the farm I found Esiekiel digging in his small vegetable patch.

'I nearly finish planting lettuce. You wait please Missie.'

I watched him water the ground with his battered watering can and then rub the sand off his hands on his worn khaki trousers.

'I ready for you now,' he said as he sat in his easy chair. 'Sit.' He indicated a patch of soft grass. 'Missie okay today? I hear about *juju* doll. Very bad.' He made himself more comfortable in his chair.

'Do you think Hannes' murderer sent me that doll?' I asked. The question reverberated in my head.

He scratched the side of his jaw. 'Missie looking for murderer of Hannes, so at same time she open up things been closed for long time. There lot of people on farm scared about past.'

'Who do you think wouldn't want me digging into the past?'

'Missie must wait … then she find out.'

A typical enigmatic Esiekiel answer. I could tell that he knew of a person or possibly several people who wouldn't want me digging up past issues. His crossed arms and tight lips expressed his reluctance to tell me. Age and experience had made him cautious.

'But do you think it could be the person who killed Hannes?' I persisted.

'Missie got too many hard questions today.'

I felt a flush of irritation but said nothing. Neither of us spoke for some time. I watched a spider make its way over a leaf and then back again as it spun its web. Then Esiekiel pointed to the sky.

'See how light shining special for you. I not seen sky like this for long, long time.'

I looked up. The sun shimmered through a halo of clouds and the blue had a velvety sheen.

'Is the spirits of the fathers.'

'I wish they'd help me find Hannes' murderer.'

'Aahh,' Esiekiel scratched his head. 'Missie got very, very hard job. Not easy find out about Little Master.'

'What do you mean?'

'He very naughty boy.'

'Oh, why?'

'On Thursday, when Tansie is day off, sometimes I look after Master Hannes. But I go to meeting in township and want leave him at Nandi but he say he want come with me. I say "No … You only little boy." He shout to me and kick the feet. He want come.'

'These meetings ... anti-government meetings?'

'Ja. Meetings closed. Only friends working near and few people from location. Ja. Hannes like very much to sing our songs. He like best sing *Pas op Verwoed.* He understand words – "Verwoed you must watch out … time is coming for you …" and he laugh. He also sing *Meadowlands.* Everybody like sing *Meadowlands.'*

I thought of whites who had sung and whistled the catchy tune with a penny whistle, without understanding the words. It was a resistance song about a group of people whom the government had moved from their homes and placed in a dustbowl with boxes as houses.

'Verwoed was Prime Minister then, wasn't he?'

'Ja. Verwoed bad man.'

I had a flash back to spring in September 1966, the farm blanketed with blossoms, when Pa ran into the house yelling, 'The Prime Minister's been killed! Quick, turn on the radio.'

The illegal immigrant, Tstafendas, who stabbed Verwoed was declared insane. At twelve years old, I thought Verwoed was a scary and strange man. He was born in Holland and Hannes and I said he should've stayed there. Whenever I saw pictures of him his mouth was open, speaking. He could speak for hours without notes in a high Afrikaans the two of us couldn't understand. Ma said he was driven by a mission from God to keep South Africa white. But I argued with her. How could God give him a mission to move all the blacks out of the city and empty the townships no matter how long they had lived there? How could anyone who wanted to do those awful things have the good of the country at heart? Verwoed's assassination occurred less than a year after Hannes' death. I knew that Hannes would've been delighted about his demise.

'You thinking far away,' Esiekiel laughed. He craned his neck at the sky again. 'Maybe big wind come.'

I sighed.

'Missie must look. Sometimes best fruit on tree is high up hiding behind branches,' he said with a shy smile, as he picked up his watering can and began watering his cucumbers.

Having been dismissed, I walked on feeling like a swimmer underwater.

That night I took Connie and Raelene to a restaurant for dinner. It was my turn to reciprocate. Away from the farm the iciness between my brother and his wife melted enough for us all to enjoy the meal. After a few glasses of wine my thoughts traveled back to those times when on Thursday nights, the traditional maid's night off, the restaurants were full.

On Thursdays Pa used to come in from work earlier than usual. He showered, dressed and even put on aftershave. It was Old Spice and I liked the way it mingled with his tobacco smell. Ma wore her fitted pastel blue dress with frills on the neck and sleeves. Pa's favorite color was blue. She wore high-heeled gold shoes and her hair up in a crest of curls. A light touch of rouge and lipstick made the pale face we were used to prettier and more alive. I called her a princess because she looked so pretty. Pa didn't compliment her but I saw the way he looked at her admiringly. His compliments were rarer than snow at the foot of the mountain.

Pa usually took Ma to one of three restaurants. Her favorite was the Indian one. He preferred the Chinese. I guessed that most of all they liked to be free of Hannes and I and to imagine they were a couple again. They were home by ten o'clock or a bit later. All this happened during a period in which they were getting along well. When the upstairs light was off, from the top of the stairs I watched them drinking wine and kissing. Hannes, usually bored with spying, went to bed. When they had emptied the wine bottle they climbed the stairs arm in arm. My room was next to theirs and I could hear the bedsprings whine rhythmically and Pa's grunting. After sounds of thrashing about, Ma cried out like a baboon in heat. I promised myself that I would never behave like that. It was animal.

On the nights Ma and Pa went out Connie was usually with his girlfriends and Vince was busy with schoolwork. Neither of them wanted us with them. I was dropped off at Grandma Lilly's but she refused to have Hannes. If Ma and Pa had taken us with them at least some of the time, Hannes wouldn't have gone to those meetings in the township hall with Esiekiel as often as he did, and I would've escaped some visits to my fault-finding grandmother.

The hall in the township stank of homemade beer and unwashed bodies. I realize now that Hannes could've been in danger if the crowd had found out who he was and that Pa was actively pro-government. Though Hannes was in his teens he needed watching because he was so mischievous. And that's why Ma and Pa had originally asked Tansie to keep an eye on him. I didn't want to think what Pa would've done if he'd found out that Hannes wasn't with Tansie as he had arranged but was attending those meetings in the township. Esiekiel ought to have known Pa would have disapproved. What was he thinking giving in to Hannes and taking him with him?

Chapter 15

Milk cans rattled outside and loud voices nudged me out of bed. In the shower my thoughts flowed with the warm water. The voodoo doll had turned the murder into a personal issue. Someone was rattled by my questions and trying to stop me prying. I was determined now to follow any clue that might lead me to the killer.

While drinking my second cup of coffee I had another intense urge to leave the house. I stood, trying to fight it, but the cup I'd been holding slipped from my hand and bounced on the table. I had to leave. There was no point resisting it. I shot through the door and down the steps without questioning where I was meant to go. Running barefoot over dirt and rough stones I was propelled along the jacaranda path towards the dam again. Just short of the water the force ebbed and, about to lose my balance, I almost fell into a prickly bush. Once I regained my foothold, I turned, making a circle, but saw nothing apart from the water surrounded by trees. If there was a reason for sending me there I had missed it. Furiously I stamped the ground under the mopane tree. A chattering sound in the tree made me look up. An adult baboon garlanded by leaves looked down at me. I stared back into the closely set brown eyes and for those moments we were locked in a consuming unknowing link. If the baboon knew something important it couldn't tell me. Tansie had taught us not to fear baboons. We tracked them, not to hurt them but to watch them and laugh at our similarities.

Back at the house Nettie handed me a message. Arnie Swart had phoned and left a number for me to contact him on his mobile. The line was fuzzy but I could hear him.

'My staff have done some research on those voodoo dolls. They are being sold in the Rustenburg–Magaliesberg area by sorcerers for big bucks.'

'More specific information would help,' I muttered.

'I'll do my best.' His voice told me that he'd done all he intended to do about the doll.

Rosie probably bought some of her mother's food. Providing additional nutritious foods for Tansie plus some basics was the only contribution I could make to her health. I was trying to build up her resistance. It was a long shot but at least, I hoped, she would enjoy it.

A storm hovered as I drove into Rustenburg. The town had spread, the old shops had gone and there were none of the guiding landmarks from my past. Shoppers had grabbed the parking spots close to the food shops but at last I found a supermarket and bought as many of the foods on my list as I could find. I filled the trolley with cooking oil, bread, butter, coffee, tea and jam, as well as biscuits. At the smaller shops that Raelene frequented, I squeezed the tomatoes, smelled the underside of the melon, tasted the peas and grapes and broke a piece of celery for freshness. Tansie didn't eat fish so I went to the butcher for beef and lamb.

Tubs of flowers and pot plants spilling onto the sidewalk outside the florist reminded me of Tansie's hut with its flowers in dark glass bottles and jam tins. In spring she was a child with me as we lost ourselves in the veld dotted with flowers. We rolled in them until our bodies were drenched in their scent, then we'd pick some, for my bedroom and her hut. I bought bunches of freesias, wrapped in shiny lilac with ribbons, and sniffed them to make sure that they still had their perfume.

Raelene knew of my intention to visit Tansie that afternoon and had asked Nathaniel to go with me. He was working in the orange groves but had arranged for Arti to go with me. Raelene had gone to a lot of trouble for me so I gave up the idea of driving to the township alone.

'*Dumela ma'am,*' Arti was a tall man with close-cut hair and a tightly trimmed beard. I hadn't met him before but had seen him talking to Nathaniel.

I returned the traditional greeting.

'Stuff too heavy for you. I carry.'

'We'll both carry. You take the big parcel.'

I knew that traditionally men did not do the carrying.

'You're Hurutshe, like Tansie, aren't you?' I asked.

He grinned.

The road was busy. People poured from the station, jostling us on the path home. Young men on bicycles whizzed by and taxis raced past carrying passengers from Johannesburg.

'They all lucky they got job to come home from. Mbeki – he's good man but he don't bring enough jobs. Too many people need work and starving.'

We were silent as we crossed the road. Arti put his arm out to steady me as I almost slipped into a pothole. He steered me towards the longer but quieter road. Children were playing in the veld and the occasional bicycle passed us. We stepped up our pace as fine drizzle fell.

'I'm hearing that Missie is looking for man who killed young master.'

'Ja. I went to Pretoria Central with my brother to speak to one of the accused men. I doubt they were the killers.'

'Ralph tell me.'

I looked surprised. He laughed and drummed his thighs with his forefingers.

'Ralph and me, we in same *bogwera* with Hannes. We all learn with Zacharias. Hannes one of us. We want to help find his murderer.'

'*Bogwera*? That's tribal initiation isn't it?'

'Ja, ma'am.'

A quiver of ice touched me. Hannes initiated into the Hurutshes' clan? How could that be? Hannes had Bushman characteristic yet he was born into a white Afrikaans family. He might have been out of place in it but he was considered white and an Afrikaner. It was unthinkable for him to be initiated into a black clan.

'Are you sure?'

'Ja, of course.'

'When was this?'

'Ma'am must ask Nathaniel. He headman of farm.'

Tansie was strong enough to meet me at the door. When I handed her the flowers, she smelled them, held them away from her to admire them and clapped her hands. Then they went into a tall glass bottle just as I remembered the others had years before. Her smile was broad. The parcels of food I brought went to Nandi in the kitchen.

In minutes Tansie's voice was drowned by rain battering the iron roof.

'*Pula,*' I said to her.

She nodded. 'Missie used to like to play in rain.'

'Mmmm.'

'I old and sick and Missie now look after me,' Tansie said with a half-smile.

'I'm your nanny now.'

I caught her eyes traveling over my body. 'Pa visit you again today.' Then she stretched back into her armchair.

'Ask Nandi for plate of biscuit with strong black tea. Tired of her piss-weak coffee,' she laughed.

I drank my tea and thought of Miriam. Ask Tansie, ask Tansie more about her, my thoughts echoed. She knows but she's not saying.

When I did ask about Miriam she rose slowly to check the windows were closed. 'Missie look like she going to lay egg if I don't tell,' she giggled softly.

I nodded.

'Is very big secret about Miriam but I been thinking. Better Missie know truth.' She took my hand. 'It start when Little Master Hannes at big school and Missie maybe so high.' Seated, her hand stretched up in line with her head.

'I must've been eight or nine then and Hannes about twelve.'

'Afternoon after I finish ironing, I going home when I see the Little Master, his clothes full blackjacks and hair with grass and leaves. I ask, "Where you been Master Hannes?" He laugh, jump and laugh. "I been watching very good show," he say. I tell him hurry inside and tidy up before Madam see him. Must be one, maybe two weeks later, I catch Little Master Hannes dirty again. "What you doing Little Master Hannes?" He got big smile and I know he doing tricks or bad things. He laugh. He say, "I seen a very, very naughty show." I try to find out what he talking about. He laugh but not say.'

'So what happened?' I asked Tansie.

'I go after him in afternoon when he go out. I walk soft and he not see me. He go under trees where ground soft and lots of flowers and bushes.'

'The place near the dam where all the lovers go?'

'Na. Nearby stables.'

'The stables?'

'Nobody come there that time.'

'So?'

'I get big, big shock. There is Miriam lying with Master Connie. They naked.'

'Oh my goodness.'

'I watch and they going there maybe one, two times in afternoon and plenty times in night-time. I not tell Little Master Hannes I know.' She made a zip action on her mouth.

This was most unlike Connie, especially in those apartheid days. Not only had he broken the law but he'd also flouted the taboos of Afrikaner society. The Immorality Act was proclaimed before I was born. In spite of the law, bits of gossip leaked out from time to time about farmers sleeping with their black workers. I was living on the farm at the time yet I'd known nothing about my eldest brother's sexual relationship with Miriam. At the time I wasn't even aware of anyone called Miriam living on the farm. Hannes usually shared gossip with me but these juicy secrets he'd kept to himself.

'Then Little Master Hannes cause big trouble.'

I was listening to Tansie as if I was miles away and she was talking about another family, not mine.

'One day he tell Master Connie what he seen. I hear Little Master Hannes and Master Connie shouting loud near huts.'

'So what happened?' my voice asked.

'Whew! Big trouble. Little Master Hannes say he going to tell the *Baas* and everyone what he seen.'

'What did Connie do?'

'He shout plenty back but it not help.'

I calculated that this must've happened in about 1963.

'And then?'

'I tired now. No more talk.' Tansie closed her eyes. I wanted to know more but I couldn't press her.

'Missie go careful,' Nandi said as I edged towards the door. She patted her pocket where the awful little bottle of afterbirth had been. She pushed an umbrella towards me. It was warm though drizzling outside.

'No thanks – I like the rain.'

I walked back slowly with Arti by my side. He chatted all the way but I barely heard him.

As I sipped a cold beer on the *stoep* Miriam was in my thoughts. She had to be in her mid forties but was still lovely, her body sensual and her skin satiny and wrinkle-free. In her teens she must've been a beauty he couldn't resist. Had she been the temptress or had he pursued her? Why was she still living on the farm if this happened so long ago? Was it kept quiet at the time? If Tansie found out about it the workers must have known too. I downed the remains of my beer, imagining their fear at the police finding out. I didn't want to think of what could have happened.

Chapter 16

Raelene had invited some of her close friends for dinner that night. She wanted to show off her sister-in-law from Australia and they wanted to meet me. I talked to them all and tried to appear interested but my thoughts were on Connie and Miriam. When at last they left I asked myself if Tansie could've made a mistake. Had she really seen Connie and Miriam near the stables? Was age affecting her memory?

Another glass or two of red wine acted as an anesthetic. I no longer cared.

I woke cold and uncomfortable in the chair. Into the shower. You've got straight thinking to do, I told myself. With Raelene's oversized bathrobe wrapped around me I sat at the desk. After rummaging in the drawers I found a pen, a block of lined paper and some scotchtape. I needed a large sheet and made one from four taped pages. Once I had placed it in front of me I committed my suspicions and the few facts I had gleaned to paper. I had to force myself to look at the murder more logically.

Once Hannes had found out about Miriam and made threats, Connie had a motive to kill his brother. So far he was the only person I'd come across with a motive for the murder and he fitted Esiekiel's description of the man he'd seen on the night – a large white male on the fat side with a protruding nose.

I wondered how long it took for Pa to find out about Connie

and Miriam. Not only had Connie gone against the morals he'd been taught but our family would have been ostracized if knowledge of Connie's liaison with Miriam leaked. The awful thought of the police finding out about Connie and Miriam kept rolling round in my head. Had Cobie helped to keep it quiet? I wondered.

I remembered going to church in my pink dress, my hair in pigtails tied with pink bows. I heard whispering among the women. I strained to hear but I couldn't pick it up. After church I nagged Ma to share the gossip but she found excuses and gave the task to my father. 'Piet you explain the unexplainable to your daughter.'

Pa muttered inaudibly, then sighed. 'All right, come Lindie, let's go for a walk.'

It was a black night, the moon veiled and the stars dim. I clutched Pa's hand. Pa sounded embarrassed as he told me about Marius de Villiers, the fish shop owner who had recently lost his wife to cancer. Lonely and too tired to cook for himself at night, he had employed a young black woman, Anna.

'The trouble was that he drank too much red wine at night and when he was a little tipsy Anna looked beautiful to him. Anna was away from her parents and the rest of her family and she was lonely too. Time passed and eventually they …'

'Ja, ja, Pa. I understand.'

My cheeks glowed in the cool air. It was just as well we were in the dark. We walked on quietly. Then I asked, 'What's wrong with that if it made them happy?'

'We have laws in this wonderful country of ours to keep the white race pure. Sexual relations between a white and a black are illegal.'

'Pure?'

'Not mixed, not colored.' I was quiet, thinking about what Pa had said. For the first time I understood the upset about Hannes.

Anna and Marius were charged with breaching the Immorality Act. With my days at school full, I forgot about them until months later when I overheard Ma tell Pa that Marius had committed suicide in his cell. That night I cried for them both and I cried from disappointment. I lived in a beautiful country but such a sad one. I had increasing trouble understanding our rules for living.

The image of the voodoo doll bothered me. Miriam could have been one of the people who would've preferred me not to find out the truth about her. Could she have sent the doll? I reminded myself that the murderer and the person who sent the doll weren't necessarily the same. What about Connie? I doubted he would have had anything to do with the doll. Connie disliked witchcraft and anything that wasn't strictly Christian.

I had asked Vince to pop in on his way home, intending to confront him with my questions about Connie and Miriam and to insist on answers. We drank beer on the *stoep* in the fading light and after polite conversation, the queue of questions in my head burst. Vince's brow furrowed and he cracked his knuckles nervously.

'Who told you about them?'

'Never mind who told me. I need answers.'

'I'm sorry you had to find out.'

'I'm sorry too but I'd rather not make any comments about Connie's behavior. Details are what I need right now.'

'Details?'

'Like … how long did this go on for?'

'It must've started about the time Connie and Raelene were engaged. You know how important it was in those days for religious girls to be virgins when they married. Well, our

Con was engaged for eighteen long months. I think that's when Miriam came into the picture. Hannes must have been twelve or so when he caught them at it. From then it was on again during Raelene's pregnancies … and who knows the rest of it?'

The question stuck in my throat but I had to ask. 'Does Raelene know?'

'If she does know, she has never discussed it with me. Maybe she pretends it hasn't happened,' he shrugged.

'I bet Hannes made a big thing of it. He would've.'

'You know what a bully Connie was and you know how Hannes felt about him,' Vince said.

'Hannes was shit-scared of Connie … but he also had no respect for him.'

'In those days catching a white man having sex with a black was big.' He rubbed the side his face. 'The racial taboos and the whole bag. I don't know if you remember the special police climbing trees to take photos of mixed couples in bed together.'

'Sure I do. And the disgusting investigations they made of sheets, pyjamas and other intimate things.'

'Hannes was in a position of power for the first time and he milked Connie dry. Early on Pa didn't know about it and neither did Ma. Hannes threatened to tell them, the priest, the congregation at church and a load of other people … if his demands weren't met. So, Connie paid Hannes hush money each month but I haven't a clue how much Hannes asked for. He also insisted on royal treatment from Connie – being served, having his bed made, his shoes cleaned and that sort of thing.'

I remembered Connie spoiling Hannes and naively I thought he was being a loving older brother. Afterwards the resentment on Connie's face let me know I was mistaken.

'How did you find out about what they were up to?' I asked.

'Connie was in a state, terrified Pa would find out, so he told me. All he got from me was a promise that I'd keep my mouth shut. I've never forgiven him for doing that to Raelene, and on his own bloody turf too.'

'When did Pa find out?'

Vince rubbed his face again. 'It wasn't long before Hannes was murdered. One of the workers made a crude joke about Connie and Miriam that Pa overheard. Anyhow, Pa stormed after Connie wanting to know more and the rest you can imagine.'

'Pa with his pro-government views ...'

'He was struck dumb with fury. Ashen and trembling.'

'Hannes was a secretive devil but he had courage. Only Hannes would have had the cheek to blackmail Connie.'

'You're right,' Vince laughed. 'I didn't say so but I was proud of him. I couldn't have stood up to Connie the way he did.'

The evening star was out when Vince placed his empty beer bottle on the cane table and stood to leave. 'Step easy round Connie. He's prickly about the subject.' We hugged, locked in our love for each other.

Vince had filled in the holes that Tansie had left out. The full story was the type of thing that one read about in the Sunday papers – another woman, sex across the color bar, intrigue, blackmail, hatred between brothers. I thought of Pa's letter. The chance that Hannes was killed by his brother and not the three men in jail could have been the real reason Pa had written to me. He wasn't interested in the welfare of the three accused men. Unwilling to dig up filth himself, he had left it to me to find out the truth. His request made sense for the first time.

My nicotine and alcohol intake in the past hours must have lubricated my thoughts. I could recall those weeks just before Hannes' death. I could feel it.

Sleep came quickly but my dreams weren't as kind. I dreamed of Connie as an adolescent running from Pa's fury. Cats were everywhere. Not purring sleek housecats but the feral kind with wild eyes and tiger teeth. Towards morning Pa, wearing his woeful face, pleaded with me but I didn't know what he wanted.

The dream was cut short when Nettie's cheerful morning voice woke me.

Part 4

Peel

Chapter 17

Hannes was with me as I took the long route to the huts through the morning veld. Flowers leaned towards the sun and flat succulents underfoot were plump with early dew. He had been so courageous to blackmail Con. I turned the thought over again and again. I hadn't appreciated Hannes and felt stabs of guilt.

Nowadays he would be thought of as a free spirit. All those novel ideas of his made my other two brothers look boring. Hannes didn't believe in homework or study or anything that interfered with his freedom. Though he spent time dodging bullies at school, his grades remained among the top in the class.

When he was nine, his inquiring mind drove him to take risks and experiment with how things worked. When he found he could pull the radio and telephone apart and reassemble them easily his eye shone on the workings of farm machinery. Pa must have threatened him so strenuously that he kept away from it.

Hannes' chronic rebelliousness resulted in him being frequently spanked. Pa gave him warnings but if they weren't heeded trouble would follow. I had to put my fists over my ears and grit my teeth during the beatings and felt my own bottom tingling in sympathy. Fortunately the hidings Pa gave me were less severe and stopped when I turned twelve. Instead he deprived me of listening to my favorite radio serials and playing outdoors.

I'd heard Pa say to Hannes, 'You can't be excused because you're different or having a hard time. I treat you boys all the same and you have to learn to behave like everyone else.'

Without planning it I found myself outside Miriam's hut. It was too late to slink away. She waved and greeted me with a lopsided smile. 'I knew you'd be back. What took you so long?' she asked.

'Oh.'

'So, you've heard that I'm the wicked *kaffir* girl who fucked your brother behind the bushes, eh?' she placed one hand on her hip.

'Nobody said that and I'm not saying it either.'

'You want to know if it's true. Don't you?' Her eyes taunted me.

'Of course I do.'

'It happened ages and ages ago. We had great sex until Hannes, the little devil, caught us at it. That put out the flame for a while.' With her bare foot she drew a line in the soft sand outside her hut.

'Ah-huh.'

'At least I got a decent house, furniture and some mod cons out of it.'

'I suppose I can't blame you for wanting that.'

'And … guess what? When Raelene got pregnant the second time Connie sneaked back. Tail between his legs.'

'Oh!'

'And afterwards when she got fat and lazy he knew where to find Miriam for a quickie.' She pulled herself to her full height, obviously enjoying my discomfort.

A male voice nagged from inside the hut.

'Men. Like babies crying for you. Got to go. Come back for tea and a chat any time.'

Stunned, I stood outside the closed door. I thought I knew Connie. Everyone had a kink or two but this was something else! My head felt thick and I stumbled back to the house.

The rest of the afternoon I spent on the *stoep*, trying to digest the load of unsettling information. Hannes reveled in gossip and telling tales. How had he managed to contain such juicy information, especially when he loathed Connie? I would've spilled it all out with glee. A compeling reason must've kept him so quiet. Money, probably, I told myself cynically.

I was still on the *stoep* by the time the sky was royal blue and fireflies flickered in the veld. A glimpse through the net curtains of Raelene placing food on the table made my gut tighten.

Connie and Raelene met through a friend. What a delicate beauty Raelene had been, with creamy apricot skin and auburn hair. No wonder Connie had been crazy about her. She played her part by supporting Connie's soccer team and wearing the team colors. Admired by his mates and always at his side, he couldn't resist her. They were engaged for eighteen months and then married.

Raelene was a wealthy industrialist's daughter from Pretoria. From childhood she had been steeped in the love of all that was Afrikaans and anti-black. She attended an exclusive Afrikaans school and had joined the Young Voortrekkers at an early age.

Her life had been soft, with indulgent parents and servants in the house. The transition to a far simpler life on the farm must've been difficult at first but I'd never heard her complain. She had two children and, when she could leave them, worked at the Rustenburg library. When Ma died she cut her work hours to spend time cooking and baking for her family.

Did she know about Connie and Miriam? Miriam sleeping with her husband would have been too much to tolerate. If she knew about them, how had she stayed with him? Sex and lies. Each day I was learning more about my family and liking it less.

Before they were engaged I heard Raelene make comments about Hannes showing the family's 'black blood'. During their engagement she visited the farm often and contact with Hannes tempered her attitude. She and Connie were married shortly before Hannes was murdered and in that brief period I had only seen her behave caringly towards him.

If Pa hadn't set me the task of investigating Hannes' murder, I would've packed and left the farm. At dinner that night I drank three glasses of wine and tore at bits of Raelene's home-baked bread. Unable to eat, I pushed the food round my plate. My eyes were down as my head screamed accusations at Connie. I had to leave the table. Complaining of a headache I rushed upstairs. I couldn't have cared what they thought of me.

Robot-like, I went directly to Connie's study in search of cigarettes. I had to have one and I had run out of my own supply. The room was simply but expensively furnished with oak bookcases, cabinets and a desk. I couldn't help noticing the collection of knives in the display cabinet. They looked sharp and evil.

Connie's desk was wide and long with ridges and beveled edges. There was a pull out bit for his computer and drawers of different sizes. I went through all the left-hand drawers and found nothing. Fortunately, or perhaps unfortunately, in a right-hand drawer near the bottom I found matches and several packs of cigarettes among his cigars and cigarillos. Intending to replace them, I helped myself and took my loot to my bedroom.

In the chintz-cushioned chair I rocked and smoked and smoked and rocked until I felt calmer. I poured more wine into one of Raelene's best crystal glasses and sipped it. Fears of leaving before I had satisfied Pa's request plagued me. If I returned home without resolving the issue of Hannes' murder, guilt would eventually force me to return to take up the investigation again.

On the *stoep* sparrows hovered, waiting for breakfast crumbs. The morning sounds of the farm and the wind playing its tune through the veld added to the pleasure of the meal.

'Surprise.' The voice sounded familiar. Before I could turn around, arms and an exotic perfume seized me.

'Priya, is it really you?'

My old friend Priya wasn't the willowy girl I had known. She had filled out and was statuesque in her sari, but her eyes still expressed her goodness. We hugged.

'I'm so sorry about your Pa. I was at the funeral but couldn't stay to catch up with you.'

'It's wonderful to see you.'

'The old ones have all gone. My father died a few years ago.'

'Things have changed in South Africa. At least now we can pop in to see each other whenever we like.'

'About time too.'

I thought about the first time we met. I was with Pa the day he rushed to the farmer's store for pesticides to kill off the pests destroying our orange trees. The pesticide was in such demand that the store had sold out of it. On the way out Pa stumbled, nearly flattening Mr Naidoo, Priya's father. The two of them discussed the pest problem and Mr Naidoo told Pa about a herbal pesticide he'd made. Pa remembered that Mr Naidoo once worked for an industrial chemist and was known for his inventions and concoctions. Being helpful, he offered

Pa some of his own mix, which Pa gratefully accepted. When Pa and I came to pick up the pesticide Priya was standing in their driveway next to about twenty tins of it.

That night Pa followed Mr Naidoo's instructions carefully applying the pesticide to the trees. The breezy night air carried the fragrance of the herbs through my window. It was glorious. The method was long and tedious but Pa would've tried anything. The next morning the ground littered with the bugs was sprayed with water. After obtaining more tins, Pa made a few more applications. Sweet smelling nights followed. One lunchtime Pa rushed in to tell us that we would be picking oranges for the next harvest. I hadn't seen him smile so widely for a long time. Though the herbal pesticide was effective and he admitted enjoying its aroma, he returned to the easier form of chemical pest control.

I told Priya about my attempts to find Hannes' murderer and the slowness of my investigation.

'If there's any way I can help, you just need to say. Hannes' death really knocked me about. Who would kill a teenager? And why?'

'Those are the big questions.'

After Priya left I bathed in memories of our friendship. We were neighbors but apartheid had separated us. We were thrown together when Pa, feeling obligated to Mr Naidoo for the pesticide, offered to help with the painting of their house. The house took several weekends to paint and with time to play and talk, the two of us discovered that we enjoyed the same games and were both daydreamers. When the painting was completed, we agreed to meet secretly every Wednesday after school. Pa would not have condoned a social relationship between us but no-one knew. Even Hannes didn't find out about it for ages.

We squeezed easily through the portion of the boundary fence between our farms that ran over a dip and hadn't been properly secured. Hidden by a cluster of tall rocks we let our imaginations guide us as we played with broken jewelery, an old bronze ornament of a dancer with many hands or a cracked statue with an elephant's head. During Christmas we ate the leftovers of Ma's fruitcake and mince pies and played with broken trinkets that fell from the tree. In October during the Hindu festival of Diwali Priya sneaked out a platter of delicious rich sweets that tasted like chocolate coconut ice. Her brother, Nitin, had returned from his pilgrimage to India with a long trident fork. She took it so that we could dress in sheets and holding the fork, pretend we were going down to the river to pray.

One Wednesday our meetings ended when Hannes followed me and threatened to tell Pa about our secret. We stopped seeing each other and I packed our treasures into a box that soon lay among the junk in the attic.

I paced the *stoep* running through my conversation with Priya. Intuition told me that some aspect of our childhood games had bearing on the murder. It was hanging there on the edge of my awareness yet I couldn't fish it out.

That night at dinner 'pass the salt', 'more juice?' or 'another helping?' was all that was said between Raelene and Connie. I ate fast to escape the unpleasant atmosphere. Placing my napkin on the table I let my mind drift until they finished their meals.

'Cat got your tongue?' Connie said sulkily.

'Yep.'

'When you arrived you wouldn't shut up and now you've clammed up. What's going on?'

'I'm tired. Got a headache,' I lied. How could I enjoy my food when I had accusing thoughts in my head?

'I'll never understand you bloody women,' he said pushing his dessert away and walking off.

'Don't you worry about your brother hon,' Raelene said, drawing back her chair.

'Thanks for a lovely dinner, but I'm tired, so if you don't mind I'm going upstairs to lie down.'

'Tell you what. You go up and I'll join you there in a sec with coffee and something to nibble. I think we need to talk.'

I had washed my face and changed into sloppier gear when Raelene arrived with Nettie behind her carrying a tray. I moved the sheet of paper with my information about the murder from the desk so that Nettie could put the coffee and chocolate biscuits there.

'Now we're set,' Raelene said, rubbing her hands.

'Good idea. It's nice and cosy.'

'I need to talk to you about Connie. That is, Connie and me.'

I waited.

'I've noticed the change in you and wondered if you've been hearing things about Connie … about us.'

'Well … er … yes.'

'So you found out about Miriam then?'

'Ja, Rae I did.' I put my arm around her shoulder.

'Even now it's bloody hard to talk about it,' she said wiping away tears.

'It must be.'

'I found out that he'd been sleeping with her after Jannie was born. I must've been thick because it didn't hit me till then, though he'd been screwing her through my first pregnancy. I think I was a new mother too wrapped up with the baby, feeding and all that to notice Connie was slipping out more than usual. By the time I had Jannie, Connie was sure of himself – he stayed away too long and I twigged that he was with another woman.'

Raelene told me that Pa saw how miserable she was and asked her to join him for a walk. He told her the full story of Connie's unfaithfulness. Then he apologized for Connie. Pa said he obviously hadn't been a good father and taught Connie what was right. It must've been a tough conversation because Raelene said that she ended up consoling him.

'It must've been a shock.'

'Like a bloody bomb hit me. You can imagine.'

'Oh Rae. I'm sorry.'

'When I look back I realize that I must've cracked up. I couldn't stop crying, wouldn't eat, couldn't sleep thinking of that black bitch with Connie. The doc put me on those tranquilizers and I took the kids and went to Ma and Pa's. I stayed at their farm until I could think things through. Of course, I didn't tell them that Miriam was a black or Pa would've killed Connie. They thought he had an affair with a white girl in the town. I doubt I'd have gone back to him if my folks hadn't made me. All that typical forgive and forget stuff,' she sighed.

'So?'

'I was back but refused to have him in my bed. It didn't suit me to leave here. God knows that's twenty-plus years ago and I've stuck to it.'

'It must be hard talking about all this to me.'

'No. We were close before you left and I still feel close to you, even though we've been parted.'

I gave her arm a squeeze.

'Your Pa chose a punishment for him. I mean Connie was an adult with kids but it didn't matter to Pa. He forced Connie into the barn as if he were a kid and gave him the hiding of his life. He couldn't go to work for days or sit for at least a week.'

'Pa knew only one punishment.'

'Ja.'

'It's a sad story Rae. I'm sorry.'

'I made a good life for myself. We do our own thing and in public we pretend to be a couple. It works out fine.'

'I see.'

'I thought you should know why there's a wall between us.' She smiled her brave smile. 'Now let's get stuck into those double choc biscuits.'

After Raelene left I brushed my teeth and went to the toilet. Duke must have crept into the room and was curled into a ball at the end of my bed. He was awake enough to stretch, roll onto his back and wiggle until I tickled his tummy. I was used to cats on the bed and left him there for the night.

Duke jumping on my stomach awakened me unpleasantly. Half asleep I fumbled in the dark for the lamp, knocking over the alarm clock and book on the bedside table. Duke dived off the bed and hid. I heard creaking sounds like someone was stepping softly over the floorboards. It sounded like Pa's step as he walked across the room in his slippers. Each night the sound had come through the thin partitions called walls.

I drew the curtains and too unsettled to sleep I lay there waiting for the cock's crow and the first signs of dawn.

Chapter 18

At the window I stretched and bathed my lungs in the fresh dawn air. In a no-nonsense mood, I was ready to look into Hannes' murder more thoroughly.

I padded barefoot to the desk with the large piece of paper with so little written on it. The open window carried an aroma of sweet frangipani mixed with tobacco. Pa was about again. I kicked the leg of the desk. My toe hurt so much that I swore loudly. Why couldn't he leave me alone?

I folded my arms and leaned forward on the desk as the logical part of me clicked into self-defence mode. For all those years in Australia, I'd had no visits from Pa or Hannes because I didn't want the contact. I knew that if I steeled myself, I could close the channel to them both. They were distracting me and I'd had enough contact for the time being at least. It had to stop.

I went downstairs to make coffee. Nettie was first in the kitchen and had put coffee on the hot plate to boil. The old-style coffee was strong and tasted good with lots of milk. I poured a mug full and drank it in the *voorkamer*.

I berated myself for not having achieved more in the investigation. My objective had to change. In my remaining time on the farm, I would throw myself into the search for the murderer with more verve. It was no longer a question of carrying out Pa's wishes. It had become my investigation.

If I didn't learn the truth, unanswered questions about Connie would plague me for the rest of my life.

The workers were having a brief mid-morning break when I found Nathaniel lounging under a tree, rolling a cigarette.

'There is something I need to ask you, Nathaniel.'

'Ja Missie?' He jumped up to speak to me.

'Please sit.' I joined him on the grass. 'I heard that Hannes wanted to be in a *bogwera* group and that Zacharias helped him.'

'Ja is true.' He looked startled. Initiation was a touchy subject, especially for a woman to broach with a black man. 'My father hear Hannes cry too much. He cry he want to belong to tribe like other boys.'

'But how could he be initiated as a Hurutshe? He was one of us … white and an Afrikaner.'

'He say to my father he born Afrikaans white but inside he black.'

'Do they still have initiation ceremonies like they did in the old days?'

'No not same today. My father not send boys into bush to learn like years before … and no cutting.' He laughed shyly and looked away. 'Some people not want boys to learn ways of tribe like before but my father say it makes boy tribesman and all boys must learn to be men.'

Zacharias was a kind man. He realized how important it was for Hannes to belong but he was in difficult spot. He couldn't have been certain if the initiates would agree to Hannes' presence. He would have had to ask them before making any decision.

'He sad for Hannes and he think long, long time. First he tell Hannes, "No *bogwera*". Later he let Hannes learn … part-time.'

'Part-time?'

'He not let Hannes join *bogwera* group one hundred percent.'

'How did Hannes manage to slip away from us to spend time with Zacharias and the initiation group? I was with him nearly all the time and when we visited Zacharias we were together.'

Nathaniel laughed. 'Saturday afternoon Master Connie and Master Vince gone with friends to soccer and *Baas* and Madam take Missie visit Ouma and Aunties. Hannes not go. Tansie she work in house and it easy to bring Hannes to my father.'

'Ah-hah.'

Hannes was so sneaky. He'd talked Esiekiel into taking him to meetings in the township when Tansie had her day off work on Thursday and on Saturdays he came to Zacharias' hut. He had done all this covertly, aware that he wouldn't find encouragement from the family, not even from me.

'Too much trouble for Missie,' Nathaniel said kindly. He must've seen the puzzled look on my face.

'I'm pleased Hannes joined the tribe part-time but …'

'Many new things to find out,' Nathaniel said softly.

I nodded. 'Are any of the men who were part of Hannes' *bogwera* group still working here?'

'Ja.'

'I'd like to speak to them if I can. Maybe they know something that'd help me find out who killed Hannes.'

'When they finish lunch I call them. They need rest now.'

I waited under the shade of an acacia thinking how strange and difficult memories were to understand. I could remember every detail of the time Rosie and I hid under the window of Zacharias' hut peeking and listening at what went on in initiation classes. The boys, looking serious, sat cross-legged on the floor around Zacharias. We laughed and joked. How could a few classes in Zacharias' hut teach the boys we knew as friends to be men?

The group was learning about the Hurutshe totem, the baboon. Zacharias told them that every Tswana family group could trace their ancestors through an animal that protected them. We watched amazed as the boys imitated baboons shrieking and chattering, jumping hanging on trees, stealing up to one another and then pouncing. They looked so ridiculous that we rolled on the grass in fits of giggles. That's when we got caught. Zacharias' head popped out of the window. He yelled at us with such fury that we ran.

'Girls you keep out of secret men's group or I catch you!'

Hannes longed for friends. There were only a few boys his age near the farm and the *bogwera* group offered him fellowship and acceptance. Nathaniel introduced me to two men. Felix was a small man with a plump middle and short thin arms and legs, like a brown beetle. Joshua was tall and lithe with a full fuzz of hair. Nathaniel spoke to them in Setswana, too quickly for me to follow.

'Yes ma'am, how can we help?' Felix said with grin and a low bow.

'I can do with some help in understanding how my brother Hannes fitted into the *bogwera* group.'

Joshua spoke first. 'It's men's tribal secrets,' he said, his mouth tight.

'I'm sorry I don't mean to be disrespectful. All I want to know is a little of Hannes' involvement.'

'Okay, it's like this. Zacharias tell us all tribe's history and religion,' Joshua said.

'Ja we hear how can live in the veld and fight like warrior. We also learn about woman and woman's ways,' Felix added, laughing loudly.

'We learn about resistance against Verwoed's apartheid government. Our leader, Nelson Mandela, was still locked up then. Long time ago, you know. If we want we can join special unit – Spear of the Nation, *Um Konto we Sizwe* –learn to blow up bridges or wreck trains ... but it not for us,' Joshua said.

I asked if Hannes had been actively involved in the Spear of the Nation. The two men shook their heads in unison. Joshua made me proud when he described Hannes' courage and strength.

'Hannes, he small but good fighter. Feet and hands very quick. He could kill, no knife, no gun.'

The two men laughed when I asked if anyone knew about their meetings. 'If *Baas* Piet find out ... ooh, there be piggies for market!' I shuddered and explained that I was trying to discover whether anyone had upset Hannes before he was murdered. They recalled that he was angry.

'He say he want to get even. People call him bad names,' Joshua said. 'Plumber come to fix sprinkler. He call Hannes Chocolate Baby.' The two laughed.

'Hannes very cross about somebody not pay up his money,' Felix added.

'Can you remember any details?'

'Sorry. Is too long time back.'

'Did Hannes say how he was going to get even?'

'He say he already get started ... but he not tell us how,' Joshua said.

The information Joshua and Felix had given me was too vague for me to extract a thread. I walked slowly over the *koppies* and past the flowering banksias. The tree Hannes and I had called the *cripple boom* was still there, struck black and twisted by lightning. On a safe section of the crumbling stone wall, I sat where we had sat as children. I dipped into my pocket for the comfortable feel of cigarettes and lit one.

Chapter 19

After noting what Felix and Joshua had told me on my sheet of paper, I had no idea of where to turn for answers. Unable to face the thought that Connie had murdered Hannes, I went outdoors and looked around for some useful activity. The garden was speckled with daisies and I'd have enjoyed sitting on Connie's huge luxurious electric mower cutting back the overgrowth. Even if he would've allowed me to use the machine, mowing was not my job. Jake was employed for that.

I wandered into the kitchen. Perhaps something rich and sweet was what I needed. Raelene's fresh baking lay under an oval plastic cover. I snatched two chocolate cupcakes iced with thick chocolate she'd baked for her grandchildren and a syrupy *koeksister.* Hannes had loved *koeksisters.* In Melbourne I had to make do with Danish pastries, which I enjoyed, but they weren't nearly as delicious.

I put my treats on a plate and ate them on the *stoep* in the pale sunlight. In spite of some positive changes I wasn't sure I liked the new South Africa. Constant reminders of the dangers of violence and awful poverty were everywhere and I loathed the restrictions that resulted – the endless high walls securing homes and warnings from everyone to be careful. I wasn't used to caged living in Australia and it didn't fit my picture of my old home. The new South Africa was yet to evolve and it felt uncomfortable. Glitzy on the outside and so rough within.

One of the workers' wives came past on her way to say hello to Nettie in the kitchen. A sleeping child was tied to her back with colored cloth in the traditional manner.

When I was about two years old, slow and easily tired, Tansie hoisted me onto her back and tied me to her, carrying me in a blanket. I was part of her, absorbing her warmth and moving as she moved. Often Hannes came along too, clutching her hand.

When Ma was out for the day Tansie took us to the township. But just as well Ma didn't find out we'd been there. It was a filthy dilapidated place that shrieked of poverty. Many roofs were dented and torn and windows boarded up with cardboard. Older men sat smoking their pipes, teenagers skulked around and children in rags ran in the streets. Smells of rotten garbage and pee greeted us round corners. But fast happy music made me forget the unpleasantness of the place. People danced and clapped to the sounds of jive and kwela. When Tansie heard the music she bent to untie me and we'd watch her dance and clap with the others. It was a relief that the leaky roof in Nandi's house had been repaired and that these days the lanes were far cleaner.

I thought of Tansie, now so ill. I had spent so much of my childhood with her that she had influenced much of my thinking.

Connie was in from work early and had brought a few cans of beer with him. He threw one to me and I sipped without speaking.

'There's something I should've told you. There's a cardboard box of Pa's in the wine cellar. He left it with me before he died.'

I drummed my fingers on the table. 'What's in it?'

'Shit. I don't know. Pa said it was to do with the family. I haven't got round to opening it,' Connie answered quickly.

'No harm done. I'll sort the boxes out. Anyway I've been dying to find out about our family for ages.'

All our family secrets were in attics and boxes. No-one talks, I thought.

'So I'll drop it into your room then,' Connie promised. For a moment he looked like a naughty boy expecting to be punished. Neither of us talked for a few minutes. I felt for a cigarette and offered him one but he shook his head. I took a long draw before I spoke. 'I've been hearing things about you.'

'You have?' he scowled as he looked down.

I stumbled over the words. 'About you and a woman called Miriam.'

'You're too quick to listen to gossip. Just like the rest of them,' he said putting his beer down on the table.

'At least you could have told me. There's nothing worse than finding out things like this about one's own family through the back door.'

'I can hear the judgement in your voice. With your fucking high expectations of us all, just like Pa. How could I have told you? Things aren't always how they look, you know.' His shoulders drooped and his face saddened.

'Well, I'm listening. I want … I need to hear it from you.'

'Look … Rae was a spoiled little girl from the city … She was all tied up about sex and with me being her first boyfriend … she didn't have a clue.' His voice petered out.

'So you found someone to satisfy your needs.'

'It wasn't like that. You make it sound so … animal. We had a bloody long engagement and I was young and stupid.'

'Uh-huh. And what about later?' I could hear the judgemental tone creeping into my voice.

'There you go – telling me how to live my life,' he said storming off.

As I lit another cigarette I wondered how I would resolve my relationship with Connie. With his infuriating knack of shifting the blame from himself he made it difficult to discover the truth. He'd always done that to extricate himself from unpleasant situations. If his grades at school were on the low side it was the teacher's fault. If he was late home he said he was unavoidably detained. Here it was naïve virginal Raelene who wouldn't have sex with him.

Yet I was angry with myself. The ugly tone of the conversation was my fault too. I hadn't even given him a chance to explain himself and I had judged him. I couldn't forgive him for hurting Raelene and he could hear it in my voice. Even if he had a good reason for his actions I'd cut him off. Talk between us would be even more strained.

Later in my room I looked at my notes. I had covered less than a quarter of a page. Hoping for inspiration I closed my eyes and tried to imagine the crime scene but no picture presented itself. 'You're doing the family escapist trick, immersing yourself in your memories of your childhood instead of investigating the murder,' I told myself. It was true.

I knew that wine wouldn't help but I poured another glass. I forced myself to concentrate on the murder. Be objective, I thought. What kind of person would stab a fourteen-year-old so violently? And why? Where was Hannes killed? Why drag him to the place he was found?

I wrote a large C on the paper, circled it and scribbled around it. Was my brother violent? Rosie said he had beaten up one of the workers. I knew he had a vile temper and probably disliked the blacks as much as ever. Did his ugly streak mean he could kill?

In my mind's eye I could see him. He was twelve years my senior and like another father, laying down family rules with a sharp voice and the occasional slap. He had shown Raelene, and later his children, his mean face. His gentle side slipped through when he was with the dogs or the cat. He petted them excessively and spoke to them lovingly. When he thought none of us were watching him he spoiled them with extra food. Could Connie have murdered his brother? There was a chasm between meanness and murder.

Outside the wind was lashing the trees and a fine layer of orange dust sprayed the air. I couldn't go out but I wanted to walk – fast. I was strung out and activity would've helped. Instead I paced the *voorkamer*, picked up ornaments and put them down. Then I went into the kitchen where Nettie was singing as she chopped carrots for the meal. I switched on the kettle and had a cup in my hand when Nettie darted over.

'I make it for you ma'am.'

'It's fine thanks … you finish the carrots.'

She looked at me sideways and went on chopping. Upstairs I went with my cup of coffee in my hand. There was nowhere else to go.

Raelene lay splayed out on the sofa snoring after a shopping trip. Connie had promised to give me Pa's box but I thought he'd forgotten about it. I didn't want to ask him for it and decided to collect it from the cellar myself. While there I would choose another bottle or two. Though Raelene did supply me with some wine, I intended to hide this reserve in my underwear drawer.

The beam of automatic light that shone when I opened the cellar door revealed Connie's renovations. The once damp dungeon of my nightmares had become a well-lit and ordered place with steps and floor covered in tan quarry tiles. I marvelled at the organized rows of wines, some of a valuable vintage. Pa's 'drink cave', as we called it as children, had been sanitised, but it still held Hannes' pain no matter how hard Connie had tried to alter it.

Hannes avoided going into the cold cellar. Shortly before his fourteenth birthday, Connie sent him down there on the pretext that Pa wanted a particular bottle of wine to give a friend. Once he was inside, Connie locked the door. Hannes was in there all that day and it was only when Ma looked for him at dinner time that Connie crept away to let him out.

To ease his terror Hannes had drunk a lot of wine and passed out on the cellar floor. Connie pretended to discover Hannes with indignant shouting. Then he asked Pa to help him drag Hannes into the sitting room. Hannes' headache the next day was bad enough, but the beating he received from Pa was worse. Though he realized Connie had set him up, Hannes didn't even try to defend himself by telling Pa what had really happened. He believed that in Pa's eyes Connie was always right. As a further punishment Pa cancelled the band for the party that was to celebrate Hannes' last birthday.

The tension between Connie and Hannes had existed over such a long time that I hadn't noticed an escalation of bad feeling, nor had anyone else commented on it. Hannes was mischievous but he wasn't intrinsically nasty. He was forced to defend himself against Connie, so when Miriam provided him with rich material he happily used it.

The box was clearly visible in a corner of the cellar. I carried it to the foot of the stairs to collect later and went back to the cellar for the wine. Once the box was on the carpet in the corner of my room I felt uneasy. I looked at it for some time but didn't attempt to open it.

The wind had become a flutter and the dust had settled. I ran from the house and visited Hannes' and my special childhood places – secret spaces behind rocks, hiding holes in the barn, tall trees that when climbed gave cover and unlimited views. The rational part of me knew that if I opened the box I would have memories to face that I had avoided for all these years.

It had taken me at least three years after Hannes' death to realize how much I had loved him. For months I thought only of ways he got under my skin or caused trouble for me. Eventually the tumultuous loss overwhelmed me and I cried for him.

Hannes played practical jokes, regularly hiding Pa's pipe or mixing up Ma's paintbrushes. He did horrid things to me like putting snails and lizards in my underwear and regularly he annoyed all of us by shrieking or loud banging. Once he put sugar in Tansie's *meilie* pap instead of salt and she was furious. We all knew he was looking for attention, but at times he was exasperating.

Hannes regularly defied authority. Pa forbade us to go near the windmill and water tank. That water was for drinking but Hannes purposely dangled his feet in it. He and I were two petals from the same flower. My thoughts were as defiant, my mind as inquiring but Hannes was older, more articulate and he had a devilish courage I didn't possess.

If only those brief links when I was still at home and he was in preschool had lasted. We spent our afternoons with Tansie and though he had his moments of jealousy of my bond with her, there were days when one of us would start a sentence and the other finish it or we'd laugh at the same things. But as Hannes matured our connectedness was severed and glimpses of his gentler side were rare.

Chapter 20

I rose and dressed quickly in the clothes Nettie had washed and ironed for me. My blue jeans had an uncharacteristic crease and the tee-shirt and knickers had been ironed too. There wasn't time for ironing tee-shirts at home.

I was ready to open the box, intrigued about finding some new information about our family but aware that I might be unearthing new horrors. As I tore at the tape, pieces of cardboard crumbled. A staple nicked my finger, drawing blood, and I licked my wound. Under wads of tissue paper was a flat object that felt like a book. I pulled out a leather-bound journal. Though old, the green suede front cover had retained most of its gold filigree border of swirls and twirls. On the first page, in black copperplate, was the heading *The Van Wyk Family History.*

A religious dedication in an old form of Afrikaans followed as well as the history of the arrival of our forefathers and the Great Trek. My hand trembled as I turned the pages. The paper had yellowed and the ink faded but the old-fashioned script was legible. Then in detail, spread over a double page, was the Van Wyk family tree. It had been so lovingly and skilfully assembled that it seemed almost sinful to throw the book into an old cardboard box.

Greedy for knowledge I studied the tree in detail. Our first known Dutch ancestors, Anika de Jooste and Gerhardes Van Wyk, topped the tree. They left Rotterdam for South Africa in 1764 and their first child – a daughter, Katerina – married

Barnie Krans. Their second child – a son, Johannes – was born in 1784. Johannes married Nelinka Van Brede.

I said the Dutch names of my early relatives over and over to myself. They sounded so foreign and different. Fortunately there were helpful notes on following pages in old-fashioned script. They told the story of Anika and Gerhardes' arrival in the Cape and of their employers, The Dutch East India Company, who had established a refreshment station for its ships and sailors on their trading voyages to the East Indies. The Van Wyks decided to stay in the Cape with others, and began farming near Cape Town. According to the notes, Johannes and Nelinka employed a free man rather than a slave, as others had, to help them in the house and on the farm. He was a young Bushman whose name they couldn't pronounce, so they called him Sonny.

Johannes and Nelinka built up a sizable sheep farm and became prosperous wool farmers. While Johannes traveled the country selling wool, Nelinka, who had no children, was bored and lonely on the farm.

Sonny had worked for the family since a teenager and was a trusted servant. Johannes, apparently a generous man, gave Sonny several gifts of lambs so that he could begin to build his own flock. What happened between Nelinka and Sonny is uncertain. It had been stated publicly that while Johannes was away Nelinka was raped by her servant. Her son Frederick was born in 1798. There wasn't much written about Sonny except that he was charged in 1797 with rape and stabbed to death in jail eight months after Frederick was born. His murderer was never found. I wondered what had really happened. Reading between the lines I could assume that Nelinka knew Sonny well as he had worked for the couple for many years. Could she have been lonely and slept with him voluntarily? Though there was no certainty that he had fathered Frederick, a look at the dates told me that it was highly likely.

The closeted mystery that Pa had kept from us was out. This was evidence of our Bushman blood. I scratched my head trying to bring to mind what I knew of the small yellow-brown people with crinkly hair. They were the earliest inhabitants of Southern Africa, and had lived mainly in the deserts, but some had moved down south. Hunters and gatherers, they lived peacefully for thousands of years until they came into contact with cattle-herding black tribes. The Bushmen's hold on land and their herds was further weakened when the Dutch settlers moved down, seeking farming land. Many Bushmen, left destitute, were forced to work for the settlers – others became slaves.

Intrigued, I returned to studying the family tree and discovering my relatives. My great great grandfather Frederick married Roxanne Van Loggenberg and their son Andre was born in 1827. Anna, born two years later, remained unmarried. Andre married Sarie in 1850 and she gave birth to Cornelius, our great grandfather. The history of our family was approaching modern times and exciting.

Cornelius Van Wyk was the first relative I'd heard of. Pa had told us as children many a story about our great grand father Cornelius, a brave Voortrekker who had distinguished himself as a warrior during the Great Trek. Cornelius married Francina, who died in childbirth, but her child, our grandfather Eric, survived.

I traced my finger along the family lines to my grandfather Eric. He married the priest's daughter Lily Cronje in 1902. Our grandmother read her Bible until the end. Oupa Eric and Ouma Lily were blessed with two sons – my father, Piet, and my uncle, Gerrett – and two daughters, my aunts Helen and Edith. We hadn't met Pa's sisters or our cousins. As a young man Pa fell out with his siblings and had not given us the opportunity to get to know them. At least he could've let us make up our own minds about our relatives.

The legend of our ancestry was a serious matter, but I couldn't help laughing. We had a Bushman as an ancestor and the Hurutshe's on the farm had more than one in their family tree. I remembered seeing Zacharias carving Bushmen figurines when Hannes and I visited him. I doubted that the little brown men had much status as tribal ancestors. The Bushmen were rejected and thought of as low class in the 19th century when they met up with black tribes in the Botswana area.

Putting my hand back into the box, I clasped hard edges. There was more. I held my prize of two large yellowed folders and placed them down carefully. Then the squelch of crepe soles outside the bedroom door interrupted my concentration. Connie's footsteps. How could I forget them? He peeked his head round the door.

'All going well?' he said eyeing the spread of papers on the desk and those pieces I'd moved to the bed.

'Fine thanks.'

'Anything interesting?'

'Don't worry, I'll let you know,' I snapped.

He left quickly and I heard his footsteps fade down the stairs. I was tired and ratty, no longer able to face my task. I lay my head on the desk, breathed the warm resins, and closed my eyes. A whirl of family names danced in my head. I wanted a moment of respite, to be away from it long enough to gather stamina for the next part. Like the rest of my family, I had a huge capacity for escapism. Only, unlike them, I usually fought to overcome it. But at that moment, all I wanted to do was to slip into a sweet snippet of the past.

I was back in the orange groves on a crisp golden morning when I saw them for the first time. Beneath the trees, I noticed a ripple in the leaves hugging the ground. Was it was a mouse or small animal? I lay in a furrow holding my breath. I had dug welts into my thighs by the time I saw them, three shimmering creatures darting between the trees and only as tall as one of Pa's beer bottles. Their pointed brown faces were too small and their features far too fine to discern details. I watched fascinated until a breeze swept them away. Once when the light was hazy I noticed them again. Zacharias had a name for them that I couldn't remember.

'When you go school you never see them no more,' he laughed. He was right as usual.

Nettie brought me out of my delightful daydream.

'Ma'am, Raelene, she worried about you. She send special sandwiches and coffee.'

'Thanks Nettie, that's marvelous. Put them down here,' I said carefully clearing a spot for the tray.

After eating I carefully opened the first folder. Painted family and individual portraits lay inside. They were antiques that must've been painted before photographs were available. Just as well there were identifying notes at the back of each. I laid out them out on the desk. The profile of Johannes Van Wyk, in sepia against cream, showed a corpulent and proud, if not arrogant, man, his face angular, mustached and bearded. Connie resembled him, though his face was fuller.

I stared fascinated at young Nelinka, resplendent in a ruffled silky gown that was full skirted and nipped in the waist.

Looking at her was like seeing myself in a mirror. I owed my oval face and deep-set eyes to her. My mouth must've come from elsewhere.

In a family painting, an older Johannes was in an armchair with lavishly dressed Nelinka leaning over him. Katerina and Barnie stood behind them with their children on the outer edge. A Golden Retriever lay in the front of the group and a smallish dark man sat on the floor near the dog. I thought that the dark man could've been Sonny.

Next was a sepia family sitting of three people: elderly Johannes, Nelinka and a man who hadn't been in the portraits up until now. Short, with darker skin than the others, almond eyes, a full mouth and tufted curly hair, he had to be my great great grandfather, Frederick.

'Oh Hansie,' I thought, 'if you're about somewhere I hope you can see this. Your body was more athletic and you were slimmer but you look just like Frederick. If you could've seen his photograph, you would've understood so much more and felt less alone!'

The second folder contained photographs taken in the late 1800s and more recently. Oupa Eric and Ouma Lily on their wedding day were a loving couple. She was a plump woman stuffed into a chiffon and lace wedding gown. Our great grandfather, Cornelius, was photographed in his uniform of Veld Kommandant from several angles. Lean and handsome, he looked so much like Vince.

At last I knew something of my ancestors. There were many family resemblances between relatives long gone and ourselves. Carefully I replaced the photographs and caressed the old album.

That evening after dinner Connie, Vince and I sat around the gleaming dining room table. The leather-bound book and folders lay in front of us.

Both my brothers looked apprehensive.

'Is this what you found today?' Connie said, running his hand along his goatee.

'It tells the history of our family.'

'Oh,' Connie said looking at me blankly.

'You're the eldest, didn't Pa tell you about our ancestors?'

'No, I assumed they were Dutch,' Connie said.

'I don't have much idea either,' Vince said. 'I asked Pa many times about our ancestors but he always avoided answering. In the end I got tired of asking.'

'You'd both better read it then,' I said, pushing the book along the table in their direction. 'It'll be a revelation.'

Connie picked it up first. He looked at it slowly and handed the book to Vince. 'You'd better have a look at it Vin. We have *kaffir* blood.'

Vince grabbed the book.

'Shit. No wonder Pa wouldn't talk about it. He should've though. We all had a right to know.'

'This is what our relatives looked like,' I said laying out the photographs on the polished wood. Names are at the back.'

We discussed resemblances and laughed over strange hairdos and clothes. Connie and Vince thought that Katerina was a beauty but didn't discuss our great great grandfather Frederick. It was as if he hadn't existed. In exasperation I pointed to him. 'What about Frederick?'

'He's as black as …' Connie spluttered.

'With Hannes so dark you should've known there'd be someone like him in our past,' Vince said.

Turning to me Connie glared. 'You've messed things up nicely with your prying, haven't you? I've always said there are some things it's better not to know.'

Vince sat with his head in his hands.

Angrily I grabbed the book, holding it tightly to my chest as I hurried upstairs. Connie was as inflexible and racist as ever and Vince disappointed me. He should've stood up to Connie, made a more positive statement about such an important matter. My brothers had dampened my excitement.

I spoke aloud, staring at Pa's photograph, 'Ja Pa, you were ashamed of Hannes and ashamed of yourself. I don't think you ever accepted that Hannes carried the dark gene in our family like your great grandfather Frederick.'

I glared at the photograph, furious with Pa for being so secretive.

I finished the last of the extra wine I had stashed in my drawer and wished I had another. Raelene had forgotten to provide the usual bottle. I stared hypnotically at the wine cellar key on top of the dressing table. I tried not to give in to my craving, but my need for oblivion made me grab the key and head downstairs. I had to pass the kitchen to reach the cellar. Connie was in the lit kitchen eating a huge salami sandwich.

'Nightwatch in the kitchen.' His mouth was full of food.

'I'll have some of that.' I pointed to the enticing fat-speckled salami. He cut a chunk and a slice of bread.

'Fix it yourself,' he said handing it to me with his fingers. I took a plate from the cupboard, sliced the salami he'd given me into manageable pieces and sat down at the table.

'Wine?' He pushed the bottle towards me. 'Why are you wandering around?' His speech was slightly slurred.

'Too much on my mind,'

He laughed cynically. 'Cooking up trouble?'

'No.'

'Trying to prove that your eldest brother killed little Hannes, eh?'

'No, hoping to find a way to prove that he didn't.'

'Hmph. Doesn't seem that way to me.'

'For God's sake Connie, I'm not out to get you!'

'Umm. When did you say you were leaving?'

I felt tears pricking my eyes but wouldn't give in to them. I swallowed the last of the salami and gulped down the glass of wine.

'See you in the morning.'

Connie hadn't changed much. He used the same techniques as he had before to ride me. But now it didn't work. I wouldn't let him get to me.

Duke was on my bed when I entered the room. I was used to a cat's delicate snore and fell asleep to it. It must've been around 3.30am when I sat up in bed in a panic. Duke raced off when I turned on the bedside light. I hunted under the bed for the pair of thongs I was using as slippers and went to the bathroom. Cold water on my face and some deep breaths calmed me a little.

I had dreamed that I opened a box containing snakes. They writhed and hissed menacingly. I woke terrified. I asked myself whether the snakes could be symbolic and, if so, what or whom did they represent? With no answers I put the light off and went back to sleep.

Chapter 21

The next morning, a mug of coffee, a cigarette and a shower helped me to dress but I'd drunk too much to face food. I felt guilty. The days had slipped past and I felt as though I had achieved nothing in my investigations of Hannes' murder. With no shift in the unanswered questions facing me, the attic was the only place I could think of that might provide answers.

I climbed the stairs and placed the wide-beamed flashlight near the entrance. Two piles of Ma's sketchbooks that Vince had forgotten to bring down partially blocked the way. Kneeling on a curled old rug, I brought the beam of the flashlight as close to the drawings as I could. The ones on top were landscapes and portraits of people I didn't recognize. Beneath those were a bundle of sketchpapers tied with a torn blue taffeta ribbon. I undid the bow and carefully rolled out the drawings. One contained pencil and pastel images of Hannes in a blue matinee jacket and leggings, crawling and gurgling. In others he sat in his high chair or stood proudly, his bright eyes staring out at me. Each page was lovingly drawn so that his fine features, delicate bones and coloring were made into special attributes. Through Ma's drawings I imagined holding and cuddling him. Only in the last book was he the Hannes I knew, with sad eyes and a droop to his mouth.

I flipped through the remaining sketches. There were drawings of me as an infant and some of Vince and Connie too, but it was to Hannes that Ma had bestowed her greatest gift of attention and love. If only he'd known how much she'd loved him as a baby. And if only Ma had given him that love later when he needed it. My throat was tight and tears flowed easily.

Once I had wiped my eyes, I cleared a path into the attic. Moving bits of broken furniture and bric-a-brac out of the way, I found a brown leather trunk banded with rusted brass, the sort that was used for sea voyages a long time ago. I vaguely recalled Hannes and I hiding in it when I was three or four. Once it was open, out poured Hannes' early schoolbooks and piles of Superman and Batman comics.

On a low table with a broken leg that was still sturdy enough to hold me, I sat studying the contents of the trunk. The base of the trunk held two old-fashioned girls' dresses, frilly petticoats and a Red Indian costume with a headdress of feathers and a quiver of arrows. Underneath was a sea captain's cap with torn braid and a boy's blue blazer. I opened a red silk cosmetic purse, containing a red lipstick, a comb and a black shiny powder compact.

As I let the images and memories meld, Hannes was a Red Indian again, sending arrows into a fat elm tree. When he tired of that costume he wore the captain's cap and jacket. Often he wore the cap when he left 'magic land', as he called the attic.

'Is your ship grounded in the dam Captain?' Pa would ask him playfully.

'No sir, we're sailing,' Hannes would answer.

Wearing the cap made Hannes feel important. With it on, he sometimes gave the servants orders. 'Clean the floor behind the door and under the table, it's dusty,' he said to Nettie cheekily mimicking Ma's voice. 'Yes, sir Captain, you clean,' she said with a laugh.

When he was about nine, he pretended to be an old-fashioned miss in the blue dress with ruffles and petticoats.

A touch of lipstick and a few bobby pins, and with his delicate frame he was turned into a young woman.

The heat of the flashlight focused my thoughts. I picked up the silk cosmetic purse. Arnie had told me about the lipstick on Hannes' lips. Hannes wore lipstick and powder when he dressed up in women's clothing to grab our attention. But there was more to it. Like many actors in costume he could lose himself while pretending to be someone else. I hadn't seen him dress up since he was nine or ten and I wondered what had caused him to revert to costume and lipstick the night he was murdered?

In the *voorkamer* the grandfather clock struck four o'clock.

'Ma'am, you want tea or coffee and piece of cake?' Nettie asked.

'Thanks Nettie, tea will be fine.'

Being served all the time irritated me. The number of servants in the house had bothered me since I had arrived – two maids in the kitchen, a housemaid, another in the laundry ironing and a gardener. Having servants was part of the affluent side of South African life and always had been. Raelene's 'staff', as she called them, all wore the uniform and cap of service but seemed happy, at least superficially. I'd been away for a long time and forgotten about servants. In Melbourne I had home help for three hours every two weeks and cleaned the place myself between times.

Nettie had worked for Raelene and Connie for many years and they regarded her as almost one of the family. Knowing Tswana life and customs I doubted she felt the same. She may have liked them, even formed an attachment to the family, but her job took her from her grandchildren and home and she'd have resented that. Like most blacks I'd known, Nettie had a resilient sunny temperament and as the job provided her with needed money, she made the best of things.

South Africa puzzled me. Black servants were still relied upon to perform tasks in the home and to look after precious children, yet in spite of pay rises they weren't paid enough for those important tasks. They were given food and had an afternoon off and possibly a Sunday or two free per month. The lot of the domestic worker hadn't changed much. Having the support of trade unions and the vote hadn't meant true social and financial equality. Not yet.

'*Dumela* Nathaniel,' I called. He waved. By the time I reached him a young man had joined him.

'Missie Linda, here is Thomas.'

'Hello,' I said.

'Thomas is ... son of Miriam,' he stumbled.

One look at Thomas and instantly I knew why Miriam was a secret. The handsome man in his forties looked like Connie. He had slightly darker coloring but I had no doubts he was Connie's son.

'You look shocked,' Thomas said, putting his hands on his hips. 'I look just like my father don't I?'

'Exactly like him.'

'Ja, well, I can't help that.'

'Does your Aunt Linda get a hug?' He looked away with embarrassment. 'At least a handshake?'

He moved forward, our hands touched and gradually our arms wound around each other. Nathaniel clapped in delight. Thomas and I looked at each other and smiled. There were no words to describe the bond I felt with Thomas. He told us that Connie had banned him from the farm and that it was best to go to Miriam's hut to talk. We walked towards the hut and Nathaniel waved as he left to supervise work on the orange groves.

Miriam was out and the hut looked empty. While Thomas made himself comfortable in a chair I had a moment to savor the pleasure of meeting him. Veils had been lifted since I had been at the farm and I wondered what I might learn next.

'I'm not allowed to be here so I'm glad to be inside where big eyes can't see me. I popped in for a mo to see Ma. That's not unreasonable is it?'

'No, I don't think so, but it's Connie's farm. I guess what he says goes.'

Thomas rattled on angrily about Connie being his father but not acknowledging him or even treating him reasonably. I tried to steer him away from the topic of Connie. Thomas told me that he was a vet and worked on the farms in the area. I pictured him tending to sick animals. He had strong hands and a gentle manner.

'You're a nice and unexpected discovery,' I said.

'Connie – I call him that – won't be pleased that you've met his bastard son,' Thomas said frowning. 'You have no idea how much trouble I have caused.'

I imagined that Connie's reaction to a mixed race illegitimate son wouldn't be positive.

'Hannes died when I was a baby but I've heard stacks about him. You can imagine that Connie tried to keep my birth quiet but Hannes stirred the pot. From what I've heard about Hannes he must have been a little devil.'

'If you'd had the opportunity to know him, you'd have liked him I'm sure.'

'Ma was living with Cheetah, Tania's father, when I was born. She's my half sister.' He gazed around the hut. 'Then little Eva came along,' he said, pronouncing the name 'Eva' loudly. Eva ran towards Thomas and hugged him.

'Knew she was hiding here. She's a real gift to us. Like a baby sister.'

'I met Eva the day I arrived.' We smiled at each other.

'Got to get going. You have a go at asking Connie about me and the trouble I caused. I'm lucky to be here. I nearly didn't make it.'

I looked puzzled.

'It started with Ma's long and painful labor. I believe the midwife said it was a bad sign. It must've been 'cos Ma's breasts dried like prunes and she had to find a wet nurse for me. All this happened to a baby who was unwanted by his mother and almost everyone who knew about his birth.'

'As bad as that?'

'Oh yeah. I've heard rumors that my Ma tried to smother me with a pillow the day after I was born but my cries were so pitiful that she changed her mind.'

'You don't believe rumors like that do you?'

'I wasn't wanted but things changed when I grew older. Not with Connie of course.'

We left the hut and walked some of the way in silence. I took his hands in mine and looked at him.

'I'm pleased we met up with one another. I'm not here for much longer but I'd like to spend some time with you and find out more about you.'

'I'll try to come round again in a few days.'

He smiled and gave me a wave that looked a bit like a salute.

I had been invited to Vince and Jeanette's for dinner that night. Their home could've been in a Melbourne suburb – dark brick, wood and glass surrounded by plants. The rugs on boards with tasteful furnishings made it attractive and comfortable.

Anita, Jeanette's maid and cook, presented an elaborate four-course dinner. Jeanette worked full-time as a secretary and I doubted whether she could have managed to produce such a feast alone without days of preparation and a lot of effort.

Old friends Kath and Mark, and Diana, Jeanette's mother, had been invited as well. Kath and I had been at school together, but after discussing the people who were in our class and our teachers we had nothing in common to talk about. The table talk slipped into a discussion in hushed tones about violence in rural areas. My mind was on Thomas and when the guests went on to discuss local politics they lost me.

Diana moved next to me. 'I was sorry to learn about your father's passing. Your parents were pillars of the society. What a loving couple and upright, God-fearing and kindly people they were. Everyone held them in high esteem. We need more people like them.'

'That's comforting to hear.'

Ma and Pa had created an outer image. Diana couldn't have known that they weren't always a loving couple in private or that they wouldn't admit to themselves that they were ashamed of Hannes' appearance. At times they resented the embarrassment he caused them, but wouldn't admit that either. Living by the 'What will people think?' dictum, they forced him to cut his frizzy hair closely and straighten it further with hair cream. He had to wear long pants and long-sleeved shirts to cover his copper skin. No one outside the family could have known. Had there been gossip about Connie, Miriam and their son Thomas? I wondered.

After the guests left, Vince and I went onto their *stoep*. The night was warm, the moon coddled in clouds.

'How's the investigation going?' Vince asked.

I pulled a face.

'You need a *ngaka* to throw some bones for you.' He laughed at his attempt at a joke.

'Not a bad idea.'

He stared absently at a branch of bougainvillea swaying in the breeze. 'I haven't got used to Pa not being here. It's beginning to hit me that we have to take over.'

'We're the next generation of Van Wyks. Pa drummed the Van Wyk history into us when we were kids. Family history was so important to him.'

'But Pa told us what only what he wanted us to know,' Vince said.

'I'm sick of cover-ups.'

'Plenty round in this neck of the woods.'

'I had a good surprise today. I met Thomas.'

Vince looked shocked. 'Connie won't be pleased you found out about him. Even less that you talked to him.'

I moved to the edge of the *stoep* and lit a cigarette. What was the point of venting the disappointment, or more accurately the frustration, that overwhelmed me? Had Pa brainwashed his sons in his secretive ways? The very things I needed to know about in order to carry out Pa's request were denied me. Vince claimed he wanted to help me with the investigation, and I believed his offer to be genuine, but when it came to tough family matters he skirted around them or did the usual Van Wyk denial dance.

'Thomas told me that Hannes kicked up hell when he found out Connie had a son.'

'I'm not sure on details but he went into blackmailing Connie big time.'

'All this retribution is so sad.'

'Connie turned bitter. After that hiding Pa gave him he got nastier and more devious. Eventually he squashed Pa by threatening to leave the farm. Pa couldn't have coped without him so he kept quiet about Thomas … pretended he wasn't there.'

'Thomas is your blood relative. What do you think of him?

'He's a great guy. I like him, but the situation is touchy.'

'Don't you see him?'

'Not really.'

'That's a pity.'

He ran his hand through his hair. 'You don't live here. Things are bloody complicated.' Vince went inside for another beer.

He was right – things on the farm were complicated. Silence and secrecy had worsened the situation. And what about Miriam? Why was she was still living on the farm with all her mod-cons? If her presence had caused so much trouble I would've thought Connie would've given her money or a new home or both just to avoid seeing her and Thomas.

But things on the farm didn't work in straight lines. It wasn't a pleasant thought but I couldn't sponge it out. Was Connie still sleeping with Miriam when it suited him? Miriam had someone living with her. I heard his voice in the background. But arrangements could always be made and Connie was the *Baas* after all and his needs came first. And she lived on the farm but didn't do anything – no work on the farm or in the house. The more I thought about it the more convinced I was that either she was blackmailing Connie or still sleeping with him. I opted for the latter choice.

Vince offered me a beer but I shook my head.

'Why didn't I bump into Thomas on the farm when I was a kid?' I asked.

'After he was born Pa insisted he be sent away, so his aunt looked after him. He's not supposed to come to the farm. Connie's orders. But he does sneak in to visit his Ma. You were lucky to see him today.'

'Thomas told me that there were rumors that just after he was born Miriam tried to smother him. Is there anything in that?'

'I wouldn't be surprised. Connie didn't want him. Her own people were horrified, particularly her real boyfriend, Cheetah. Then there was Hannes calling her names.'

'A difficult time for her.'

'The story is that her aunt caught her trying to kill the baby and stopped her.'

'Oh, I see.' Vince's version of the story seemed more realistic.

It was past 1am when Vince drove me home. As soon as I entered my room I knew that it wasn't the way I'd left it. My suitcase and items I had scattered on the desk had been moved. The white paper lay in a slightly different position. It couldn't have been Nettie dusting and cleaning because she promised not to touch any of my things. It had to have been someone else. Raelene, or Connie?

Part 5

Juice

Chapter 22

In the back garden the sounds of insects were magnified in the heat haze. A chorus of workers sang the story of their lives, of love, violence on the streets and poverty, AIDS and death. At every occasion, sad or joyous, singing was the blacks' means of spontaneous expression. Being naturally melodic, they were in key and pleasant to listen to. When Pa went to a meeting, or to the co-op, the workers broke into songs about oppression and their hopes for freedom.

As hard as Pa had tried to keep the workers concentrating on their jobs rather than politics, when the activist Eddie Morake and his wife Seraphina came to visit their relatives on the farm, every black stopped work. Tansie hurried me back to the house. I did manage to spot Eddie's round shiny face with the biggest set of teeth I'd seen. He worked the building crowd with a forced smile, shaking hands and nodding as he slid past. Meanwhile Seraphina carried placards from the back of their jeep. In African languages, English and Afrikaans the placards demanded better working conditions, shorter hours and more pay.

The crowd spoke with one voice, one message – *more money*. The workers' eyes shone with hope. Pa didn't wait, he called the local police. Swiftly they bundled Eddie and his wife into their jeep and sent them away. With Eddie gone and the police herding them back to the orange groves, the workers trudged back to work.

'Pa, who's Eddie?' Hannes asked that evening.

'The story goes that Eddie Morake was in the crowd during the Sharpville demonstration earlier this year. Esiekiel says that Morake and his wife travel around telling the blacks their stories and whipping up trouble.'

'Sharpville?'

We sat near his chair and waited for him to pull off his boots and sip the froth off his beer.

'Okay,' he sighed, moving around in the cane chair. 'I have to get comfortable before I talk about this miserable subject.'

He took a few slugs of beer and told us how in March that year the police had shot at hundreds of blacks gathered in demonstration against pass laws that restricted their movement around the country.

'The worst thing happened,' he said. 'Without warning the police fired into the crowd. Sixty-nine people were killed and about three hundred injured.'

'Oh no, Pa,' I said.

He finished the last dregs of his beer. 'I support the government but there are times they don't know where to draw the line. Now I don't want to hear any more about it.'

Nettie tiptoed up to me. 'Sorry Missie, you sleeping? Phone for you.'

'Take it in the kitchen,' called Raelene.

The kitchen screen door banged in the background.

'Come on, I think it's that policeman for you on the phone,' Raelene whispered.

Arnie Swart wanted to know if I had made any advances in the investigation. Unfortunately, I had to answer that I'd discovered nothing more than bits and pieces that didn't amount to much.

'If you want some help ... just say. And of course that dinner invitation is still open.'

'Not right now, but thanks.'

How could I discuss my fears about Connie with Arnie? Even if he had heard the gossip about Hannes' threats and known about Thomas he was keeping quiet about it. Any discussion about the murder would be a farce without all the facts on the table.

I sat on the *stoep* sipping coffee and mulling over the murder. Miriam was back in my thoughts. If she attempted to smother the baby could she have killed Hannes? Hannes could've seen her as the temptress who seduced his brother for her own ends – a comfortable home and possibly money. He was fond of Raelene, the pure one, and must have seen Miriam as vile.

Miriam had gained enormous power by sleeping with Connie. Not only over him but the whole family. Perhaps she used it by demanding money. Connie and Miriam had committed an immoral, illegal act that would bring shame on the family name if discovered but, more seriously, it could have resulted in a jail term for both. It's hard to believe that Hannes would've gone as far as wanting to see his brother in jail and the family disgraced, but he may have threatened to expose them. In any event, with Hannes' sharp tongue I could see him taunting her and making life as unpleasant for her as possible. Perhaps she killed him to keep him quiet. Facts had been unraveling like a torn sweater. Perhaps I would find out more about Miriam in my time left on the farm.

My thoughts shifted to the brutal stabbing. Was the killing the murderer's way of drawing attention to how he felt about Hannes? Was the murder impulsive, a crime of passion, or was it premeditated? Would I ever have answers?

I asked myself whether I'd followed up all possible avenues of investigation. As I ticked them off mentally, I realized I hadn't been in Hannes' room. I couldn't expect to find anything substantial after all this time but it I had to satisfy myself that I hadn't been sloppy. His room was next to mine and the two older boys had slept across the passage. Over the years the room was used for the occasional visitor or one of the grandchildren but it was virtually as he had left it. I forced myself to open the door and found myself in a room resembling the room Hannes slept in with its soul ripped out.

Ma had changed the blue curtains with ships to yellow ones with white daisies. The navy linen bedspread had been replaced with a yellow candlewick one. Perhaps they were her attempts to change the atmosphere in the room or attempts to forget.

My search began with separating the mattress from the bed base. I found nothing. After replacing the mattress and tidying the bed, I moved the bookcase filled with romance stories away from the wall. Behind the paperbacks a dog with its mouth open had been scratched into the wood and then filled in with blue ink. I looked closely. Its mouth was open in laughter. To the side of the table next to the bed I found another laughing dog. The dog caricatures made me sad. It was the real Hannes covering up how bad he felt by laughing or being cynical.

The farm was still between 1pm and 2pm when Connie and the manager had their lunch and the workers had a break. Many went home to eat and take a nap. My usual haunts felt different without the noise that humans made. I could hear the calls of birds and insects distinctly and even the crackle of leaves or sticks underfoot made sharper sounds. I was almost sure that I'd heard an elephant's trumpet in the distance. There were several animal reserves in the area.

The ugly image of Miriam placing a pillow over her baby's face remained with me. By the time I neared her hut the workers were yawning and stretching as they made their way back to the orange groves. Her head popped round the door and she waved.

'Nice to see you again. I had a bit of snooze and now I'm up and ready for visitors.'

Though I wanted to ask her the questions bothering me, I wouldn't have known where to start. How does one ask a woman if she killed one's brother?'

'What's wrong Linda? You're looking unhappy today.'

I shrugged.

'I hear you met your bastard cousin the other day.'

'I was so pleased I met him. Thomas is … a delight. And things couldn't have been easy for him.'

With her hands on her hips she proudly recited Thomas' achievements – top of his class in vet school, president of the local association, liked by all the farmers in the area.

Thomas had an engaging smile and was a listener. His own difficulties may have helped to develop his empathy. I had taken to him immediately and could understand his popularity.

'Did he tell you the stories about me trying to smother or strangle him as a baby?'

I looked away, feeling uneasy. 'Ja. I've heard those stories.'

'They're true. All true. When I first got pregnant with him Cheetah was furious. He'd been away to visit his relatives in Jo'burg for a month so he knew the baby wasn't his. He had found out about Connie and me … and … he wanted to get rid of it. Ja … he'd have done anything to get rid of the white man's baby. So, he went to a *ngaka* for help. A smelly old man with feathers all over him turned up here. He threw bones and gave me medicines he promised would make me abort the baby.'

'What happened?'

'The medicines tasted terrible and made me sick but the baby grew. Cheetah even punched my stomach but my belly still got bigger. It was too late for an abortion so we agreed. I'd have it and we'd kill it once it was born.

'The day after he was born, I did try to kill Thomas but he cried so much and I cried too. I couldn't go through with it. My auntie who was staying with us helped me. She talked to Cheetah and me that night and he agreed to let the baby live.'

I refused Miriam's offer of coffee and walked from her hut as fast as I could. The repugnant picture of the couple trying to kill their unwanted child had sickened me. How Thomas had become a warm, caring person after such a beginning was miraculous. Miriam was a physically attractive woman but beneath that was stark ugliness.

I was stuck. Cobie, Pa's old friend, was the only person I felt I could turn to. I could discuss family business with him openly and he'd be honest with me.

'Lovely to see you,' he said giving me a kiss on my cheek. 'Come sit.'

We sat on the sofa and I shared my fears about Connie with him. He knew about Miriam and Thomas so there wasn't much to explain.

'You can understand why your Pa let those poor black devils rot in jail. He was dead scared to mention Hannes' hold over Connie. He was furious with Connie but Connie was still his son. He was the firstborn and your Pa protected him.'

'Pa spoiled him and it didn't help him to develop a sense of responsibility.'

'It was your Ma too, bless her. She adored him and gave in to all his whims.

'So Connie ended up a selfish bastard.'

I told him about Hannes' drawing of the dog.

'He was laughing at us all then,' he said, 'swallowing his sadness.'

As one of Cobie's clocks chimed the hour he changed his tone and stood. 'Coffee time.' He disappeared into the kitchen and I overheard him giving orders. Ten minutes later his maid served coffee and cake. After drinking the hot Turkish-style coffee out of small porcelain cups, I tried to tie Cobie down about Connie's role in the murder. I desperately needed an honest answer.

'We know Connie's got a mean streak, but kill Hannes? There's no evidence, no witnesses. Who can say?'

'So what do you think I should do?'

'You have to keep at it, if only to clear Connie's name.' Cobie drummed the table with the palm of his hand. 'You're deep in it now so don't leave it up in the air or you won't rest. If you want to discuss things I'll be here for you.'

Eyes bored into me as I sat down to dinner.

'That arrived for you.' Connie pointed to the sideboard. It was an arrangement of roses. We called the coral and orange beauties 'Tequila Sunset' back home. Nettie stood holding the soup tureen and watched me.

'An admirer and after such a short time here,' Raelene said.

I wrestled the card free. *'For a lovely lady. Arnie.'*

'Please put the flowers in the *voorkamer.* I don't want them in my room.'

I battled to force food down. Once Connie had retired to watch re-runs of soccer, Raelene and I sat drinking coffee. I spoke quickly, swallowing words in my embarrassment as I told her about the Detective Inspector's advances and invitations to dinner.

'Do you fancy him?' she asked.

'He's attractive in a rough way.'

'Well then,' she sniffed. 'You're a grown woman.'

'The attention is nice.'

'What about his invitation to dinner?'

'No. He's after sex.'

'That puts you in a spot if you need his help,' she said.

'He knows it too.'

'Tell you what … let's invite him to have a meal at home with us,' she said with a big grin.

'Wonderful idea. I love you Raelene.' I gave her a hug.

My thoughts were elsewhere. Patterns in families don't change, I thought. Pa had turned to me as an accomplice to edge him out of a tight spot before. The time the bailiff made an appointment to see Pa about his mortgage payments seemed like yesterday.

A drought brought two poor seasons and Pa was behind in payments. An hour before the bailiff arrived Pa asked me for a special favor.

'Put on your party dress, the pink fluffy one, with your lace socks and comb your hair around your shoulders. When the bailiff knocks at the door ask him in and take him into the *voorkamer.* Tell him you'll ask the maid to fetch me. While he's waiting offer him tea and some of Ma's ginger cake, then play a few tunes on the piano.'

'But I'm not that good.'

'Do your best. After a while the maid will return saying that I had to rush off to the co-op to buy pesticide.'

I followed Pa's wishes and after the bailiff left I ran upstairs to take the dress off. I felt dirty.

Chapter 23

Rain had brought flowers, leafy tendrils and a mass of weeds to the brittle veld. I picked wet jacaranda blossoms, popping them as I once had and sniffing their faint perfume on my fingers. Blue borage was flowering and I followed its trail as it crept along hedges, over trunks and boulders. I found myself outside the cemetery. The sand heap over Pa had sprouted weeds. I tugged at roots in clods of soil and threw them onto a barren patch. As I rubbed my hands on my jeans and clicked the cemetery gate behind me, I heard my name called. It was Miriam.

'Sorry I can't stop to talk. Cheetah likes his lunch on time,' Miriam muttered in Setswana.

'Just one quick question. Was Cheetah here when Hannes was murdered?'

'He sure was. Sorry. Got to get going.'

As the light dipped over the hills I left the cemetery. I sat on Pa's old bench watching the last rays of light and listening to the call of birds mingling with the songs of the workers on their way home. A sudden loud snap was followed by a shuddering thud. I felt as if an electric shock had hit me and I was thrown into nothingness.

When I opened my eyes my head throbbed and I had a pain down my side. I tried to stand but a dizzying weakness and a stab of pain stopped me. I must've been on the ground for at least an hour and all I could do was to lie there, call out for help and wait to be found. A tree had fallen and clobbered me on the head, knocking me out.

The sky was navy when Nettie and Nathaniel heard my calls for help. They had set out to look for me with a wide-beamed flashlight and a blanket. They lifted me carefully and, making a stretcher from the blanket, carried me back to the house.

'Spirits looking after Missie,' was all that Nettie said.

I had blocked Pa and Hannes from my conscious thoughts but perhaps they had been there to protect me.

The house lights and outdoor spotlights were blazing. Connie had been looking for me in the front garden and Raelene had made a search of the back one. By the time they realized I had come home and was on the couch in the *voorkamer,* I had collapsed again, but at least I was conscious.

Raelene insisted on calling a doctor in spite of my mumblings that all I needed was rest and I'd be fine. I had fallen asleep when a tall antiseptic-smelling man peered down at me. I lay there limply while he examined me. He pronounced me in shock, with a bump on my head and a badly bruised rib. Though he suggested an x-ray, he backed down when I refused doggedly.

Raelene fussed over me with hot sugared tea, biscuits, extra blankets and an icepack for my head and Connie paced the room looking worried. He didn't talk to me but brought a mohair rug from the bedroom to warm my icy feet and propped up my pillows. In fact, Connie's tenderness surprised me.

As I drifted off I saw Connie watching me from the chair. Noise from the kitchen of Nathaniel and Nettie disagreeing loudly about the fallen tree, woke me. Nathaniel said that he had examined the tree in the flashlight light and had come to the conclusion that it had a definite cut that meant it to fall in the direction I was sitting. Nettie laughed and said that surely I would have heard several strikes with an axe. Nathaniel argued that the tree had probably been cut earlier. It had fallen in a spot in the garden where I'd sat nearly every day and mostly at twilight. All that was needed to down it was a push.

The next morning I was still in my dressing gown and had spread myself out on the *stoep* as comfortably as I could. I was dozing when footsteps woke me.

'Bloody hard to get some rest around here,' I said with irritation in my voice. Arnie Swart moved away quickly and sat in one of the cane chairs.

'Sorry. I'll wait while you sort yourself out.'

'Tell you what,' Raelene said tying on the apron as she bustled round us. 'I'll send out some coffee for Arnie while he waits and some to wake you up too.' Slowly I lifted myself from the couch. My head was tender and my side ached but at least I could stand. In a few minutes I managed to wash superficially and throw on my jeans and tee. With my runners under my arm I went back to talk to Arnie Swart. Groaning softly I pulled them on and laced them.

'Sorry to have kept you. I'm ready for questions now.'

'You're in real bad shape,' he said. What's this about a tree falling on you?'

'Who called you?' I wasn't in the mood for questions.

'Connie was very worried and rang me.'

'Connie rang?' I remembered his concern the night before.

Arnie went over the attack with me in minute detail.

'Do you think someone's trying to …?'

'To harm you?' he cut in. 'There's a strong possibility. I hear there are axe marks on the trunk and the perpetrator has chosen a tree that you regularly sit under. You'd better be very careful.'

'It sounds ridiculous.'

'You've been asking lots of questions about Hannes' murder and stirring up the past. You could be pressing on someone's corns. I'm sending Sergeant Phefo round to examine the tree. He's working on that doll that you were sent too. We have to find out if the two are connected and if they have anything to do with this murder you're looking into.'

I wasn't firing yet. 'Connected … of course, they could be. I am glad you're doing something about it. It makes me feel safer.'

Feeling shaky I walked him to the door. I was in one piece and very lucky, I told myself. If I wasn't such a bulldog I'd have left the farm immediately. But I felt I was on the murderer's track and duty held me there.

Late that morning Sergeant Phefo came to take measurements of the tree and the distance it had fallen. He photographed the cut in the trunk and a mark made on the side of the tree. The cut was deep and clean and he said it was likely to have been made by an axe during the night. My movements must've been watched. Someone wanting to harm me merely had to wait for me to sit in my favorite place and then, without making a sound, push the trunk in my direction.

Sergeant Phefo searched the area close to the tree, carefully picking up and placing any foreign material into plastic bags. He also took some copies of footprints. He explained that the material would be handed to the forensic department for testing. When I asked him who he thought had cut the tree, he said, 'Be patient and I'll have some answers for you.'

'Do you think this tree thing could be tied to the doll and even to Hannes' murder?' I persisted.

'It's possible but nothing is certain at this stage. Be patient.'

Sergeant Phefo left me feeling unsettled. With the window of the car down, I drove through the streets of Rustenburg and the surrounding veld. My mind whirred as my thoughts flitted from the doll to the tree episode.

It was midday when Raelene tore herself from her post in the kitchen and insisted I accompany her to the shops. I had no shopping to do but I was pleased to see her out of the kitchen. She wanted a formal dress for a special occasion and dragged me from shop to shop in her hunt. Whatever she tried on wasn't the right color, fit or price. We trudged through the over-lit concrete and glass malls to yet another shop. While Raelene was trying on the umpteenth batch of dresses, I phoned Cheetah. His nickname alone made me keen to meet him.

'Cheetah, handyman services. Fast and reliable,' he answered.

I introduced myself. Cheetah made a point of telling me how busy he was but did offer to talk to me between jobs at lunchtime. We agreed to meet later at Miriam's hut.

Miriam was serving Cheetah his lunch when I arrived. Sleek and sinewy, I could understand how he'd earned his name. He pulled up a chair for me and offered me coffee. I sipped the mixture with its strong chicory kick while we talked.

'You're wasting your time hunting around for Hannes' killer. It was Connie. I'm sure of it.'

'How can you be so certain?'

'Connie was furious when Hannes threatened to tell your Pa that he and Miriam had been … well … screwing. When Hannes finally told your Pa, Connie gave Hannes such a shaking that his teeth nearly fell out. He just about ran for his life.'

'Really?'

'Jeez that little devil stood up to Connie, warned him he'd tell everybody about Miriam if Connie didn't pay him to keep his mouth shut. I thought Connie was going to blow up. "I'll see you dead before I pay you one fucking cent, you bastard," he yelled. Hannes laughed and laughed.' Cheetah's eyes moved in his head as he relived what he'd heard.

'You're absolutely positive Connie threatened to kill Hannes?'

'Hundred percent sure. And he threatened Hannes many more times. I heard it. "You little shit, I'll drown you in the dam like a rat, if you don't quit trying too blackmail me." When Hannes was killed I wasn't surprised and I knew who did it.'

'Be careful what you say,' Miriam interrupted, placing a hand on Cheetah's shoulder. 'You talk to much.'

'I called Connie a fucking murderer to his face. We had one helluva fight that day.'

'But you didn't see him kill Hannes, did you?'

'No but have a look at Connie's collection of knives. That'll tell you something.'

I had seen Connie's knives in a cabinet in his study. I shrugged. 'What would Connie want knives for?'

'He hunts on the *kloof*.'

I sighed. A nail in Connie's coffin.

I needed proof rather than accusations. That afternoon I drove back to visit Cecil, the ex-coroner, at his retirement village. I hadn't phoned for an appointment and hoped to find him at home. He was in the garden reading. He turned back the page of his book, closed it and rose slowly.

'Nice to see you again. I can read any time but visitors are rare these days.'

'I'm here to ask for more of your help.'

'I'll get you a chair,' he said pulling a second deck chair close to his. 'I'm all ears. How can I help?'

Going on what Vince had said I took a deep breath and tried my luck. 'I would like to know more about what you and Pa were whispering about over Hannes' dead body.'

'I told you before, I can't talk about it.'

'If it was about Connie and Miriam, I know the story.'

Cecil sighed and smoothed his brow. 'Oh, all right. Almost in tears your Pa told me that he thought Connie could have killed Hannes in a rage. He didn't go into details but outlined the sordid bloody mess with Connie's black girlfriend and how Hannes had found out about it. He begged me help him to keep things quiet. So I made sure the body was covered and tried to underplay the violence of the killing in the report.'

'Let me guess. You were Broeders so you felt you had to help.'

He lowered his head. 'Ja. We had been in the Bond together for years. Irrespective of that I felt certain Connie was guilty ... but I should've asked a lot more questions than I did.'

'So thinking the way you did about Connie ... without hard evidence you let the three blacks take the rap. How could you?'

'I'm not proud of myself.'

'I wouldn't be either.'

He looked at the gardenias.

'Do you still think Connie killed his brother?'

'I wouldn't know. Haven't thought about it for years.'

I turned round quickly and left for the car.

The aroma of something spicy for dinner led me into the kitchen. Raelene was cooking a meat stew called *baboetie.* In the study, Connie was watching a soccer match on television. Shouting and waving his hands he yelled instructions to the players and referee.

'How's my sister the detective from Australia feeling this evening?' he said turning away from the television for a moment.

I gave him the thumbs up sign and went back to the kitchen. Rows of tempting cookies were cooling on wire trays.

'You've made so many … who eats them all?' I asked.

'I give them to the grandkids and Vince has a sweet tooth too. Don't worry, they get eaten.'

I forced myself away. I'd eaten too many myself already.

Chapter 24

The bedroom curtains swayed in the sharp morning air. Wind raced through the veld, stirring grass, breaking twigs and flower tops. The small bit of information I had gained about Hannes' murder might as well have been a swirling stalk. If I thought I was investigating the case I was deluding myself. Instead of struggling on I lay in bed in a dreamy, almost-wakeful state, thinking about visiting Tansie. Hannes and I were often in Tansie's straw-roofed hut at sunset. When Ma and Pa were away Tansie was expected to care for us in the house but preferred taking us to the *kraal* for a night or two. Ma and Pa didn't find out, so we were all happy.

We watched groups of chatting women prepare the evening meal and stirring pots of *mielie meal* on the communal fire. Some distance from the fire Tansie had put down two beer crates for us to sit on. She was still feeding eighteen-month-old Zebedelia and had Rosie to care for and had no time to worry about us. I liked the sound of the name Zebedelia. The name was taken from the huge Zebedelia orange estates in the area.

When the food was cooked Tansie led us into her sleeping and living area, which doubled as a kitchen. Her bed dominated, with its white frilly bedspread and cushions she'd embroidered. Under each of the bedposts were two bricks. She, like many blacks, believed that the bricks made the bed too high for the *Tokalosh* – a mythical small man with a large penis – to climb into it during the night. Near the bed, on a turned over crate, she displayed religious pictures and statuettes of the Virgin Mary.

She belonged to the Church of Zion, a Christian church that attracted black worshippers. On Sunday, her day off, she wore the blue and white church outfit. She joined the blue and white procession led by a person carrying a large cross as they marched to the church in the town.

We ate with Rosie, having fun rolling our *mielie meal* into a ball and dipping it into the stew with our fingers like she did. Then we had sweet coffee and sometimes a Marie biscuit as a treat. The men drank sour smelling beer from a stack of bottles near the window.

Tansie smiled lovingly at Zebedelia's little face, peeking from layers of wool. When a brown breast popped out from her clothing and the baby's mouth sucked rhythmically, making gulping noises, Hannes giggled with embarrassment. Tansie sang to Zebedelia in soft tones as she fed her. I had vague memories of Ma feeding me and was jealous.

Before the sun was up the men ate separately and left for the farm. I forced down another serve of *mielie pap* with milk and sugar followed by coffee before Tansie took us back to the house.

That afternoon my arms were filled with healthy foods – grainy bread, fresh vegetables and parcels of meat, as Arti and I made our way to Nandi's house. Apart from children playing, the streets were quiet. But on all the walls posters were plastered advertising a meeting that night about land rights. Two speakers were to address the people at the soccer stadium outside the town.

Tansie was sprawled in her armchair. 'I very happy you come. I very tired today. But tomorrow I want to go church. Maybe I better. Nandi already iron my dress,' she said pointing to the blue and white outfit with the stiff lace collar. 'It fit too big now but belt pull it right.'

When I was passing through the teenage questioning phase I asked Tansie how Nandi could be a witch and at the same time an elder of the church. Tansie explained that the church outwardly disapproved of witchcraft but that in Africa the two approaches existed side by side. If the church tried to force people away from traditions, she believed the people would leave in droves.

Tansie had been showing me photographs of her grandchildren at different stages, when Rosie arrived. Rosie looked tired and her hair, usually immaculate, was messy. Her purple skirt and red cardigan screamed at each other – unlike her usual careful color co-ordination.

'Ma's test results weren't good last week. I' m going to take another lot of blood. She doesn't seem to be responding to the medication as well as I'd thought and I'm worried.' She clutched her cardigan.

I squeezed her hand.

'You look exhausted.'

'Very little sleep, and then I lost three kids with AIDS this morning. They haven't much hope of survival when they're born infected with HIV by their mothers. It's tragic. The children's wards are full of kids carrying the virus.'

'I've spent a long spell nursing in casualty but I doubt it's ever been as bad as that.'

She sighed. 'I'll take Ma's blood and then I have to go.'

Rosie opened her case and took out a syringe. Then she woke Tansie to take her blood. Within minutes Tansie had flopped sleepily back into the chair.

Rosie looked through the window at her car parked outside the front door.

'Tyres and hubcaps still there ...'

'Did someone come with you today?' she asked.

'Ja, Arti.'

'Wouldn't he like to come in?'

'I doubt it. He said he wanted to catch up on some sleep.'

Then with an apologetic smile she declined Nandi's offer of tea and rose to leave. I grabbed her hand as she opened the door. I had forgotten to tell her about Zacharias' kindness in allowing Hannes to join the other boys to study for initiation. She was surprised that a young white was accepted into the tribe. It hadn't happened before.

'It couldn't have been kindness alone that made Zacharias bring Hannes into the group. Hannes must have had special qualities or the others wouldn't have accepted him,' she said.

'You're right, he was smart and agile and he felt close to the boys in the tribe.'

After Rosie left I was about to leave too when Nandi whispered, 'Missie Linda, come to yard. Flowers beautiful, eh?' She proudly caressed newly opened roses. 'Tansie plant them two years back.'

I bent to smell them. 'Lovely.'

'I see family spirits sit with Missie. They look after Missie even if she not want them.'

I thought of the time I closed myself off from them.

'They quiet now but they not leave you.'

'That's a comfort.'

'I hear you meet Thomas. He very good boy,' she smiled and patted me on the arm.

'Ja, he is.'

'Missie still looking for man who murder Little Master Hannes?'

'I haven't found the killer yet.'

She lowered her voice. 'You know Cheetah?'

'Ja.'

'When Thomas was baby, Cheetah fed up with Miriam, Master Connie and Hannes for always making trouble.'

'Sure.'

'You know what Cheetah do? He go straight away to *ngaka* and ask him to teach them big lesson – special lesson for Little Master 'cos he young still and have time to learn.'

'So what did the *ngaka* do?'

'He mix jar dried leaves with water. "This punish them good," *ngaka* say. When Cheetah come back to farm he put ten drops in coffee for Miriam. Alice is working inside house for Madam. He pay Alice one live chicken to put fifteen drops in coffee for Master Connie and twenty drops for the Little Master.'

'Did Alice do it?'

Nandi drew closer and whispered from behind a hand she held over her mouth.

'She do it and look what happen. Little Master Hannes die two weeks after. Miriam have stillborn baby maybe one year later.'

'And Connie?'

'He and wife have big trouble and they no more sleep in same bed at night.'

'So you think Hannes is dead because of that stuff the *ngaka* made for him to drink?'

'*Muti* not kill him but make him like rabbit that no run fast when you hunt him too long.'

'You mean it made him weak, easy to catch?'

'Ja.'

'And Miriam?'

'She not ever have any more babies.'

I left Nandi feeling uneasy. Whether what she'd told me was mumbo jumbo or had a grain of truth in it didn't seem to matter right then. The idea of the unseen forces at work on the farm was disquieting.

Before dinner Connie beckoned to me. 'What have you been visiting Cecil for?'

'Checking out information.'

'He and me ... we don't talk you know. Haven't for years.'

'He didn't say a thing about it. I wouldn't have known.'

'Smart ass,' he muttered.

'I'm trying to find out the truth of what happened to Hannes and will talk to anyone who has something to tell me.'

His voice was cold. 'You keep away from him.'

I didn't say that if it weren't for Pa's letter I'd have left his farm days ago.

Wine couldn't quieten my racing thoughts. I wished Wil had been there with me that night. He'd have cut through the strange events that had surfaced on the farm. He'd have known truth from fable and helped me to plot a sound direction.

I had to admit to myself that I'd been equally to blame for our break-up. I had been caught up with work and not given him the attention he deserved. No wonder we had drifted away from each other. The frangipani blowing in through the lace curtain, the trees swaying in the warm breezy night, carried thoughts about the past.

Chapter 25

In Melbourne I didn't attend regular church services. Interested to find out if the church of my youth had changed, I decided to accompany Raelene and Connie to church on Sunday.

The Nederduits Gereformeerde Kerk was a large and impressive building with stained-glass windows, not the simple stone church of my youth. But apart from superficial alterations, the service hadn't changed.

Back then, small-town attitude, the politics and the unbending narrowness of the church's teachings made Hannes an oddity, someone to whisper about behind hands and stare at. Even though I tried to be open-minded about the people I shook hands with on my return visit, I bore resentment. As the sermon about 'love thy neighbor' droned in the background, I couldn't help wondering about the doctrines of the church during the period of apartheid. Our calvinistic church passively sanctioned all aspects of the regime. This meant that blacks were banned from attending church services in our area. They had their own churches in the townships.

Arnie Swart had suggested I ask Hannes' classmates if they knew anything about him or his murder. I thought of Ben who was in Hannes' class and had been one of his protectors. Vince had told me that Ben had become a successful journalist, an arty type, once considered a hippie by conservative residents of the area. During the apartheid years he opposed the government vehemently and his articles against it earned him the label of 'Communist'.

My memories of Ben didn't fit Vince's description of him. The class heart-throb was olive skinned, green-eyed and handsome and the girls mooned over him. He didn't interest me. I was already going with Wil.

Ben's phone number was listed and I called him. On Sundays the farm shut down and Connie was at home. An invitation from Ben to visit that afternoon suited me. I wanted to be as far from the house as possible. Ben's place was along a dirt road near the hills and was tricky to find.

'At last – Linda Van Wyk. I've been waiting to get you into my den for years.' He kissed me on the cheek and squeezed my hand. Lover boy is still around, I thought.

'It's good to see you, Ben. I'd never have recognized you though.' Long grey hair met a beard that covered most but not all of the crinkles on his face. Ben was nothing like the brash person I remembered. I had to smile. He had been polite and not commented on how different I looked. The easygoing young woman with the plump cheeks and flowing locks well past my shoulders had gone, replaced by a shorter-haired and more intense person.

'You have a delightful home,' I said, looking at his wooden cottage with whitewashed walls and tiny square glass windows. I stared at one of the landscapes on the wall.

'If you're wondering … ja, it's your Ma's. I bought it ages ago and love it.'

'You seem happy here,' I said looking at the piles of books, CDs and papers.

'Life is good and I have plenty of work so I can't complain. But you didn't come here to hear about my journalistic career. It's Hannes, isn't it?'

'It's a long story. I'm investigating his death. The men jailed for killing him weren't the killers.'

'I smell a story in that, but you're after something from me, aren't you?'

'I'm after your help.'

'I'll do my best,' he said leading me out into his unplanned garden.

'Hannes died at the end of the harvest. You were around the farm with the kids from school working casually for pocket money. Do you think any of them could've turned against Hannes and harmed him?'

He told me that most of the kids had laughed and jeered at Hannes and that some of them were actively antagonistic but he doubted any of them had killed him.

'They were a pissweak bunch,' he said. 'The only dangerous one was Joey de Villiers – a huge kid who was the class bully. Joey and Hannes got stuck into each other now and again but Joey died eight years ago.'

'Only Joey then?' I asked.

'Let me think ...' He combed his beard with his fingers. 'After school Hannes had a go at a few of the blacks who were goading him. They called him a *moffie* because he was friendly with Terrence.'

'*Moffie* ... you mean gay don't you?'

'Ja, that's it.'

Arnie had asked if Hannes was gay. I had never thought of Hannes as gay and couldn't remember him showing any of those characteristics. I suppose I had to consider his dressing in women's clothes and using make up, but his dressing up had never been because he wanted to be female. It was just for fun, and a way of demanding attention.

'Who's Terrence?'

'Hannes hung around with Terrence, a black kid only a few years older than him. No-one spoke to Terrence so Hannes' friendliness towards him must've been noticeable I guess.'

'I haven't come across him.'

'He was a casual worker on your Pa's farm. Later he moved on to work with the horses. He's still doing that.'

'Thanks. I'll find him.'

'Tell me, how's your brother Connie?' He had an edge to his voice. Though it seems ridiculous if I think about it now, I was loyal to Connie and didn't give Ben the opportunity to fish.

He gave me sidelong look and muttered something about blood being thicker than water. I changed the subject and admired his colorful garden, a mix of native and self-seeded plants.

'Since you're here I thought you might want to revive some memories and visit the Reserve. It's only a short walk.'

'I'd love to,' I said glancing up at the mountains. 'I haven't seen much since I arrived. It's been a difficult time.'

'Ah yes, I forgot to offer my condolences.'

We took the path from the cottage that led us to higher country. Heathers and lantana spotted the veld and a kudu darted past us.

'A sign of good luck,' Ben said.

The ravine was sheer and stark. Puffing, I followed Ben up the slender path, stray bushes brushing past as I climbed. My bruises from the falling tree ached and I realized too late that I shouldn't have attempted the climb. At the top, I held my breath – a steep drop and view of veiled peaks, waterways and ridges, an embroidered tablecloth spread before me. Surely, it couldn't have been as beautiful before. I ignored the pain in my side and did my best to imprint the scene in my mind.

'You've picked a perfect spot to live,' I said a little wistfully as we climbed down.

'It's lovely here but not too secure. I've been mugged many times coming up here on my own.' He concentrated on negotiating his way and then threw a question at me. 'You married that quiet blond boy you hung about with didn't you?

'Ja, Wil. We've split up now.'

'I wouldn't have let you go if I were him. You know I've always been attracted to you. Even at school I wanted to steal you from him but he laid first claim.'

'That was a very long time ago,' I said with a laugh.

Ben helped me over the uneven ground. We were about to climb over a rock when he pinned back my arms and pulled me to him. His hairy mouth was on mine but I jerked my head away. Breathing in and summoning strength I didn't know I had, I gave him a shove.

'What the fuck do you think you're doing?'

'Just what I've always wanted to do,' he said, looking down.

I made it down the rocky path to my car parked outside his house and drove off.

Ben was well into his fifties and behaving like a teenager. I wasn't used to men my age and older making advances. Arnie Swart was no spring chicken either and he was pursuing me too. Sex. Had I forgotten that some men in their fifties and sixties were still on the prowl?

As I drove home Wil was on my mind. Wil and I had hardly been separated since our early school days. We were together throughout junior school and most of high school. Each day we walked home together and split up at the Portuguese fruit and vegetable stall. Sometimes the owner gave us fruit that was a little too soft or misshapen. Our farms were only a five-minute walk from the stall in opposite directions.

Intimacy was the glue of our relationship. Though sex was the powerhouse, the sharing of our ideas and feelings oiled the machine. I longed to feel his body next to mine and to love him completely.

It was in spring and we were fourteen when our childish kisses and fumbles turned into adult sex. We were protected from the wind and prying eyes in our cuddling spot, a hollow close to the furthest fence around the orange grove. The warm earth full of blossoms and the orange trees provided shade. It was perfect. Pa and the workers were too far away in the top groves to notice us.

Some details were so clear – like the heap of blossoms Wil made into a pillow for me and his sweet kisses on my hair and face. We kicked our sandals off our sunbrowned feet and Wil removed his belt because it was digging into me. I know that we hadn't planned to experiment but when lust fired our bodies our young minds couldn't control it. On that day we couldn't wait and in our hurry we were clumsy. The initial knife-like pain inside me soon turned into pleasure and after recovering from the shock that we'd 'done it,' we repeated it often. It was thanks to Wil's good sense that I didn't fall pregnant – he stole condoms from his father on a regular basis. But then Wil was always practical.

Back at the farm, I went straight to the kitchen. Raelene was preparing dinner. The oven emitted familiar comforting aromas.

'I need something chocolaty,' I pleaded.

She nodded knowingly. 'Help yourself to a slice of mud cake in the fridge. That should do it.'

I cut an obscenely large slice and licked off the icing. Then, grabbing at bits of the middle I pushed them into my mouth. Calm came after I'd swallowed it all. I ticked myself off. I'd eaten more cake in the past few days than I normally would in two months.

'Something wrong?' Raelene asked tentatively.

'No,' I lied. 'Everything's fine. It was just a massive craving.' There was no point in telling her about Ben. I shook the crumbs from my clothes and sat digesting it.

That night I slept restlessly, dreaming of grey hairy monsters and falling down the sheer cliff.

I was in the *voorkamer* watching television when Nettie rushed up to me.

'Next door Indian lady, she come up drive in big hurry.'

I noticed that Priya had not yet earned the title of madam as far Nettie was concerned.

'Hi. I remembered something that could be important.'

'Come sit down.'

'I can only stay a minute but I wanted to tell you something that came back to me when our tap leaked yesterday,' Priya puffed.

'Tell me.'

'It was about the run in Hannes had with the plumber, Tiny Van Loggenberg.'

'Tiny? I'm trying to place him.'

'He'd just done his apprenticeship with old Schalk, that misery. Don't you remember Tiny? A mountain with big hands,' she said.

'How could I forget the rude bastard?'

'Hannes played tricks on Tiny for months. Mucking up the irrigation system for fun. Lucky for him your Pa never guessed, because it must've cost a packet calling the plumber so often. The water went crazy again a few days before Hannes was killed. Tiny couldn't fix it until he got some help. This time it wasn't Hannes' fault but Tiny thought it was.'

I shook my head disbelievingly. 'I don't know how one person could get up to so much mischief.'

'It was comical – that hulk yelling at Hannes, less than half his size and width. I watched them from our side of the fence.'

'What did Hannes say?'

'Hannes tried to explain that he had nothing to do with it but Tiny didn't believe him. He picked Hannes up with one hand and shook him really hard.'

I laughed.

'Hannes came prepared with one of those long sticks the blacks use for self-defence. He'd dropped it in the veld next to him and Tiny couldn't see it. Hannes felt for the stick and … you know how quick he was.'

'Ja so.'

'Kind of bouncing on his toes he hit Tiny's arms and legs, poked at his stomach and hit him in the balls. It's so clear I can't think why I didn't remember it. It was just too much. Hannes flitted like a mosquito and Tiny couldn't defend himself. Finally Tiny picked himself up and lumbered off cursing and yelling at Hannes that he'd get him.'

'Do you think Tiny could've carried out his threat?'

'He was almost purple with fury. You know what a monster he was.'

'I'll check it out. You never know.'

Priya rushed off but had left me wondering how she knew about Hannes' run in with Tiny and I didn't. Perhaps Priya's memory was playing tricks. I needed to verify what she had told me.

That afternoon I went to look for Esiekiel.

After greeting me, Esiekiel gave me a long look. 'Missie OK?'

'Ja Ja.'

'Missie be careful – tree nearly bite you.'

'I'm fine.'

'Maybe the *ngaka* put curse on tree … make it fall.'

'Somebody cut the tree with an axe. It wasn't a spirit or a curse.'

Esiekiel looked away. Then he took a handful of earth in his hand and crumbled it.

'Land very dry now. It rain little bit but dry up quick. Too hot,' he said, looking up. 'Every day sky too blue.'

'Sorry to worry you all the time with my questions.'

'Missie no worry. I pleased to help.'

He looked at the sky again, waiting for me to speak. The cobalt shimmering sky delighted me. Unless time and memory had confused me I had seen such luminous skies only once or twice on the farm. Zacharias was excited. He said that the spirits were sending a strong message about events to come. But he wouldn't give details about the message. I wondered if the shimmer could be due to the especially warm spring.

'Do you remember the plumber, Tiny?'

'Ooo, Ja. He so big but voice so small.' He laughed. 'I no like him. He shouting, swearing at workers.'

'He must be old now.'

'Ja, he not work here no more. Andries, other Afrikaans man – friend *Baas* Connie – he now plumber here.'

'I heard that Hannes caused Tiny big trouble with the water sprinkler.'

Esiekiel confirmed what Priya had told me about Tiny. Hannes had gone out of his way to upset the plumber by putting jacaranda blooms into the sprinkler valves. He did this many times and each time Pa phoned Tiny to come back to fix the sprinklers.

'Did Pa find out Hannes was doing it?'

Esiekiel shrugged.

I had become a pest. Esiekiel and Nathaniel were polite when I asked questions but they had to be tired of me. I had no option but to ask questions, to use their fragments of memory to solve the murder.

'Did Hannes cause Tiny trouble near the time he died?'

'For two weeks Hannes fill up drains with the rotten oranges. He very naughty. Tiny come to fix maybe three times. He getting very mad at Hannes. Day before Hannes die sprinkler break and Tiny got too much work to fix it. He bring Andries help fix it. Tiny very cross, he think Hannes break it … but it break by itself. Sprinkler old and got holes.'

I remembered Tiny but it was annoying that I didn't remember his troubles with Hannes while both Priya and Esiekiel knew about it. It occurred close to Hannes' death – the period that I had wiped out.

'Did Tiny have a big argument with Hannes?'

'I hear from other people but I not see.'

'Do you think Tiny could've killed Hannes?'

'I no like him. He strong man and got big, big temper.'

The plumber on the farm now, is he Andries Scheepers?'

'Ja, that's name.'

'I'll find out more.'

'Missie must check every bad man.'

'You're right.'

Connie had set up a modern sprinkler system that worked more effectively but when we were growing up the old style of sprinkler was our source of cool and fun on hot days. Hannes, Tansie and I ran squealing and screeching under it. Ma was there too and sometimes Vince if he was home from school early.

Wet clothes and hair didn't worry us. Too hot in her studio, Ma danced and sang under the fine spray. During the heat wave Pa joined us too. We'd not seen much of Pa letting go and enjoying himself and we laughed at him until our tummies ached.

I didn't want to become too optimistic about the possibility that Tiny could be the killer. When I returned to the house I phoned Arnie Swart. He would know if Tiny had ever been charged for abuse or worse.

'Ja I know Tiny, and I can tell you without looking it up that he's no angel. He's been charged with assault two or three times and had a few restraining orders against him. His late wife complained regularly that he beat her up but she wouldn't charge him. I thought she was crazy but it wasn't my problem.'

'Has he assaulted a young person?'

'Ja, one of the charges made against him was for almost beating a teenager to death outside the movie house. The boy was in his way, they argued and Tiny got stuck into him.'

'Ah-hah.'

'I see where you're going with this. You think he could've killed Hannes.'

'Could've. Hannes kept on wrecking the water system on the farm and drove Tiny up the wall.'

'I suggest that you try to find Tiny's old apprentice and talk to him before you approach the big man.'

After talking to Arnie Swart I went to my room and sat at my desk. Miriam and Cheetah had joined Connie on the list and now I added Tiny's name with a question mark beside it. Unfortunately it was still Connie that had the strongest motive for killing Hannes.

Chapter 26

With an arm full of flowers from the garden I visited the cemetery. I was placing roses on Ma's grave when Miriam startled me. I went on putting the rest of the flowers on Pa's grave and ignored her. Without a word to her I closed the cemetery gate and turned back to the house. She followed me.

'Have you come to any conclusions about the murder yet?'

'Not yet.'

'I'm being straight – Connie must be one of your suspects?'

'Listen. It's none of your busi…'

She put a hand up to stop me. 'Don't get so uptight with me. I'm trying to help. I don't think he could've done it. The Connie I know – he's tough on the outside but underneath he's like butter. Have you ever see him slaughter a sheep, or goat? I haven't.'

I was staring at her. 'Such a softie?'

'He's never had to do any killing on the farm. Nathaniel was paid in time off to do all the slaughtering for Connie.'

'But some men have a taste for the kill.' I thought of his collection of hunting knives.

'He's a weak man and that's why he couldn't resist me,' she sniggered.

I searched for Nathaniel to verify what Miriam had said about Connie. Nathaniel was supervising a team planting new orange trees in an area Connie had cleared. He acknowledged me with a wave and as soon as he could, broke away from the group and ran up to me.

'Ja Missie, something wrong?'

'Sorry to worry you. I want to check something with you. I'll be very quick.'

'Ja, *Baas* Connie not happy I leave planting.'

'I'll clear it with Connie that I called you away. I've been talking to Miriam. She says Connie paid you to do all the slaughtering on the farm. Is that true?

Nathaniel laughed. 'It so very true Missie. I kill lamb and also chicken for *Baas* Connie. When *Baas* Piet still here, he do it himself.'

'Did my brother pay you to help him?'

'Not money. He give me plenty time off.'

'Thank you Nathaniel.'

Even if Connie had found a way out of the unpleasant tasks of killing chickens and lambs it didn't prove that he hadn't killed Hannes. Feeling in need of a break I walked as far as the wall Pa and Esiekiel built and sat on it. I watched the workings of the farm. Connie was an experienced farmer and with the help of his manager the farm was smoothly run. The two men kept on track with time and the seasons so that everything necessary to have a bumper harvest, from pruning and feeding to keeping the trees pest free, was achieved.

Connie was in the orange groves, the servants were having their lunch and I noticed Raelene had her apron on and flour on her hands. It was the ideal time to slip into Connie's study to examine his display of knives. Arranged in a cabinet, the blades of the hunting knives shone through their plastic covers.

I had no knowledge about knives so I counted them. There were twenty, the largest a little smaller than a knife I'd use to slice bread.

Having looked through his desk before when I'd hunted for cigarettes, I took the opportunity to emulate detectives I'd seen on film and had read about – I decided to check my brother's financial dealings. I was becoming desperate to uncover something that would clarify his role in Hannes' murder.

This time I looked under the desk and found scuff marks. Under the pull out computer was a knob of wood, large enough to grasp in one hand. I tugged the knob but nothing happened. When I moved the chair closer to the desk, put my feet on the scuff marks and used the extra leverage, a box-like drawer dropped down under the desk. I tried to open it but it was locked.

Like Pa, Connie was exceptionally neat. The desktop was free of all clutter and drawers were filled with assorted stationary all placed in containers. Two tall filing cabinets dominated the room. The cabinet nearest the door had belonged to Pa but the one next to it was Connie's. In the top of Connie's cabinet, farming and personal correspondence was organized in files. The bottom was filled with old cheque stubs and cash-books.

To find Connie's cash books dated back to the first day he had helped Pa to the period when he eventually ran the farm, was more than I could've hoped for. Sifting through bunches of cash books held together with elastic bands was a tedious task. There were two sets, one covering farm expenses and the other home expenses. I found what I was looking for in those dealing with home expenses dated 1963 to 1965. Payments for servant's wages, food, gifts, church and school funds and a number of personal needs were all noted. The amounts increased before Easter and Christmas but there were no other payments that interested me until February 1963 when I found a note that R25 was paid to 'H'. In those days the Rand was worth far more. The R25 payments to H continued every month until March 1964, when Thomas was born. Then the amount paid to H was increased to R100 and it was paid to him every month thereafter until August when Hannes died.

I'd been told that Hannes had blackmailed Connie but the shock of seeing it infuriated me. I was angry with myself for having waited so long to check something so important and so obvious. I banged the cabinet shut and dashed out.

My dreams that night were of Connie's secret drawer full of guns – revolvers, shotguns and ammunition. In my dream I was sifting through his things when the drawer stuck and I couldn't close it. I looked inside and selected a revolver, a small black one that fitted into my hand. I was about to hide it in my handbag when Nettie drew the curtains.

In the shower, I thought about the dream. 'Why dream about a gun?' I asked myself. Was it my need to protect myself, or perhaps the intense anger I felt? Thinking about it wouldn't bring an answer.

Before lunch, a car drove up to the house, parked in the shade and a woman stepped out. I gauged her to be in her early sixties though at first glance she looked forty. It was her longish, styled blonde hair, well-exercised figure and modern clothing that ate away her years.

She rang the doorbell, tapping her foot nervously as she waited. Nettie spoke to her but didn't ask her in. Raelene appeared and the woman followed her inside but wasn't there long. They walked out together, each looking tense and uncomfortable. Intrigued I followed them as they walked towards the cemetery.

At the cemetery gate Raelene left the woman and returned to the farmhouse, almost bumping into me.

'I was following you,' I owned up.

She sighed.

'Who is she?'

'I'm not sure how to tell you this ... ' Raelene was making circles in the sand with the tip of her shoe.

'Tell me straight.'

The woman's name was Gloria. Raelene said that Gloria had been Pa's girlfriend and she wanted to spend some time at Pa's grave. After hesitating she added that Pa had been seeing Gloria for some time, even when Ma was alive.

'Did Ma know?'

'I expect she must've.'

'Poor Ma.'

She kicked at the sand this time. 'The men in this family ...'

Back on the *stoep* I tried to absorb the shock of Pa's unfaithfulness. I scanned my memories of my parents' relationship – the yelling, door-banging, frequent arguing and then the making up. The blissful days of peace that followed an argument when they'd do almost anything to please each other. I heard Ma's soft voice through the wall again and the sounds of their lovemaking. When they yelled at each other I waited for the atmosphere to settle in the same way one waited for a sandstorm to blow itself out. Tired of living on the edge of a rock that could plummet at any second, I shut them out. They no longer disappointed or upset me.

I pictured Ma with her morning downturned mouth and Pa stony-faced, gulping down his breakfast without a word. Connie staring at the floor, Vince grabbing a slice of bread and a banana before he rode off to school.

Some nights raised voices from Ma and Pa's bedroom made fluttery feelings in my stomach dance up to my throat. I crept into Vince's bed and nestled against his warm body. The next day Ma would try to appear cheerful. She put lipstick and rouge on her pale face to cover the way she felt. It was useless – we knew that her sad ragdoll look meant that Pa had upset her. If I asked her what was wrong, she smiled her false smile and shook her head. I can't recall her saying anything derogatory to us about our father.

One Thursday in the month Pa used to attend a Broederbond meeting. He'd put on his flannels, his only tie with a clean shirt ironed by Nettie and his brown corduroy jacket. He'd put a sheaf of papers he'd been working on into a briefcase and then leave the farm without explanation. We all knew he was going to a BB meeting. Each month the cell met at another person's home. He usually returned late and that's when Ma and Pa argued most. I could hear it all through the wall. BB this and BB that. One night Ma threatened to leave and take us two younger ones with her if he didn't resign from the society. Of course he didn't. Not then.

At seven Hannes wet his bed when Ma and Pa had a row. He was so ashamed that he lay awake in the soiled bed until dawn. Then he pulled off the offending sheets, bundled them up and tip-toed downstairs to the laundry and left them in a plastic bag where he knew Jenny, a young washerwoman, would find them. She felt sorry for him and washed his sheets. On his way back to his room he took fresh sheets from the linen press. I was still too young and uncoordinated to be of any help. Hannes heaped the sheets and blankets on the bed and crawled under them to snatch a bit more sleep. It was up to Tansie or one of the maids to make the bed.

Those who didn't know him well could have been taken in by his outward show of confidence but the comment Dr Parker made at Pa's funeral about Hannes being anxious was more accurate. Over the months we all came to rely on Hannes' nervous bladder as barometer of tension between Ma and Pa.

Ma was as proud as Pa was stubborn. There was no sign from either of them that the months of Pa's drinking and the bad feeling between them had ended. The war dragged on.

After a meal the boys whispered in a clutch around the heater. Though they pushed me away I sat near enough to hear Hannes ask with a catch in his voice, 'Do you think they'll split up?'

'Never. Don't you worry about it. They'd be too afraid what people would say about them,' Connie said.

I heard Vince whispering, 'Isn't there anything we can do to get them back together?'

'Na. They'll work it out. Keep out of it,' Connie said.

My heart thumped wildly. What if they split up? I bit my lip hard to prevent myself from crying.

For months Ma hadn't bothered to comb her hair in the evening or change out of her day clothes as she used to, but at the end of winter there was a difference. She put on a flattering dress for dinner, sprayed her hair with perfumed lacquer and wore lipstick. To me it seemed as if Ma had wrought a miracle. Pa cut down his drinking and showered after work again. The barbed remarks that had marked dinnertime were gone. Winter evenings on the *stoep* or in front of the fire with both Ma and Pa present were fun again. At least I slept easily through the night and Hannes ventured out of his room. He played tricks on us again but not with quite the same vigour.

Ma, who claimed to dislike cooking, spent time in the kitchen preparing delicacies I still dream about. The best part was the tender way they looked at each other.

I thought of the elegant woman who had come to pay her respect to Pa. It was just as well that I had been unaware of their affair.

Later, a knock on my bedroom door disturbed my memories. Connie glowered at me from the doorway.

'You've been in my study. Find something?'

'Yes, I did. Payments to H – Hannes I suppose – from 1963 to 1965 … the time when I've been told you paid him to keep quiet about your woman. You paid more when Thomas was born.'

Connie glared at me angrily with cold eyes I barely recognized.

'Linda ... you'll be sorry one day about your meddling.'

He banged the door. If he'd tried to frighten me he'd succeeded. Cold and trembling I crept under the doona. It was my fault, I had antagonized him. I should've kept my mouth shut, I told myself.

Chapter 27

After consulting the map of the town, I set out to find G & S Plumbing and Andries Scheepers. From outside, his place was grey and uninviting. I waited in a filthy reception area that must've doubled as a lunchroom. It smelled of bolognaise sauce and curry and its dusty floor was dotted with cool drink bottles, papers and food wrappers. Andries was out on a job but the girl in the office promised he wouldn't be long.

After almost an hour, Andries walked in complaining loudly about a woman who hadn't wanted to pay the full price for his services. Andries was a short muscular man with a bald head and closely spaced shining eyes. After introducing myself and explaining why I needed to talk to him, he asked me to follow him into his office. The clean wood-paneled room surprised me. Files, papers and boxes on the carpet were arranged in tidy heaps. The rest was immaculate. He offered me coffee but I refused politely, thinking of the filthy percolator.

Apparently Tiny did a bit of gardening at the retirement home where he lived. Years ago he had given up his work as a plumber due to arthritis in his hands. I asked Andries to tell me about Tiny.

'He was the last of the partners that left this firm when I took it over and I can tell you I was pleased to see the back of him. We're cousins but that doesn't stop me saying what a bad-tempered bastard he is. We had a staff turnover like you can't imagine. The staff hated him and clients didn't want him in their homes, so we gave him the heavy industrial jobs where he didn't have to see a living soul. Shit yes, I was pleased to see him go.'

'Do you think he could control that temper?'

'Even now Tiny has a very short fuse. When he drinks that's another story. I don't think he can control himself then. He's a strong devil and killed his dog with his bare hands one night when he was boozing.'

'Why?'

'God knows. Hearing about it made me feel sick so I didn't want to know the details. Look, he can be crazy if you stir him. He's had a good few fights in his time. I learned you don't argue with Tiny.'

I shrank from the picture he was painting.

'He and Hannes didn't get along too well, did they?' I said.

'Whew! That's a bloody understatement.'

Though the nasty episode between Hannes and Tiny was in that sealed chamber, I did remember how much I disliked Tiny. Nevertheless he was an adult who must've been in his thirties then and I showed him respect. Pa had drummed the 'respect for your elders' dictum into our heads. He must've drummed it into Hannes' head too. But Hannes followed his own rules and in doing so frequently found himself in boiling water. Where was Pa when the run-in with Tiny occurred? Possibly he was frantic about the water supply to his orange trees and was either distracted or didn't care just then what Hannes was up to.

While Andries was willing to help, I'd keep on asking questions. The murder inquiry that had been a task Pa set me had become my obsession by now and I had to find answers.

'Can you remember anything about Tiny and Hannes in the days before Hannes died?' I asked.

'The two of them were at one another's throats. Hannes had been playing tricks on Tiny for months and it was all Tiny could take. He was a bull seeing red.'

'I heard how Hannes mucked up the sprinklers.'

'Ja, your brother was full of mischief.'

I smiled wryly. 'Did you see them fighting days before Hannes died?' I asked.

'Well, as it happens, when Tiny had a go at Hannes, I did see him picking up a long stick and hitting and poking at the ape man. It was hilarious. I nearly pissed myself.'

'Did Tiny make any threats against Hannes?'

'Who wouldn't after that?' he laughed. 'He was raging, but I can't remember what he said.'

'It was a long time ago,' I said.

'Ja,' he sighed touching his shiny head.

'Was Tiny on the farm the day Hannes died?'

'Ja he was there. I was with him.'

'Can you remember what time of day you saw him there?'

The plumber scratched his hand. 'I think it was afternoon that Tiny came back to check on the watering system. He didn't want another call from your Pa the next day.'

'Was it early or late in the afternoon?'

'Sorry … I don't know … but I can tell you he and Hannes were still at each other.'

I left with the address of the retirement home. I wasn't looking forward to meeting up with Tiny. He had strength and venom, and fitted the profile of the killer I had in my mind.

My brain raced day and night as I sought answers. I was worn out and tried to skip dinner with Connie and Raelene by eating earlier in the kitchen but my plan flopped.

'So, hungry, eh?' Connie said as I slurped up the last of my fruit and ice-cream. 'Join us at the table for some wine and coffee.'

I sat through the meal, talking to Raelene and answering Connie in monosyllables. At last Connie threw his napkin down and stretched, Raelene went into the kitchen and I was alone with Connie. I pushed my chair back to leave when his hand clamped my arm.

'Where are you rushing off to?'

I didn't answer.

'Can't even give your brother a few moments of your time, eh?'

'Connie!'

What could I say to my brother? Being in his company made me feel uncomfortable.

'Don't you think I know that since you heard about Miriam you've no time for me? On top of it, I'm your prime suspect!' His grip on my arm had tightened and his face was beetroot.

I was afraid. 'Don't enrage him, just sit quietly,' I told myself.

'So what have you to say, eh? What have you found out about the murder? Don't give me bullshit.'

'Nothing substantial yet.' I managed to free myself from him and rubbed my arm.

'Ten to one you'd like to leave to stay with Vince, but you're not leaving until you come up with something. Forget going home until you do.'

'Don't be ridiculous, I can't stay indefinitely. My ticket home is booked and I have to get back to work.'

'Do you think I'm going to live for the rest of my life with a sign 'murderer' hanging over me? Sort it out.'

His glare was a mix of hurt and anger. Without answering

I scurried from the dinning room and then took the steps two at a time.

In bed I breathed more easily. The way Connie frightened me was ridiculous. He'd turned me into a scared child again. Was all his aggro defensive or was there more to it?

Thoughts about the murder rolled in my head like stones in a barrel. Pictures of Connie stabbing Hannes with his big white hands were glued in my brain. Dressing up, wine and lipstick.

It was taking so long to find an answer and my fear was that at the end of it all I'd be no closer than the day I thought Connie was the killer. The tediousness of needing to check each inkling of a clue was getting to me.

Chapter 28

The next morning, armed with sun block and a hat, I went out onto the *stoep* to assess my progress. I couldn't concentrate. I wasn't sure if I had run out of ideas or was frightened into inactivity by Connie the night before. I tried to comfort myself by thinking that even if I hadn't found Hannes' murderer, at least I had gained a different perspective on my family and the farm, and as I shifted from past to present I was discovering myself. I couldn't talk myself into feeling satisfied. I pulled the hat down and stretched out in the sunshine.

A walk was what I needed to stir my thoughts. As I made for the orange groves along carpets of fallen blossoms, I was blessed with memories of the last harvest I had spent with Hannes only weeks before he died. The oranges were full and sweet and their scent enveloped me.

During that harvest the farm was overrun with helpers, the largest group was German students, spending a year traveling and working through Africa. Then there were the usual local fruit pickers and teenagers who helped out in the afternoons for pocket money.

After sunset the farm came alive with chatter, music and dancing. Elvis was singing as pickers bobbed and twisted, holding and spinning to the fast music. I had seen Ma and Pa dancing to boring *boere musiek* at church functions but it had none of this energy.

'Let's have a go,' Hannes said pulling me onto the floor. I sensed I was clumsy but Hannes was a natural. Supple and athletic he let go of my hand and danced his own steps.

I smiled to myself and let the images of the past fade. Lost in memories I almost missed the budding of violets under the water tap and zinnias that had opened. Near the huts Eva, Miriam's 'adopted' daughter, ran up to me. She stood awkwardly, first on one foot, then on the other. 'I been waiting every day to find you,' she said.

'Oh?'

She tugged shyly at the hem of her red shorts. 'I made something for you.'

'How lovely.'

She dipped her hand into the tiny cotton sling bag she was carrying. Flowers and leaves popped out of it. 'Here, for you.' She thrust something hard into my hand. It was a cross made of two bits of wood tied together with grass. 'It keep you safe from evil spirits.'

'Thank you darling Eva. Thank you for looking after me.'

'You Thomas' auntie. You my auntie. I must look after you.'

I kissed her cheek and she ran off. No words could capture my feelings at that moment.

When I entered Nandi's house that afternoon, Rosie and Zebedelia were in the front room. Tansie was resting. Rosie and I hugged and touched fondly while Zebedelia watched disapprovingly. She and I were almost strangers. When I left the farm Zebedelia was still a child. Now she was slim and glamorous in slinky clothes.

'Ma isn't good today … tired and down,' Rosie said, looking concerned. 'I've just taken another lot of blood for testing.

We'll have to wait to see what these results are like. The last lot showed a decline.'

'Mmm.'

'Maybe you can perk her up,' Rosie said smiling at me.

Zebedelia glared at her sister. 'She's not family,' she muttered.

I ignored her and went into Tansie's room. She was asleep with a puffing snore. When I returned to the front room I heard the sisters arguing.

'We blacks are coming down with diseases like flies,' Zebedelia said. 'After all, why should the white countries care?'

'That's not entirely true Zeb. It's too simplistic an argument,' Rosie said quietly.

'Is it? All the drug companies want is to make a fortune from us ... '

Zebedelia had left her chair and was pacing the room. I couldn't blame her for feeling distressed. With extreme poverty came overcrowding in unsanitary conditions and disease followed. Blacks throughout Africa were dying. If it wasn't TB or malaria, it was AIDS, sometimes a combination. There were too many people hanging on the edge, no easy solution to the poverty cycle and not enough medication to go round. I turned to Rosie.

'What's your health department doing about it?'

'They've set up treatment in clinics for TB in the cities but they haven't got it right in country areas yet. As far as AIDS goes, the government slowed things down by refusing to admit that the HIV virus causes the illness. We went through that ridiculous phase of being told by the health minister that olive oil and lemon juice, parsley, African potatoes and garlic would do the trick. We need masses of anti retro-virals desperately but as it stands the poor with AIDS can't afford to buy the small amount available.'

I shook my head. 'Dreadful.'

'They do nothing about crime either. They shove it all under a blanket. It's more than ten years since Mandela and the ANC were voted in. The people voted for ANC again and nothing will be done for the next ten years,' Rosie said.

Zebedelia leaned against the wall as we spoke, her face bathed in criticism. She had lived through the backlash of apartheid and the hopes of change, only to be disappointed.

'Let's have tea until Ma wakes up,' Rosie suggested.

'She's full of talk but I can't drink tea with her! I'm not a hypocrite.' Zebedelia's eyes narrowed as she glared at me again.

'Come on, Nandi's made us tea,' Rosie said steering us towards the small round table. Nandi had covered the rough wood with a tablecloth and taken out her best cups and saucers with blue flowers on them. A plate of packet biscuits was in the center of the table.

'All you rich whites in this area have done very well on our … Hurutshe land.'

I could see Zebedelia was upset. I hadn't expected such an attack and didn't answer. I couldn't tell her that I understood or that I sympathized with her feelings, that Wil and I had been against the apartheid government and migrated to Australia years ago because we realized we could do nothing about the unfairness and suffering around us. That when positions for nurses in Melbourne were advertised we jumped at the opportunity. We had been whites living privileged lives and our perspective on that time was a white perspective. We moved on and left people like her behind. For her, anger and disappointment were constants.

I couldn't help feeling sad. How could I deny what Zebedelia had said? My forefathers had seized Hurutshe land that had been scorched by the Zulus. They developed those barren tracts into farms and gave work to the black inhabitants. Blacks working for whites – that was the system, as we called it, in South Africa. As a result the workers became poorer and most of the land owners richer. With the new government in the country, blacks were reclaiming their land.

'Look Zebedelia, I came to see your mother, not to argue with you. I don't blame you for feeling angry. So much that's unfair – even inhuman – has taken place in this country. But let's leave it at that for today.'

Zebedelia picked up her bag and walked to the door.

'I'm going, Rosie. I'll be round to see Ma another time.' She banged the door behind her.

'I'm sorry,' Rosie said.

'Don't you apologize. She's entitled to say what she feels and most of what she says is true. You know that.'

'But she's so hurt, so angry.'

'Don't try to shut her up on my behalf. I don't belong here anymore.'

Rosie nodded. 'Thanks for being understanding.'

'I'll have a peek into Ma's room. Maybe she's awake now,' Rosie said.

Tansie was awake but feeling weak and tired. She looked wasted and her head flopped against the pillow. I spent only a few minutes at her bedside. Before I left she grabbed my hand, 'You do something please. You go to Zacharias, his grave for me. Near the huts. He will know,' she said, speaking as if he was still alive.

'I promise. I will.'

Nandi walked me to the car. 'Tansie must go visit *ngaka*,' Nandi said in just above a whisper.

'Why the *ngaka*?'

'White medicine not enough. I ask her tomorrow if she wants to go.'

'It might be an idea for me to talk to the *ngaka* about Hannes' murder. Maybe he can tell me something new,' I said half-jokingly.

'Maybe he can help. Not to laugh.'

I hadn't thought of visiting a *ngaka* for help with the murder. Seeking help from doctors, counselors or alternative therapists had become commonplace in Western society. There was much about Hannes' murder that didn't add up. Perhaps a *ngaka* would be able to view it from a new perspective.

As I drove home, my mind was on images of traditional witchdoctors with headdresses of feathers and animal skin skirts that I'd seen in my youth.

At the intersection of the narrow road from Nandi's house and the main road, I waited for traffic to ease so that I could cross. An elderly man driving a blue car in front of me, moved cautiously across the intersection and I followed. The arrival of a car from a dirt service road was sudden and alarming. It raced up to the blue car and jerked to a stop a meter or so away, cutting it off. A black man wielding a gun jumped out and pointed the gun at the side window.

'Open the fucking window or I'll shoot through the glass.' After a time lapse I heard, 'Hurry up. Wallet.' The man with the gun grabbed the wallet and ran back to his car. He was off down the dirt road in a cloud of red dust.

Behind me cars hooted, others tried to get around the stoppage along the side of the road. The man in the blue car was too shaken to move. It took ages for him to pull over on the same dirt road that his assailant had used for his escape.

As I passed the blue car I looked inside. The man was ashen faced. I would've like to stop to help him but the roads were too dangerous. Considering myself lucky, I drove back to the farm at a speed well above the limit. Right then I could've phoned the airlines to book my ticket home. The seemingly fruitless search for Hannes' killer, the tension between Connie and myself and all the unexplainable things that had happened made me want to run.

That night I dreamed of the mugger. Beneath his mask was Connie's face. The man in the blue car was Hannes. When I woke I wondered, if Hannes had lived, how long it would've taken him to change his mischievous ways and become adult. Perhaps, I thought whimsically, the glimpse of sweetness I saw in him would've returned.

Part 6

Pulp

Chapter 29

Another day with a bright sky. Nathaniel looked up from hoeing the ground where he was to plant a new strain of lemons. He craned his neck at the heavens.

'*Modimo* is happy.'

I explained that I was going to visit his father's grave on Tansie's behalf.

'I come with you.'

Zacharias' grave was a mound topped with a painted wood white cross.

'Big funeral for him. They come from Pretoria, Jo'burg – all over,' Nathaniel said, as he returned to his work.

Zacharias would have been proud of both his sons. Nathaniel was well liked by the workers, though he didn't have the power or the authority of Esiekiel or Zacharias. Nathaniel's weakness – his addiction to marijuana – had lost him respect.

I stood next to Zacharias' grave, trying my best to convey Tansie's message. From what I understood of Tswana beliefs she wanted the ancestors, *Bodimo,* to intercede on her behalf with *Modimo* – their god. She expected him to know what she needed.

Zacharias had been headman and the oldest member of the group of workers on the farm. When he died in his nineties, the workers asked Pa for permission to bury him behind the huts next to his wife Lena.

Zacharias told us stories that delighted us. The stories must have been handed down through the generations and embellished along the way. Our favorite story was about the huge scaly crocodile that greedily ate the sun at the end of the day until the world turned red and purple and then black. The next morning the creature would swim in the river, flick its long tail and regurgitate the ball of light so that the sun could return.

During his life, Zacharias, though kind and helpful, retained a remoteness. He was an excellent organizer and ruled the group of Tswana on the farm tightly but justly. He was in trouble only once I knew of, and needed our help.

Government officials considered he was too old to work on the farm. He was ordered to leave and return to the Tswana homeland, Botswana, although he was born in Rustenburg and his family lived there. This move by the government incensed Pa. His intention was for Zacharias to end his days on the farm.

'I not want to go. Better I die,' Zacharias had said.

The word 'die' frightened me. I didn't really understand what happened when a person died. Pa explained that the spirit leaves the body and goes to heaven. I was told that my Great Aunt Durna died six months before and she was buried in Potchefstroom. I couldn't imagine Durna dead. She was an obese woman oozing out of her clothes at the neck and arms. She spoke loudly and fast and liked to be the center of attention. So dominant, that to me she was still with us. But if Pa said her spirit had gone to God, it must've. I thought of my cat Red and wondered if he was with God too. Tansie said that in her tribe the living could speak with the spirits of dead ancestors. It was too confusing for me to grasp then.

Pa mentioned Zacharias one night at dinner. 'The government is acting ridiculously in expecting an old man like Zacharias to uproot himself and go to Botswana because of their red tape. It's cruel.'

'You're usually so pro-government Piet. I'm surprised at your attitude,' Ma said with a half smile.

Pink patches on Pa's cheeks swelled and reddened. 'How can I support the government on this? No sane farmer could kick a person off his farm who has worked for him for years, because he's old.' Pa had a strong sense of right and wrong and fiercely adhered to it.

Weeks later Pa sat down to dinner looking pleased with himself. 'I've sorted it out. Zacharias will stay. He has a new job. The orange bags that go out to the marketplace need our stamp on them. That'll be his job – putting our stamp on the bags. He can take his time over it and will be paid for the work. He'll be able to stay on the farm with his people as long as he lives.'

'He must be relieved,' Ma said, putting her arms round Pa.

'Ja, he is. All I have to do now is phone the government office and tell them not worry him again because he's one of my best workers.'

I had put off a visit to the retirement home to see Tiny and had to force myself to go there. The home was larger than I expected and the lawns and flowerbeds luxuriant and park-like. Old people sat under trees in their wheelchairs or battled to walk leaning on frames.

I spotted a big man digging up a bed of frazzled daffodils. Each plunge of the shovel was labored, as if it hurt.

As I neared I heard him cursing. I had to stand directly in front of him and then cough before he put his shovel down and slowly straightened his back. When I told him who I was he nodded. Then I explained that I was investigating Hannes' murder.

'I haven't lost my marbles yet like the other residents here. I remember that little devil Hannes well.'

Before I could ask about him the days before Hannes' died when he'd been called to the farm to fix the sprinkler, he spoke loudly with an edge to his voice.

'You've come here because of my reputation in those days. I'll make no secret of it – I hated that little brother of yours, and he knew it. Your Pa was my customer, and a bloody good one, so I had to watch myself with that little shit or he'd have known all about it. He drove me bloody mad … but I didn't kill him. Too much respect for your Pa to do that. Piet was a hard man with money, but a good man underneath.'

He spat into the daffodils and walked off. Tiny was horrid. I felt I needed a shower after being near him but I knew he hadn't killed Hannes.

In the fading light red hibiscus dominated the town's gardens and the scent of frangipani filled the jacaranda-lined streets. I had arranged to meet Vince at a pavement café and loud music led me to it. I found him under a red and yellow umbrella sipping a cappuccino. We kissed and I sank into the chair. The noise level was almost unbearable but the vibe was exhilarating. I turned this side and that to take in the scene – whites and blacks caught in conversation or calling each other across the tables. In secluded booths mixed color couples huddled and kissed.

'I thought you'd like to see our changes working out.'

'This is wonderful … wonderful … amazing. I can't find a word for it.' My face had warmed with joy.

Vince looked hard at me. 'So what's bugging you, *sis*? You look as if you haven't slept for nights.'

'It's this thing with Connie that's getting to me.'

'I've had talking about it. I thought we'd have a fun time together.'

On the way home Vince turned on the radio and listened to the cricket. He was six years older than Hannes and had wanted little to do with him. Hannes hung around his older brothers like an itch. He listened to their phone conversations and stood at doorways to pick up secrets. Vince knew Hannes was subjected to bullying and racial taunts but rarely did anything about it. Occasionally he came to Hannes' aid, but he could have been a more reliable protector.

I thought that Vince had been ashamed of his brother's appearance and now felt guilty that he hadn't done more to help him. Connie was a prefect, talented academically and at sports. In his final year he was head prefect and he, of all people, could've put a stop to the discrimination against Hannes. But like Vince he removed himself.

Without support from Ma and Pa Hannes fought a single-handed war. What about the principal? He intervened when other children were persecuted, but did nothing for Hannes. It was as if it was Hannes' fault that he was different.

The harder I tried to suppress my anger the more it fired. I stared out of the car window trying to concentrate on the landscape. The worst thing I could do after our discussion at the café was to accuse Vince of not caring or burst into tears.

'Hey, come back,' Vince gave me a nudge. 'This murder thing has taken over. You don't want to talk about anything else. Obsessed isn't the word.'

'Sorry Vince. I know, I can't let it go.'

'I've something in the boot I think it will interest you. A wooden crate like the ones we used to pack oranges in. Pa gave it to me months ago and it's been in my garage since. Con did ask me to give it to you, but I forgot.'

I felt my hands clench. He knew how important any clue was to me. But I didn't answer. I'd gain nothing from being a nag. He pulled up in front of the farmhouse and pressed the boot lever.

'I'll carry it up to your room for you.'

Connie and Raelene were watching television. Connie's eyes were glued to the box. He didn't bother to get up when he saw us. Vince slipped out the door and Connie waved.

'He's finally got round to bringing Pa's box for you,' Connie muttered. 'About bloody time.'

Raelene patted the couch but I hovered. I didn't want to spend an uncomfortable hour or two glued to the television with the two of them.

'She wants to be as far as possible from her brother the murderer,' Connie snapped.

Raelene stared at me.

'It is rubbish, isn't it?'

I didn't answer her. I couldn't tell her that Connie still remained my key suspect, that I was hoping that I'd find he had nothing to do with it.

'She should know I wasn't involved, shouldn't she?'

He looked at Raelene. She nodded and continued arranging biscuits on the plate. Connie coughed uncomfortably.

'By the way, the attorney phoned to ask us all to come to his office for the reading of Pa's will. Okay with you if I work out a date with him?'

'Fine,' I said. The wooden crate interested me, not the attorney.

Chapter 30

More secrets in boxes. I sniffed the wooden crate. It smelled of oranges and mould. Using the steel ruler on the desk, I snapped back the top strips of wood. Under layers of newspaper was a grey exercise book with a torn cover. I held my breath as I turned back the cover, scribbled on in blue and red ballpoint. On the first page was an ink drawing of the laughing dog I'd seen in Hannes' bedroom. In a rounded childish hand was the name Johannes Willem Cornelius Van Wyk. Pages were dated in the form of a diary. I'd forgotten about the diary Hannes had begun writing when he was nine years old. I flipped through to find the last entry, two days before he died.

My poor darling Hannes. I began to read.

Mannie with the big ears, you've got the cheek to call me 'Black Boy' – I'll get you for that. Pik you're a real dumbo. All you can do is parrot the bad names everybody else calls me. Who do you think you are, saying behind my back that I'm a colored? How dare you pick on me when your little brother is a moron?! Judy you stink of cows and sheep and you've got the bloody nerve to call me kaffertjie. I hate you. Even you Stephanus, with that clubfoot of yours, turn your back on me! Little shits all of you.

Ben, you're the only one who stands by me. You're the biggest and when you tell them to leave me alone they're scared of you. I hope you'll always be my friend. I think you're real hot on Lindie and hang around me because of her. I've seen you watch her and lick your lips. You haven't a hope. It's Wil she wants.

You stupid teachers make out you hear nothing and so the devils get away with calling me names. You're as bad as they are because you don't care.

He wrote about all the family.

Lindie doesn't know how lucky she is that she was born fair-skinned and pretty. Everybody likes her. She's getting too full of herself lately. It's not my fault I'm like this – a brown monkey. Why did God punish me? I hate my skin and this hair frizz. Anyone could see Pa loves Lindie best. 'My koeksie', he calls her and gives her hugs and kisses. Again not fair. She gets what she wants every time – a tricycle for her birthday. A pony. When did I get anything I wanted? Pa doesn't have much time for his little darkie. He doesn't care what I'm going through. If he did, he'd help me do something. All he can tell me to do is to be a man. Do men have to suffer like this?

I think Vince understands. He's stood by me when bullies were around trying to get me. He warned them to leave me alone or else. That got rid of them but it was only a short time till they were calling me names again. I wish he'd come back to make sure I was okay. He doesn't know how badly I need help. Sometimes I think he's ashamed of me like the rest of them.

Connie only cares about himself and girls. He hasn't a clue what's happening to me and if he did I don't think he'd want to know about it. It's crazy but he'll be head prefect one of these days. I'm sure of that. If he wanted to he could do something to stop them bullying me but he's ashamed of me too. He doesn't understand what it's like, he's good at everything and popular. If only he'd teach me to be good at cricket or soccer – at something. He could if he wanted to. I'd be more popular then.

Ma hasn't time for me or anyone, her painting comes first. She should care more, look after me but she won't change. I've decided not to worry about her any more. I've switched her off in my heart.

Six months before Hannes' death a name Ben had mentioned appeared in Hannes' hate list – Terrence, a teenage black whose father worked on the farm.

How dare Terrence call me 'brother'. I'm not a black like him. I'm one of God's Afrikaans boys. 'Your folks spawned a darkie like me,' he says. It's not funny. I'm nothing like him. He's got nerve to think he's my equal. He's black and a worker on my Pa's farm and he must learn his place. I should've told Pa when he punched me.

The rest of the diary was filled with schoolboy riddles, jokes and odd facts that interested him. I stared up at the photographs on the wall.

'Ma, Pa. Hannes suffered too much. We're all to blame. We shouldn't have let him suffer like this.'

Emotionally spent, I closed the exercise book diary and placed it on the side of the desk. The box was filled with toys Hannes once played with. The green rubber snake was so realistic it was frightening and one of his favorites. A box of Monopoly – the board game he liked best – and his collection of cars, a bus, an ambulance and parts of a train filled the rest of the box. I packed the toys into the box and left the diary on my desk. I looked longingly through the window. I had to breathe fresh air.

The veld flowers on the way to Nandi's house were in bloom and I picked a large bunch for Tansie. This time Nandi allowed me to see Tansie. She wore a dressing gown and was part lying and part sitting in an armchair with her feet up on a stool. A woollen blanket was thrown over her in spite of the heat. We kissed and I sat beside her.

'Missie Lindie you go visit Zacharias?' she asked, her face creased with concern.

'I promised didn't I? And I took some jacaranda with me.'

'He like that very much.'

'Tansie, why did you ask me to go to him for you? Nandi or one of your children could've done it for you.'

'He on your Pa's farm. Also you and Hannes like him more.'

'But I don't belong to your tribe.'

'No matter. You good person and you understand.'

We drank the coffee that Nandi brought us and then played cards. I didn't know the name of the game but I hadn't forgotten the rules. Tansie was as quick and sharp a player as ever. Her memory for the cards I threw out and her shrewdness won her three games out of the four.

I left her singing softly to herself.

I was outdoors early. My mood was high and the sun shone with the added intensity I was becoming used to. The trees appeared larger and the floral perfumes were more concentrated. My world couldn't have been more perfect, if only I knew who Hannes' killer was.

Nathaniel was on the rise above me pruning a wayward orange tree. He waved.

'*Dumela,*' he greeted me enthusiastically.

I returned the greeting and asked, 'When you're finished can I talk to you for a few minutes?'

'Nearly finish Missie. Farm short workers today. Big meeting in town last night.'

'The meeting about land rights?'

He jumped down. 'So many come that they put big television for people outside can hear.'

'A good meeting?'

He shrugged. 'For some people it good.'

There was an uneasy pause.

'Is there someone called Terrence working on the farm?'

'Ja, he be here many, many years.'

'That must be the one I'm looking for.'

Nathaniel held his side. Little spurts of laughter escaped like bubbles. He made delicate fluttery movements with his fingers like a bird flying. At last I caught on. He was telling me that Terrence was gay. I ignored Nathaniel's implication.

'What is his job?'

'He look after horses and ponies.'

The rural scene at that end of the property was like a painting, tall trees swaying, shading luscious pasture with horses and ponies munching contentedly. One of the horses was well groomed with muscles rippling and held itself like a pedigree. I guessed it might be a racehorse. Pa had kept racehorses. The other two were riding or workhorses. I wondered if the ponies were for Connie's grandchildren.

Before taking the path to the stables, I rubbed the smaller brown pony's mane. It could've been Chokkie, a pony Pa had brought home for me as a present. I remembered the afternoon that Pa had come back from Van Neikerk's with a big smile. 'I've brought something for my favorite girlie.' I'd held my breath. He had opened the cart attached to his van. Inside had been a pony – small, plump and the color of milk chocolate. Though he had probably been named before I called him Chokkie. I had looked into his wide, dark eyes and instantly fallen in love with him.

'Let him settle for a few days,' Pa said handing me sugar cubes. Every day I had nagged Tansie to take me to Chokkie. I had been thrilled when the pony let me stroke his muzzle and run my fingers through his short mane. Eventually he'd learned to come when I called. He had been affectionate, nuzzling my hand or rubbing against my shoulder, but Chokkie had also had a stubborn streak. If he'd set out in a particular direction only loving tones and lots of sugar cubes had ever persuaded him to change it.

It had been mid-summer with the grasses high and the wild flowers in full bloom when I'd ridden Chokkie for the first time. I had learned to move with him and to feel secure on his back. Tansie had remained close as I explored the farm from a new height. I'd giggled when I had brushed low-hanging boughs and climbed hills to view new vistas. At the time, my body was growing and my dexterity increasing. Those months were the happiest I remember. I had Tansie to myself, as Hannes was at preschool. She prepared lunch and after a ride we'd eat in the shade of the orange trees. We had made rings of the deep green leaves and flowers for Chokkie's head and plaited his mane with brightly colored ribbons. He was beautiful. Sometimes I had pretended he was a warrior horse or a fairy pony with wings. My play was never to be such fun again.

How could I let Pa down? I know I had been his favorite. If only I could, I would demonstrate my love and respect for him by fulfilling his last request. I wiped sweat from my forehead and flicked my fringe back. I asked myself, what I would do if my investigation proved that Connie had killed his brother … shrug it off? Tell Arnie Swart and everyone else that I had reached a dead end and that the blacks must've been guilty? Would I be able to speak to Connie ever again? 'You started this Pa – I wish you'd let things be!' an angry voice buzzed in my head.

I noticed that Connie had built new stables. The thatch and wood had been replaced by a brick structure. There was place for eight or ten horses and strong padlocks on the doors. A man was mucking out.

'I'm looking for Terrence.'

'He other side. I get him.'

A few minutes later a gangly man walked towards me. From a distance he looked young but close up his face, paler than most of the Tswanas on the farm, was lined and mottled. He must've been over fifty.

'You looking for me?' he eyed me warily.

'I'd like to talk to you.'

'Okay, let's sit on the grass.'

We picked a shady spot under a poplar tree where the filtered light made my bare legs green and spotty.

'I'm Linda, Connie's sister. I grew up here but I've been away for a long time.'

'Ja, ja. I don't see …'

'You remember my brother Hannes?'

'Of course.'

'I'm looking into the circumstances of his murder.'

He shielded his eyes with his hands when he told me that he had loved Hannes and that he was a 'very special person'. I reminded Terrence that it was harvest time when Hannes was murdered and asked if he remembered anything about it. He sighed and picked at the long grass.

'I think of it sometimes ... how things turned out.'

He talked about the orange picking competition between himself and Hannes. He said that Hannes was more enthusiastic and had won.

'Then we got bored and were arsing around. You know Hannes could be sharp … and me … I'm the same. He called me names and I called him names back. He'd punch me and I'd give him one back. Some days he got the shits and said he hated me and wouldn't talk to me. Then like a change in the weather he got over it.' He looked up remembering.

'What happened then?'

'Two days before he died we had a massive fight. It was one hell of a slanging match and we got stuck into each other. We weren't talking the day he was killed. I always felt guilty about that.' He looked down at the grass. 'I could put up with him but some of the others couldn't. He'd make trouble for them if he thought he'd score his Pa's attention. During that harvest he was so bloody full of himself and he treated the others like shit.' His eyes were still focused on the ground, his face expressionless.

'Come on!' I slapped my thigh. 'What did you two fight about?'

I wasn't satisfied with Terrence's answers. What was the real reason they were fighting and calling each other names? It must've been something important if they didn't talk to each other the next day, the day he died. And who were the others that Hannes upset?

'Ah, it's too long ago.'

I looked hard at him. 'Please Terrence, I need you to be more specific.'

He pulled at the grass until he had a particularly long stalk and slipped it between his teeth.

'Look … I'm sorry, but I can't remember.'

I would have to try another tack, be more direct in my questions and no more open ones. I felt I had to make him answer.

'Were you on the farm with the others late on the afternoon of the day that Hannes was murdered?'

At last his eyes met mine and he began to talk. During the harvest month he had left the farm before the rest but not later than five o'clock to exercise Thunder Boy – Pa's great hope to win one of the minor races in Turffontein in Jo'burg. Jackie Neerdling, the trainer, paid Terrence to run him daily. On the day of the murder Terrence left the farm alone and went directly to the stables.

'One or two of the others might've sneaked out with me but I can't say.' He opened a button of his checked shirt and then wiped his brow.

'And where was Hannes when you left?' I asked.

'There was still enough light so he could've been picking oranges. I didn't see him so I can't be sure.'

His sustained uncertainty heightened my suspicions. I tried another approach.

'So tell me about you. I hear you've been working here for ages.'

Terrence told me that he was a musician who played the clarinet and lately had been only working part-time on the farm.

'The job feeds my old Ma and *sissie*.'

I took a deep breath and asked the question one more time. 'Sure there's nothing else you can remember about the day Hannes died?'

'No, I'm sorry,' he said placing his hand on his chest.

Terrence was troubling me. If he was gay, did he have a clandestine relationship with Hannes? Arnie Swart had implied Hannes' homosexuality. I didn't know what to believe. Could they have had a violent argument? But surely Hannes was too young for this type of relationship … What was he up to? Perhaps he was influenced by Terrence.

The idea was abhorrent but I'd found out so many strange things about Hannes.

There was enough light to look for Chokkie's grave near the pine windbreak. I had buried all my pets there. I was hoping to find the crosses I'd made with their names but all that was left were grass-covered bumps under the trees.

In my room I put the 'incident sheet' on the desk. I tried to act like a real detective, adding a capital T, but I didn't circle it. Not yet. Strands of my conversation with Terrence kept coming back to me. He had remembered unimportant things but forgotten the important ones. Though I was new at the detective game I wasn't green enough to accept the story about leaving early to run Thunder Boy without checking it out.

Then there was the lipstick Hannes had been wearing the night he died. Could it have been connected to Terrence? Hannes dressed up in clothing he found in the trunk, both men and women's clothing, and sometimes he painted his face. This was for dramatic effect, I argued with myself, and had nothing to do with Terrence.

I thought of Esiekiel's original description of the killer – light-skinned, large and heavily built. Terrence didn't fit the profile. I wanted to believe that Hannes had found Terrence interesting and different but that he'd had nothing more than a friendship with him.

Chapter 31

I found Nathaniel resting under a shady tree.

'Ja Missie. What you want ask me?' his smile was quizzical.

'How did you know I wanted to ask you something?'

'You got on the question face today,' he grinned.

I was a nag, I knew it. I swallowed the moment of embarrassment. 'Can you remember if on the night of the murder Terrence left the farm earlier than the others to take a horse for a run?

'Sorry Missie, I not remember. I too busy with harvest,' he said slowly.

I felt the disappointment show on my face.

'Missie must not worry. Terrence not kill Master Hannes. He not strong.' Nathaniel's hand went from his heart to his head and then to the bulging muscle in his arm.

'Okay Nathaniel, thanks. I'll talk to you another day.' The smell of marijuana smoke followed him – how could I rely on his information?

I marched to Esiekiel's hut. He had been headman at the time and I'd have to ask him what he knew about Terrence. Esiekiel was snoring when I found him sunning himself in his chair. He shook himself awake when he heard my footsteps.

'I happy to see you Missie.'

'I'm happy too.'

Esiekiel put his head in his hand and waited for me to speak. I told him that I'd been to see Terrence and that I'd asked him what he knew about Hannes' murder. Esiekiel pulled a sour face.

'You don't like him?'

'He not always tell truth.'

I told Esiekiel that Terrence maintained he had left the farm at five o'clock to exercise Thunder Boy, who was training for a big race in Jo'burg.

'I not see him leave early but that horse, Thunder Boy, he not run in Jo'burg year Hannes die. He run year after. I win plenty money from Thunder Boy. I remember good,' he cackled.

'A-ha.' I'd have to check.

Esiekiel shook his head and then made the same fluttering movement with his finger as Nathaniel had.

'Ja, he's a *moffie*,' I said.

He nodded. 'Also he playing music and riding horses with young boys. For years now we watch Terrence but never catch him.' He made the crude sign for sex that I remembered from my junior school playground.

'I don't want to think of it.'

'He friend with Master Hannes. They very young, happy … always talking and laughing.'

At least Arnie Swart had reassured me that Hannes had not been interfered with on the night of his death, I thought. Esiekiel couldn't remember anything further about Terrence so I left. I had only taken a few steps when he was snoring again.

By that afternoon my confused head buzzed. I decided to pay a visit to Cobie. He had understood Hannes and I relied on his objectivity. Cobie had been for a walk and greeted me breathlessly. He was surprised to see me again.

'Hold it,' he said, unzipping his tracksuit top. 'Let me sit down, have a glass of cold water, then I'll give you all my attention.'

I told him as much as I knew about Terrence and my fears about a sexual involvement between Terrence and Hannes.

'Well, you can take it from me – that's crap, if you'll pardon the expression. From what I know of Hannes, he was as gay as I am. He may have been fascinated by this bloke or friends with him … but that's it.'

I told Cobie that Esiekiel implied that Terrence was a pedophile and that the men on the farm were watching closely so that they could catch him in the act.

'In my years at the station there weren't any complaints about him. Things could've changed. Ask Arnie.'

'So you think I shouldn't worry about it?'

'Well, did this Terrence tell you they were lovers?'

'Noooo … '

'Then forget it. You're just muddying the water with supposition. It's facts we need!' He knocked the table with his glass.

'I guess you're right.'

Cobie asked if I remembered the De Villiers family who had owned the panhandle alongside his old farm. They had a young blonde daughter, too pretty to forget. Cobie pointed out that he had seen Hannes eyeing her. He laughed when he recalled the time he and Vince were inspecting the sheep. They saw Hannes and the blonde girl in a huddle against the shed wall.

'We called it smooching in those days. When the two of them heard us they ran like sheep with a wolf after them.' Cobie and I laughed. 'So much for being gay, my dear.'

'So you're sure.'

Rosie had been his closest friend, holding his hand when he was nervous, smiling at him encouragingly when he was clever or giving him a nudge when he was silly. Now that I knew another girl interested him too, the cards were stacked against anything more than friendship with Terrence.

Cobie's maid brought us tea. As we sipped we talked about Connie. He took pleasure in painting a picture of the Connie I knew nothing about. The loving father who attended all his children's sporting meets and helped to coach them for exams. Apparently Connie built model airplanes for his grandchildren and encouraged them to enter flying competitions. I had seen glimpses of the softer side of Connie, a quick smile or quick tap on the arm, but I had no idea he could be so caring.

By the time I'd driven back to the farm my head felt as if a constant engaged signal was beeping inside. Instead of going up to the house I perched on the stone wall Pa had built with the workers. I watched the spectacle of the sun slipping and its golden light oozing over the mountains. I was pleased I had told Cobie about Terrence. He was someone whose opinion I valued for its logic and objectivity.

While I was savoring my second cup of breakfast coffee, Nettie came to tell me that I had a visitor.

'She say she called Rosie.'

'I'm pleased she's here.'

'You want me bring her inside?'

'Please. Rosie's an old friend.'

I'd always been close to Rosie. Even when she was little she was independent and didn't care about her appearance or what others thought of her. Tansie had a tough time making Rosie look after the two dresses she owned. She wore them with tears and holes and wouldn't mend them. Her concerns were about where the stream water originated or when her favorite birds nested. She turned over rocks to watch the insects underneath them and she lay in the veld until buds opened. She continually asked questions. Zacharias told her all he knew about creation and she wanted to hear more.

'You come,' Nettie grunted, rudely half pushing Rosie into the room. Nettie stared as I stood to greet Rosie and kissed her cheek.

'Hope I'm not disturbing you,' Rosie said, looking at the breakfast table.

'Not a bit. Sit with me while I finish my breakfast. Coffee, a muffin for you?'

'No thanks, just coffee.'

'Some fresh coffee please, Nettie.'

Nettie muttered to herself softly.

'You're here early. Nothing wrong with Ma, I hope?'

'No, she's holding her own. I'm on an afternoon shift and decided to pop in.'

'Good. I'm pleased to see you.'

'Actually I'm here about you,' Rosie said.

'Me?'

'I'm worried about you. You've been looking worn out. This business with Hannes isn't doing you any good. I thought you were supposed to be having a break here.'

'It's a change.'

'Hunting down clues is exhausting. On top of that you're flipping in and out of the past. I've watched you daydreaming.'

'Well, I've needed to go back … to put things in place.'

'My opinion … give up that investigation and calm down before you get sick.'

'How can I? Anyhow I'm too committed now.'

'Your Pa, and Hannes too ... have a hold on you. The only way to free yourself is to see a *ngaka*.'

'I'll think about it,' I said. 'Thanks for worrying about me.'

Rosie was like Tansie, straightforward and caring. I was so proud of her achievements. She meant well trying to stop me wasting my energy but I knew I couldn't give up my search until the last moment. And as for my past, I'd relive it until I stopped needing to.

We moved from the breakfast table to the television room. Rosie sat in Connie's favorite leather chair and gazed around the room. I'd forgotten that she had never been inside the house. When we were children, she'd knock on the kitchen door and we'd talk in the back garden or garage. If we met at night she'd throw stones at my window to wake me.

Rosie asked for a tour of the house. We started with the *voorkamer*. It had retained its old-world quaintness and she clapped her hands in delight. The grandfather clock that had belonged to Oupa caught her attention and she examined it carefully. She was thrilled when it chimed briefly on the half hour. She'd often heard me talk about the clock. She paused in front of one of Ma's paintings. I'd told her a lot about them too. Smoothing her hand over velvet and satin and touching wooden surfaces she followed me from room to room. Then she asked to see my bedroom. She had imagined it many times. Inside the small room with only a bed, desk and chair she looked disappointed. She pointed to the portraits of my parents.

'Your guardian angels are looking after you.'

She examined the passage between our bedrooms and counted the steps down the staircase.

'When I was little this house was a castle – huge in comparison to our huts. From what I saw through your windows, it was luxurious. You were the princess with your long hair in ribbons and your pretty dresses. Hannes was the prince. I imagined what you ate each day and how you lived in the castle. I was jealous until I overheard your parents arguing. Once I was peeping and saw you crying and Hannes was alone in his room looking sad. That's when I realized I was lucky. I only had my Ma and sisters to worry about. We were poor but happy together and none of us took notice of Ma's boyfriends or of her interfering brothers. You know what a wonderful Ma she is.'

Rosie could help me clear up my confusion about Hannes' sexuality. She was his girlfriend, after all, but I didn't know how to frame questions to such a delicate topic.

'You look as if there's something stuck in your throat that you can't swallow or cough up. Come on – you know that you can say anything to me.'

'It's about … er … your close relationship with Hannes.'

'Picking your words? You're going to tell me you're confused, aren't you?' Rosie sat back in the chair, sipping a second cup of coffee and told me secrets we had never shared. I thought we'd shared everything. She explained that sexually Hannes matured younger than many boys. Shyly she admitted that they began experimenting with sex at twelve or so.

'Some nights we slipped out to meet. I don't know how he got away from the house but I waited till they were all snoring then I crept out of the hut. Our spot was under the trees near the dam. You know it. He had arranged things well. In the hollow of a tree near there he kept a stash of sweets and biscuits in a plastic bag. We'd have a feast.'

'Were you with him the night he died?'

Her eyes clouded. 'Ja. When everyone left we were in our place … and had a cuddle. It was late so he walked me back to the hut. We kissed outside the door … and that was the last time I saw him.' She wiped tears from her eyes. 'So long ago but it still gets to me.'

She looked at my confused face.

'Sorry, I should've told you earlier that it's likely that I was the last one to see him alive.'

When I asked about Terrence, her face clouded.

'Terrence tried to draw him into a gay relationship but thank heavens Hannes had the sense to give the guy the flick. Hannes may have flirted with the idea but he wasn't gay. We both knew it.'

I put my arms around Rosie and hugged her. She had made a complex topic simple for me. Together we picked a large bouquet of veld flowers for Tansie and made our way over to her house for a visit. Nandi, looking worried, told us that Tansie had been in bed all day. When Rosie came out of Tansie's room her bleak expression needed no words.

'She's tired. I don't think you should see her today,' Rosie said gently. I picked up my handbag, about to leave, when Tansie called for Rosie.

'She's asked you to visit Zacharias for her one more time.'

We drove back to the farm in Rosie's car. This time we hardly spoke. After Rosie had left I found Connie's store of beer in the bar fridge. Balancing a can, a glass, and peanuts and chips I headed for the *stoep.* The medicine has to help Tansie. She mustn't die. She can't, I told myself. I had lost her once before. My head spun like a child's top.

Memories of Vince's thirteenth birthday swung back to me. Ma and Pa had taken us all to a Chinese restaurant in Rustenburg to celebrate. It was my first taste of the delicate and unusual flavors and I ate little. Pa was relaxed, told jokes and even allowed Vince a few glasses of wine. Driving home we saw a drunk black man supported by a woman in tight clothes, high heels and make up. The woman was Tansie. Dad exploded with curses and called her a drunk and a prostitute.

'She'll have to go and tomorrow. She won't be looking after any children of mine after what I saw tonight.'

Pa wouldn't listen to our pleas to hear her side of the story. In church I prayed that Pa would let her stay but he could be stubborn and refused to budge. My crying started that night and continued for months. I was bereft, my life empty without Tansie. Hannes moped about unhappily. The cruelest thing was that we weren't allowed to say goodbye to her.

I had spent more time with Tansie than with my mother, so I'm not surprised that I loved and needed her. Hannes was also attached to Tansie but not as close to her as I was.

After wiping my salty hands on my jeans I drank the dregs of the beer and went in search of jacarandas. Luckily I found a jacaranda protected from the wind that was still dressed in its blooms. Most of the others had lost theirs. I snapped off a long flowery twig, wrapped the stem in foil and took it with me to Zacharias' grave. When jacarandas were in season he'd have a mass of the blue flowers in a tall pot near his chair. They didn't last but he replaced them daily.

Tansie didn't have to tell me why she wanted me to visit Zacharias' grave for her. I understood. It was to do with ancestors. Last time she asked me to visit the mound with a cross for her, she had told me that, 'He would know.' I hoped he would know this time too.

Thunder Boy was still on my mind. I phoned the Turffontein Racecourse in the hope that they had archival records of races going back to 1965. After I was passed from one to another, a clerk in archives promised to search the microfiche for races in August 1965. But when I tried to tie her down to a time she was vague. Even after explaining my haste I didn't expect a phone call.

Within an hour she phoned back.

'I can find no record of a horse called Thunder Boy listed in any of the races in August 1965 but he ran four times in 1966 and won another race in 1967.

Esiekiel was right, of course. But why had Terrence lied about the race? What else was he lying about?

Chapter 32

Once Connie was asleep in his after-dinner chair, Raelene whispered, 'Follow me.' We went into the kitchen. Nettie had cleaned it and left for the evening. Raelene looked uncomfortable. I waited.

'I'm taking a big chance here … I've decided to give you something of your Pa's that Connie kept stashed away at the top of his closet. I'm sure he didn't want you to see it … and … it could have the answers you're hunting for.'

'Connie hid it from me?'

'Ja. An old zip-up airline bag. I'll get it for you.'

She went inside for a minute or two and returned carrying a navy blue bag. She told me to go through it quickly and take the things I wanted. Connie was tired that night and had been drinking and wouldn't notice. She would put the bag back in its hiding place the next morning.

I tugged at the zip. It opened smoothly. Another box of secrets, I muttered to myself. How many could there be in addition to the box in the cellar and the crate Vince almost forgot? Out came a biscuit tin decorated with toy soldiers that contained papers, string, a door handle, nails, tins of tacks and a screwdriver. Among the junk was a bankbook in its cover. Entries of small amounts that had been birthday or Christmas presents had been deposited regularly since Hannes was one year old. What interested me were the amounts of $25 that appeared each month from February 1963 to March 1964.

Then R100 was paid into his account. The R100 payments continued until August 1965 when he died. This corresponded with Connie's bookkeeping. I wished I hadn't found absolute proof of the bribes. I could understand why Connie had hidden the bag from me.

Under a wad of yellowing newspaper were photographs and papers, Ma and Pa's marriage certificates and a black and white photograph of their wedding that I had not seen. Pa was dressed in a morning suit looking solemn and his eyes were misty. A smiling Ma was pretty in a lace dress with a long matching veil. Next was a folder with all our birth certificates. I had a copy of mine at home.

As I opened a thick album devoted to Hannes – his photograph taken on his fourteenth birthday grinned at me. On the next page his death certificate was bordered in black. The pages that followed were packed with photos of Hannes from his infancy to his teens. Many were new to me. Pa had caught Hannes with a whimsical expression. He was about eleven then and all of us were on holiday at the dam. Then there was Hannes daydreaming, when he was away with the birds or *'met die voeltjies'* as Pa said. I'd not seen the photos of a teenage Hannes with Tansie, Rosie, and those of him and me arguing. We both had mean expressions.

A bundle of Hannes' school reports held by string lay at the bottom of the folder. Certificates of merit he'd received for mathematics and science were clipped together. He'd been smarter than I remembered. Ma and Pa hadn't praised him nearly enough for his excellent academic achievements.

By the time I reached bottom of the bag that held the police reports, press cuttings that described the murder, the trial and all the letters of condolence, I could not hold back my tears. For so long I had numbed myself to forget. I dived onto the bed face down and sobbed. The wound had opened and I saw it all like a movie.

Hannes had joined the group of orange pickers as soon as he came home from school. He had worked all afternoon and was last seen at sunset that evening. It had been unseasonably hot and the pickers stayed on as late as possible.

Orange picking was a sociable time and the usual rules of being home early didn't apply. When Ma discovered that Hannes was not in his bed the next morning, she wondered if he had spent the night with a friend or left early for school. She phoned his friends and contacted his teachers but no-one had seen him. Pa thought he may have gone off with the group of overseas students who picked oranges for extra money but they hadn't seen him either. Worried, Ma phoned all the hospitals and clinics in the area. Still no sign of Hannes.

Pa called the police. Response was fast and a band of men formed lines searching the entire property and the neighboring farms. By nightfall they hadn't found Hannes.

As ruby light spread over the farm the next morning, the search continued. I left the main search group to hunt for Hannes in his usual hiding places. After the tree house in the back garden, I went to the *koppies*, looked in the arms of trees where we often hid, under bushes and in rocky hollows. I felt unsteady climbing to the ledge near the farm's entrance, and cursed. I had worn sandals instead of my sturdier shoes. Feeling a sudden urgency, I pulled myself up, grabbing at the slippery veld grass. A bunch of weeds came away in my hand and I tumbled. With a jolt I struck a heap of soft earth. Flies buzzed around it lazily.

The smell was the first thing I noticed. It was sweet and putrid like rotting fruit, the same stink that clung to the grass days after Pa had slaughtered a sheep.

The flutters in my chest turned to thuds. I knew. The trees, the ground and the plants held the traces of a dreadful thing that had happened. I had found him. From what seemed to be a distance, I heard my own shrieks.

People converged on me from different points on the farm, scattering rotten oranges, tree roots, leaves and clods of grass as they tore at the heap. They dislodged a constraining branch and I glimpsed staring eyes, a flash of silver and something pink and sparkly. Ma wailed and tears dribbled down her face. A policeman used a loud hailer to call off the search. Those draining the dam dropped their hoses and black workers prodding the land put down their forks and waited. All eyes were riveted on the mound of earth.

Pa lifted me up and put his arm around me.

'It's him – Hannes,' I heard someone say.

'Shush, shush,' Pa said as he stroked my head.

Right then I was sure that they were not talking about my brother. It couldn't be him.

'You shouldn't be here. Go back. Up to your room,' Pa said softly. All I wanted was to be told that it wasn't my brother that I'd seen on the ground. I hid behind a rock and watched. Pa's knees buckled. He unbuttoned his coat and tearfully laid it over the body. Shaking his head and muttering to himself he turned away.

Police gathered and later men in white coats wearing masks arrived. The coroner's van screeched up the gravel driveway and two people jumped out carrying a stretcher. Pa and the coroner whispered. After zipping the body into a white plastic bag they put it into the van and drove off. Women workers had begun to thump the ground and wail.

I looked up at the darkening sky and made my way to the house, passing through the open door and climbing the stairs to my bedroom. Shivering I sat on my chair. Ma had made the floral pink and white chintz cushion with the lacey frill. Closing my eyes as tightly as I could, I sank into the softness, rocking rhythmically.

I didn't cry or feel sad. I can't recall feeling anything, for months. Eventually it was Hannes' physical absence that forced me to accept that he had died.

Ma sobbed and even Pa cried. Vince was on his way back from camp and Connie had disappeared. All the workers looked sad and wore black armbands in sympathy with our loss.

The day after the body was found, Pa and Esiekiel dug the grave. Ma pulled me away from the flying orange dust and told Tansie to take me back to the house. It wasn't the place for me, she said tearfully.

Three days later, a sealed white coffin with gold handles was placed in the *voorkamer.* The coffin was smaller than adult ones yet larger than a child's coffin. I'd been to little Angelina's burial and seen her small white coffin. Ma told me that the undertaker had recommended they close the coffin this time. She explained that Hannes lay on white satin and was dressed in the clothes he wore to church. Though she told me that he would rest in the square hole in the cemetery, I couldn't imagine my once active brother in the white coffin.

Family and friends took turns to sit up with Hannes through the night before the burial. Ma struggled to explain the custom of the night watch and that it was my last chance to spend with my brother's physical body before he was buried. I sat with the others, nodding off from time to time.

In the morning I battled to wake. Ma wiped my face with a cold cloth and hurried me to dress for the funeral. Vince had returned overnight and looked pale. The clothes I usually wore to church, my good dress, lace socks and patent leather shoes were laid out ready for me. I joined Ma, Pa and my two older brothers on our walk to the cemetery. I didn't feel as if there was anything special about our slow procession. It was as if we were on a Sunday walk in the country.

So many people had gathered that they couldn't fit into our small cemetery and stood in rows in the veld. Vince and Connie gave eulogies at the graveside and the priest recited *The Lord is my Shepherd.* The workers made a guard of honour and women in dark clothing wailed. Ma and Pa may have appreciated the workers' sentiments but could not have understood the significance of their actions. Hannes was more than the *Baas'* son, he had been initiated into the Hurutshes, even if it was a partial initiation. He was one of them and they mourned him.

As the coffin was lowered and earth was thrown on it, I heard Ma scream. Pa had handed round a basket of white rose petals and there were sniffles and tears as petals covered the coffin lid. He had held back whole roses for family members. I threw mine automatically and thought no more about it as it landed on the head of the coffin. Soon, all that was left of Hannes was a small orange mound.

At the house, only family and close friends lingered. Looking uncomfortable, they shook hands or kissed Ma and Pa and mouthed the same words of sympathy. Pa couldn't bring himself to celebrate Hannes' short life.

When hiding behind the velvet curtain didn't protect me from being kissed and having my arm stroked, I ran downstairs and climbed into the cubby in the tall tree and hid. I took blankets, pillows and food for my cat and myself. If Vince hadn't found me, I would have stayed there for days.

The house was heavy with guilt. Vince said he shouldn't have gone to camp that week. Of all people, Ma said, she should've known something was wrong with her boy. Pa felt he ought to have taken more notice of Hannes' complaints of bullying. Connie didn't say much. Ma and Pa were too miserable to care whether we obeyed house rules or even ate properly. Unasked black hands kept the home together when Ma and Pa were lost in grief and unable to function. Vince was old enough to care for himself but Connie checked where I went and came to fetch me. He seemed to enjoy playing parent.

For at least two months Ma sat in the *voorkamer* staring. After that she paced the room for another month or so. Then she locked herself in her studio and told us all to keep out. Pa worked on the farm from sunrise to sunset and in the evening took over the accounts from Ma. He hardly ever spoke to us. The worst part was that they had stopped talking to each other.

Pa was the only one who attended the trial of the three men accused of killing Hannes. Each day after court he'd swear about the *kaffirs* who killed his boy. 'Hanging would be far too good for them,' he said. Then he locked himself in his study.

During the trial, and for days after it, Pa slept on the cold stone floor, refusing the comfort of his bed or the fire. He was punishing himself but his relationship with his God and his feelings about his dead son were too complex for any of us to understand. All he said to me was that God was everywhere and watched his sinners.

About a year later, life on the farm regained its rhythm but it was never the same without Hannes. Somehow Hannes' death mellowed Pa. He lost interest in the Broederbond and no longer met with his pro-government friends. In the orange groves he stopped yelling at the black workers or forcing their pace. The change was welcome but the price was hefty.

It was dark but I had to go outdoors. Feeling drained, I sat on the garden bench and looked up at the star-speckled sky and the sliver of a moon. Perhaps they knew why I'd sealed off my pain for all these years. Eventually the images of the past began to meld.

Chapter 33

A message to phone Detective Inspector Swart surprised me. I thought he'd fulfilled his obligations to his old colleague, Cobie, and wiped his hands of my investigation.

'I was talking to Sergeant Phefo about you the other day. He reminded me that he was in the team that worked on Hannes' murder. He's come up with some interesting stuff. We'll come round later.'

'What about dinner with the family afterwards? You haven't taken up Raelene's invitation yet. I know she'd be delighted to have you and the Sergeant to dinner tonight.'

'We'll leave Phefo out of dinner, if you don't mind, but tell her from me thanks for the invite. Expect us later this afternoon.'

The sky was swept with pink and orange when a police car rumbled up the drive.

'We better get going before the light fades,' I said to the two policemen.

'Take us to the dam,' Sergeant Phefo said.

They moved around the dam, looking at it from different perspectives.

'It's a long time since I was here last. I wish I could remember more but I do know that a pair of blood-spattered red high-heeled shoes lay near here. I'm clear about that.'

The Sergeant pointed at an area on the grass bank.

'There was a lot of blood round here,' he said, touching the side of the dam bank a few meters from where he said the shoes were.

'Bloody good memory,' Arnie Swart said.

'We're lucky all the stuff that was found here went into the evidence box. I found some fine pink silky material with sparkles and a very strange fork, like a garden fork but bigger and longer. It had one long prong and two short ones. The tags said they were found between the bank and the little house.'

'You mean the farm manager's house over there?' I pointed.

'Ja, that's it.'

'You're lucky Phefo's a whiz. Got a photographic memory for visuals.'

The fork sounded like the Hindu trident Priya and I used to play with.

As the sky darkened we headed back to the house. The computer in my brain battled to add the new bits of information to the picture. So … Hannes was wearing red high-heeled shoes, pink sparkly material and possibly carrying a trident. An image with an Indian flavor began to form.

'I'm off home now,' the Sergeant said. 'Contact me if I can help in any way.'

'Phefo's pretty abrupt, but don't worry about it. He's got a good heart and he's a top cop.'

Later Arnie and I had a cold beer on the *stoep*.

'Any new developments?' Arnie said, holding his beer up to the fading light.

I told Arnie about my meeting with Terrence and that I was concerned about Hannes' relationship with him.

Arnie assured me that he knew 'the crims in the area'. Terrence had been investigated as a possible pedophile but his team had found nothing that could incriminate him. Arnie suggested I wipe him off my list as a suspect. I couldn't let go. It could have been my own pig-headedness or an intuition that made me want to dig deeper.

After the meal Arnie had a couple of beers with Connie on the *stoep.*

'Phone me if you need help,' he said, taking his coat from the chair.

In my room I stuck a second large sheet of paper together and drew an oval for the dam at the top and towards the bottom a rectangle representing the grassy patch where Hannes had been found. Sergeant Phefo had given me some useful information about the crime. I put a cross at an arbitrary point between the dam and the manager's house and sketched in the red shoes, material and trident. None of it made sense yet.

Everything I needed to know about Hannes' murder was there in the subtext but I couldn't see it. If I concentrated on something else for a while possibly it would reveal itself.

A view of the trees heavy with blooms lured me outdoors. I was determined to relax and with Ma's lopsided hat perched on my head, I banged the kitchen screen door behind me. Humming to myself, I kicked stones along the path.

The rattle of wind was sudden. The sun looked poached. At the crumbling stone wall near the dam, I froze. Only a few meters from me was a long snake, its head raised to attack. Then miraculously it slipped through the veld in an opposite direction. Forcing my legs to work, I shifted to a solid bit of wall. Feet held high, I hardly moved.

I tried to make sense of what had happened. It seemed unlikely and illogical but perhaps this was a sign. I was in Africa,

I told myself, and the blacks believed in omens. I toyed with the possibility that I was being warned of something important about to happen and that I would be protected. In the end rationality won and I decided that the snake in my path was coincidental and that chance had played its hand in removing it.

In Australia I had managed to shed most of my fear of snakes. There were so many creeping creatures near our house in summer that I was forced to come to terms with them.

In earlier days, at the height of my snake terror, Hannes had caught a snake that he made a pet. He was about fourteen and thrilled with his snake. 'It's only a baby,' he simpered when he showed it to us for the first time. Terrified, I hid under the bed. It might've seemed a small snake to him but it was the length of my arm when extended and at its thickest the width of three fingers. He found a cage for it that had been used once for keeping rabbits and secured it with extra wire. Cedric was the name he gave his pet, after a lanky boy at school that he said was a creep.

Cedric became so used to Hannes that he didn't seem to mind being draped round Hannes' neck or dangled from his arms. Hannes hadn't shown any fear of him. The snake's apparent fondness for Hannes must've been due to its diet of live field mice that Hannes kept in the barn. As Cedric grew wider and alarmingly long, Hannes gained status at school, showing off his pet during breaks. Owning Cedric gave Hannes a burst of confidence. He strutted about, head held high, and made more than his usual quota of sharp and offensive remarks.

One afternoon, when Pa left for the farmer's co-op, Hannes took the opportunity to have some fun and took Cedric down to the orange groves. The blacks feared snakes and believed that they had evil powers. Only special people like *ngakas* owned snakes. During the work break he let Cedric out of his cage and, showing off, draped the snake round his neck like a collar. There was silence as eyes were fixed on it and the workers' mouths dropped open when Hannes collected Cedric in a coil, ready to be put back into his cage.

A few days later we heard Hannes scream, 'Cedric's dead! He's been killed!' Hannes said pointing to slash marks on the snake's body. 'I bet it was one of the blacks.'

We didn't find out who killed Cedric but a week later Hannes was dead too. I wondered if finding the snake killer would lead me in the direction of the murderer.

The wind stilled and once again the sun beamed from another unusually lustrous sky. With Ma's sun hat on my head I crossed the veld to the stables. After stewing about Terrence's lies, I was ready for a confrontation with him.

I found Terrence chopping wood, wielding the axe easily as he sliced through thick tree trunks. This was not the weakling that Nathaniel had described. Terrence glanced in my direction but didn't acknowledge me until he had completed his task. Then he wiped his hands on his overalls and nodded. He didn't look pleased to see me and took his time tidying up before he came to talk to me.

'If you've come with more questions don't bother. I haven't the time to talk. I'm meeting a friend in Rustenburg and have to change,' he snapped. 'What's wrong with you anyway? Can't you leave things alone?'

'No, I can't. You know damn well that I'm trying to sort out who really killed my brother.'

He wiped his hands on his overalls again.

'Your questions will have to wait.'

'Before you dash off ... I checked with the Turffontein Racecourse. Thunder Boy didn't run in 1965. So what were you really up to when you stopped work?'

'Checking up on me, eh?'

'That's right.'

'I was with a kid from one of the farms near here ... David. We had a thing going.'

'And where is David now?'

'Gone and forgotten. Left for the Cape years back.'

'Pity.'

'Got to go now.'

His smile was too broad. I left with the air thick between us. Through a break in the trees I noticed Terrence driving through the gates. Immediately I retraced my steps to the stables. I didn't know what I would find there, but I had to look.

Terrence cared for the horses day and night, and must have had a room nearby, I reasoned. To the left of the stables was a walled area with a fireplace, shower, toilet, laundry trough and bedroom. I tried the door to the bedroom but it was locked. The key wasn't under the mat but it was under the plant pot.

The door opened easily and I entered the sparse room. Behind the bed and spanning the whole wall was a collage of photographs of nude young boys. Some were seven or eight years old and the oldest ones must've been around sixteen. I swallowed hard to prevent myself from vomiting. Apart from a bed, a camera on a tripod, a chair and a lopsided bookcase there was a large chest of drawers. Clumsy with anxiety I fumbled as I opened the drawers. Clothes filled the top ones and there were scraps of paper and more photographs in the middle. My surprise came when I jerked the bottom drawer open. Blades of assorted sharp knives glistened. Quickly I shut the drawer and moved on to the lopsided bookcase. Skimming the books and videos with pornographic titles that crammed the shelves, I almost missed the green arch lever files tucked under piles of CDs. There were five green files, one for each period of five years, from 1960 to 2005. Dust sprayed as I pulled out the one marked 1960 to 1965. Between plastic leaves were more photographs. These were more intimate. Faces, genitals, bottoms, young people having anal intercourse and oral sex. I forced myself to scan the folders in case there were photos of Hannes. At last I found his face smiling at me. At least his face was all of him that I could recognize.

I ran back to the house. In seconds I had dialed Sergeant Phefo's private line and told him about my find.

'You did well. I'll get some men out watching him and if we catch him at it, we'll get a warrant and search the place. You never know what we'll find.'

His last sentence hung in the air. My interpretation was that his men might even find something that had a bearing on Hannes' murder.

'Terrence is the one, he has to be,' I told myself as I sat on the *stoep* drinking a cold beer. I had to face it – he and Hannes must've been sexually involved, had a row and then Terrence must have stabbed him with one of his knives. It was his knife the three blacks picked up, not Connie's. I had another beer and sat back.

Chapter 34

A dream woke me shortly after first light. I had been opening and closing drawers and files in Terrence's room, looking for proof that he'd killed Hannes, but I couldn't find Hannes' blood on any of the knives, or an article of Hannes' clothing.

'Lies but no proof,' I muttered as I opened my eyes. With a huge sigh I turned over and went back to sleep.

Tansie was in her easy chair wearing a pretty floral dress. She didn't seem as enthusiastic to see me as usual and her mood was negative.

'I think I be going soon. Hurutshe fathers call me.'

'They won't take you before you're ready. Don't make it too easy for them.'

'You right,' she said with a thin smile. 'I make them wait.'

'You are looking better.'

'I sure now. I want see *ngaka.* He help inside here.' She pointed to her heart. 'Please, you stay,' she said. 'I rest, close eyes.'

I was terrified of losing Tansie. The misery and loss Hannes and I felt when Pa sacked her scarred us. We were overjoyed when she worked for our family once again.

During one Sunday lunch Pa said, 'I hear your old nanny is back. Your Ma and I have talked it over. We know how much you two miss her and we think maybe we judged her too harshly. I've sent Esiekiel over to her sister's place to ask her to come round this afternoon. There must be some job we can offer her.'

'Pa, I love you so much!' I said, flinging my arms around him.

'Pa, I'm so happy,' Hannes said.

I don't know how Ma had convinced Pa that offering Tansie a job was his idea but it didn't matter. I waited until the meal was over to give Ma a hug.

At exactly three o'clock Tansie knocked on the back door. I was first to fall into her arms. We hugged and she rattled off endearments in Tswana. I understood enough to know she loved us and was pleased to see us.

'I have present I make for you and you.'

She handed us each a brown paper bag that contained a bracelet like the ones men and women of the tribe wore. I still have it. She worked in our house for many years.

Tansie had fallen into a deep sleep. I was about to kiss her forehead and leave, when Rosie arrived.

'I was hoping to find you here today.'

'I've got a bit of time off work – thank heavens.' She took me by the hand to the couch. 'Sit, let's talk.'

After I'd told her about my find in Terrence's room, she threw her arms in the air. 'Enough about that creep Terrence.'

'I agree.'

'I brought something to show you. The cheapie ring Hannes gave me when we were madly in love.'

It had a bright pink stone and the imitation gold was worn.

'I was only allowed to wear it when I was with him and had to swear not to tell.

Tansie coughed softly. She was up and asking for tea. Nandi placed a floral porcelain cup next to Tansie. 'Drink before it get cold,' she said, as she fussed with Tansie's clothing.

'Tablets Rosie bring not strong enough. Want *ngaka*,' Tansie said.

'I'll make an appointment for you,' said Rosie. 'You can come along if you like Lindie. There's a top *ngaka* near the dam. You may find him interesting.'

'Good idea. Make an appointment for me too but make it soon.'

I'd always wanted to consult a *ngaka*.

I joined Tansie on the couch. We sat next to each other without speaking. The semi-naked urchins banging garbage bins outside didn't bother us. She took my hand and caressed it.

'I very lucky find you again.'

'I'm lucky too.'

Her loving touch was the same now as then. She had always treated me as family.

When I left the house two children were sitting on my car guarding it. They received a handsome tip.

It was light enough to rush down to the dam and look for the tree where Rosie and Hannes met. I found a tree with a hollow that birds had nested in. Carefully I put my hand into the space and felt around. Out came dried veld grass, twigs and a rusty metal tube. Lipstick. The find struck me like a whirlwind. Could it have been the lipstick Hannes wore on the night of the murder?

The moon was full that night. Pearly light slipped under the curtains and spilled in splotches on the floorboards and chair. My mind teased at the murder. Had there been a full moon on the night Hannes was killed? The light would have made lighter skin easier to see. I knew I wouldn't sleep unless I found the answer. The study was a few doors down the passage. After logging on to the internet it didn't take long to establish that, yes, the moon had been at its fullest that night.

We were late for our appointment with the family attorney, Christian Myburg, who was to read Pa's will. I remembered Pa and Christian sitting on the *stoep* drinking beer, laughing and discussing soccer. Back then Christian was lean, with a full head of blond hair and a sun-tinted cow's lick. If not for his voice, the bald-headed, stout man in his striped three-piece suit would've been unrecognizable.

He waited for us in the imposing boardroom. In silence we arranged ourselves around the oblong table. 'I'll avoid the legal jargon where I can and get straight to it,' he said. 'In your father's words … "To my eldest son, Cornelius, I bequeath the farm and all its properties."' Connie breathed a sigh of relief.

" 'To my other children, Vincent and Linda, I bequeath one each of my two houses in Rustenburg. They are to do with them as they see fit." ' Vince smiled.

" 'And in the case of Thomas Van Wyk-Mosegi, I bequeath R5,000." '

Vince and I looked at each other and at Connie. His head was down and he fiddled with the cuticle on his thumb. Pa knew that Thomas wouldn't be left anything from Connie and had tried to correct for that.

Christian hesitated as he read the next section and moved his chair back with a scrape on the wooden boards. " 'To the descendants and the families of Zacharias Modiste and the Tswana peoples of the Hurutshe tribe, I bequeath the land that was owned by my father Eric Van Wyk. That is, Lot 23 on the old Rustenburg side road. Many years ago this land was Hurutshe territory and it is now being returned to them." Your father has included a hand-drawn map of Hurutshe territory prior to the Great Trek and the areas of Hurutshe land appropriated at the time by Afrikaners for farming. I have made photocopies for you.'

The landmarks were the mountains and streams. The map told the story of the trekkers' seizure of black territory better than words.

'Your father adds that he expects his son Cornelius to help in the setting up and running of the Hurutshe's farm until it is a viable concern.'

I was delighted about Pa's will. My Pa growled a lot but was a fair man. Hannes' death had been the catalyst for change in him. I knew that the Tswanas would treat our family graves on the farm with respect. Their culture revolved around ancestor worship rather than money. Would Connie give his skills generously to help them to set up the farm? I doubted it.

'Your attention, please.' The attorney raised his voice. 'Furthermore your father states ... "To Mev Marina Steenkamp, of 15 Jacaranda Avenue, Rustenburg, I bequeath R25,000.' "

'Who's she?' whispered Connie.

'You know ... the woman Pa had an affair with for so many years,' Vince whispered.

'Affair, what affair?' Connie said, looking startled.

'I'll tell you later,' Vince whispered.

'That finalizes the reading of Piet Van Wyk's last will and testament.' The attorney took a sip of water and smoothed down his waistcoat. 'Any questions?'

'Have any of the other *boere* returned land to the blacks?' Vince asked.

In a boring voice the attorney rambled on. Yes, there had

been land returned to the blacks but he couldn't be specific. Land ownership was being looked at differently in the last few years and some groups had made claims on mineral rich deposits and won. He cited an example of the Tswanas winning such a claim. Then he added that there had been a meeting about land rights at the soccer stadium weeks before, which was so well attended that hundreds were turned away.

The attorney waited, then coughed and stood. 'I'll be getting on with my work then,' he said, urging us out of the door. As an afterthought he said, 'If any help is required with the sale of those two houses let me know. And if you need any help at all with the gifting of the farm to the blacks as your father instructed, I'd be only too happy to assist. Thank you for your attendance today.'

Connie's face was fiery as he stormed out. Vince wasn't pleased about giving away family land either.

The clouds of blossoms now lay rotting. It was time to prepare the rich earth to grow sweet oranges. Workers sang as they aerated the ground or mixed essential nutrients. A liquid team, moving neither fast or slow, they had no idea of the terms of Pa's will and how their lives would change. I imagined the disbelief and then joy on the workers' faces when they heard about the land Pa had left them. Connie and Vince wouldn't tell them immediately. They would need time to get used to losing Oupa's farm.

So far my brothers had not initiated any discussion about our Bushman ancestor and I doubted they would. They hadn't freed themselves of the sickness of apartheid yet and Pa's decision to return the land to the blacks was a spiked thorn for them. Hannes had been born at the wrong time. Today there would have been no comment about his color. His being different may have been applauded.

How delighted Hannes would have been with Pa's decision to return the Hurutshe land. I felt certain too that he would've been as pleased as I was that the farm remained Connie's. It had always seemed that way.

Reluctantly I joined my brothers at a café over sandwiches and coffee to discuss Pa's will. Connie sat at the head of the table and Vince and I on either side.

'I'll start off by saying I'm not at all happy with Pa's will,' Connie said in a loud voice.

'You know I don't agree with it either but if that's what Pa wanted, carrying it out is the least we can do,' Vince said, sitting up straighter to make his point.

Their faces were creased in childish dissent and tension hung in the air. They found discussion difficult. I was reminded of the time I'd run from the house, climbed the *koppies* and hid under the quartz ledge where there was a hollow lined with grass and pebbles. Among the tall rocks I felt safe while the two older boys turned on each other and the house became toxic. I'd given up hiding when after a week they still weren't talking. A week later than that, when the iciness still prevailed, Pa in his sternest voice called them into the *voorkamer*. The three of them were in there for ages. Ma and I were beginning to worry when we heard laughter – the kind that comes from deep inside the chest.

'Pa left you this farm, Con, expecting you to do the right thing, and expecting you to give them advice and supervise the early stages of farming,' I said.

'Who's going to tell the blacks about it?'

'You will have to do it. You're the eldest and they work on your farm.'

'Shit,' he muttered. 'Who do I tell and how?'

'Haven't a clue,' Vince said with a hint of a smile.

'Tell Nathaniel you have something important to talk to him and the others about. Say that you want him and some of the elders to come up to the house tomorrow night to talk to us at about 7.30.'

'So you expect me to entertain them in the living room and serve them coffee?' he sneered.

'The *stoep* will be fine,' I said, ignoring his remark.

'Get the attorney to explain it to them,' Vince suggested.

'Do you know that almost my entire work force is Hurutshe Tswanas? I'm going to lose the lot.'

'Maybe not. Some may not want to go. Wait and see,' Vince said.

Connie's mouth tightened in resignation. He had no choice but to speak to Nathaniel and to ask Christian Myburgh to come to the house the following night. He stood and, without giving either of us a backward glance, turned and walked to the counter to pay for our meal. Vince would have to keep an eye on Connie and stand up to him, I thought. He had kept Connie in check in the past when it was necessary.

'I can imagine that Ma must have influenced Pa ... just chipped away, changing his views. She was in favor of giving the land back to the blacks years before he wrote his will,' Vince said.

'They were opposites in so many things but they were close friends.'

'In spite of Pa's infidelity?' I said.

'Ja. I think so.'

'How can a couple be close if there are secrets?' I said, feeling sad.

'It was just as well Ma didn't find out that Oupa Eric had belonged to the Ossewa Brandwag during the war. Pa refused to join but kept it secret from Ma that Oupa was a member.'

Ma would've been horrified and I can imagine how my British grandparents would've reacted if they had found out that Oupa was a member of the renegade group that tried to undermine the British war effort – sabotaging railway lines, blowing up bridges and the like. They even stooped as low as tarring and feathering soldiers returning from the front. The soldiers were South Africans who volunteered to fight the Nazis while the OB members sat comfortably at home plotting unrest. I hated to think that Oupa may have been involved in that sort of activity.

'Didn't the government lock them up for the duration of the war?'

'They did, but Oupa slipped out of the net.'

Two police vans sped up to the farmhouse with dust flying behind them. Nettie led a young policeman I hadn't met before to the orange groves where Connie was supervising planting. The policemen spoke to Connie briefly and drove on to the stables. I rushed to the stables and hid behind the nearby clump of trees. After a while Terrence came out handcuffed and his possessions followed. A young black boy with his head down followed slowly. I felt sorry for the boy, who was entangled in something he couldn't have anticipated. Intrigued with the round up, I slipped out of my hiding place. Terrence spotted me and roared obscenities at me.

'Bitch! You stuck your fucking nose where it didn't belong and now I'm in this shit!'

He railed on until a policeman pushed him and his things into the back of one of the vans. Out of puff, Connie came up behind me.

'So they've picked up Terrence for questioning?'

Connie relied on Terrence to run the stables. He had groomed Pa's and now Connie's horses. From the look of amazement on Connie's face when the police took Terrence away, it was obvious that he hadn't a clue about any of Terrence's other activities. I took a deep breath. Then I told him how I had crept into Terrence's room while he was out and seen pictures of young boys on the wall. Connie was shocked.

'Shit, I knew he was gay but nothing like this.'

He was miffed when I told him that I had raced back to the house to phone the police.

'You should've told me first. This is my farm and I was the one to phone the police.'

'You're right, but I didn't think things through at the time. Sorry.'

His face dark with anger. He insisted on knowing if I'd found anything to suspect Terrence of Hannes' murder. Things were moving too quickly for Connie and he liked to do the steering. Rather than annoy him further I kept my find of the photos and knives to myself.

'Nothing specific … let's leave it to the cops.'

Chapter 35

Light saturated the room. Nettie had her usual cheery smile and placed my breakfast down next to me. As I rubbed my eyes the words, 'Phone Phefo, phone Phefo,' echoed like a drumbeat in my mind. I sat on the edge of the bed struggling to put the fragments of my last dream together – a mish-mash of red shoes, ponies and Sergeant Phefo. I had to see the evidence from the archives, feel the soft sparkly material, gauge the size of the red shoes. My breakfast untouched, I grabbed a gown and raced down the stairs. The kitchen clock showed 8.50.

Sergeant Phefo was understanding but didn't know when he'd find the time to show me the contents of the evidence box. Perhaps it was the urgency in my voice or my connection with Cobie that convinced him to visit late that morning. He arrived holding a garbage bag.

'It was the easiest way to take the stuff out of the station without questions being asked,' he said placing the bag down carefully on the slate of the *stoep*. Then he took off his cap, threw it on the chair, wiped his brow and opened the top button of his uniform. He wriggled into a comfortable position and sighed a relaxed sigh.

'I didn't think I'd make it here today.'

'I'm grateful you did.'

'I've had it with violent crime ... and I thought ... what the hell ... I'd take a break and come out.'

'Good idea.'

'Anything cool to drink?' he asked.

As anxious as I was to open the bag, I stilled my curiosity enough to offer him an iced lemonade. With Nettie's dislike of the police and reluctance to serve her fellow blacks, I brought a tray with the drinks from the kitchen myself.

'You're dying to open the bag. Can't even wait to finish your drink,' Sergeant Phefo said with a chuckle. 'I don't know what you expect to find in there but let's open it.'

The items were wrapped in the plastic bags they'd lain in for twenty years. There were handwritten notes tied to each with string, stating where and when the items were found. The trident fork Priya and I had played with as children stuck out of the bag. It was scratched in places but its prongs were as sharp as ever. I examined the red shoes. Crimson and high heeled with tucks on the front that looked new except for smears of blood on the left one. Turning them over to establish their size gave me jolt. Size six and a half. In my mind's eye I saw Hannes' fine frame and small feet. They'd have fitted. The sheer, blood-stained material – enough to be wound into a generous sari – was the pink of geraniums in flower, and had a border of sequins.

I shook the garbage bag and let a knife slide out. I shuddered and let it lie there like a venomous snake. Concentrate, I told the blur in my head. I sat up and stared at the bloody knife. I didn't have the technical knowledge to pinpoint anything unusual about it. It had a long pointed blade and a curved black handle and could've belonged to Connie, Terrence or anyone else.

'The knife got to you?' Sergeant Phefo said kindly.

I nodded.

'I must go back and I'll have to take all this with me. One of us will contact you soon.' He packed the bag and carried it back to his car.

Touching and seeing the evidence of Hannes' murder increased my determination to unravel his case.

Sue and Evan Van Loggenberg's invitation to lunch came in time to allow me to process what I'd discovered that morning. I looked forward to seeing Sue, who had been in my class at school, and Evan, who'd been a class above. When Evan drove up to collect me in a red Porsche, I was taken aback. His look was youthful and sporty and his clothing carefully chosen.

Buck were everywhere on the gentle hills of their farm at the foot of the Magaliesberg. I tried unsuccessfully to block the thought that the graceful creatures were to be slaughtered and their venison would be sold to overseas markets. Bambi was still with me. The terraced gardens and mansion of a farmhouse told of their wealth and the desire to flaunt it.

After lunch on the patio, we shared memories of weekends spent at his parent's tobacco farm.

'Those were wonderful times,' Evan sighed. 'My Pa had open house in those days. The place buzzed with Pa's friends popping in and mine too. Do you remember Hannes turning up wearing a cap of some sort; a captain's cap, a baseball cap or occasionally an Indian topi?'

I screwed up my face struggling to remember.

'Caps were magic for him. When he wasn't wearing a cap he'd be shy and blend into the background,' Evan added.

'Once he had us all in fits of laughter. He put on a white topi, like the one Nero wore, and he did this Indian accent,' Sue laughed. 'Don't know where he got that hat.'

'Pa must've invited a kid who turned out to be one of the group who bullied Hannes at school,' Evan said. 'This kid tried his luck at pulling faces and insulting Hannes in front of all of us. You should've seen the fury on Hannes' face. Wearing the captain's cap he punched the bully's bloody lights out. It did Hannes a load of good. You should've seen the victory smile on his face.'

I could picture Hannes, hat perched on his head and grinning with pride. He was small but had learned to protect himself. He ducked and weaved and placed his hits where it hurt. He didn't fight fair either – scratching, biting or pinching when a big brawny classmate picked a fight.

'I'm pleased Hannes found a way to get even,' I laughed.

But Hannes wasn't as happy every time he visited. Sue recalled a time he burst into tears. He told Sue that he was scared of going home and asked if he could stay for a few days.

'Why was he so scared?' I asked.

'Connie, of course.'

'Big mouth and full of bluster,' Evan added.

'When was this, Sue?' I asked.

'I can't be exact, but not long before he died.'

Connie was drinking a beer on the *stoep* when Evan dropped me at the gate and sped off.

'Now that he owns a Porsche I'm not good enough to stop and have a beer with, eh?'

'Have you thought that he didn't want to talk to you?'

'It's your fault. You stir the shit wherever you go.'

He was right. I was a stirrer and always had been. Even as a small child I'd spoken out if I didn't agree with others or thought things were unfair. In that way Hannes and I were similar.

'Sue told me Hannes was terrified of you. Why?'

'Can't you understand? I was sick of paying Hannes to keep his mouth shut. Pa and Ma knew about Miriam and Thomas by then. So I warned him that enough was enough and that he'd be sorry if he didn't stop.'

'How did you intend to stop him?'

'I don't know. Shake him up … or give him a belting … but you can't imagine I'd have killed him …'

'Humph. Fucking bully!' I yelled rushing past him and up the stairs.

That night wine and cigarettes were my companions as I glanced over my notes and added the bit about Connie's admission that he had threatened Hannes. Terrence and Connie were now neck and neck in the suspect stakes.

That afternoon Priya took me to the local showpiece, the Pilandesberg Game Reserve, known for its ancient extinct volcano. Four buses and three Kombi vans disgorged lines of tourists. We strolled through the aviary filled with hundreds of varieties of brightly hued squawking birds. When we stopped for coffee Priya noticed a poster advertising a tribal singing and dancing show.

We sipped our coffee out of plastic cups and talked while waiting for the performance to begin. Priya was interested in a detailed rundown of my progress with the murder investigation.

The way she stared at the coffee grains left in her cup, told me she was trying to remember something.

'I've got it! The poster of singing and dancing triggered my memory,' she said excitedly. 'It's Hannes – a year or so before his death he came round. He made me promise that I wouldn't tell anyone, not even you.'

'That's weird.'

'He asked if he could borrow a topi. My father had an old topi he wore for special occasions at the back of his cupboard, so I gave it to him.'

'Well that explains some of it.'

I told her about the parties Hannes attended at the Van Loggenbergs and the caps and the topi he wore.

'I wish I would've thought of this stuff before ... I'm like that, I don't remember things unless something triggers them for me.'

'Don't keep me in suspense.'

'Hannes paid me another visit later in the year. It was only days before he died. He begged me to lend him one of my saris. I was reluctant because they're so delicate but in the end I gave him one I didn't like that my mother had bought me and I showed him how to pleat it. He shut me up when I asked what he was going to do with it.'

'Was it sparkly and pink?'

She nodded.

Priya had no idea that Hannes was wearing the sari she had lent him the night he was murdered. She couldn't have. The coroner, Cecil Redlinghuis, and Pa were Broeders and when Pa begged him to cover my brother's body immediately, he did so without making the usual examinations of the body and its surrounds. After the police had made a cursory assessment, Hannes was rushed off to the morgue. The coroner fulfilled his promise to hush up the details of the murder.

'I noticed her tense expression.

'How is your mother?'

'Not too well. She developed heart problems after she was attacked.'

'Attacked?'

'Shush.' She pointed to the dancers as they ran onto the stage. They were young men and women, mainly Tswanas. They sang, calling and answering each other as they made music with ankle rattles or by clapping and beating the drum. After the performance we drove through the reserve. The wildlife didn't have the impact on me it deserved. My mind was on the pink sari.

At the entrance to the farm Priya parked the car and we sat close to each other chatting about the past.

'We'll try to see each other again before you leave.'

'Partings stink,' I said, giving her a quick kiss.

I slid out of the car and without turning back ran up the driveway to the house. As soon as got in I returned a phone call from Arnie.

'I thought you'd like to know, Terrence Melefane went before a magistrate this morning. There is a case against him so he will be held in remand until the trial in three months time.'

'Bloody pedophile. Hope he's put away for a long time.'

'Thanks for helping to bring him in.'

'My pleasure.'

'You've grown tougher. I can't imagine you'd have snooped on him when you first arrived.'

I laughed. 'Now that you have him, can you question him about Hannes' murder? I reckon he could be up for that too.'

'Okay, I'll do my best to find out more about his movements at the time.'

Part 7

Seeds

Chapter 36

Nathaniel raced up to me. 'Missie, why Master Connie call meeting on *stoep* tonight? He selling farm? We all have no job? I very worried.'

'No, no. Please don't worry Nathaniel. My brother is not selling the farm and you won't lose your jobs.'

'Missie sure?'

'Absolutely. My brother has some good news for you. You will be very happy about the meeting, I promise.'

'Thank you Missie. I wait.'

Vince, Jeanette and our attorney Christian Myburgh joined us for dinner that night. Though Raelene was an excellent cook, I didn't taste the food. None of us spoke.

The purple dusk sky seemed to engulf us as we waited on the *stoep* for Nathaniel and the elders. I suggested placing a jug of ice water and glasses on the table and Connie conceded to that. In spite of the cool breeze my breathing was labored. For all of us, in our different ways, this occasion would be an exceptional one. My thoughts weren't with Connie's prejudices or Vince's uncertainty but with my overwhelming love for Pa. At least Connie had accepted that he'd have to carry out Pa's wishes.

It was almost night when Nathaniel and six Hurutshe elders appeared from behind the bushes, proud and expectant. If only I could preserve that moment, chisel it into my memory forever, I told myself.

Connie stood as they climbed the stone steps towards us.

'Come … sit down,' he said. He greeted Esiekiel, the oldest, Ralph, Phineas and Felix. The other two I didn't know.

They sat opposite us looking uncomfortable, their eyes down. They had made the effort to dress for the occasion in white shirts and dark pants. We all waited tensely until Connie spoke.

'I'm sure that you are wondering why I asked you to come here tonight to meet with me, our attorney, my wife, and my brother and sister …' The men's eyes were fixed on Connie. 'I asked you to come to hear what Mr Myburgh, our attorney, has to say. He has read my father's will and has something important to tell you.'

The chair creaked as Christian stood. 'Well, according to the last will and testament of your former boss, Mr Piet Van Wyk, there are two things for me to inform you of. Firstly, this farm previously owned by Mr Piet Van Wyk has been passed on to his son Connie. Mr Connie Van Wyk now owns this farm. Secondly, and important for you, Mr Piet Van Wyk left the land at Lot 23 on the Old Rustenburg Road to the Tswana families who lived and worked on his farm from 1958 until he died in 2005. The control of the land goes to the headman Nathaniel Modiste and members of the Modiste Family.'

The faces of the blacks were expressionless. Ralph dug Nathaniel in the side with his elbow and whispered something. Then the others talked among themselves. They were having trouble understanding. I felt a surge of energy. That moment Pa was with me again and I spoke loudly.

'Hold it – I'll do my best to explain.'

The Tswana I'd learned as a child flowed back and speaking slow pidgin, I explained that Connie was the legitimate owner of the farm. Then I told the blacks that my Pa had left them the farm on the Old Rustenburg Road, that had once belonged to my Oupa Eric. The farm covered an immense area and their eyes registered surprise, then fear. They looked confused. To own a farm was something strange and unknown. The will had created something wonderful and yet terrible.

'Show Nathaniel the section dealing with the gifting of the farm in Pa's will. He reads well and if he sees it himself I'm sure that will help,' I suggested.

'Come to the light,' Vince said making a place for Nathaniel. The attorney pointed out the relevant passage. Carefully Nathaniel read and re-read the section. Then he translated it twice for the others. They all nodded. Vince, speaking slowly, explained that their *Baas*, Connie, was expected to help them to start up the farm. Nathaniel looked down.

'Why? Why *Baas* Piet he do this for us? He white man … law not force him?' He asked his eyes clouded with tears.

Again I used my poor Tswana to explain that Pa wanted to give back some of the land that had been taken from them by our family so many years ago. The attorney produced an ancient map of Hurutsche land, clearly showing the farms appropriated by the trekkers and our ancestor Cornelius Van Wyk. Pa's farm – now owned by Connie – and Oupa Eric's old farm were highlighted in yellow.

The group of blacks stood near the trees in a huddle discussing the will. One turned away and wept, two hugged each other. We all felt the passion of the moment, sniffing and wiping away tears. Even Connie looked pink.

The six men returned to their seats. Vince offered each a glass of water and they accepted it gratefully. The attorney explained that as recipients of the land they had to sign the papers. Again I translated. As headman, Nathaniel signed his name.

Nathaniel bowed his head. 'Thank you Bass Piet. Hurutshe fathers will look after his family,' he said. Then Nathaniel took the deeds from the attorney, thanked us and left with the others.

Wired up, I went up to my room rather than have coffee and cake with the family. I missed my home, my close friends and Snoekie and Helga, the two Burmese. It was time I was back in my messy house free of servants. I looked forward to the cloudy mornings, the unstable Melbourne weather, softness of the bush and my noisy neighbors. I missed it all.

Chapter 37

In the morning sunshine, the farm was unusually still apart from the breeze rattling the thorn bushes. The orange groves were deserted. A tired-looking old woman milking the three cows was the only one about.

Connie surprised me. 'They're all sleeping off hangovers. I expect you don't go from a pauper to a land owner every day. We'll all have a holiday.'

I climbed the rocks where I had a view of the huts. Nathaniel spotted me and waved. Minutes later he joined me.

'Wonderful thing happen last night.'

'Ja. And I'm very happy for you.'

'Tonight we have big, big party. Please you come?'

'Thank you. I'll be there.'

'Life of all of us change.'

'For the better. You can work on your own land now.'

Nathaniel bent down and held his head in his hands. 'Is very hard Missie Lindie. Before I am angry. We have to work our land for white man. We have nothing. Tswana proud people.'

Together we looked out at the orange groves, the veld and the Magaliesberg Mountains.

'Is good.' He said with a contented sigh.

'Very good.'

I took the path back to the house past the boulder commemorating the last place Hannes lay. After standing there for some time I felt at peace.

I spent most of the morning in the kitchen making four large pavlovas filled with cream and fruit – a sweet contribution to the festivities that originated in Australia. Raelene generously provided the ingredients and helped to add final decorations to the meringue desert with bits of chocolate. I wrapped each pavlova carefully and Nettie agreed to help me take them down to the huts before the party.

The moon shone on the celebrations. The jacarandas were ghostly grey as I walked towards the new huts festooned with fairy lights. Loud music and aromas of grilled seasoned lamb filtered through the veld. The area inside the circle of huts, the *boma,* was packed with guests by the time I arrived. There were lamb spits roasting, *boerewors* were on the *braai* and chickens had been marinated and grilled. Hot *mielies,* watermelon and vegetable delicacies were laid out. Huge pots of mielie pap and meat stew with onion and tomato bubbled on the open fire. Huge ice-filled laundry tubs kept beer and Pepsis cool.

Nathaniel and the other men grinned and joked as they greeted their guests. Their women had decided to mark the occasion by dressing in traditional long printed dresses with beaded necklaces and headscarves wound high on their heads. They looked good enough to be in any travel brochure. The band turned up its volume, drawing guests to join the dancing. They were a local group with a regular gig in a hotel in Rustenburg who had given their time for the festivities. The music was typically South African in its mix of jazz, rock 'n' roll and tribal music. I thought of Connie and Raelene battling to sleep in the house and shrugged.

'Come dance. Enjoy.' I joined the others on the make-do dance floor, feet stomping, fingers clapping and clicking. I was the only white present but I felt comfortable. Their delight in their new acquisition gave me immense pleasure. During a break Nathaniel stood on an oil drum and spoke of Pa's will, the group's good fortune and the task that lay ahead. Although he spoke in Tswana I understood the gist of it. He received tumultuous applause and friends and relatives rushed to shake his hand. Halfway through the evening all the drinks had been consumed and relatives rushed off to buy more beer from the hotel off-license.

Later the celebration turned raucous with hoots of joy and banging on whatever made the most noise. A police car dove by slowly and then drove off again. I remembered how New Year's Eve in South Africa had always been accompanied with banging and whooping in the streets by black revellers. It was dawn when I was escorted back to the house.

'Policeman here for you,' Nettie called from the kitchen. I was in the back garden reading in the sunshine. I ran up to meet Arnie. He took his time collecting his briefcase and stubbing out his cigarette in the car ashtray.

'So. Any news about Terrence?'

'Yes and no.'

'Well? Spit it out instead of teasing me.'

His laugh was deep-throated. 'Okay, I won't make you wait any longer. We interviewed Terrence and he sang beautifully. He's a pedophile alright. We've got enough on him to build a case that will put him away for years.'

'That's good news.'

'And to a large degree it's thanks to your detective work.'

'What about Hannes?'

'He says he fancied him big time but Hannes made it plain that homosexuality wasn't for him. He'd experimented once or twice and said he'd never try it again. Apparently Hannes told him to get lost.'

'That could've been why they weren't talking the day before Hannes died. But the big question is still unanswered. Did he kill Hannes?'

'We checked out his story. His friend David's gone but the older brother Jack is still on the farm, Meintjiesdrift. He helped us back then when we were searching for Hannes. He confirmed that Terrence was at Meintjiesdrift with his kid brother David the night before.'

'So you're certain.'

He nodded. 'Poor Jack – he was sick all over his boots when it clicked that Terrence was a rock spider. We checked his background and history and you'd be interested in what Terrence told me about your Ma.'

Arnie told Terrence's story. Terrence had been the washerwoman Gladys' youngest son. I remembered Gladys, an older woman with three grown-up children who had left for the city. In those days her youngest son, Terrence, had the nickname Tickie, after the bit of silver that bought more sweets than a penny and less than a sixpence, which was a fortune to us. The small bony kid that rarely spoke didn't resemble the adult Terrence at all. Gladys used to tell everyone that Tickie was the cream of her youth and that's why she loved him so much.

When her husband Josiah was killed in a mining accident she and Tickie were left almost penniless. That's when Ma helped. She paid for Tickie's school fees and books. I remember the withdrawn child in the back garden waiting till Ma began baking so that he'd get a misshapen cookie or muffin.

And I recalled Tickie making music with sticks and tin

cans. She was so impressed at his ability that she bought him a clarinet and paid for a set of lessons.

A few years later, Gladys died and Terrence left the farm to live with his grandma on the other side of the town. It was there, Arnie said, that he had been introduced to the sleazy side of gay sex. When Terrence found he couldn't make a living playing his clarinet he returned to the farm. Pa noticed that he spent time with the horses and gave him the job of mucking out the stables. He has been on the Van Wyk farm ever since.

After dinner I took the old family album and the two folders of photographs of my ancestors out of the drawer. I had an appointment with the *ngaka* the following day and was uneasy about the visit, even though I had told myself that it was going to be an interesting and educational experience. The feeling that my family were somewhere in the background watching over me eased my anxiety.

Rosie had taken the day off work to take us to the *ngaka*. I settled into her comfortable car but she drove too fast.

'Ma, you okay there?' she turned slightly to speak to Tansie.

'Better if you go slow,' Tansie said, hanging onto the door handle.

'I'll do my best to keep you happy,' she said, slowing down a little.

'So how far away is this *ngaka*?' I asked.

'Only about another quarter of an hour's drive from here,' Rosie said.

I didn't know what to expect from the *ngaka*. I remembered a witchdoctor, as they were called then, coming to the farm to visit a sick worker. Tansie told me that the strange-looking man was a holy man and that I shouldn't be afraid of him. I laughed and that was the only time I can recall her giving me a slap. A *ngaka* should be respected, she told me crossly. Later, she explained that every part of his unusual costume was to aid his contact with the ancestral spirits so that he could ask them to heal the sick man. He did look weird though, with his headdress of ostrich feathers and a goat's bladder protruding at the back of his head. He wore goat horns filled with herbs and medicines around his neck, strips of goatskin crossed his chest and were bound around his arms. Most fascinating was the cow-tail whisk he flicked to summon the spirits.

'*Ngakas* are different these days. People visit them alongside Western doctors,' Rosie said. 'I don't feel any threat from them.'

'They're like priests then?'

'Sort of, but healers too. You know how it is when you're sick, sometimes there's an emotional reason for it. They work out what's upsetting you and that's useful.'

'Like a psychologist?'

'Ja sort of. Some *ngakas* can tell the past and the future. Moses does both. He's also worked with the police finding crime sites and re-enacting crime scenes.'

'I'm looking forward to meeting this phenomenon.'

Rosie pulled up at the side of the road to consult her map.

'His place must be up here somewhere.'

We were in the mountains surrounding the Harebeespoort Dam. At each bend I caught a glimpse of the immense stretch of blue merging with the sky.

Tansie had been humming softly to herself, when she jabbed Rosie and pointed to a side road. The sign was in English, Afrikaans and three of the eight official black languages. *Moses Mojelwoa: Ngaka, Sangoma, Healer, Herbalist and Psychic.*

'They say he's the best in the area, maybe in the country. He was born into a family of healers. His father, grandfather and great grandfather were *ngakas* before him but he wasn't satisfied with their knowledge. He studied psychology at university as well as Western naturopathy and herbalism.'

'With all that he must be pretty knowledgeable.'

'And smart,' Rosie added.

Moses' clinic was on the ground floor of his home. I expected him to live in a hut or at least a mud-brick home but the modernity of his double-storey brick house and well-cared-for garden surprised me. Tansie was shocked.

'Big house. He make too much money from sick people,' she said.

We parked across the road from the house in a reserve where wild peach trees blossomed late. Back in the tall mopanes I could hear the chatter of baboons.

Moses' waiting room was full and, as with most doctors, we had to wait. We tried to ignore the piped reggae music, which became repetitive. I had read all the magazines when at last he appeared at the door and called Tansie's name. He was in his early thirties. Apart from his long dreadlocks he was dressed conventionally in jeans and a checked shirt. His only concession to witchdoctor regalia was a necklace of goat's horns.

While I waited my turn, I looked out onto the dam and the powerboats racing. I pictured Hannes water-skiing. About a month before his death we had all gone to the dam for the weekend. For Hannes the water was magic and a time to show off his agility. He flew on his skis, doing turns, somersaults, jumps and twists, smiling and shrieking with pleasure.

The strange thing was that he attracted birds whenever he was on the water. That day there were so many following him that they momentarily dulled the sunshine. Towards the end of the day a vulture appeared. Pa looked uneasy. Vultures were known to inhabit the mountain crags but why it came then was a mystery.

At last, Tansie emerged radiant. Moses called my name and I followed him into his room. We shook hands and he pulled back a chair for me. It was my first consultation with a *ngaka* and I felt apprehensive.

'Hey chill, I won't cast a spell on you. Not immediately anyway,' he laughed. His laugh was high-pitched, almost squeaky. I attempted a smile.

'So you're a healer too … a doc, nurse or someone like that,' he spoke with powerful assurance.

'I'm a nurse.'

The room was peppermint green and soothing, like a doctor's consulting room except for the dark bottles, roots, herbs and masks hanging on the walls. In the far corner, a decorated space surrounded by a grill contained oil lamps and small pottery vials.

'You're looking at my shrine,' he said. It was more elaborate than Nandi's makeshift shrine and it faced east for prayer.

He turned his attention to me. 'I can feel that you're emotionally attached to the woman I saw before you.'

That piece of information would have been easy for him to gather. After all, we had come together and he'd seen the way I'd looked at her. I waited for new tricks.

'Cool, so you've come from another place but your roots are here,' he said in his flat accent.

'Ja,' I waited.

'So where you from?'

'Australia but I was born here.'

'Cool.'

My accent hadn't changed that much and from my speech patterns one could hear where I came from. I wondered if Moses was really that good.

'You haven't come to me for healing. You've got a massive problem that's got a grip on you day and night. You even dream about it.'

I told myself that it was easy to see that I was stressed. Anyway, why would a white woman come to see a black healer if something important wasn't worrying her?

'So it's my psychic skills you're after?'

I shrugged.

'Well I don't stuff around … you know … play guessing games. My spirits tell me you have a weight on your shoulders. You've got a problem with someone who has passed on.'

I had made up my mind that I wasn't going to tell him about Pa's letter, the murder and the trouble I was having fitting the pieces of the puzzle together. I waited, wondering if he'd uncover it. Though I'd promised myself that I would keep vigilant for any hocus pocus, I sensed my sharpness leaving me. I was a little girl again, visiting the doctor.

'You're holding back and it's making you as uptight as hell,' he said, shaking a small brown bottle before opening it. He unscrewed the top and the pungent air transformed the room into a garden. I thought I could smell bergamot, basil and something musky. He clicked on a CD of melting sounds and simultaneously dipped the lights. My rational, cynical self left me.

'Now we can unwind.' His voice was syrupy. As his voice dominated I slipped into a cushioned place. I couldn't do a thing about it. I was interested only in the pleasure of floating.

Then with a fierceness I could not have anticipated, my knotted emotions welled up. My chest heaved and tears rolled down my cheeks but my arms and hands felt too heavy to blot the wet away. When I woke Moses was fiddling with his dreadlocks. He told me that I'd been 'out to it' for about twenty minutes. To me it felt like ten.

'You're humongously tense. Some of it has eased but there's plenty more. No wonder you've got problems sorting out whatever is biting you.' He shook his head and the dreadlocks followed.

'What do you mean, tense?' I felt my voice sharpen.

'Don't get on your high horse, just listen. The spirits tell that your channel is blocked.'

'Channel? What channel?'

'You're unable to receive the information the spirits show you. You dig up clues but your intuitive mind is not giving you the answers you need.'

He was right. I'd had enough interference from Pa and Hannes and shut them out.

'Come, come, we have work to do,' he said as he cleared bits of paper from the floor. When we had a clear circle he rubbed his hands together.

'I'm going to throw the bones so that the spirits can guide you.'

I must have looked skeptical.

'Try to keep an open mind,' he said.

I must have been about eight when I collected my own set of bones. I went to Zacharias for guidance with my handful of animal bones – foot, ankle, and heel bones from sheep or cattle. He selected ten bones I could play with. I rolled them in one of Ma's old laundry bags and when I'd found a similar set for Priya we pretended to be witchdoctors.

I was eleven or twelve when Zacharias explained how reading bones as well as stones and nuts had always been part of Tswana life as a form of divination.

Zacharias showed me his own set. Two bones the length of a finger had three notches or nodules at both ends. The smaller bone represented a female. Sides of the bones had special meanings concerning health, money and so on. Bones that were even smaller were for children. Two nuts, again one larger than the other, represented the spirits of the ancestors. A set of bright stones was thought to mean wisdom and good fortune. Zacharias had explained the process of throwing the bones and reading them so I knew what to expect.

Moses uncorked another two bottles with sharper fragrances. While I told myself that Moses would come up with nothing of value, part of me longed for a positive result.

He reached for a leather pouch, then stretched out his hand to a nearby shelf for a handful of nuts and stones. He gave me the nuts – they were old walnuts.

'You can't always tell by the package,' he smiled.

Then he handed me two bright stones. One looked like a golden tiger's eye and the other was an amethyst crystal. Then he clapped, calling the spirits of his ancestors to enter his body and aid him. He shook the pouch and emptied the contents into the palms of his hands. By then he was breathing deeply. I knew from what Zacharias had taught me that through the breathing, he was directing his energy to the bones. Dramatically he threw the bones onto the floor.

Muttering to himself he worked back and forth over the surface of first the large bones and then the smaller ones. His voice seemed to come from a distant place and I felt myself drift again. Then he pointed to the nuts and stones I held.

When the bone reading ritual was over, he sat back in his chair.

'The bones have shown me that someone has tried to get rid of you – scare you off – but it didn't work … you're still hanging in there. You have an important task to complete. They tell me you will climb through the fog you're in now and work to find the one you seek.'

'Can't you tell me more?'

'Not really. To help you to sharpen your powers of deduction, I'm giving you some herbs. Take them. The herbs together with the work we did today will call your spirits and they'll help you to find your answers. Meanwhile, I'll commune with the ancestors on your behalf.'

'Um … thank you.'

'You'll find your dreams and intuition bringing you what you're searching for.'

'I hope so.'

'Normally I'd ask to see you again but you're leaving for home soon …'

'Fine, but … herbs … what kind?'

'Hey, chill. Just ordinary Western herbs you know – valerian, hops, passionflower and so on. No witchdoctor *muti.* Anyway you don't have to take them if you don't want to.'

I felt myself blush.

'Hey, don't stress, we all like what we know.'

He went to the shelves and brought back two bottles.

'So two of each before dinner and two an hour before sleep and your mind will stop chasing itself. Let the spirits do their work.'

I thanked Moses again and gladly paid him a ridiculous fee. Rosie had fallen asleep in the waiting room. I woke her and we headed for the car park and the calling baboons.

My thoughts echoed. 'If you'd let your feelings flow and left the imagining side of your brain open to what you knew, you'd have worked all this out yourself long ago.'

In the car I ran through my meeting with Moses. I had to take a chance. He was my last hope. Rosie watched me anxiously.

'You'll go back home without nails,' she said, pointing to the chewed the nails of my right hand. 'Did the *ngaka* upset you?'

'No … but he must've hypnotized me. God knows what he told me …'

'Does it matter? You want help to sort out Hannes' murder don't you?'

'I suppose so.'

'Use him to find your answers.'

'Thanks Rosie, you're right.'

Chapter 38

I took the pills and was thrown into a dreamless sleep. Hunger stirred me at dawn. I showered, dressed hurriedly and with no-one about, went into the kitchen for a bowl of cereal, toast and instant coffee. After unlocking the elaborate latch system and deactivating the alarm, I went out.

Through Connie's prissy garden, past the over-trimmed shrubs, weedless slate path and down the jacaranda avenue I followed the veld path round the acacias to the stone wall. I sat there in the pale sunlight.

First playful tugs and then bolder ones dragged me from the wall and urged me along the path. Hannes was back. At the dam his hold on me loosened and I was dumped on the grass. I was close to the spot where the Sergeant found the blood-covered red shoes. Hannes had dragged me there before and I had seen nothing. This time the scene was peaceful – birds digging for worms, the dew on buds drying. Nothing was out of place or unusual.

I was angry and spoke fast and loud.

'Why have you brought me to this place again? There's nothing here. Heaven knows what you were up to before you died or what you're up to now. I do know that I've found out some very weird things about you. Lots I dislike. No, let's rather say that I find them abhorrent – things you told none of us. And you've left me to uncover it all years later. Bloody hell Hannes! Why did you have that fucking token initiation into the Hurutshes? Weren't we good enough? Didn't you feel you belonged? You could have told me. All the time you left me thinking that the two of us were close. My God … Hannes.'

I paused to wipe away angry tears. 'What were you thinking of dressing up like a woman in Priya's sari, wearing those red shoes and the lipstick? Why fucking lipstick? Were you crazy? Sure, you liked to dress up, wear hats, but this? This doesn't make any sense. I know people have hurt you and said awful things and you had plenty of hassles, but you went too far.'

My ranting went on until I felt the pull in me again. 'Leave me alone Hannes,' I yelled. 'I'm sick of it. I've had enough!'

When he left me I rolled onto the grass and slept.

'You've been hiding in the grass having a nice little bit of shut-eye but your snoring gave you away,' Thomas said, waking me with a prod of his toe. He was paying a quick visit to his mother and said he had spotted me on his way to his car.

I stretched for his hand and held it between both of mine.

'I was lucky to find you. I wish we had more time together,' he said.

We spent the next hour talking. We were building memories.

Jeanette phoned mid-morning to ask me to meet her after work. We met at a fashionable coffee haunt in Rustenburg. Visions of passersby were successfully obscured with the heavy lace curtains. This older world of luxury and timelessness was a meeting place for friends or a secret hideaway for lovers, who chose the velvet booths. We took a quiet table close to the wall. Jeanette looked pale and her movements were jerky.

I was fond of Jeanette but had found her tense and distant. I wondered if something was bothering her, then dismissed the thought. That day she spoke more freely. She told me that she felt nervous much of the time and slept badly. Her awareness of the violence around her made her anxious. We were distracted as we chose from the selection of cakes and tartlets. Then Jeanette spoke hesitantly.

'I know I can talk to you.' She had screwed her tissue into a ball. 'There is something I have to tell you. I've been building up the courage.' She tried to swallow her coffee but couldn't. Holding on to the edge of the table, she made small gulping noises. 'It's Vince. He's been having an affair with one of the young physios renting his rooms.'

'Vince? How could he?'

'Someone saw them together and told me. It's been a terrible time. I've had it on my mind day and night.' She wiped away tears. 'At first I told him to get out … but when he made her leave the rooms and promised not to see her again I allowed him back … but not into the bedroom. I'll have to trust him again first.'

'I'm really sorry. I hope he's learned his lesson.'

'We're trying … to start again.'

I had no words that could console her. Jeanette composed herself after offloading her painful information and left for home. Shaken, I ordered another cup of coffee. Like a virus, she'd passed on her hurt to me and put a dent in my love for Vince.

Duke jumped onto my bed and I let him snuggle up. There is nothing as comforting as a furry cat to cuddle. With the lights out I could just make out the framed edge of Pa's photograph. My eyes burned.

'What's wrong with you Van Wyk men? You hurt your women so easily. Why do you do it – boredom, sexual excitement? The thrill of the chase?'

In Raelene's sunny craft room, Ma's paintings of Hannes stood like sentinels where we had left them. The intensity of the pain portrayed struck me more forcefully than the day Nathaniel and Vince had carried them in from the attic. In the end I forced myself to make choices and selected five to go into the crate I was shipping home. The rest I left, hoping for an exhibition.

There was a tall pile of Ma's drawings that I hadn't looked at yet. What a formidable task. Formidable was the only word I knew that fitted. As I turned the drawings over I was picking through Ma's emotional life for a period of twenty years or so. It was an uncomfortable feeling, scrutinizing her as she revealed herself in line, shade and color. The critic in me came to my aid, letting me sort objectively so that, in the end, I believe I placed aside only the very best drawings. I left the rest for the family to chose from.

Since my brothers hadn't bothered to sort the possessions of my dead family members it was a chore left for me. Apart from the boxes and the airline bag that Pa had given to my brothers, there were several dusty suitcases and bags of my family's belongings that had been chucked into the attic. Connie had suggested I give anything wearable to charity and throw the rest out or burn it. All he wanted was some family photos. Vince asked for photos too, a few of Ma's drawings, one of Hannes' baseball caps and Pa's pipe.

Armed with a heavy-duty flashlight I went up to the attic. Without much trouble I found Pa's possessions towards the back wall in an over-stuffed suitcase labeled 'P. Van Wyk'. It hadn't been opened and undoing the clasps required all my strength. Pa's pipe and tobacco lay under newspaper. I put them aside for Vince. Pa's blue fountain pen, a valued gift from my grandfather, and his leather-bound bible were underneath. Those I kept for myself. I turned over the layer of protective paper and found the tan scarf he wore on icy mornings and a small velvet bag. The bag contained a pair of silver cuff links and a tiepin. I'd seen Pa wear them only once, at Marie Prinsloo's wedding. The bag and scarf went into my crate, together with his personal diaries. His accounts and notes on running the farm I put aside for Connie, in case he changed his mind and wanted them. The clothes in the case could be donated to charity. Years earlier Pa had given away all Ma's possessions except the few I had found in the attic trunk.

The biggest task facing me would be going through Hannes' records, comics and schoolbooks. His clothing had been given away. His collections and school things filled an old suitcase. I selected the Elvis and rock and roll recordings I fancied to send home. There were several hundred comic books. He had read only adventure comics like Superman, Batman and Dark Avenger.

Caught in the elastic bands that bound a pile of comic books were two of Hannes' sketches. One depicted a scowling thickset man with a bottle in his hand. Instantly I recognized Uncle Gerret, who had doubled as Pa's manager. In the other drawing Uncle Gerret lay on the floor pierced with a long three-pronged fork. A pool of blood had seeped onto the floor. Below the drawings Hannes had written, *This disgusting vermin must be exterminated.* It was signed '*Hannes, The Avenger*'. A trident fork stood next to his signature.

I didn't have time for the impact of the note to register. The flashlight flickered and cold air whooshed past me. Knocking myself against edges of boxes and furniture, I grabbed the sketches and rushed out. Panting, I closed the attic door behind me. A cigarette helped to ease my shivers as I tried to regain my composure.

The attic had offered up another secret. I would ask someone braver than myself to collect the flashlight and items I had put aside.

After a glass of claret, I had another look at the sketches. Exterminate Gerret? Had Hannes planned to kill him or did he have some other sinister plot? But how could he do that? He was only fourteen. The intensity of Hannes' hatred of Uncle Gerret and his desire for revenge threw me. I was back where I started. Nothing made sense. I wandered into the kitchen for something sweet. Raelene had left a rack of chocolate muffins out to cool. I took two upstairs with me.

As I licked the chocolate icing off my muffin I thought about Uncle Gerret. He was tougher on the workers than Pa had been and they were wary of his loud voice and definite stride. With production in mind, Pa didn't look too closely at his brother's methods. The workers continued to sing as they worked but they muttered about the Big White *Baas* wanting them to work faster. Once Pa gave him a slice of the profits, Uncle Gerret worked even harder and drove the workers until the air in the orange groves lost its sweetness and voices were laced with bitterness.

I didn't understand why Uncle Gerret and Aunt Flora weren't invited to visit and we had never been to their house. One evening on the *stoep* after work when Pa had his feet up I asked him about it. He stared at the silhouette of the mountain, a prehistoric animal in the twilight. When at last he answered, his words were carefully chosen and the message clipped.

'Your uncle and I … we go back a long way. We can never be close but we work well together … and I'm grateful for his help in getting the farm going. I won't have anything to do with him outside of work and that's the way it is. I don't want to hear another word about it.' His voice was tight and scratchy.

I wondered if the reason Pa kept his distance from his elder brother had to do with his childhood. He had told me that my uncle went to a boarding school and when he had completed his studies he left the farm to work in the city. Pa was four years younger and by the time he was old enough for school Oupa said the price of lamb at the market had dropped to nothing and floods had turned the *mielie* crop rotten. Cash was so short that my Oupa and Ouma only just managed to pay for his uniform for the local farm school. After he had finished his schooling Pa didn't leave the farm, though he wanted to follow Gerret to the city. Oupa was aging and an extra hand was desperately needed.

It was understandable that Pa was resentful. 'Can the city slicker with the fine education please help with the spraying?' was the sort of cynical remark that slipped out if Pa had a beer or two for lunch. It was clear that Pa didn't want to talk about what had upset him about his brother.

Uncle Gerret was the sort of manager who kept tabs on everyone. He forgot himself at times and, instead of explaining, he gave Pa instructions. Pa would walk away purple in the face but say nothing – that is, until he exploded. I could hear them yelling at each other from the house to the veld. After that, the silence between them went on for weeks. Once they talked again Pa must've made it clear that he was steering the farm.

The pattern of Pa's life was set. He rose at dawn and worked until twilight darkened the mountains. Only occasionally did he return to the house for lunch.

Pa was my rock. His power was in his thick thighs, alive with black hairs, and his sinewy arms that could lift me onto his shoulder in a single smooth move. Appearance was important to Pa, who shaved and slicked back his hair each morning. Though Uncle Gerret had started off neatly dressed in fresh clothing every day, the change in him was noticeable. He began to come to work smelling and his clothes looked slept in. Hannes and I had difficulty understanding why he was moody at times and wouldn't even talk us. The workers laughed at him, lifting curved hands to their mouths, and made drinking noises. He lost interest in the way the work was done or in the quality of the oranges.

'Gerret's gone bad on me,' Pa whined to Ma.

'Try talking to him. Find out what's eating him,' Ma suggested.

'Na, what's the point?'

'He's your own blood, Piet. Don't even think of making him leave.'

'He was a drunk but I thought he'd got cleaned up. He promised he didn't touch the stuff anymore. Now look at him.'

It was Ma who spoke to Aunt Flora and warned her that my uncle could lose his job if he didn't get a grip on his drinking. Uncle Gerret went to see the local doctor, who helped him to keep sober so that he could manage the farm competently. After a battle he regained the respect he had lost. But in 1964 Aunt Flora died and he began to drink again. By the time Hannes was murdered a year later, the doctor could no longer help him.

Ma was in my dreams through the night. 'Gerret, Gerret,' she whispered. The thought of breakfast made me nauseous. This time it was Ma urging me out onto the path past the now bare jacarandas and on towards the dam.

In the early cool I walked briskly and was at the dam within ten minutes. Flowers were raising their heads to the sun and geese were feeding their young. The scene looked as peaceful as before, until a door banged and a man yelled a string of

Afrikaans expletives. Frikkie Lourens, Connie's manager, was leaving the house to work on the farm. The sharp message must have been for his wife in her dressing gown, who peered at me from the door. She recognized me, waved and stepped back inside.

'What had happened between Hannes and Uncle Gerret?' I asked myself. There was obvious animosity between them but was that enough for my uncle to kill Hannes? It didn't add up. 'And where did Connie fit in?' I asked myself.

It seemed ridiculous to even think that Connie had coerced his uncle into murdering Hannes. I recalled Vince hissing *skadu* behind Uncle Gerret's back. Yes, Gerret was Connie's shadow and Connie asked him to do his dirty work. When Pa and Ma went on a rare holiday, Connie was left in charge. Naturally Pa expected Connie to run the farm in his absence but Connie made life easy for himself. He gave Uncle Gerret complete responsibility for overseeing the staff, carrying out any sackings and handing out wages. But surely Uncle Gerret had a mind of his own, I thought as I left the peaceful scene at the dam.

Luckily, Cobie was at home that afternoon. As Pa's closest friend, I hoped he could tell me more about the relationship between Connie and his uncle, Gerret.

'You know that Connie is bone lazy but smart. Connie could squeeze extra work out of Gerret with a few bottles of red. Your Pa must've known it but turned a blind eye. He often complained to me that your Ma had spoiled Connie but there wasn't much he could do about it.'

'Wasn't Gerret one of the Broeders?'

'Those were the golden days of the Broederbond. I'm ashamed to say that I joined. Connie followed your Pa and joined as well. You can imagine Gerret's joy when Connie offered to put his name forward as a prospective member.'

'Oh yes, I can.'

'They sat together at meetings and worked together on the same committees.'

'So they became chummy?' I was picturing the two big men together. They had their size and aggressiveness in common.

I told Cobie that I thought it possible that Uncle Gerret had murdered Hannes, but that perhaps Connie had initiated it. Cobie shook his head.

'I can't see Connie planning the murder ahead of time and then getting Gerret to carry it out. Hannes' murder wasn't a premeditated crime. It was a murder in a rage with vicious stabbings, the body dumped and wine thrown over it.'

'So you doubt Connie could have manipulated Uncle Gerret into killing Hannes?'

'Gerret's not cool enough to organize. He's got a wild temper.' Cobie pushed his chair back, stood and stretched. 'Let's break for tea.'

Cobie's maid had laid a table in the shady part of the garden with tea and scones. I enjoyed talking to Cobie and listening to his stories about past cases. He used logic in his detection of crime and didn't follow gut instinct at all. The difference in his approach to mine was interesting and helpful.

Cobie began to talk about one of his hobby horses, the Broederbond. He explained that when the scandal about Miriam and Thomas spread to the Broeders, Connie and Pa's reputations were damaged beyond repair. Of course, this was not long before they decided to resign anyway.

'I was so appalled by the way the Broeders treated Connie and your Pa that I resigned on principle too. But guess what? Gerret stayed on and left Connie out in the cold.'

'So what happened?'

'Gerret's head swelled. He thought himself too good to be

a manager and talked of starting up his own farm. Of course he couldn't have pulled it off. He drank too much and didn't have much upstairs. He couldn't keep staff either with his temper.'

Then Cobie crossed his arms. If he knew more about Uncle Gerret he wasn't going to tell me.

On the way back to the farm, I remembered seeing a woman in Uncle Gerret's cottage some mornings. I thought her name was Lettie. Had she witnessed the murder, seen or heard anything? With Gerret a bit older than Pa, if she was still alive she would be in her eighties now.

I went down to the orange groves to find Nathaniel. When he saw me he came right over with that questioning expression of his. I asked him if he remembered my uncle's girlfriend. He nodded and lifted his hands to his head.

'Ja. We called her Yellow Hair. One day she run away from *Baas* Gerret after big fight.'

'Have you ever seen her in Rustenburg?'

He shook his head. I wondered if Arnie Swart knew of her whereabouts. I phoned him and asked him to visit as soon as he had the time. He promised to drop in later that afternoon. I placed some of Raelene's cookies on a plate and had the coffee cups ready.

He arrived around three o'clock on his way from a crime scene. He looked strained and his clothes were crumpled. A farmer and his family were murdered during the night.

'What a pleasure to sit out here on the *stoep* in the quiet and sunshine,' he said after the second cookie. He eased himself back in the chair and ran his hand through his hair.

'Have you eaten?' I asked.

'I'm fine. Just enjoying the simple things of life.'

'You've had a bad day?'

He shuddered. 'Don't want to think what they did to the kids. It looks as if someone broke into the farmhouse after dark and killed the lot of them. I'll save the details.'

'I don't know how you do this.'

He pushed out his hand as if he was waving all awful things away.

'Tell me, how are you going with your detective work?'

'I've hit a few tough spots but I don't want to bother you with it too much today. Just one or two small things.'

'Go for it. It'll be a break.'

'When you first told me about Hannes' murder you thought the body had been moved.'

'Ja. My notes told me there were some drag marks on a sandy strip near the grass where he was found. They were the width of the body and it looked as if a male's heavy work shoes had made the rippled marks on the ground. There were some animal prints there too but I managed to match one of the shoe treads to a strip in the sand and it fitted. Forensics didn't carry out tests to back me up so I can't be certain. You know we abandoned all that when we arrested those three blacks. We didn't even look at their shoes,' he said with a frown.

It was unfair – there had been too few police to do the job well. And then the belief was that most crimes were committed by blacks. I had almost forgotten to ask him about Gerret's girlfriend, Lettie.

'I remember she spent time here with him,' said Arnie.

'Is she still in the area?'

He laughed. 'Once she split up with Gerret she aimed higher. She used her full name – Leticia – bleached her hair and got real thin. Then she was lucky. Met and married a rich farmer, De Wet, but she wasn't happy. She was one of those women who kept on having plastic surgery. It's a long story and

I shouldn't laugh. She's dead now … was drunk and fell into the pool and drowned.'

'That's sad.'

'Well then. Is that all you wanted to know?'

'One more thing. About the attack on Hannes. You said it was vicious. Was it unusually vicious?'

'It was the sort of thing someone in a wild rage would do.'

'Dreadful!'

'Ja, but at least death came quickly. Well, this has been a breather for me, but unfortunately duty calls.'

'You don't seem to like your job much.'

'I've had enough. I'm out of it as soon as I get enough stashed away.'

He jumped into the car, gave a salute and roared down the drive.

Sadly I walked along the driveway, through the gate and along the grass to the boulder that Pa had erected in Hannes' memory. I must've been sitting on the grass for an hour or two until I noticed a vermilion streak in the sky.

Chapter 39

I woke early. A halo of rose had just begun to peep over the mountain ridge. At the desk I read and re-read the evidence and bits of information I had collected. And where did Hannes' drawings of Gerret fit in? There had to be something I was overlooking. Feeling stiff and restless I left the papers. After deactivating the alarm I rushed out to a new morning sky and the rich smell of the earth. Nathaniel ran up to me near the garage.

'Missy finding man who killed Little Master yet?'

'I think I will find him in the end.'

'Better be before Missie go,' he said, with a worried frown.

'Ja, you're right. Not much time left.'

Connie's snoring reverberated through the *voorkamer.* His feet were on a leather ottoman and an open newspaper covered his body. He looked almost vulnerable.

'Eh, what's the matter?' He sat up with a start, yawned and rubbed his stubbly cheeks. 'Been staring at me and thinking bad things about your brother, eh?'

'On the contrary.'

'Just hold it. I've got to pee.'

While I waited I went into the kitchen and put the kettle on for coffee. I fumbled with the cups. Connie was entitled to an explanation but I wasn't sure if I could give it. As I poured the hot water over the instant granules I told myself to do the right thing. Then I carried the two cups back into the room.

'We've got to talk, Con … sometime.'

'Damn ... I'm already late for work,' he said, glancing at his watch. 'But with that very serious look on your face … Lourens can handle things for a while. They'll call me if something urgent crops up.'

'It's like this … When I first began to investigate Hannes' murder … whatever way I looked at it … you turned out to have the strongest motive. I've never wanted it this way and I've been trying to disprove it … but I couldn't. You've remained the key suspect … that is, until I found Hannes' drawings in the attic implicating Gerret.'

'What drawings?'

I explained how I had found the drawings in the attic and described them. Then I told him about the evidence box Sergeant Phefo had brought round with the trident fork, the sari material and lipstick. Connie listened and said nothing as he paced the length of the room for what seemed ages. After I had told him about my feeling that our Uncle Gerret may have been implicated in the murder he sat facing me.

'Of course I didn't kill Hannes,' he said loudly.

I waited.

'What you say about Gerret … makes sense. I don't know about the lipstick and all that. It sounds weird.'

'Ja.' I nodded. 'It is.'

'But I do feel guilty about Hannes.'

'How come?'

'I don't know if you remember Nana Joyce and Pop's visit about a month or so before Hansie died?'

'I can remember parts of it. The rest is vague.'

When our maternal grandparents migrated to South Africa from England they settled in Cape Town. They visited us occasionally. During the visit that Connie was talking about they had planned to stay with us for about a month and then holiday elsewhere.

'You know the welcome tea party Ma made specially for them?'

I looked at him blankly. 'I can remember their suitcase full of presents but not a party. Sorry.'

'Gerret, friends from the town and some of the neighbors were invited. On his walks Pops liked chatting to the neighbors, so Ma asked the guests to join us. When we were all having a good time Hannes dropped a bombshell. In a loud voice he told everyone about … me and Miriam …and about Thomas. Nana and Pops were church elders … and you can imagine their shock. I will never forget the look on their faces.

'Gerret got Hannes out of the room real quick but Nana and Pops turned away from me. They wouldn't hear a word in my defence. Not that there was much I could say. I was clearly in the wrong. They gave Ma and Pa what for about not bringing me up decently.'

Connie had been carrying these memories for so long and not spoken about them. When he thought I suspected him of the murder he went into his *laager* as defensively as our Voortrekker forefathers in danger placed their wagons in a closed circle. It would've been so much easier for him to talk about it and clear his name. But that was Connie.

'This is where I did the wrong thing … and I feel guilty. You can imagine how furious I was with Hannes. The next day when I heard Hannes making smart-arse remarks to Gerret, like he usually did. I kept quiet. I saw Gerret grab him and take him behind those big bushes near the orange groves. Then I heard Hannes screaming. I shouldn't have allowed it … let Gerret lay into him. I was the elder brother … it was my job or Pa's to set him straight. I took the easy way out. Gerret went overboard and left Hannes bruised.'

'I remember the bruises but didn't know how he got them. He wouldn't say.'

It was useless pointing a finger at Connie's past weakness, wishing he had been more protective. At least he realized he had been in the wrong and had given me another snippet of the story.

He yawned and looked out the window at the blazing sunshine. 'I'd better move it.'

Tobacco swamped the fragrance of jasmine. I put my pen down. I had been re-reading my notes about Hannes borrowing Priya's sari. Her face grew large and smiley in my mind. Something made me recall Priya mentioning that her mother had been attacked many years ago. Whether it was a prompt from Pa or not, I had to follow it up. After breakfast I phoned Priya to ask her about the attack on her mother.

'It was your Pa's farm manager … that bastard Gerret. He crept into our kitchen one morning when my father was working and tried to rape my mother. Can you believe it? He had a thing about Indian women and everyone knew it. He didn't get near my mom though. She gave him a dent on the head with a saucepan full of hot curry to remember her by.'

'Did you report him?'

'No he ran off and we didn't want to make waves. Ma should've charged him but he got away with it.'

'Did he steal something or …'

'No. You remember how attractive Ma was in her sari.'

'Ja, she was lovely.'

I didn't have time to mull over my conversation with Priya. As soon as I'd put the phone down, Sergeant Phefo arrived.

'Sorry I've taken so long to come back to you. When I had a moment, I looked up past cases of voodoo dolls sent to victims. At the same time I was assessing the material we have on the falling tree. There's a scribble on a smooth bit of wood at the side of the tree. So far we can't find a match for it but I'm working on it. We see a lot of these attempts to frighten people round here. It's likely that whoever sent you the doll made that tree fall. Sorcerers who use evil witchcraft, and there are several of them, often make the dolls. They're so full of themselves that they just have to leave a mark, a letter or scribble that will identify them. They think they'll never get caught – but that's how we get them.'

'Like a calling card.'

'That's it. I'm narrowing it down. I should have an idea who it is soon.'

After lunch I went to see Tansie. Taking the car and paying a group of children to watch it was a less time-wasting solution than walking there with a chaperone. Tansie had just woken from a sleep and was grumpy. A cup of tea and her favorite gingernuts and her smile returned. By the time Rosie arrived Tansie was telling jokes.

I mentioned to her and Rosie that I was trying to find out as much about Gerret as possible. Tansie lifted an eyebrow.

'Missie think he do the murder?'

Then Tansie told us that when she had helped out during the harvest she'd seen how upset Hannes was about Gerret.

'That Gerret he crazy – swearing and shouting. He bad, bad Afrikaner.'

'Why do you say that, Ma?' said Rosie, giggling and egging her on.

She lowered her voice. 'He like Indian ladies … too much.'

'So what?' Rosie said.

'One day he rape Indian lady near big fountain in town. She too frightened of husband to call police. Another time Gerret chase Indian lady near fish market but she get away.'

Rosie's face was screwed up in disgust.

'One day he go over fence to farm next door and try nonsense with Mrs Naidoo but she quick with the curry pan.'

We laughed.

We ate dinner at sunset. After gulping down his dessert of fruit and ice cream, Connie disappeared with a pack of beers and I went up to my room. For comfort, I moved my sheet of paper from the table to the floor. I placed a bottle of wine, a glass and my cigarettes on a tray next to me and leaned back on cushions to study my notes. Within twenty minutes I was asleep.

I dreamed that I was at the dam with Hannes. He pointed to a camellia bush, its pale blooms ghostly in the moonlight.

'Hide behind there,' he whispered. Insects buzzed as he unzipped a small canvass bag, took out a pair of shoes, a pink sari and a tube of lipstick. He took off the clothes he had been wearing, folded them and put them into the bag. Once he was dressed in the sari and shoes he put the bag under a bush. Every now and again he gave the sari a hitch and wobbled on the high-heeled shoes. He disappeared behind a tree for a moment and emerged holding the trident. All I could see of his face was the fire of anger in his eyes.

He lingered outside Gerret's cottage building up courage, and then, using the end of the trident, knocked on the door. A surprised and delighted Gerret peered through the net curtain at the person in the sari. When he opened the door and recognized Hannes, they were locked in fury.

I woke sticky with sweat. In the soothing shower I played the unusually vivid dream scene over and over. Did my dream depict what actually happened? A fourteen-year-old boy, slight in build, dressed up in a sari and high heels, wearing lipstick and carrying a trident went to the manager's cottage and knocked on the door? If the dream was accurate, his Indian attire had attracted Gerret's attention sufficiently for him to open the door. Different scenarios of what could've occurred next played in my mind but I kept returning to this question. Had Hannes choreographed it all like a violent play? Would he have gone to all that trouble if he hadn't planned to injure Gerret with the trident or kill him?

It was only eight o'clock and too early to go to bed. The image of Gerret's cottage nagged and nagged at me, demanding action. How could I visit the cottage at night? I argued with myself. It was still early, my internal dialogue continued. I dressed and went down the stairs to look for Nettie. I found her chatting to a friend in the backyard. I interrupted and asked if she'd come with me to the manager's house. I didn't need to explain. All I had to do was ask. I waited for her to finish her conversation and we took the path to the cottage. I hadn't seen Magda since schooldays.

Magda peered out of the half-open door. When she recognized us she asked us in. With embarrassment she pulled a hand through her messy hair and tightened the cord of the gown. As Frikkie was asleep, we quietly followed her into the kitchen. She had been boiling milk for cocoa and offered us a cup.

She wasn't on the farm when Hannes died but she'd heard about his murder. I explained that it was possible that the murder had taken place outside her cottage at night. There were no words to explain the driven feeling that had brought me out but the determination in my face must've quietened any annoyance she felt about my late visit. When I asked for her help she agreed, as long we didn't wake Frikkie.

Nettie sat in the kitchen drinking cocoa while I examined the net curtain. It covered the window next to the front door and was a similar curtain to the one that would have hung here many years ago – clotted in parts and thin from washing. The outer light over the door that burned throughout the night hadn't changed.

From outside the cottage I could only make out vague movement and broad shapes in the house. Then I stood inside near the window while Magda was outside and I checked exactly how much I could see of her. Fortunately she was wearing a salmon colored dressing gown, close enough in color and shape to the sari Hannes had worn on the night of his murder. The color of the gown and her blonde hair were clearly visible but her features were indistinct. Gerret would have seen the sari, the red shoes and lipstick and could have come to the conclusion that an Indian woman was outdoors. The probability that he'd also been drinking, as he did most evenings, would've made his judgment wobbly.

Magda yawned and, though she offered us another cup of cocoa, we left. As we walked back I thought how dramatic Hannes' strategy to lure Gerret to the door had been. After all, he could've pulled a hat down over his face as a disguise and knocked on the door saying he was lost or had run out of petrol. But Hannes had chosen a more colorful way of getting back at his nemesis. That was Hannes. He must've reveled in the planning.

The visit had served its purpose by making my dream more credible. I knew I was on the right track, the next step was to prove it. The only way I could do that was by confronting the murderer.

Cobie was still eating breakfast when I phoned him for Gerret's address. With a touch of irritation in his voice he promised to look for it after his walk.

'I'll come to the farm before noon. I'll give it to you then.'

In spite of his age he still had a driving licence and drove an old Austin that he enjoyed calling 'antique'. That day, like many others, he had stalled on one of the hills near the farm. He was late and flustered.

Once we had discussed the clear skies and lack of rain he produced a piece of paper with the address. He hesitated initially and then using his serious voice apologized for not telling me everything he knew about my uncle.

'In the old days Oupa Eric was having trouble selling his lambs at market. He wasn't the only one. But that wasn't the reason that there wasn't sufficient money for your Pa's high school fees. Don't forget Gerret was four years older than your Pa. Once Gerret had matriculated he left for Jo'burg and started an apprenticeship with a motor mechanic. He was clueless about cars but good with his hands … so he learned quick and earned well. When his boss died he wanted to buy the garage. The bank wouldn't give him a loan so he went to his Pa with a cock and bull story about how much money they'd cream from it.

'Your Oupa knew nothing about money and asked my opinion. I'd been in a small food business that didn't do too well before I became a policeman but I could spot a shonky deal. I looked at the figures and didn't like them. The garage was in a crummy position at the bottom of a street where no-one went. I told your Oupa not to give Gerret the money.

'Gerret drank himself into a rage, lashing out at everyone

and calling his Pa mean and me a busybody. Your poor Oupa couldn't take it. Finally he gave Gerret the money. Gerret left on Monday morning with a big smile.

'Anyway, once Gerret bought the garage the trouble started. He spent wildly on painting it up and had a big sign made. He took on an apprentice too and waited for the work to come in but the garage didn't take off. It could've been that he charged too much and didn't know how to talk to the customers. We did know that he wasn't shy about spending his money on himself – ladies, gambling ... who knows? Whatever the reason, he was soon broke and looking for a job again.'

'Did he pay the money back to Oupa?'

'Of course not,' Cobie sniggered. 'And that's what your Pa had against him.'

'I see.'

'It's more complicated than that though.'

When I began to speak he held up his hand to still me. He smoothed his tracksuit pants as he launched into a family story.

'He couldn't forgive Gerret for making them all suffer because he wanted a step up in the world. Your Pa wouldn't talk to Gerret for many years. Later he tried his best to patch things up by offering Gerret a job on the farm. Things warmed up briefly between them when they were in the Bond together, but it didn't last. Gerret developed big ideas of branching out on his own, which incensed your Pa. He had these schemes of a starting a tobacco farm on some vacant land down the road but he had no hope of setting it up. He was a drunk without a penny, hoping to draw the cash off others. Your Pa saw him going along the same path he'd been down before.

'Your Pa's hate for his brother returned with a vengeance. The two of them had one almighty fight and Gerret left the farm swearing. Hannes was home from school on some pretext and had witnessed the fight and heard the curses.

'After that, any words between the two brothers were ugly ones. Gerret continued to work on the farm but he drank himself silly and so he'd turn up late for work, sometimes not at all. Hannes must've been about twelve or thirteen at the time and he heard his Pa muttering about Gerret.

'Gerret had never liked Hannes and had picked on him over the years. Whether it was about Hannes' size or his color, Gerret found something nasty to say. Your Pa would put an arm around Hannes and tell him to ignore his drunken uncle.

'Hannes knew he was on safe ground when he fought back by whispering about his uncle behind his back or calling him bad names in front of the workers. When Gerret found out what Hannes was up to he was furious.'

'Phew.' It was about time that Cobie told me the full story.

'The feud had reached boiling point – *die vet was in die vuur.* Anything else thrown into it and it could've boiled over.'

I wanted someone tough and trustworthy to accompany me on a visit to Gerret. Esiekiel was a perfect choice. I found him outside his hut, asleep. I walked softly so as not to jolt him but as I neared he sat up.

'Have to learn to wake up quick if want to live till old man,' he grinned.

When I told him of my intended visit to Gerret he tried to dissuade me, but when he realized my determination he reluctantly agreed to join me. After lunch we headed for Reit Vlei, Gerret's son's sheep farm. The farm, sandwiched between two tobacco plantations, was a three-quarters of an hour drive. Traffic was unusually heavy and at the entrance of the farm we waited for a seemingly endless line of lambs to cross to the paddock. While we waited, Esiekiel used the opportunity to ask the shepherd about the layout of the farm and where to find Gerret.

We found Gerret's white-washed cottage behind the farmhouse. Next to his gate, a garbage bin, a pile of beer cans and wine bottles greeted us.

'This sure house of *Baas* Gerret,' Esiekiel laughed. 'On farm he carry little bottle in pocket. Drinking all day. He go back to house lunchtime, fill it up. All day drink and pee, drink and pee,' he laughed again.

'Will you come in with me?' I asked.

Esiekiel put his hand to his chest. 'Not worry, I watch out for Missie.'

I knocked on the door and when no-one answered I knocked again and harder. After a long wait we heard rumbling. The door opened. Gerret was panting a little as he leaned on his walker.

'What do you want?' he scowled.

He hadn't recognized us so I introduced myself and Esiekiel.

'We'd like to talk to you.'

'I'm in no mood for talking,' he said attempting to shut the door.

'We do need to have a chat,' I said more forcefully.

'I suppose you can come inside.' His walker groaned as he pushed it into the front room. We followed and sat down. Gerret made a slow transfer to an armchair. He had shrunk and lost most of his hair but what was left was combed across his head. His blue eyes were as I remembered them.

'What is it you want?' he asked again.

I explained that I was investigating Hannes' murder and would like to ask him some questions about the night Hannes was killed.

'It's too long ago. How the hell can I remember?' I noticed he'd clenched his right hand until the knuckles were white.

'Please try to remember. There are things I must ask you.'

'I can't remember what I had for breakfast. Can't you leave a sick old man alone?'

I noticed the daily newspaper spread over a footstool and a radio turned down to a low hum on a low table. He was physically weak but in still in touch with the world around him.

'Look, it's a blank. I can't remember ... and you can see yourselves out.'

There was nothing more I could say. I walked out of the room and out of the house with Esiekiel following.

In the car Esiekiel shook his head. 'That old man he fox. He liar. He remember everything.'

'How do you know?'

'I watch hand and eyes. The body slow but eyes quick, move round in head ... back to past time. Hand is tight and holds back temper. He remember good,' Esiekiel frowned.

That afternoon, I told myself that I had taken my investigations of the murder as far as I could. If any further action was to be taken it would have to be by the police.

I made a point of walking along the path past the boulder commemorating the last place Hannes had lain. The bed of grass surrounding the stone was high and speckled with white daisies. I stroked the stone and placed stray forget-me-nots at the foot of it.

After leaving a note for a sleeping Raelene, I drove to the police station. Maneuvring the car through choking traffic, I rehearsed what I would say to Arnie Swart.

Outside the brick building people hung about smoking. I edged my way through the door and found it crowded with mainly black men and a few whites standing around. The stink of cigarette smoke and body odor bombarded me.

After checking in at reception I joined the queue on a wooden slatted bench. Heavy-shoed police officers carrying papers squeaked past on the linoleum floors. Down the hall I heard unpleasant muffled sounds.

It was a long wait until the duty sergeant steered me down the corridor into an office with a dark stained-wood door. Looking cool in his short-sleeved shirt, Arnie Swart put his pen down and looked at me.

'Delightful as usual,' he said, fixing his eyes on my breasts.

I ignored the comment and sat opposite him.

'So what brings you to this hellhole so bright and early?'

'At last I've worked out who murdered my brother … but I do need your help.'

He pushed his swivel chair back, put his hands behind his head and his feet on the desk. 'I'm listening.'

I spoke slowly and told him exactly why I thought Gerret was the prime suspect and the three blacks had nothing to do with the murder. I reminded him of comments made about a large man with white hands and face. After going into the background of bad feeling that had escalated between Hannes and Gerret prior to the murder, I described how Hannes had dressed up as an Indian woman to unsettle or possibly harm Gerret. I mentioned the lipstick case I'd found in the tree hollow near the dam, Priya's sari, the trident and the travel case Hannes must have used for his change of clothes. The detective said nothing but nodded when I pointed out Gerret's history with Indian ladies. When I told him about Hannes' drawings signed 'The Avenger' he put his hand up to stop me.

'You could be right about Gerret but most of your evidence is flimsy. In spite of the drawings, we don't know what Hannes had planned and what occurred that night in the manager's cottage. And we haven't a single witness.'

I told him about my visit to Gerret. 'He makes out he's past it and can't remember. I can't prove it but I know he's lying.'

'It happened so long ago … but I guess we could question him.' He looked at his watch.

'I know resources are thin.'

He rubbed his forehead, sighed and looked through his diary. Then, speaking in Afrikaans, he made a phone call.

'So, Phefo will bring him in for questioning … and then … we'll see.'

'That's a step forward,' I said.

'Don't expect too much.'

I thought Arnie had finished talking when he asked me to wait. He disappeared for some time and when he returned he had a folder under his arm. He flipped through the pages.

'Gerret was inside for rape and aggravated assault about fifteen years ago. We've had our eye on him for years. We had some solid information that he played a part in importing drugs ... but we couldn't nail him. He's pretty old now and it's unlikely he's still involved but you never know what contacts he still has.'

'Importing drugs?'

'Ja. We wouldn't mind getting him. We've tried for long enough.'

So much for special favors, I thought.

He levered his chair back and forth. 'Best bet is for you to make a statement. Then … if we can squeeze a confession out of him … and you never know … we may just get a conviction.

It's a long shot but if it works we'd be doing society a favor.'

'I'll make that statement tomorrow morning.'

Chapter 40

After breakfast Connie sat on the *stoep* staring moodily at the orange groves. At least half the workers had left to clear their own land and make it ready for planting and those who remained in Connie's orange groves worked slowly and unenthusiastically. The farm was operating on reduced power and his schedule was well behind. Worse still, he had lost his drive for work.

The air between us wasn't friendly but conversation was slightly easier.

'Have you heard from Nathaniel about his plans?' I asked.

'He's trying to sort out a supply of labor for the two farms. It'll take time.'

Connie wore a resigned expression. Pa's will had brought about unwelcome changes. The *Baas* wasn't used to having to wait to be notified of his workers' plans.

'You didn't have much of a holiday here, did you?'

'I didn't come for a holiday. You know that.'

Neither of us spoke for some time.

'I think I've unraveled most of the story of Hannes' murder. I spoke to Arnie Swart and he wants me to come down to the station to make a statement.'

'A statement?'

'About Uncle Gerret. From the pieces I've put together … and the rest is deduction … it looks like he committed the murder.'

'You're sure?'

'Ja, but I'm not sure of the details.'

'You can't go alone. I'll come with you.' He looked at the sun masked by clouds. 'Be ready in two hours.'

It was a relief to have Connie at my side, even if things were still strained between us. My last visit to the police station had been unpleasant and if Connie could make it easier I was grateful.

He would've realized how difficult it had been to sort through the muddied facts that seemed to point in his direction. As unpleasant as the process had been for him at least it looked as if he would come out of it cleared of the murder.

I took my favorite route along the now bare jacarandas. Their fern-like leaves would appear soon. At the water's edge I kicked off my sandals, flattened the tall pollen-sprinkled reeds and scrambled into the water. A plump pink water lily floated towards me and I bent to touch my face with its petals. As I straightened, I glanced into the water and for a second, it couldn't have been more, Hannes smiled at me.

The police station was crowded. The police were drowning as they fought current crime. If Pa hadn't known Cobie well, a case as old as Hannes' would have remained in the archives. Connie's large frame seemed to slide through and past the crowds and somehow his demands for attention were noticed faster than mine had been. After only a brief wait in reception Sergeant Phefo led us to a small interviewing room. At least Connie was forced to take notice of the details in my signed statement that made the case against our Uncle Gerret.

The Sergeant lined up all the papers and stapled them together. He put them in a file and looked at me.

'I have some news for you. The voodoo doll and the tree were the work of a sorcerer, Letsego, who makes his mischief from his home near the lake. The young detective constable who has been working on the doll decided to send it to the crime lab. He thought they might pick up something useful. They didn't get a thing from its inside but they did manage to find a partial print from one of the button eyes. And there's a positive link between partial prints on the doll's eye and those on a smooth bit of the tree trunk. From our records we were able to trace the prints to this sorcerer. There is no doubt of his guilt.'

'Have you brought him in?'

'Yes. His story is that he found you one helluva nuisance. Your snooping mucked up his financial arrangements, brought them into the light.'

'Really?'

'He had a good collection going from a whole lot of people on the farm. Protection money. If they paid up nothing bad would happen to them.'

'Did Connie pay?'

Phefo laughed loudly. 'Sure. To ensure that his children and grandchildren were protected. Don't forget, Connie still has Miriam on the farm and he made sure Letsego would keep quiet about it. Letsego collected from her too and Cheetah paid him to keep his nose out of his business.'

'A little gold mine.'

'So what'll happen to Letsego?'

'He'll be charged for extortion and endangering your life. He's likely to go to jail.'

I picked a generous bunch of flowers for what would be my last visit to Tansie. Connie drove me to Nandi's house and promised to fetch me later.

'You go home soon. I see on your face,' Tansie said, taking my hands in hers.

'Ja, very soon,' I said, forcing back tears.

'Not be sad. I always with you and you with me … even when I gone.'

'I know.'

'*Modimo* he keep me here for little while.'

The sound of someone coughing interrupted our conversation. It was Rosie. She grabbed me and began tickling me as she had when we were children.

I struggled to free myself.

'No, you're not getting away.' She tickled me until I was giggling furiously, kicking and flaying my arms. 'There … that's enough. You're far too serious. I've been wanting to do that since you arrived.'

Gasping for breath I had to wait to answer her. 'You're right.'

'Music and laughter … best therapy,' Rosie said heading for the tape recorder.

We sat in the front room nodding and singing the words to our music, the music from the sixties. Nandi made us tea and we enjoyed titbits of local gossip. Rosie told me about her latest lover, much younger than herself, and we laughed again. We were pretending that Tansie would recover and that we didn't have to part.

We exchanged phone numbers and email addresses. I couldn't say goodbye to Tansie, it would've been too painful for both of us. We held each other without speaking. At the front door Rosie whispered, 'We'll keep in touch.' I hurried out of the house and joined Connie in the car.

Howling interrupted my sleep. Wolves or jackals, I thought, pushing the curtain back and staring into the black. Nothing at first and then a familiar chattering sound. Baboons were in the trees beneath my window.

Wide awake I sat in the rocker thinking about Tansie and Rosie. I felt as if I was leaving my family. Would I ever see Tansie again?

Nettie shook me. 'Wake up ma'am. Policeman downstairs.'

I felt the blood drain from my head as I rolled too quickly across the bed, forcing myself to stand. Once my teeth were brushed and a comb dragged through my hair, I pulled on the gown I'd borrowed from Raelene.

'Morning. And a lovely fresh morning it is,' Arnie Swart said.

'Any news?'

'Plenty.'

'So?' My fingers drummed on the table.

'Phefo took a team down to Gerret Van Wyk's place with a search warrant and they combed the place. They found papers proving his past drugs involvement and some possible contacts. So thanks to your bringing up that old murder this has been … er … a very positive operation.'

'Glad you got something out of it. You don't want any more drugs on the streets.'

'Indeed.'

'Did you find out anything about the murder?'

'Phefo took him in to the station for questioning about that yesterday.'

'And?'

'Suddenly he remembered that a hunting knife had been given to him by his father.'

'Well. Did he confess in the end?'

'He put on a big act, wailing and beating his chest. Then he admitted stabbing Hannes. Said he'd never forget that night. You should've seen the look on his face when he told us about it. Well, he'd had a few drinks … but he reckons he was far from drunk. When he opened that door and recognized Hannes togged up in the sari and high heels he was furious … flew into a rage and swore at him. It was just Hannes playing one of his pranks, he thought, and aimed a punch at him to teach him a lesson, but Hannes was much too fast for him. That pointy fork of his … well, he was ready to attack with it and if Gerret hadn't stabbed him it would've pierced him. The bloody thing's deadly. I've seen it.'

'So now it's self-defence is it? From a fourteen-year-old.'

'Mmmm.'

'So where was the knife?'

'It's not clear but he thinks it was in a leather sheath around his waist. He'd been using it that week. He and a couple of the workers had been after rabbits who'd been eating the small crop of *meilies* they'd planted. Usually he changed his clothes and had a shower when he came in from work but he remembers that he was late that night and hungry so he let the shower go.'

Hannes had intended to wound or even kill Gerret. It was crazy. This new information had shaken me. Of the many questions flying around my head, I asked myself, 'Why had Gerret stabbed Hannes so viciously and so many times?' It wasn't as if he hadn't recognized Hannes in the sari and high heels. Hannes had gone too far, but why had Gerret stabbed him to death?

'Some water? You're looking pale.'

'I'll be fine thanks,' I said, pulling the dressing-gown cord tighter. 'Did he tell you why he stabbed Hannes … so brutally?'

'He muttered that he couldn't remember.'

'From the start I haven't been able to understand why anyone would stab a fourteen-year-old to death in that hideous way.'

Arnie nodded. It had happened too long ago to find answers. Hannes was always playing one trick or another, particularly on people he disliked. This time he planned more than a trick, he tried to harm someone who couldn't control his rage.

'What did Gerret say about moving the body?'

'He remembers every detail – the sari, the shoes. He rubbed off most of the lipstick then dragged it to the grass near the road, as far away as possible from his cottage, so that he wouldn't be connected to the murder.'

'The bastard.'

'Some bad news,' Arnie sighed. 'He's got Hodgkins Lymphoma. The prognosis is bad … he won't be around for more than a month or so. As you know, two of the blacks wrongly arrested are dead and the other is dying. At least he's looked after in jail. Who knows, if he's let out he might die sooner with no treatment or money.'

'Shit, shit, shit.'

'Sorry, but I doubt that justice will be done here. We're better off leaving things as they are.'

'No. As long as Gerret lives he must pay.'

Arnie Swart rubbed his chin.

I ran down to the orange groves. Connie was back at work, supervising the planting of new trees.

He scowled when he saw me.

'Arnie Swart is certain Gerret's the murderer.'

'You're unbelievable,' Connie shook his head. 'Can't talk about it now, new trees have to go in. Set up a meeting for tonight with Vince and we'll talk.'

The three of us sat around the oval wooden table as we had before.

'So what's all this about Arnie Swart and Hannes' murderer?' Connie asked.

Before I could answer Vince cut in. 'Has Swart proof?'

'He's got a confession,' I said.

'Come on, tell us.'

After I had told my brothers how Hannes had planned to get back at Gerret for his vile behavior by tricking him, I explained how Hannes had carried the trident and planned to harm Gerret in some way, or possibly kill him, but his plan had backfired and Gerret stabbed him with his hunting knife. Vince looked shocked and Connie picked at the skin around his fingernail.

'I could've told you that Gerret was a bastard but I'd never have guessed he was the murderer.'

'So tell us how you worked it out,' Vince said.

I gave them a shortened version of how the clues came together to point to Gerret.

'Without you we'd never have known the truth. Neither of us did much to help you and we should've,' Vince looked down.

'We've got Hannes' killer and that's what counts,' I said.

'Has Swart charged him?' Connie asked.

'Apparently he'll be dead sooner than Arnie can do all the paperwork to get him into court to face a judge and jury. Arnie has no intention of doing anything about that innocent man in jail either,' I said.

'He's letting Gerret get away with it because he's too fucking lazy,' Vince said, his voice rising.

'I'm going to see Cobie Mulder. Gerret must be formally charged even if he has to rot in a prison hospital. Swart's taking the easy way out, hoping Gerret'll die soon,' Connie kicked the table.

'We'll see Cobie together … and the press must be told,' Vince added.

'At last. You're moving on it.' I couldn't help my cynicism.

I pulled my suitcase down from the top shelf of the closet. I had just put my gold jewelery back on and bundled my dirty jeans into the bottom of the case when Connie knocked on the door. He grinned.

'The shit hit the fan at the station. Cobie took the case to the Chief. He's threatening to take it to the Minister of Justice.'

'So?'

'So … Swart got rained on from up high. He's been told to bring Gerret in and charge him. Until Gerret's tried they'll detain him in a jail with hospital facilities. That's if he lives long enough.' He rubbed his hands. 'The black prisoner will be given the option to stay in the prison hospital or join the community.'

'Much better.'

I stood at the window edged with bougainvillea and gazed at the farm. It was swathed in sunlight, the orange groves merging into the mountains. My camera was loaded with undeveloped film of the farm but this view I wanted to commit to memory. At the small wooden desk I put the pens into the drawer and gathered my sheets of working paper. I tore them into bits and threw them into the wastepaper basket with a pink flower on it that I had used as a child.

With a cigarette in one hand and a glass of red wine in the other I weighed up my feelings about my visit. The energies of Pa and Hannes that had been with me had retreated and I felt easier. I thought about my struggle to understand Hannes' murder. My investigation had given me the opportunity to prise open family secrets. I was leaving far richer than I had come.

I was taking home new concerns to come to terms with – Hannes' capacity for rage and the certainty that my Uncle Gerret had murdered him so brutally. But at least the burden of Pa's last request of me was satisfied. Apart from tearing myself away from Tansie, I had no regrets about leaving. I was longing to hear the purr of my two Burmese and quietly restore a garden grown wild in my absence. My feelings about the changes in South Africa were mixed. The country was in a state of flux, I thought. It was an exciting yet dangerous place – still emerging. Another visit in a few years might prove interesting.

For the last time, I drove out of the farm gates and towards the Old Rustenburg Road. I took the turn-off to the farm the Hurutshes now owned. The front gate of the farm was no longer buckled and the driveway had been levelled and swept of stones. It was Sunday and most of the black workers were there, some clearing, others chatting. Nathaniel proudly showed off the work completed. Tall grasses had been cut, weeds yanked out and paths neatened. Seedlings had been planted in a fenced-off area for later transplanting and the dilapidated house had been cleaned and wore glass in its windows. I was amazed at the amount achieved in such a short period.

Nathaniel's wife, Mina, had invited me for afternoon tea in the old house. Mina, their children and relatives stood within the doorway to greet me. Everything was very proper. The cleanliness inside of the house was striking – walls whitewashed and floors scrubbed. A table was covered with a lacey cloth and chairs were in place for tea. Mina served tea in a pretty porcelain tea set and offered cake. We talked but conversation, like the rest, was so formal – they must have been trying particularly hard to please me.

Outdoors, I heard whispers about a Tswana ceremony about to begin. Within minutes women who seemed to be standing doing nothing moved as one to form a ring. Two of them pulled me into the middle. They sang, moving together then apart, stomping or clapping. The men watched from a discreet distance, not wanting to interfere with the women. Having danced with women years earlier, I knew what was expected and joined the circle, moving with them. When the dancing stopped Mina urged me back into the middle and facing me held something out to me.

'This is for you from us,' was all she said, placing a heavy object in my hands. It was a leather bodice and apron that women of the tribe wore for dancing and ceremonies. Trying to keep my emotions in check, I held the two pieces up to my body to show they were a good fit. It was a gift belonging to Tswana heritage, one that would always be precious. The group clapped and whistled. I continued dancing as they would've wished.

When the ceremony was over Nathaniel walked up to me. 'I so very happy,' he said pointing to the leather garments.

'Thank you Nathaniel,' I said, knowing he'd probably played a part in suggesting the gift to Mina and the other women.

'I hear police sure now Gerret kill Hannes. He in jail and wait for trial. Maybe he die first.' He clicked his tongue disapprovingly.

'That's how it goes.'

'No worry. *Modimo* fix him.'

'I hope so.'

'I sad you go home,' he said.

'We have shared so much.'

'Very much.'

We shook hands for the first and last time.